COLLISION

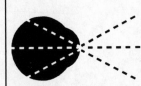
This Large Print Book carries the
Seal of Approval of N.A.V.H.

COLLISION

WILLIAM S. COHEN

THORNDIKE PRESS

A part of Gale, Cengage Learning

GALE
CENGAGE Learning·

Farmington Hills, Mich • San Francisco • New York • Waterville, Maine
Meriden, Conn • Mason, Ohio • Chicago

Copyright © 2015 by William S. Cohen.
Thorndike Press, a part of Gale, Cengage Learning.

Thorndike Press® Large Print Thriller.
The text of this Large Print edition is unabridged.
Other aspects of the book may vary from the original edition.
Set in 16 pt. Plantin.

LIBRARY OF CONGRESS CATALOGING-IN-PUBLICATION DATA

Cohen, William S.
    Collision / by William S. Cohen. — Large print edition.
        pages cm. — (Thorndike Press large print thriller)
    ISBN 978-1-4104-8313-3 (hardcover) — ISBN 1-4104-8313-4 (hardcover)
    1. Political corruption—United States—Fiction. 2. Conspiracies—Fiction.
    3. Large type books. 4. Political fiction. I. Title.
PS3553.O434C65 2015b
813'.54—dc23   2015020746

Published in 2015 by arrangement with Tom Doherty Associates, LLC.

Printed in Mexico
1 2 3 4 5 6 7 19 18 17 16 15

To Carl Sagan
(who inspired us to look to the stars and
find there our dust)

If some day in the future we discover well in advance that an asteroid that is big enough to cause a mass extinction is going to hit the Earth, and then we alter the course of that asteroid so that it does not hit us, it will be one of the most important accomplishments in all of human history.
— Representative George E. Brown, Jr., House Subcommittee on Space of the Committee on Science, Space, and Technology, March 24, 1993

On March 19, 2013, a month after a meteor explosion over Russia and a close encounter that same day with an asteroid, the House Science Committee held a hearing. A member of the committee asked NASA administrator Charles Bolden what he would do to deal with an Earth-threatening asteroid that was discovered with three weeks' warning.

"If it's coming in three weeks . . . pray," Bolden answered. "The reason I can't do anything in the next three weeks is because for decades we have put it off."

1

Cole Perenchio pulled the blue-and-white gym bag from under the seat and stood, tilting his head to avoid the overhead bin. He was six foot seven and as slim at age fifty-six as he had been when, for three years, he was top scorer for the MIT Engineers. He ducked again as he left the Delta aircraft and entered the walkway tube to Reagan National Airport. His only luggage was his gym bag carry-on, so he went directly to the taxi pickup line. When his turn came, he told the driver, "Roaches Run."

The driver turned and spoke through a thick plastic shield: "You kiddin' me, bro? You want Roaches Run? You can just damn well walk. And I'll get me another fare that's really goin' somewhere."

"How much would it cost me to go to Capitol Hill?" Perenchio asked in a weary voice.

"Twelve bucks plus tip," the driver said.

Perenchio reached into a pocket of his blue windbreaker and took out a piece of paper torn from a small notebook, along with a roll of bills. He peeled off a ten and a five, which he handed to the driver through a compartment in the shield. "Now take me to Roaches Run," he said.

The taxi pulled out of the airport exit and onto the northbound lane of the George Washington Parkway, went about half a mile, and then turned onto a causeway leading to a slice of land jutting along the shore of the Potomac River. Across the dark strip of water Perenchio could see the Washington Monument rising into the night sky.

"Okay, mister. Here's Roaches Run," the driver said. "You just want to get out *here*?"

"See that Lincoln over there?" Perenchio answered. "Go over there, and please put on the overhead light." He held the piece of paper up to the light. "Turn there. I want to see the license plate."

The taxi turned slowly toward the grid of a parking lot in which there were five scattered cars, all of them long, black town cars that shone brightly in the taxi's lights. The driver stopped behind a Lincoln. Perenchio leaned forward to check the District of Columbia license plate.

"Thanks," Perenchio said, getting out of

the taxi. He leaned his head toward the driver's half-opened window. "Now go over a couple of rows and wait for me. I'll be back in, at most, fifteen minutes. Then I want you to take me to my hotel. I'll give you the name when I come back."

As he approached the Lincoln, he heard the door locks click. He opened the rear right door and the interior dimly lighted up. A man seated on the left awkwardly held out his right hand as Perenchio folded himself into the rear seat and the light went out. Seated, Perenchio reached across, his hand engulfing the other man's.

"Sorry the flight was late," he said.

"No problem. That's the point of Roaches Run," the other man said, his face emerging from the shadow. "I give Leo here" — he nodded toward the driver — "the flight number. He keeps track of the flight, and, when he figures that it's twenty minutes away, he calls me, pulls up in front of my house in Alexandria, picks me up, and drives here. It's like a holding area for cars on call, town cars, under contract with firms like mine. You said you wanted privacy. So I suggested that we meet here instead of picking you up at the terminal."

"I remember this place from when I was a kid and my father was stationed at the

Pentagon," Perenchio said, his tense face suddenly breaking into a smile. "He'd take my brother and me here, usually on Sunday, and we'd watch the planes zoom in and out of National — not called Reagan then. They were close! It was like you could stand on a picnic table and touch 'em. But, you know, Hal, I didn't know the name of this place until I got your message. Roaches Run. Funny name."

"It's a fish, the roach. People fish for them here in the little bay," Harold Davidson said.

"Thanks, Hal," Perenchio said, smiling. "You've always known things like that."

"Well, here we are," Davidson said, ignoring the remark. He had a round, smooth face that merged into a bald head. His dark skin was slightly darker than that of Perenchio, who had a Creole father and an African American mother.

"I thought we could drive to my house, have a drink, something to eat — I hope you're still big on pulled pork. And we —"

"All I want, Hal, is a chance to talk with no one around. Right now," Perenchio said. "We're sealed off from the driver, right?"

Davidson pressed a button on the console near his door handle, and the light went on again. He pointed to another button, and a small red light flashed on and off next to

12

the word DRIVER.

"Standard practice. He can't hear me until I press that button. These cars all have them," Davidson said in an instructional tone that Perenchio remembered from their college years. "Look, you're my client. Everything is between you and me. We have a client-lawyer relationship. So, if you don't want to talk somewhere else, just start talking here. Now, what's on your mind? All you told me on the phone was that you had something you couldn't tell me over the phone. Now you can't tell me face-to-face." Davidson grinned and leaned toward Perenchio.

Perenchio reached into the gym bag and took out a black carrying case. He opened the case to show Davidson a Dell laptop, then zipped the case closed. "Keep this," he said. "It's all in that. You're in some kind of trouble at the law firm."

"How do you know that?"

"It's in here."

Davidson reached down for his suitcase-size briefcase, opened its hinged maw, and tried to slip in the laptop case. But it stuck out, its black shoulder strap hanging down the side of the briefcase. "How come you didn't use a thumb drive?" Davidson asked. "Lot easier to carry."

"You always have better ideas, Hal," Perenchio said, a touch of anger in his voice. "I need to give you the laptop, the whole laptop. That's it, okay?"

"Okay, okay," Davidson said, still fussing with the briefcase.

"All I can tell you is that it belongs to SpaceMine and it's very important. I mean, White House important," Perenchio said, lowering his voice. "I want a meeting with someone from the White House who can guarantee me immunity and get me into the federal witness program."

"I need more information than that, Cole. What the hell is this all about?"

"I can't tell you. All I can say is it's about something that could kill us all."

"Look, Cole. I trust you, trust your scientific mind. But tell me *something.*"

"I'll call you at your office tomorrow. Have the laptop open in front of you. I'll tell you how to activate and decrypt the information. Then you'll see. It's all there. Set up a meeting between now and Friday. At the White House."

"Hold it, Cole," Davidson said, his voice suddenly turning stern. "I won't be in my office tomorrow. I'll be in New York all day. A meeting with a client that I cannot break." He took his cell phone out of his pocket

14

and looked at his calendar. "It's got to be the next day, Wednesday. Ten thirty a.m."

"Damn it, Hal. Don't treat me like one of your clients. There's no time to lose. And what am I supposed to do all day?"

"Walk around. It's a great city. Maybe see Ben Taylor," Davidson said.

"I don't have time. Now I've got another day to kill. Yeah, kill. Funny saying that. I'm afraid to walk around. Really afraid, Hal."

Davidson reached out to pat Perenchio's shoulder. "Relax, Cole. Try to relax."

"Relax?" Perenchio asked with a bitter laugh. "Yeah, maybe I'll have time to write my will." As he opened the door he added, "See you Wednesday. And don't let that laptop out of your sight."

Perenchio got out of the car, walked to the taxi, and got in. The taxi recrossed the causeway and returned to the parkway, heading toward Washington. Davidson's black car followed.

So did another black car. Seated behind the driver were two men. One of them opened a cell phone, brought up a number, spoke briefly, and pocketed the phone.

2

Sean Falcone had finished his sixty-minute morning workout with weights and aerobic exercises. He could still bench-press 250 pounds. That was a lot less than he could a year ago, but he was in better shape than when he was fifteen years younger. And he looked it.

Now, sitting in his apartment and drinking his second cup of coffee, he glanced at the *Washington Post* front page and saw that Congress and President Blake Oxley were in another budget fight. *Today's Wednesday,* he thought. *The crisis will ease tomorrow when Congress begins to disappear for the long weekend.* Unexpected thoughts like that made him happy to be out of politics for good. And why not? He'd spent six years as a guest in Vietnam's Hanoi Hilton, a hellhole that made Guantánamo look like the presidential suite at the Ritz. Then he hit a four-year stint as Massachusetts' attorney general, followed by membership in what used to be the world's most exclusive club.

Falcone allowed himself a silent "Ha." The Senate was once a place so honored that members left its rolls defeated or dead. On a shield or in a coffin. No longer.

It had become a place where dreams died, where hope for change and conciliation were ground down into the dust of rancor and bitter recrimination. So after twelve years, Falcone wanted out. He quit the club, thinking that freedom was his at last.

It was a false hope. President Blake Oxley had asked Falcone to serve as his national security advisor. What was he to do? When the President asked an old Army Ranger to serve his country one more time, did he really have a choice?

After plowing through Oxley's first term and halfway into the second one, Falcone submitted his resignation. In those six years he had handled dozens of crises, the biggest being the most bizarre and the most secret: finding the plot behind the accidental explosion of a nuclear weapon that virtually destroyed Savannah, Georgia.

It was Falcone's worst nightmare: a nuclear bomb destroying an American city. Who caused the attack? How could they have done it? And why? And how should America respond? The questions demanded answers and fast. The pressure on President Blake Oxley had been immense. Someone had to pay for the worst human-casualty toll since the United States bombed Hiroshima and Nagasaki.

Immediate speculation pointed to Iran. Some leaders in Iran's military had used extreme rhetoric, but they weren't insane. If responsible, Iran would be incinerated in a matter of minutes. That didn't make any sense to Falcone. But very few things did when it came to the kaleidoscopic changes taking place in the world.

Oxley had to act. And if he didn't, congressional leaders threatened to declare war against Iran and impeach Oxley if he failed to act upon the declaration.

Falcone managed to work with an Israeli assassin and *Washington Post* bigfoot reporter Philip Dake to discover a plot that had been orchestrated by a fringe group to attack Iran with a nuclear weapon that had dropped from a U.S. Air Force aircraft in 1959 off the coast of Georgia without detonating. The Air Force had declared the bomb lost and unarmed, assuring Congress and the country that the weapon, buried deep in the seafloor, posed no threat. But the bomb accidentally detonated when plotters attempted to extract it and move it onto a ship masquerading as an exploratory vessel.

Americans initially blamed the disaster on Iran and nearly waged war against that nation, which had no responsibility for the nuclear explosion that destroyed Savannah. The accidental denotation was more than enough evidence to cause Falcone to question every temptation to use America's formidable nuclear arsenal.

The experience had taken its toll on Falcone. He wanted out. Oxley persuaded him to stay on longer. But six years in that job was too much. Falcone, without discussing it further with Oxley, announced his decision to resign as national security advisor and left the White House.

The President held no hard feelings, but Ray Quinlan, his chief of staff, who disliked and frequently feuded with Falcone, considered Falcone's announcement an act of betrayal.

Falcone had no doubt that he had done his duty and that enough was enough. The President had accepted Falcone's resignation reluctantly and had told him that he was expected to be on call when needed.

Falcone had been eager to get back into the private world. It wasn't as if he'd have to stand in an unemployment line or go on welfare.

When he retired from the Senate years ago, Falcone had joined DLA Piper, a newly minted mesh of older law firms that had decided to go global in a hurry.

He had been a star performer there and would have been welcomed back. But a number of the former partners with whom he was close had retired or moved on. He decided it was time for him to do the same. He had been approached immediately by Sullivan & Ford, one of the world's largest law firms.

The firm had nearly one hundred offices scattered across the world, from Uganda to New Zealand, from Silicon Valley to Cairo, and employed more than four thousand lawyers, including three in the London office who had been knighted by the Queen. The average profit per equity partner this year would be $1.9 million. The firm's senior partners assured Falcone that his compensation would be much higher. They made him an offer he couldn't refuse.

But there were two conditions Falcone said were nonnegotiable.

First, no lobbying. He had just read in the

Atlantic that back in 1974 only three percent of retiring senators and House members became lobbyists. Now half the retiring senators stayed in Washington to get rich lobbying, as did forty-two percent of the retiring members of the House. He wasn't ever going to join the herd that camped outside the doors of the House of Representatives or the Senate, pleading or cajoling members for votes. His door would always be open for those who sought his counsel, but his former colleagues on Capitol Hill and in the Oxley administration knew where to find him.

Second, he would not keep time records for billing the firm's clients. Whether he devoted days or less than an hour to a case, his value wasn't going to be weighed by the clock. Sullivan & Ford's partners had no problem with his not wanting to lobby. They figured he could still make a call or two without breaking any laws. Several partners complained about his refusal to record how he spent his time, but they swallowed hard and folded. His name on the firm's letterhead would add a mark of distinction. He was seen as a man with worldly gravitas — and that was money in their pockets.

Even though Falcone refused to lobby, he still kept in touch with the makers of laws and shapers of policy and was often seen at events that drew Washington's elite — State Department receptions for foreign leaders, White House dinners for heads of state, the Kennedy Center Honors, change-of-command ceremonies at the Pentagon. He also served on the President's Intelligence Advisory Board. And, with little or no publicity, he went on missions as U.S. special envoy to hot spots where the President wanted an extra set of eyes.

Now, on this October day of blue sky and Indian summer, Falcone began walking briskly from his penthouse atop the high-rise at 701 Pennsylvania Avenue to Sullivan & Ford's gleaming steel and glass ten-story building at the foot of Capitol Hill.

He started his workday, sleeves rolled up and sitting behind a large handcrafted mahogany desk, embellished with replicated lions' heads and insignias from the age of King Arthur. The desk was oddly out of place in a building that screamed of geometric angularity and Spartan efficiency. More than efficiency, Falcone wanted substance, solidity, something that conveyed a respect for the past.

He had spotted the ornate desk while on a trip to London and had it shipped back to

Washington. It was expensive, but it was just one additional price that his fellow partners were willing to pay to persuade him to join the firm.

From the window behind him he could see the dome of the Capitol, a quarter mile away. On the wall opposite his desk was a sixty-inch flat-screen television that contained an unusual capability. When it was turned on, ten different news channels appeared in small boxes along the set's border, with the preferred channel occupying the center of the screen. At the moment, the preferred channel was GNN, Google News Network. GNN had worked out an exclusive agreement with a relatively new enterprise, which called itself SpaceMine. The name had debuted about three years earlier in a great splash of GNN-generated publicity. Ned Winslow, once GNN's premier news correspondent and reportorial rival to CNN's Wolf Blitzer, had become a huckster. He belonged in the field or behind an anchor's desk. Maybe it was a matter of ratings, but whatever the reason, Falcone was disappointed with Winslow's new role. Content used to be king on television. Now, it was just schlock and awe.

Winslow breathlessly hailed SpaceMine for "taking the world into a new realm —

the commerce of space." SpaceMine's founders, he went on to say, planned to mine asteroids. "These gems of the heavens," he said, "have higher concentrations of precious metals, such as platinum, than any known ore mine on Earth."

At no time did Winslow ever describe how SpaceMine would chip away the asteroids' treasure. Instead, he ran a cartoonish NASA video that showed huge robotic machinery and vehicles gouging ore out of a landscape consisting entirely of rock.

The press conference that had launched SpaceMine had been dominated by the hologram of SpaceMine's CEO, Robert Wentworth Hamilton, the world's fifth- or sixth-richest man, depending upon what list of billionaires you accepted. There were also two former astronauts and three investment bankers, who looked particularly uncomfortable being projected as spectral holograms. In the following months, GNN had begun producing *SpaceMine Special* and sold rights to television networks throughout the world.

SpaceMine seemed to be everywhere — a Facebook site with an ever-growing army of friends; a constantly spouting Twitter with 1,627,435 followers. "SpaceMine" appeared at the top of responses to any Googled query with the word "space" in it. Every special fostered videos and endless comments on blogs, some of them genuinely spontaneous and others written by SpaceMine's digital hires.

Each special was a kind of reality show devoted to talks by Hamilton or an astronaut and images of SpaceMine workers at scattered, unidentified sites performing vaguely described experiments or building components of what was called the Asteroid Exploitation System. In the latest special, Hamilton compared the enterprise to the Manhattan Project, which took several routes toward development of the atomic bomb "before deciding which one would quickest lead our nation to its goal."

Millions of viewers got used to GNN's use of holograms, which carried SpaceMine into the borderland of scientific fact and science fiction. There was an aura of secrecy: no interviews, no identification of Space-Mine sites. Because SpaceMine was so much a product of GNN and cable television, newspapers and network television retaliated by giving the corporation little coverage.

About a year ago, a GNN *SpaceMine Special* had been devoted to discussing the potential launching of the corporation's

25

initial public offering. Hamilton, in his usual hologram form, urged viewers to stay tuned for a progress report on the company's IPO plans, "giving anyone on Earth the opportunity to share in the equivalent of a new 'gold rush' in space."

Some stock analysts, whose judgments were not particularly reliable, speculated that SpaceMine could exceed the phenomenally successful $30 billion IPO achieved that year by the Bradbury451 Group. The hype had given SpaceMine a few days of publicity well beyond GNN. But Wall Street yawned and soon moved on to other news.

Falcone was no fan of television, reality or otherwise. He occasionally watched newscasts by CNN, BBC, CCTV, and Al Jazeera to see how different channels covered essentially the same news. He had not paid much attention to the SpaceMine specials until today, when, for professional reasons, he found himself watching and recording one. Hamilton was now a Sullivan & Ford client. The move of a superclient like Hamilton from one law firm to another was as secretive and complex as a CIA rendition operation. One day the client was at Firm X. The next day the client was at Firm Z, and neither X nor Z had any documents that showed who had engineered the transfer or how it was made. Falcone had learned about the acquisition of Hamilton a few weeks before, when a terse, confidential memo had been sent to Falcone and the other senior partners.

Falcone had no direct connection with the new client. He was watching the SpaceMine special out of curiosity and jotting notes on a yellow pad in the assumption that someday he would be asked to offer some counsel to Hamilton, such as the probable reaction of political and financial decision makers to a corporation operating in space.

If a corporation is a person, what is a corporation that is no longer a fulltime Earthling? Interesting issue, the lawyerly part of his brain mused.

SpaceMine had been late to the game of exploiting space assets in our galaxy. Other firms, such as Gold Spike and Moon Struck, had bolted out of the gate the moment that Congress canceled NASA's ambitious plans to send men to Mars and beyond in the quest for scientific knowledge that could benefit mankind.

Falcone did not hold Robert Wentworth Hamilton in particularly high regard. It was nothing personal between them. He just resented how our political system had been corrupted by men like Hamilton. Politicians were like crackheads begging for a fix. Not for cocaine, but for money. People like Hamilton were eager to feed their addiction and turn them into grateful lapdogs.

And now Hamilton had hired Sullivan & Ford to handle all of the legal work associated with his latest adventure into space. This time it was millions for advice, not votes. *Given my druthers,* Falcone thought, *I would have told Hamilton to pound sand with his checkbook.* But it had not been Falcone's decision to make. And, besides, he had to remind himself that it wasn't personal. Just business.

As Falcone sat there watching SpaceMine's latest info-commercial on GNN, he remembered his recent lunch with the *Post*'s Philip Dake at the Metropolitan Club, one of Washington's premier establishments, where new and old power players could meet to drink, dine, discuss politics, or close business deals. He had spotted Hamilton sitting at a table located at the far end of the main dining room. He was in deep conversation with Senator Kenneth Collinsworth of Texas, the powerful chairman of the Senate Committee on Appropriations.

At the end of their lunch, both men rose

and shook hands. Falcone suspected that a deal had just been struck. No money had passed hands, of course. The money would come later in the form of a large check from a political action committee masquerading as a nonprofit, tax-free organization dedicated to some innocuous-sounding social welfare cause.

Hamilton didn't have to wait long to reap the benefit from the time spent dining on a Cobb salad in the company and surroundings of the club's elite members. A week later, President Oxley's NASA budget for space exploration was cut by nearly sixty percent. The cut included NASA's multiyear asteroid plan: the launching of an unmanned spacecraft to capture a small asteroid and tow it closer to Earth. Astronauts would later travel to the asteroid to examine it, providing science with the first on-site assessment of a near-Earth object.

Collinsworth's budget cut shouldered NASA out of asteroid travel and pretty much handed it over to SpaceMine. It was all done in the name of fiscal austerity. It was all so civilized, so legal, and in Falcone's mind, so perfectly corrupt.

Dake had worked closely with Falcone during the White House investigation into the Savannah disaster, the subject of a book he had nearly completed. Dake had typically held back details from his *Post* stories, saving them for the book. Falcone agreed to look over the manuscript before Dake submitted it to his publisher.

"All I want is tributes and praise. No criticisms," Dake had said, giving Falcone a quick smile.

"You'll get what you deserve," Falcone said. "And what will you be up to next?"

"Oddly enough," Dake said, "it's that gentleman who just left."

"Collinsworth?"

"Oh, God, no. Not that shyster. He's bound to be indicted one of these days. *Then* I might use my talents on him. No. I'm thinking about Hamilton."

"So, it's not by chance that you and he were at lunch in the club on the same day. I imagine you have an understanding with the maître d'."

"My life is adorned with coincidences," Dake said with another smile. "Seriously, Hamilton is a fascinating subject. Even more fascinating for me because the son of a bitch is so elusive, so totally shielded from the public."

"Some billionaires have a way of being invisible," Falcone said. "Comes with the territory."

"He's a challenge, all right. So far, all I have is some background on his father. Well, the death of his father." Dake leaned back, and Falcone knew that Dake was taking the floor.

"When Hamilton was fourteen, his father disappeared. Henry Hamilton was the owner of a small, independent bank in a Boston suburb. He had gone on a whale-watching ship out of Gloucester. A mile or so out, while all the patrons were on one side of the ship watching a whale spout, he was apparently on the other side. No one saw him go over the rail. His body was never found.

"There were rumors that he had staged his apparent death. Hamilton was just old enough to read the *Globe*'s stories, which cautiously mentioned speculation about the disappearance. But the insurance company finally paid off the fifteen-million-dollar policy. There were also rumors about the health of the bank. But the chairman of the bank board took over and managed to keep it going.

"The life insurance payoff was the beginning of young Hamilton's fortune. Eventually, he bought the bank. He financed private investigations into his father's death.

Supposedly, he is haunted by the belief that his father is still alive."

"Interesting," Falcone said. "But if that's all you have, you've got a long way to go."

"Well, I have some more. I talked to one of the investigators. He turned up the fact that Hamilton was born illegitimate and was adopted by the childless Hamiltons soon after birth. They took elaborate measures to appear as blood parents. The wife dressed up in maternity clothes. The husband managed to get some clerk to create a birth certificate showing the Hamiltons as his natural parents. The investigator told me that the adoption had come as a shock to Hamilton. Mama had never told him. That, I'm convinced, is the source of stories that he thinks that in a previous life he was the historical Alexander Hamilton, who was also born illegitimate. And, like the historical Alexander Hamilton, he has a deep belief in a personal God."

"Well, does he expect to be killed in a duel?" Falcone asked.

"In a rare interview — in a little Christian magazine he bankrolled — he was asked how he would describe his faith. He said, 'I have a tender reliance on the mercy of the Almighty.' The interviewer didn't realize that those were Alexander Hamilton's dying words after Aaron Burr shot him."

3

Falcone came out of his reverie as Ned Winslow's voice seemed to take on a messianic tone. "We are on a commercial voyage to a new place for minerals that are getting rare and expensive to mine on Earth," he said. "I'm literally speaking of a new world, a world where a mile-wide piece of rock called an asteroid contains platinum and other minerals worth about eight trillion dollars. Palladium goes into cars' catalytic converters, converting harmful gases into harmless gases. We're just around the corner from palladium fuel cells that will combine hydrogen and oxygen to produce electricity, heat, and water. Palladium is the future!"

There was a time when NASA had a monopoly on America's imagination, a time when bold rhetoric of a young president inspired us to put a man on the moon, Falcone mused. But thanks to Hamilton and other government-get-out-of-the-way forces, space now ranked low on the list of budgetary issues being juggled by the White House and Congress. The economic recovery touted by the chairman of the Federal Reserve had proved anemic.

In his latest State of the Union address, the President had reintroduced his plan to send astronauts to an asteroid by 2025, putting NASA back in the man-in-space business. *Well, Congress shot that down again.* Reluctantly, the Oxley administration had been forced to yield a leadership role to the new space buccaneers.

The moneymen were now in charge. NASA was in the backseat of a grounded spacecraft. That meant that SpaceMine and the others probably wouldn't have to worry about government interference.

When it came to Oxley, one never knew if his heart was behind his words, but Falcone genuinely hoped that Oxley would supercharge his support of NASA's plans and take on his political opponents. The exploitation of space wasn't science fiction anymore. It was real, and the government damn well needed to stay involved in it.

It was getting pretty crowded up there. And space was no place to be playing demolition derby where there were no rules and no judges. The mining of the moon and near-Earth asteroids was bound to lure adventurous capitalists, and they would try to make their own laws, as had the gold seekers who stampeded to California and Alaska two centuries ago.

There was a theoretical barrier in the form of the Outer Space Treaty, which called for international regulation of space activities. The treaty had been around since 1967, but it focused primarily on preventing the use of space for military purposes by states and their governments. Concern for the commercial exploitation of space was, no doubt, deferred for later negotiations, considering the magnitude of the costs and complexities of the issues involved.

Falcone made a note to call his friend Dr. Benjamin Franklin Taylor, a NASA veteran who was assistant director of the Smithsonian's Air and Space Museum and prospective science advisor to the President. Taylor would know whether SpaceMine's entry into the race might stir up new interest in the treaty among scientists.

Falcone was sorting through his thoughts about all of this when Ned Winslow announced the arrival of Hamilton's hologram "to make what is undoubtedly the most astounding announcement since Neil Armstrong walked upon the moon."

Hamilton seemingly stepped out of the hologram and appeared as a slim, middle-aged man in a dark blue suit, white shirt, and blue-and-gold striped tie. He stood before a huge image of the night sky.

"Twelve months and eleven days ago," he said, "from Earth Base SpaceMine, we launched a rocket that last night delivered a payload of scientific instruments to Asteroid USA, the first object in the cosmos to become commercial property. To all of us at SpaceMine, Asteroid USA is now a branch office, an entity of free enterprise. Capitalism — *American* capitalism — is now in space."

Hamilton turned and aimed an object the size of a TV remote. A laser beam shot across the star-studded backdrop and stopped in the great *W* of Cassiopeia, a constellation named after a vain Greek mythological queen, identifiable by its "W" shape in the northern sky.

"This is the approximate region where Asteroid USA is located, far away in the northern sky. Soon, SpaceMine's Asteroid USA will begin sending a signal — *U-S-A* in Morse code — that will be heard on shortwave radio at approximately four-eight-seven-nine kilohertz." He paused before adding in his oddly singsong voice: "You will be hearing more about Asteroid USA and SpaceMine in the near future." Hamilton paused again for a moment, and then went on.

"Future. What a wonderful word. To put it simply, we are months away from beginning a mining operation on an asteroid. In an amazingly short time, SpaceMine is about to do what the U.S. government — NASA — said was something that would take decades to do. The NASA plan called for putting the captured asteroid into orbit near the moon so that astronauts could visit it by 2025. That asteroid — in the government version — would become a sort of boot camp for humans who would learn how to live and work in distant solar sites, including Mars. Asteroid USA — the capitalist version — will do that far sooner and be a source of wealth, fantastic wealth.

"This is the most important venture — the greatest adventure — ever launched by an American entrepreneur — or an entrepreneur from any country on Earth. May God bless America and Asteroid USA."

Hamilton disappeared and Winslow reappeared. As usual, Winslow did not question Hamilton or give GNN viewers any background on Hamilton's statement.

Winslow began narrating a documentary about SpaceMine. Falcone, although intrigued by Hamilton's announcement, decided this was the right time for an intermission.

Near a doodle of a hologram man on his yellow pad Falcone jotted Hamilton's name and hit the hold button. The building was laid out as a hollow square inside a glass-walled atrium. Partners' tenth-floor offices were strung along three sides of the atrium, their doors opening onto an inner corridor. On the north side were a large conference room and staff offices. Falcone left his office on the south side and turned left toward the west corridor.

At the beginning of the west corridor were a reception cubicle and two elevators, one a private express to the tenth floor. When Falcone turned, the express elevator's door opened and two men stepped out, escorted by the receptionist, Ellen Franklin. Falcone said hello to her as she returned to her cubicle chair. Across from Ellen, on a black couch, sat a young woman wearing a blue dress and an elderly man in a yellow shirt and brown suit, apparently waiting to see a partner.

The two men from the elevator looked straight ahead and made no attempt to acknowledge Falcone as he passed. Continuing down the corridor, he heard one of the men speaking to Ellen. He had a slight accent of some kind. Falcone made out the words "Al Jazeera" and "Harold Davidson," the name of a partner.

They look foreign. Not quite Middle Eastern, not Asian. But, well, not American. The unexpected thought momentarily troubled him; he told himself that the thought had been instinctive, not prejudiced.

As he continued down the corridor, he tried to understand his moment of bigotry. *Or was it something else?* He could not dismiss a sense that there was an aura of hostility about the men, and he wasn't quite sure why that sense sometimes suddenly flared. He had a habit of sizing people up from how they looked, how they walked, and how they engaged with other people. Maybe it was just the thing that scientists called pheromones, airborne odors that sent signals to another member of the same species. Or maybe he was just too quick to prejudge people. Whatever the reason, he didn't have a good feeling about them.

4

Falcone had reached the door of the restroom at the end of the corridor when he heard a booming *thump, thump, thump.* The sound reverberated throughout the vast atrium, momentarily stunning Falcone. Instinctively, he crouched and turned toward the sound.

Only a second passed, but Falcone's thoughts seemed to be swimming in molasses. Then a rush of adrenaline cleared his mind.

Jesus Christ! He knew that sound. He had heard it a thousand times before.

He saw the backs of the two men as they emerged from Davidson's office, leaving the door open. One man carried an M16 with a folding stock, now unfolded. Falcone had carried an M16 as a U.S. Army Ranger in Vietnam. For years he had struggled to suppress the smell of rot and death and the nightmares that haunted him.

Now, the memory of a shadowy village flared for an instant. The M16 originally had a magazine that held only twenty rounds but quickly got amped up to thirty bullets that at point-blank range ripped through a body, inflicting horrendous wounds. The gunman had enough bullets to wipe out the tenth floor even if he did not carry extra magazines.

Davidson's open door blocked the men's view of Falcone as he ran down the corridor toward them. Time seemed to stop, as it did at moments like this back in the jungle. He was planning as he ran, the way he did in an ambush. At six feet tall and a solid 190 pounds, Falcone coolly assessed his chances against the gunman. *I can take him, grab the gun, and hope the other guy is unarmed or slow on the draw.*

The two men took a couple of strides toward the elevators and stopped. The people sitting on the couch were motionless, frozen by shock or fear. Ellen ducked behind her desk, pulling her phone console with her. Before she could press a button, the gunman raised the gun and fired. Bullets etched a bloody line across the young woman and the elderly man.

The gunman turned toward Ellen, his back to Falcone. The other man pressed the express elevator's button, holding the door open for the gunman. He spotted Falcone, whipped out a handgun, and fired four shots in rapid succession at Falcone, who dropped to the floor, shielded by a planter. The bullets shattered the glass wall behind Falcone's head.

Falcone sprang up, cursing, "You sons of bitches!"

Rushing the gunman, Falcone hit him low and drove him to the floor. As he went down, the gunman fired a burst, shattering Ellen's glass cubicle. Falcone landed on him, pressing his knees into the gunman's back. Falcone seized a handful of black hair, jerked back the gunman's head, and smashed it down, bloodying the parquet floor.

The other man fled into the open elevator and disappeared.

The M16 was on the floor, under the gunman and pointed toward Ellen's shattered cubicle. He pulled the trigger, spraying the lower panel of the desk with an arc of bullets. Ellen screamed.

Falcone let go of the hair and grasped the trigger finger, bending it until it was dislocated and stuck up at an odd angle.

Screaming in pain, the gunman rose to a crouch with Falcone still on his back. Ellen crawled out from her splintered desk, her white blouse turned scarlet, her face bloodied.

"Hold on, Ellen," Falcone said, feeling her right hand go limp.

At that instant, the shooter, still holding his gun, stood and spun toward Falcone. Deprived of his trigger finger, the gunman hesitated long enough for Falcone to stand. Falcone clutched the hot barrel, burning his hand. Ignoring the pain, Falcone twisted the gun and shoved the gunman against the waist-high glass partition that encircled the atrium. He drove the stock against the gunman's jaw so hard that his body lifted off the floor, teetered on the thin partition, and then plunged over.

For several minutes Falcone stood, looking down at the man's body, holding the gun, ready to kill the next one . . . and the next one. *You never know how many there are. You kill one, then another. . . .*

5

During the agonizingly slow descent, Ahmed Kurpanov braced for whatever was on the other side of the elevator doors. He had the bag containing the laptop slung over his left shoulder. His right hand was in the pocket of his zipped-up leather car coat, his index finger on the trigger guard of the Glock.

The door opened to a lobby overflowing with panicky men and women rushing out of the building. Kurpanov stood at the open door, paralyzed by the sight of Dukka Sadulayev's body. His cousin lay near the deserted reception desk, where they had checked in less than fifteen minutes before. *It will be so easy, Dukka said. So easy.*

Dukka was still alive in Kurpanov's mind even when he saw him there, lying on his back, eyes open, face bloodied. Then Kurpanov's eyes brought reality: *His blood. All that blood. He is dead.*

45

Most people stepped around the body, but Kurpanov saw a fleeing man step on the outstretched left arm of his big cousin.

"Dukka! Dukka!" Kurpanov said softly, tears welling in his black eyes. In a sudden spasm of hate and revenge, his hand tightened on his weapon and he thought of killing that man and as many others as he could before joining Dukka in martyrdom. But the spasm ended as quickly as it came, and Kurpanov, hand out of his pocket, chose escape by blending into the crowd. "Peace be upon you. Mercy of Allah and his blessings," he whispered in Chechen as he walked past Dukka's body.

Two DC police officers, guns drawn, shoved their way into the lobby. "Tenth floor! Tenth floor!" someone shouted. One of the officers pushed Kurpanov aside and grabbed at the closing elevator doors.

Outside on the sidewalk, the crowd spread in all directions. Kurpanov stood for a moment looking at the spot where the car was supposed to be. He could hear the distant scream of sirens. *I am naked as in a dream,* he thought, searching through the memorized words of the Qur'an for solace — *"O people! I have seen the enemy's army with my own eyes, and I am the naked warner; so protect yourselves!"* And then his mind plunged deeper into hatred and fear. *That idiot of a Russian driver. He drove off.*

6

The elevator doors opened and two police officers stepped out, guns drawn. Falcone, crouching, turned, the M16 aimed at them.

One officer pointed his gun at Falcone, while the second one aimed his weapon high and fired, bringing down a rain of glass from the atrium's ceiling. "Drop the gun!" he yelled. "Drop the goddamn gun!"

Falcone, still locked in Vietnam, placed the gun on the floor, raised his hands, and shouted, "American! American!"

"Stand up," one of the officers said. "Slow. No fast moves." He turned away and with his free hand switched on the radio attached to a shirt epaulet. His voice calm, he said, "Ten thirty-three. Ten thirty-three. Responded to 911 shooting report, 676 Eighth Street Northwest. Multiple shootings. Tenth floor. Looks like three or more dead. Ambulance and tactical backup urgently requested."

"Okay. Lower your hands," the other officer said, still holding his gun aimed at Falcone. "Take out your wallet and show me ID."

Falcone slowly reached into a back pocket, pulled out a wallet, and took out a Sullivan & Ford business card. "I work here," he said, handing over the card.

"What the hell were you doing holding a weapon?"

"I took it from a shooter. He's down there," Falcone said, pointing toward the atrium.

"The body in the lobby," the other officer said, lowering his weapon. "What the hell happened here?" he asked.

"There were two men," Falcone answered. "I . . . The one down there is dead, I guess. The other shooter took the elevator."

The officer switched on his radio again "One shooter believed dead. Other shooter left the scene. Armed and dangerous. Here is a description of him." He held the microphone up to Falcone's face.

"About five foot ten," Falcone began. "Trim. Early twenties. Black hair, dark eyes. No facial hair. Looks . . . looks foreign. Darkish complexion. Almost Arab-looking or Asian. Somewhere in between. Sort of triangular face. Khaki slacks, blue shirt, no

49

tie. Wearing zippered black car coat — down to his knees. The gun he fired, it looked like a nine-millimeter Glock. And he was carrying something" — Falcone paused, recalling what he had seen only a few minutes before — "on his shoulder. It looked like the kind of case you might carry a computer or an iPad in. Maybe that's what he was carrying his gun in. I don't know."

The officer took back the microphone and asked Falcone, "Anyone wounded?"

"No wounded. Five known dead, including the gunman. I'm sure there's another one in that office," Falcone answered, nodding toward the open door of Harold Davidson's office.

Looking around, the second officer asked, "Security camera?"

"No," Falcone said. "None in the lobby. None in the building."

"That's odd."

"Not for a law firm. Some people who come here don't like their pictures taken."

The first officer spoke into the microphone again. "Tech office. Start getting security camera images in the area around the building. Urgent."

He turned to the other officer. "Check for another body," he said, pointing to the open door.

Turning back to Falcone, he said, "That hand of yours looks pretty bad. You should try to have someone take care of it."

7

Through the earpiece of a smartphone Ahmed Kurpanov suddenly heard a torrent of Russian words, beginning with repeated *"eto piz."* "Yes, Viktor, things are fucked up. But speak English."

All three had agreed that on this job they would all speak English so that Viktor could practice and the three of them would not stand out. For Dukka Sadulayev and Kurpanov, who had lived most of their lives in America, the language switch was no problem. For Viktor, the driver of the team, English was still a work in progress. He had studied English by watching *GoodFellas* over and over. Joe Pesci was his favorite foulmouthed mobster.

"No parking," he said. "When you goes — left — car, a fucking bitch cop came, said 'no parking' and made me move. Now I try circle around on these fucking streets with numbers and letters for names. Many cop cars all over. Keep walking, turn right at corners. I find you two."

"One. Only one," Kurpanov said, speaking into his phone. With his phone to his lips, he looked just like several people standing outside the Sullivan & Ford Building and talking into their cells. "Dukka . . . Dukka is gone. Dead. Some guy jumped him from behind, shoved him over. Ten floors down."

As he spoke, two more police cars pulled up and officers sprinted toward the entrance.

"Shit! Sorry, sorry, Ahmed," Viktor said in a deep-voiced staccato. "Fuckups, fuckups killed him. Worst job we had ever. Keep walking, turning right. I listen to cop radio. Many, many cop calls. They say on radio look for young man. Black hair. In a black leather coat carrying something."

"Yeah, it's all fucked up, Viktor. Everything fucked up," Kurpanov said, melding into the crowd fleeing the building.

"Get rid of that fuckin' bag and coat," Viktor said. "Keep turning right at corners. I find you."

Kurpanov pocketed the smartphone and continued walking down H Street, his thoughts crowded with anger.

Dukka didn't have enough time to plan right

for this job. What was so damn important that we had to rush? Dukka always had a plan B for every operation. But there was no plan B for this one! Dukka said it would be simple. No need for a backup. Just drive from New York, kill a weird black guy, and grab his laptop. Why didn't we do it at the airport? So simple. But this other black guy shows up and Dukka says we have to wait. Get more instructions.

What the fuck was so important about one little laptop? Build a bomb with it? Find out the names of all the members of Congress who were screwing their girls or boys? Why couldn't it have waited another day? Dukka dead, killed by that fucker who jumped him. I should have killed that prick, should have stayed.

What will Uncle Khasan say? And Basayev? He punishes workers who make mistakes.

Who's in charge now? That asshole Viktor? Can he get us back to New York?

Sirens, flashing lights. Kurpanov felt the panic building in him, flowing over reason, making his hands shake. *Dukka, Dukka. He would know what to do. Dukka would tell me don't run.* So Kurpanov continued walking, trying to make himself invisible.

At the next intersection, Kurpanov turned right and saw an alley with a Dumpster in it. He ducked into the alley and put the bag containing the laptop and his Glock in a tight space behind the Dumpster. He hesitated before doffing the coat. *From Uncle Khasan. Worth seven hundred dollars, he said. He didn't exactly buy it. Still . . . his gift.* Kurpanov neatly folded the coat before placing it on top of the bag.

He did not know that the Dumpster was under frequent surveillance — not by the police but by guests of the city's largest homeless shelter, a many-windowed, three-story building that overlooked the alley.

8

Six minutes after the first two officers responded to the numerous 911 calls, others began to appear, their cars parked at odd angles in front of the building. Then three detectives, who had been on a nearby robbery case, ran in. Another car parked and a captain stepped out to take command, issuing orders that rapidly turned the entrance panic scene into a crime scene marked off by yellow tapes and stanchions that were being unloaded from a police truck. Down the street, fifty yards from the entrance, police stopped television trucks, which lined up, beginning to form a media site that was drawing reporters and photographers behind stanchions.

Two ambulances backed up across the sidewalk in front of the entrance, doors open, lights flashing. They were followed by two black armored vehicles that disgorged a dozen SWAT officers in black helmets and bulky black uniforms covering body armor. The captain, standing at the reception desk, made the elevators part of the crime scene, sent one SWAT unit directly to the tenth floor on the express elevator, and ordered uniformed officers to take over the public elevator and begin a floor-by-floor, office-by-office search of the building for other victims or other shooters.

Assistant Chief Louise Mosley, two stars on the shoulders of her uniform, arrived and strode into the lobby. She was shorter than her driver but wiry and quick-moving, leading him by a couple of paces. "Put a lockdown on all traffic for ten blocks around the building," she told the captain. "A checkpoint at every intersection. As soon as each floor is cleared, get those officers out on the street looking for the guy in the black coat. Keep the building sealed until you hear otherwise. Get the press office to send out an armed-and-dangerous bulletin about the shooting. I want a major warning. The shooters might be going after lawyers all over town. I'm heading for the tenth floor."

When she stepped out of the elevator, Mosley paused to look at the bodies and spoke quietly to her driver: "Stand by here until the crime-scene guys and medical examiner get here. We need IDs on these victims as soon as possible. When the techs finish doing their thing, get these bodies out of here so people we talk to aren't spooked."

"What about the guy on the lobby floor?" the driver asked. He had turned his back on the bodies; his face was ashen.

"I have a hunch he's not local. Tell the ME that the body down there is high-priority. We need the full perp exam on him. Photos, prints, DNA, powder-presence test. With the other guy on the loose we have to move quick, treat this as a crime in progress."

The sergeant nodded and looked as if he was about to throw up.

Mosley softened her voice, saying, "This your first mass homicide, Mike?"

"Not exactly, ma'am. I was first on the scene for those three kids in Anacostia a couple of months ago," he replied. He had seen many — too many — bodies. Nearly all of them Young Black Males, as they were tabulated on the crime reports — kids lying in their blood, sprawled on the sidewalk, in a go-go club's parking lot, in a bus-stop shelter. And all of them across the Anacostia River, the other Washington.

"Those kids, that was the usual Anacostia drug deal gone wrong," Mosley said.

"Yeah," the driver said. "This one is all-white . . . well, mostly white . . . and downtown. And it looks like it's going to be complicated. Very complicated."

9

Falcone and the two officers who had first encountered him were now joined by a SWAT officer. The M16 was still on the floor in front of Falcone. A few partners had ventured out of their offices around the atrium. Mosley stepped to the middle of the corridor and, shouting across the atrium, said, "I am Assistant Chief Louise Mosley of the Metropolitan Police Department. This is an active crime scene. A shooter is still at large. Please return to your offices. You will be asked for statements. Thank you."

Mosley pointed to one of the officers and said, "Update me." He briskly repeated Falcone's account of the shootings.

"Where's the other body?" Mosley asked.

Falcone led Mosley to Harold Davidson's office. They stood for a moment on the threshold. The office was well lit and eerily neat. What was left of Davidson was behind his glass-and-chrome desk, his face blasted away. Three .223-caliber bullets had tumbled through his skull and then into the floor-to-ceiling window behind him, shattering it. Blood, flesh, and bones covered the portly man's white shirt, maroon tie, and red suspenders.

Molsey, a handkerchief in her right hand, closed the door. "Nobody ought to see this who doesn't need to," she said. She looked into Falcone's face. "Glad to have a witness who's still alive."

They walked back to the elevator. Pointing to the weapon on the floor, she asked, "That's the shooter's gun?"

"Right," Falcone said.

"We'll leave it there until the crime-scene guys get here," she said. "What about that bag he had?"

"What bag?" Falcone asked.

"It's still on the floor over there, a big canvas bag," she said. "You didn't notice it? You're a pretty observant guy."

"When I had him down I was focused on the gun. But, yes, there was some kind of bag. I remember now. When I first saw him walking into the office, he was carrying it. . . ."

"It says 'Al Jazeera' on the side, written on by something like a Sharpie. Any ideas

61

about that?"

"No, Chief. Except it was big enough to hold the M16."

"Yes. Thank you, Mr. Falcone." She noticed that Falcone was in some pain and kept squeezing his left hand, which was bright red and raw. "I'll have the ME put something on that hand of yours." She turned to the officers and, with a wave of her hand, said, "You three check with Captain Jefferson in the lobby and join the hunt for the other guy."

As the trio approached the elevator, the doors opened and two men stepped out, police-badge holders jutting from their suit-coat breast pockets.

"Detective Lieutenant Tyrone Emmetts and Detective Sergeant Samuel Robinson of the Homicide Branch," Mosley told Falcone. She paused, and shifted to her command voice: "Tyrone, I want a formal statement from this man, Falcone, who killed the guy on the lobby floor. Sam, the usual drill. Get identities and contact information of everybody here. There are a lot of people. We'll need statements from all of them. Get help from the branch if you need it. A lot of big-time lawyers, so good luck. Most of them were behind closed doors and didn't see anything. But they may have heard something. We'll also need to know what those people on the couch were doing here. And if anybody knows anything about that guy who wound up on the lobby floor. Do the usual paperwork. I'll keep closely in touch with the Branch. This is a big one, Sam."

Falcone pointed toward the end of the corridor and said, "I need to go there."

Mosley looked at him quizzically.

"Toilet. I need to . . ."

"Okay," she said. "Which office is yours?"

He pointed and said, " 'Falcone' on the door."

"I'll meet you there."

Falcone walked off, and in the restroom went over Mosley's questioning. She was good, the kind of interrogator who makes you feel guilty. *Al Jazeera. What the hell is that about? Those guys didn't look like any television journalists.*

When Falcone entered, Mosley and Emmetts were seated in front of his desk in the burgundy wingback chairs that usually contained his clients. "First of all, Mr. Falcone," Mosley began, "this seems to be an interrupted mass shooting of lawyers. Our strategy in shootings like this is to anticipate. I've ordered a general warning about the second shooter. Maybe he's going after lawyers. So this is urgent. Any idea why this firm? This floor?"

"No, Chief. None at all," he said. He had a theory about the crime, but he decided not to share the theory with Mosley.

"Did you feel you were . . . disrupting something?" Emmetts asked. "That there would have been more shooting if you hadn't stopped them?"

"Yes. I felt . . . I felt that we were all sitting targets."

"But *why*? What were they doing? Why shoot up a law firm? Why —"

Someone simultaneously knocked on his door and entered. A tall man strode over to the chair that Mosley occupied, reached out his right hand, and said, "I am Paul Sprague. I am greatly sorry that I'm disobeying your reasonable request to remain in my office, Chief Mosley. But I came here because I am obliged to find out what happened. I'm Sullivan and Ford's managing partner, and I am responsible for the lives of the men and women in this building."

Sprague then pulled up a wooden chair from a corner and sat down. In his perfectly tailored gray suit with a *Légion d'honneur* rosette in the lapel, he conveyed the confidence of a patrician, a man born to

64

deference and accomplishment.

"I've . . . I've seen the bodies — Ellen, the couple on the couch," Sprague said. "Horrible. Horrible. And I understand that Harold Davidson . . ." He paused. "We can directly identify one of the other . . . victims, of course. Ellen Franklin. As to the man and woman on the couch . . . I assume that they carried identification . . . and that they had some business with someone on the tenth floor . . . but . . ."

"The crime-scene techs will handle the obtaining of their ID documents, Mr. Sprague," Emmetts said, "and then we'll handle the notifying of their next of kin and making positive identification. Naturally, we will want to find out why they were here."

Sprague, ignoring Emmetts, pivoted toward Mosley. "Naturally, we will cooperate, Chief Mosley. But I am sure that you understand our need to adhere to the common rules of client-lawyer confidentiality."

Mosley did not respond. She rose and, ignoring Sprague, said, "I'm heading back to headquarters. But I'll be in constant touch with the investigation. Goodbye, for now, Mr. Falcone."

Sprague reached across Falcone's desk and picked up the yellow pad while saying,

"Thanks, Sean. I'll just turn to a fresh page and make some notes." He looked toward Emmetts and smiled. "I'd like to start at the beginning. Is it possible to . . ."

Emmetts shrugged, looked down at his notes, and gave Sprague a sketchy account of what Falcone had said so far. Falcone then finished his description of what had happened.

"Thank you, Mr. Falcone," Emmetts said. "Now, one other matter. You killed a man, Mr. Falcone, and we are all glad you did. But you're going to have to make a separate statement about that unknown male's death. And we will have to ask you to come to headquarters. Your prints are on the murder weapon, and we'll need to fingerprint you."

Sprague turned to Falcone, again ignoring Emmetts. "Mind if I represent you, Sean?"

"Well, I might really need a good defense lawyer," Falcone replied with a tight smile. "But I guess you'll have to do."

Sprague nodded and smiled back. He was a tall, slim man in his early sixties. His bearing and diction proclaimed privilege and a probable New England–Choate–Yale–Yale Law biography. But that was only part of his biography. He was born and brought up in a trailer in a little town on the Oklahoma panhandle and had known hungry days and lonely nights. He attained his scholarships because he was brilliant and polite, and he had attained his senior partnership not only because of his career as a superb lawyer but also because he had an uncanny ability to drain fear, fraud, and even greed out of a dispute, leaving only the purity of reason and common sense. He was Falcone's favorite squash opponent, but Falcone would not like to have him as an opponent in court. Falcone's hand, now thankfully dressed with an antiburn cream and bandaged, was still throbbing. His head ached, and he felt blood trickling down his left cheek. He reached into his pocket for a handkerchief, and held it against a cut on his forehead. He longed to go home.

Sprague stood, and now clearly in charge, addressed Emmetts: "I assume you'll need an operating base for interviewing people and so forth. I've arranged for the police to have an empty staff office on this floor. It's Room 1038, just off the conference room on the north corridor."

Emmetts's radio crackled. He stepped out, closed the door, and then stuck his head in to say, "Crime scene and a team from the medical examiner's office. Have to brief them. Please remain in your office, Mr. Falcone. And then I'll get you an escort for the trip to headquarters. Goodbye, Mr. Sprague."

"We have a lot of talking to do, Sean," Sprague said as soon as the door closed. "And you need something for that cut." He reached for the phone, pressed the button for his interoffice phone, and said, "Ursula, please bring the first-aid kit to Mr. Falcone's office — and your laptop. Thank you." Looking at Falcone, he added, "I'll be right back for our talk."

Still clutching Falcone's yellow pad, Sprague left.

10

Back in his corner office, Sprague summoned three associate partners from the eighth floor. Working from a list on a yellow pad, he assigned one to write a draft of Davidson's obituary, which he would sign off on and send to the *New York Times* and *Washington Post.* Sprague also told the associate to start working on arranging a memorial service for Davidson at the National Cathedral.

The second associate was to go to Ellen's mother, give her the condolences of the firm, help her make funeral arrangements, and offer to help with Ellen's insurance and pension account. He was also to prepare the draft of "a short message about the incident" to be sent to all Sullivan & Ford offices around the world. He would also sign off on that.

He told the third associate to organize a meeting of the Senior Partners' Executive

Committee in the conference room. At nine a.m. tomorrow. But she pointed out that people were still streaming out of the building and that many tenth-floor occupants, after being questioned by police, would want to go home and not come in tomorrow. Sprague, acting as if nothing notable had happened, shrugged and told her to call the meeting for the day after tomorrow. And he told her to immediately send out the kind of all-personnel message used for holidays, making tomorrow "a day of remembrance."

He instructed Ursula Breitsprecher, his executive assistant, to take charge of incoming phone calls, keeping track of condolences and clients' concerns. She was to politely inform every reporter or television producer who called that because of the ongoing police investigation there would be no comment from Sullivan & Ford.

Sprague, accompanied by Ursula, then went to Falcone's office. Falcone was sitting at his grand old desk, back to the door, staring at the Capitol dome and the graying sky. He turned to Sprague and felt that his cool and methodical behavior had somehow produced a shield of reason that held off the madness of the shootings. Sprague matter-of-factly told him about his instructions to the associates.

"And now for you. You okay?" Sprague asked, as if, Falcone thought, Sprague had been practicing triage and now had come to treat a case that needed immediate, specialized treatment.

Sprague took out his cell phone and clicked three images of Falcone's wound. Then Ursula handed him a small blue box with a red cross on its lid. He took out a cotton swab, wiped Falcone's wound, squirted antiseptic on it, and applied a large Band-Aid.

"Now we talk about the killing," he said. "I have asked Ursula to check out recent and classic homicide cases in which the killer claimed self-defense or justified homicide." Ursula sat at the corner chair and opened her laptop.

She moved gracefully and surely. He had heard that she had been a teenaged ballerina in the Leipzig Ballet when the Berlin Wall fell. Traveling alone, she managed to track down a distant relative in Philadelphia. She worked her way through the University of Pennsylvania by teaching dance. Office gossip, which Falcone usually ignored, said she was having an affair with a South Carolina congressman.

"We go with justified," Sprague continued.

"Self-defense is a bit risky. There's no 'stand and defend' law on the books in DC. This isn't Florida, Texas, or a dozen other states that give you a license to kill. In real life, self-defense rarely ends in homicide. And when it does, some wise-guy prosecutor always asks, 'Why was it necessary to *kill* John Doe? Why not just restrain him until the police arrive?' "

"Jesus!" Falcone said. "You sound like a goddamn . . ."

"Lawyer," Sprague said. "Which is exactly what you need."

"The guy had an *automatic weapon.* You make it sound like he was the victim!"

"The autopsy will show that his trigger finger was disabled," Sprague continued. "Poor fellow. He landed faceup, and, from what I gather from a lobby security man I called, his nose was broken and his face bloody. Looks like you brutally attacked him and deliberately threw him to his death."

Falcone started to sputter a response. Sprague held up his hand in a traffic-cop gesture and said, "We go with justifiable. You were a hero. You intervened during the commission of a crime. You came to the defense of others. You *prevented more murders.* You were *injured.* When a person commits a justifiable homicide, that person

72

is not guilty of a criminal offense.

"Detective Lieutenant Emmetts does not realize that if the investigating police officer sees the death as justified homicide, he can just sign off, using his own judgment. No prosecutor. No court hearing. No further legal issues. I will get that assurance from Detective Lieutenant Emmetts. There is absolutely no need for you to go to police headquarters now. I'll schedule a time at our convenience."

"Okay," Falcone said wearily. "I'm sure you're right. Look, I'm bushed, and —"

"There are only a couple of other issues," Sprague said. Nodding at Ursula, he opened the office door and handed her the yellow pad, saying, "Thanks so much, Ursula. As usual, you were superb. Go along to the office the police are occupying. I will see you in a moment."

"What other issues?" Falcone asked as soon as Ursula closed the door.

"You and I are in a client-lawyer situation here, just to remind you. So anything you . . ."

"Jesus, Paul, I know about client-lawyer privilege."

"Just being cautious, Sean. I must be absolutely certain that you never saw the gunman, never had anything to do with him

73

or with the guy who escaped."

"I never saw that bastard before. Or the other guy."

"Okay. Two other matters. Delicate. First, I must tell you that when I glanced at the yellow pad I borrowed from your desk, I saw notes about SpaceMine and Robert Wentworth Hamilton. Also a note about someone named Taylor."

"What the hell were you doing snooping on me?" Falcone asked angrily.

"Come on, Sean. It was an accidental discovery. But a lucky one. I'd rather not have Hamilton or SpaceMine dragged into this. And who is Taylor?"

"Dr. Benjamin Franklin Taylor, assistant director of the Air and Space Museum — and a friend. Why the hell should you care?"

"I care because I need to know *everything* about what's going on. This has been a traumatic — potentially disastrous — incident for the firm. As you can imagine — well, it's *unimaginable* — Mr. Hamilton is one of our important clients — if not our *most* important client."

"I'm well aware of Hamilton's importance, Paul. I was watching that announcement because I was curious. GNN had been promoting a 'major news break' for the past couple of days. I also figured that Space-

74

Mine or Hamilton might need some ideas about whether the SEC might get involved. Incidentally, SpaceMine wasn't mentioned in that confidential memo about our new client. Does our work for Hamilton include SpaceMine?"

Sprague paused, deciding not to respond to the mention of Hamilton. He then continued his line of questioning. "When you first talked to police, when they put out the description of the second gunman, did you mention that you had been watching the SpaceMine special?"

Falcone thought for a moment. "No. I started out by telling them about walking down the west corridor, seeing the two men in the reception area, and continuing walking to the restroom. No mention of Space-Mine or Hamilton."

"Fine. Now, what you saw — or *thought* you saw — the second man was carrying. How did you describe what you saw?"

Falcone hesitated before he responded: "I said he was carrying something . . . but not in his hands. It was slung over a shoulder, like the kind of case you use for a laptop."

"That's what you saw . . . what you said? So it looked to you that the man might be carrying a laptop in a case?"

"Yes. For God's sake, Paul, this is getting

tiresome. What the hell are you trying to get at?"

"Harold had a desktop in his office and a laptop, both registered as property of Sullivan and Ford, just as you and most of us have. On my way here from my office, I disobeyed Chief Mosley by looking in Hal's office — horrible, horrible. There was no laptop there. That *could* mean that Harold didn't bring the laptop into the office."

"Or," Falcone said, "it could mean that Hal did bring it in today and the guy took it."

"Right. That's what we must assume."

Sprague rose and drew his chair closer to Falcone's desk. "If necessary, I'll handle your description of the gunman as speedy information, not part of your formal statement, which you will be making in my presence. When you make that formal statement, I suggest that you simply say the man was carrying a briefcase, period. On the other matter, I'll be there in case he strays away from your claim of self-defense in the death of the gunman."

"And in case I start to say anything that you and Sullivan and Ford don't like," Falcone snapped.

"Well, you bring up the second — the final — issue. The needs of the firm are paramount to all of us, as are the needs of all our clients. Regarding Hal's laptop, I do not want our clients to learn that a computer containing confidential client information is missing."

"Hold on, Paul. I said something like 'the kind of case you carry a computer in.' If Harold was killed so that the killer could get his laptop, that is supremely important to the police investigation."

"Perhaps, Sean. Perhaps. But at the moment the police are investigating a crime in progress. The second man is at large. I don't want you to harm or thwart the police investigation or withhold vital information. Saying he had a carrying case of some kind is part of describing him. You don't know what was in the case."

"I was up against guys like you when I was a prosecutor," Falcone said, shaking his head. "Defense attorneys who were always skating at the edges. I'll follow my conscience, and I will heed the needs of the firm."

"The firm is facing a crisis, Sean. We can lose clients, big clients. And we can lose personnel, even partners. I don't want to rely on what the police or the media make of this crime. We need our own narrative, Sean. I want you to conduct your own investigation of what happened here and make a confidential report that will be presented to me as managing partner."

"Will I be allowed to question you?"

"Yes, of course. But . . . I don't see what I can add. You were the witness, the guy who stopped a massacre."

"I may have to ask you some questions about Davidson, about his clients."

"Of course. I'll cooperate in every way, Sean. Now I have to go talk to the detectives."

"I assume that Ursula is shredding that yellow pad with Hamilton's name on it."

"Don't make assumptions, Sean. Just ask questions and get answers. But remember, Ursula is my confidential assistant and the firm's rules say she doesn't have to answer to anyone but me."

11

Viktor Yazov saw two police cars blocking the intersection half a block ahead and decided to take a chance. His black Mercedes-Benz S600 was conspicuous, and if he tried a U-turn, he'd be even more conspicuous. He was not carrying a weapon, but within a hidden compartment in the driver's door was a Sig Sauer P226 that had been stolen from a Navy SEAL during a brawl at a bar in lower Manhattan.

The police-scanning radio was invisible, concealed within the wiring of the regular dashboard radio. He had a New York chauffeur's license in his wallet, a chauffeur's black cap on his head, and a New York registration in the glove compartment. He knew from experience that a routine police-car computer check would not turn up any criminal record for him. The armor and the bulletproof glass were discreet. And these were street cops, not feds nosing around.

He stopped behind a taxi whose driver was giving the cop a hard time. When the taxi was waved through, Viktor moved slowly up to an officer standing at the side of his car. Viktor showed his license and registration, doffed his wraparound sunglasses to show his friendly eyes, and produced a grin gleaming with two gold teeth. He could truthfully say that he had not seen a young man in a black coat. The Mercedes rolled on, turning right at the next intersection.

Viktor had begun his career in Moscow, when, following in his father's footsteps, he was accepted into a pool of drivers who specialized in providing safe, high-speed service for young oligarchs. They enjoyed the status of a flashy, armored vehicle driven by someone who knew exactly when to offer a bribe and how to make himself invaluable as a guide to the seamier side of Moscow life. One of his clients called the Mercedes his whoremobile.

One night, a client, high on cocaine, began engaging in sexual play with a young woman he had picked up at one of the hottest clubs in Moscow. Viktor was used to having the ample backseat turned into a playground. But this time the play became lethal when the client lost control while experimenting with sexual strangulation. The client was a middle-echelon member of the Foundation for Social Assistance to Athletes, also known as the Orekhovskaya gang, and Viktor realized he was at a crossroad: Call the police or help the client dispose of the body and become a driver for the gang.

He made his choice and became well known as the best driver in the Moscow underworld. Soon he was hired as the principal driver for one of Russia's richest and most powerful oligarchs, Kuri Basayev.

Dukka gone. Now what? To stay alive in Basayev's organization, you could not make a mistake. Viktor knew Basayev as a man to be feared, a man who killed his enemies, a man who punished mistakes with exile or, sometimes, death sentences. What happened today would not please Basayev.

12

While Viktor was in Washington in a near panic, Kuri Basayev was far away. When what Basayev called "a special operation" was going on, he always was far away — usually somewhere at sea aboard his yacht. Special operations were relatively rare, and Basayev regretted them, especially on American soil. But sometimes they had to happen.

Like other Russian oligarchs, Basayev had acquired a fortune by having the political connections that provided the inside knowledge needed to be at the right place at the right time. Even with that advantage, however, the oligarchs were hit hard by the financial crisis in 2008. Kuri Basayev's investment losses forced him to expand his underworld empire in Russia and in the United States.

On a day about two weeks before the Sullivan & Ford shootings, Basayev had shown that his wealth was ample enough for him to acquire a new residence in New York. Accompanied by the manager of his principal hedge fund, Basayev had appeared twenty minutes late for his meeting with the president of the city's largest real-estate firm. The meeting was in the penthouse atop the eighty-five-story NYNY on Fifth, the latest Manhattan aerie built to provide appropriate New York City shelters for billionaires like Basayev.

The towering palaces were not homes. They were places where foreign visitors could spend a few days and nights enjoying New York and the great wealth that buys the city's splendor. They were not part of the New York society. They never appeared at charity galas, museum fundraisers, or gallery openings. They tried to play in the shadows, unseen by the eyes of the media.

The realtor reverently greeted Basayev and led him and his trailing advisor to a large, glass-walled room called the library lounge. Its shelved walls already contained dozens of books selected for their jacket colors by the room's designer. They sat in high-winged chairs around a table that was a polished slice of redwood. A slight echo bounced off the twenty-two-foot ceiling as the realtor described the penthouse's panoramic views, its rosewood flooring, and its walls of Italian marble.

"NYNY on Fifth," he continued, "will become a classic landmark, one that is not eccentric or bizarre, but an intelligent building that is in dialogue with the outstanding cityscape it is entering. In this architectural gem, magnificent but discreetly opulent, you'll discover . . ."

"I am aware of this building's many virtues," Basayev interrupted. Swinging his right arm around in an encompassing gesture, he said, "I will buy this place." He nodded to the advisor, who opened his slim briefcase and extracted a check for $90 million, drawn on a Belgium bank owned by Basayev.

He rose and walked around the room, leaving the advisor and the realtor to go over the details of the purchase contract. He stopped for a few moments before a floor-to-ceiling window that framed Central Park, a skyline silhouette, and a patch of clear blue sky. Then he turned and said, "Fine view. Goodbye."

Quickening his step, he walked toward the hall that opened to the elevator, where his security men awaited him. One spoke into a cell phone. The two men were both over six feet, unusually tall for Chechens, though they had been shaped by Chechen genes that made them black-haired, black-bearded, broad-shouldered, and barrel-chested. They wore black leather jackets, black jeans, and black Air Jordans.

They followed Basayev into the elevator and flanked him when they emerged and crossed the long, blue-carpeted lobby. At the bronze door that opened onto Fifth Avenue, the two men shouldered aside the doorman and stood for a moment, scanning the sidewalk's swirling currents of people. One of them pointed toward a man standing nearby, looking conspicuous as the only person standing in a flow of people on the go. The bodyguard said something in Chechen and laughed. He nodded to Basayev, and the three men stepped out.

They walked ahead of him as they strode toward a black limousine that slipped out of the traffic and pulled up parallel to them; three cars behind was a dark blue Chevrolet. The man who had been pointed out by the Chechen walked rapidly toward the Chevrolet.

At that moment, another man dashed across Fifth Avenue, cut in front of the limousine, stepped before the advancing trio, and stopped. The bodyguards had seen him and chased him before. He was a paparazzo — but he did not have a camera. For a moment, they were puzzled. Then one of them noticed something attached to the right lens of his sunglasses — and realized, Google Glass!

As one of the bodyguards ran forward, the paparazzo rapidly blinked. The bodyguard towered over the paparazzo, snatched his Google Glass off with one hand, and punched him with the other. As the smaller man fell, the bodyguard hurled the Google Glass to the ground and stomped on the tiny computer built into the frame of the sunglasses.

While the paparazzo writhed on the sidewalk, Basayev and his guardians entered the limousine, which pulled into the Fifth Avenue traffic and began crawling south.

Each time the paparazzo had blinked, the Google Glass had recorded the image and transmitted it to his cell phone in a pocket in his suit. The cell phone transmitted the images to a computer in his office in SoHo. Three days later, two of the images appeared in the *New York Post,* accompanying a story about the Russian oligarchs' "invasion of superposh Manhattan real estate."

One photo showed Basayev, a handsome middle-aged man, tanned and fit, with a beard that was little more than a five-o'clock shadow. His close-cropped hair was graying and receding. He wore Top-Siders, a half-buttoned white shirt, and dark blue slacks. Basayev was frowning, his right arm raised as if warding off a blow. The *Post* caption noted that he had just "emerged from a new Fifth Avenue skyscraper, whose lavish penthouse he had bought for a reputed $120 million."

The other photo showed one of the bodyguards charging toward the camera, his jacket flaring open and revealing a shoulder holster.

"Note that the bodyguard is carrying heat," said the *Post* caption. "A New York Police Department spokesman revealed that the Glock in that holster is legal. The bodyguards have concealed-weapon licenses as employees of On Guard, the personal-security company owned by Basayev."

The story described Basayev as one of Russia's richest oligarchs, ignoring his Chechen identity. That identity was especially important to American law-enforcement officials, who saw Basayev not only as an up-and-coming Russian mafia boss but also as a potential importer of Chechen terrorism. The man who jumped into the Chevrolet was an FBI agent as-signed to the New York Police Department's

Joint Terrorism Task Force.

Kuri Basayev was a distant relative of Shamil Basayev, a notorious Chechen terrorist. But Kuri Basayev became one of the few successful Chechens who was accepted by the thin layer of the Russian ruling class that included financiers and killers. He was a man of two worlds with vague borders: finance and crime. On his legitimate side he had earned a reputation for shrewd investing that produced enormous fortune with a global reach. He had also played a veiled role in Vladimir Putin's rise to power in 2000 — a connection that led to Basayev's control of oil companies, ore mines, and media corporations.

His criminal career was more difficult to track. But the expansion of his underworld empire became known to New York police when they discovered signs that he had his own representation in Brighton Beach, Brooklyn, headquarters of the American branch of the Russian mob. Residents with or without police records appreciated the way the swaggering Russians kept the streets safe from muggers and FBI informers.

The latest newcomers were two young hit men who had arrived from a Chechen community in Idaho. Viktor showed them around what residents called "Russia by the Sea" and was impressed by the way the two cousins managed to fit into a place that did not welcome strangers, especially Chechen strangers.

Through an arrangement that Basayev had made, his men lived and worked separately from the established mob. So far Viktor had been behind the wheel for five of the cousins' hits — quick jobs in New York and New Jersey: shots to the back of the head for reasons unknown. Now Viktor wondered what would be the reward for this special operation.

13

Falcone was about to leave his office when his unlisted private phone rang. DC POLICE appeared on the caller ID screen and he picked up the phone. *Private, my ass. Nothing's private anymore.*

"Mr. Falcone. This is Sergeant Clarence Reed. Please open your e-mail. I urgently want to send you some surveillance-camera images."

Falcone sighed. *I wonder what the NSA will do about these e-mails.* Less than a minute later, on the monitor of his desktop computer he saw a dozen or so men and women walking rapidly or running. In the background he could see the entrance to the Sullivan & Ford Building. The image froze and the phone rang.

"Sergeant Reed again," the voice on the phone said. "You are looking at an image from a Starbucks exterior surveillance camera on First Street, about one hundred yards south of the Sullivan and Ford Building, just after the shooting. You can see, near the entrance, the first officers leaving their vehicle."

"Right. I see them," Falcone said, leaning closer to the computer screen. "Hold it. . . . No . . . I don't think that's him. . . . I can't be sure."

Falcone was wary of making any snap judgments, given the power of the new social media. He remembered how a false identification was made in the wake of the bombing in Boston two years ago. The young man, who was mistakenly identified, had his photo plastered all over the media. He got so much harassment that he ended up committing suicide.

"I understand," Reed said. "Thanks anyway. We'll be doing a facial-recognition scan on this guy anyway and put him into match-up mode against our watch lists — FBI, CIA, Homeland Security. Please stand by for another image."

Falcone stared at the computer monitor, looking at the image, now no longer stopped in time. The man on the screen — he had to be in his early twenties — walked on, not hurrying, not drawing attention. *Maybe he was the killer. Maybe he was already planning his next victim.* "Possibly him. Still not sure.

It's just hard to say."

Reed, still on the phone, said, "Now here comes an enlarged image from the windshield video of a patrol car turning onto Second Street near D and heading north in response to the 911 call."

"Right," Falcone said. "The police car passes a black car heading south. Can you read the license plate?"

"Unfortunately, no. Very muddy back plate."

"On a Mercedes town car?" Falcone asked. "Very unlikely."

"Yeah. Not the first time I've seen mud on the plates of a getaway car. So we have a black car — Mercedes. We blew up the image. No indication of a passenger. Driver has on what seemed to be a chauffeur cap. Maybe New York plates. But we can't be sure. So that's what we've got. The gunman was probably on foot, waiting a pickup. And God only knows where he is now. Well, Mr. Falcone, thank you for your help. We'll keep in touch."

14

When Viktor saw the road crew and the big orange DETOUR sign, he stopped and sighed. He was forced to turn left and go south, when he wanted to turn right and head north. Another turn around another block, another plea from Ahmed — *Viktor. I'm on E Street, near Eleventh Street. Where the fuck are you? Cops all over.* The GPS on Viktor's dashboard showed he was not too far away from Interstate 395. *Get to Ahmed, pick him up, head north . . . to New York Avenue, then out of this goddamn city.* Basayev's tech guy, who had wired the police scanner so that it worked inside the regular radio, had also added to the GPS an app that showed most surveillance-camera locations. *Jesus! Cameras all over the fucking place.*

At Eleventh and D, Viktor spotted Ahmed leaning against a telephone poll, his head swiveling back and forth, back and forth. *If*

*a smart cop saw that nervous son of a bitch,
he'd take out his gun, walk right up to him,
and start asking questions.*

"Get in! Get in!" Viktor commanded. "In
the back. Like a big shot."

Ahmed opened the rear door and hurled
himself into the backseat. "Let's go! Let's
go!" he shouted.

"We need to get that fuckin' laptop,"
Viktor said. "Show me —"

"We need to get the fuck out of here,"
Ahmed shouted. "Out! Out! Let's go, for
Christ sake."

Viktor had parked at a bus stop on E
Street, engine purring. Cops usually ignored
town cars that stopped to await clients.

"Where the hell you put it?"

"I put the bag and my coat behind a
Dumpster in an alley on Second Street, near
E Street."

"And the gun?"

"Yes. And the gun."

Viktor looked at the GPS and ordered a
new destination. "That alley is five, six
minutes from here, if no big fuckin' orange
signs." Viktor studied the GPS map and saw
a parking garage two blocks away, off
Pennsylvania Avenue. He steered into traffic, drove to the garage, plucked his ticket
from the machine, drove down the ramp to

a space, and backed into the space. "My father tell me, front out, always front out. Back in so you can move fast after."

Viktor looked at his Rolex, which once had been on the wrist of a hedge fund manager who had tried to cheat Kuri Basayev. "We sit here an hour, maybe two," he said. "Things cool. Then we go to that alley and we get the goddamn laptop." He patted the GPS map. "And we head north. On the turnpike we get hamburgers."

15

Falcone walked down the corridor toward the restroom, looked around, and then took a few steps toward the stairway. He had had enough police for the day, and he didn't intend to run into any of them on the elevator. At the fifth-floor landing he decided to give his weary legs a rest. He opened the door a crack, saw no one near the elevator doors, and headed toward them. An empty car arrived. He hit P1 for the basement parking garage.

The Sullivan & Ford Building, as an architectural critic wrote, looked "glassy and classy" on the outside. The basement garage was just as clean and classy. And nearly deserted, Falcone was glad to note.

He walked up the street-level ramp, which ended next to the building's E Street entrance, around the corner from the entrance with the stanchions, the yellow tape, and the knot of police at the doors.

Satisfied that he had eluded the police and the TV and print reporters, Falcone turned right and took his usual route to his apartment on Pennsylvania Avenue.

As he congratulated himself on his successful escape, the word persisted in his mind. Falcone suddenly realized that he might be stepping into the gunman's escape route. *For some reason, he misses the pickup car. He comes out of the building, maybe walking a little slower than the people who are fleeing. He sees that the car isn't there. He goes to plan B, maybe talking to the driver to work out some place for a pickup.*

Back in his days as a prosecutor, Falcone had a reputation for nailing criminals by making hunches come true. He tried to explain that his hunches arose from his attempts to get inside a felon's brain — "soul-burrowing," a *Boston Globe* feature writer called it. Falcone knew, deep in his soul, why he had become a relentless prosecutor who would never bargain, never make a deal: He kept making up for the fact that he had lost his first two cases — aggravated rape and vehicular manslaughter. He had vowed that never again would he allow law to thwart justice.

In the rape case, a judge ruled that the

young woman had gone to the frat-house party voluntarily and had consumed liquor voluntarily and, according to witnesses, had entered the accused man's bedroom voluntarily. "This can hardly be a case of rape, let alone aggravated rape," the judge had ruled in dismissing the case. "Aggravated rape calls for the victim to 'resist to the utmost' and for the alleged rapist to 'make threats of great and immediate bodily harm.' The accused said he had made no threat, and his alleged victim does not have a clear memory of what had happened. The prosecution's exhibit of torn clothing is irrelevant, given the lack of witnesses to what happened behind the closed bedroom door."

The vehicular homicide case had not even reached a judge. Just before the scheduled day of the trial, someone in the governor's office had ordered that the case be handled by another prosecutor. The new prosecutor dropped the charge, because "the tragic accident had not involved a crime, namely no gross negligence, no drunk driving, no reckless driving, no speeding." Not included in the explanation was the fact that the driver was a nephew of the lieutenant governor.

After those cases, he had a kind of epiphany: He would stop thinking like a lawyer, stop thinking like a prosecutor, and start thinking like a criminal — a smart criminal who not only broke the law but also tried to outwit the law.

Now, as he passed Starbucks and a police car sped by on First Street, he found himself instinctively imagining himself as the gunman who tried to kill him. *No car. I have to walk and hope to find the car. I'm a pro, but I'm feeling a little panicky. I am alone, and that was not in the plan. Cops all around. That guy I shot at, he'll give the cops a description: young, black hair, usual stuff. And the coat, the bag. Hide them.*

Falcone turned right on E Street to Second Street. He was on the stretch of the street specially named Mitch Snyder Place after the homeless advocate who turned the block-long former federal building here into a massive shelter. *Hide. A place to hide them. Look for cameras.* Falcone looked around and then remembered. *No cameras. Perfect.*

A few months ago, the police, reacting to the number of arrests made at or near the shelter, had installed surveillance cameras around the outside of the building. The Community for Creative Non-Violence, dedicated to protecting the rights of the homeless and poor, went to court and succeeded in getting the cameras removed. He guessed he remembered because the anti-camera activists had argued that if the police put cameras on private premises where people gathered, then there should be cameras in front of private clubs like the Metropolitan.

He was now opposite an alley next to the shelter. He saw a Dumpster and on a hunch started toward the alley. In the shadowed light, Falcone saw the silhouette of a man walking away from him. As he moved quickly to catch up to the retreating figure, he shouted out, "Hold on. Wait up, mister."

The man could be in his forties or his seventies — dank, gray hair curling over his ears, cheeks sunken beneath a sparse, gray-streaked beard. He wore an unzipped black leather coat over a faded-green T-shirt ringed with dirt and sweat. A computer bag was slung carelessly over his shoulder.

"That's a nice-looking coat," Falcone said. "You want to tell me where you got it?"

"Fuck you, buddy. I found it. That makes it mine."

"No," Falcone said. "That coat belongs to a killer. So does that bag and whatever is in it. That makes you a criminal unless you hand it over to me now."

"Bullshit, mister. You don't look like no cop to me," the man said, trying to sound

100

menacing, as he came closer to Falcone.

He smelled of liquor. Cheap wine, Falcone guessed. "So you got the coat and the bag out of the Dumpster over there?"

"None of your business where I got it."

Falcone reached out and grabbed the man's arm. As he did so, he quickly concluded that the man's appearance was deceiving. Beneath the sleeve of the leather coat that was ill-fitting and too small, Falcone felt a forearm that was thick and iron-hard.

"Fuck off, mister! Get your hands off me!" he shouted, jerking his arm away with stunning speed and power, catching the corner of Falcone's eye with a closed fist.

Blood gushed out of a cut that had been sliced open along the scar tissue Falcone had acquired years ago as a collegiate boxing champ at Syracuse University.

The man seemed as surprised as Falcone when he saw the blood dripping onto Falcone's white shirt.

"Sorry, but I told you . . ."

"Son of a bitch," Falcone cursed, and lashed out quickly, grabbing the man by the throat in a vise grip and squeezing hard.

Unable to breathe, the man started to gag and sank to his knees.

"Yeah, and I told you to give me the goddamn coat and bag. Give them up or I'll break —"

"Okay, okay," the man rasped, choking on his words. "I didn't get the coat and bag from inside the Dumpster, but behind it." Getting back to his feet, he dropped the tough-guy pretense. "Young guy hid it. Like he was going to have someone pick them up. Maybe someone like you."

"I'd appreciate it very much if you give them to me. There's a reward," Falcone said, trying to remember how much money he was carrying.

"Well, maybe I want to keep them."

"Look, Mr. . . ."

"Mr. Jones."

"Okay, Mr. Jones. I'm Mr. Smith. I don't want to report stolen goods and get cops involved. I'm going to give you one hundred dollars cash, and you're going to give me the coat and the computer."

"Just the computer," the man said. "I need the coat."

Falcone moved swiftly. He slammed the man against the Dumpster, stuck his hand into the pocket of the coat, and felt the handle of a gun. He pulled the gun out, stepped back, pushing the gun into the man's stomach.

"Look, Mr. Jones, I don't have time to

fuck around. What's your real name?"

"Crawford. Thomas Crawford," the man said, sputtering. "I'm a vet, like a lot of guys here. Two tours in Iraq. One in Afghanistan. I don't want any trouble, mister. I —"

"Just take off that coat and give it to me, along with the computer bag," Falcone said, speaking softly, embarrassed that he had lost control so quickly and had been about to hurt a complete stranger. A stranger who had worn the same uniform he once had. "I can't tell you why I know, but there just might be a detective here soon, and he's going to ask you how you got these. Just tell him the truth about finding them. And tell your buddies that there's going to be a VA person here soon."

The alley was deep in shadow. A chill wind stirred, sending a cluster of paper and dead leaves across the man's ragged sneakers. In slow motion, as if coming out of a trance, Crawford handed over the computer bag, which Falcone slipped over his shoulder with his bandaged left hand. Then he slowly removed the coat, which Falcone grabbed with his free hand.

"Turn around," Falcone said.

Crawford instantly obeyed. Falcone took out his money roll and slipped the gun inside his belt under his suit jacket. He pulled out five twenty-dollar bills and stuffed them into a back pocket of stained and worn jeans.

"Count to fifty before you even think of moving," Falcone ordered. He pressed a white handkerchief on the cut that had been opened over his eye and walked rapidly down the alley to the street.

Ten minutes later, Falcone was in his apartment. He had managed to stop the flow of blood and had sealed the cut with a thin Band-Aid. Next, he placed a bag of frozen beans over the cut to keep the swelling down, as he pondered exactly what to do.

He could call Chief Mobley or he could call Sprague. He had not actually charmed Mobley, and Sprague was his lawyer. He chose Sprague. But first he opened the laptop.

Suddenly, a flashing black-and-yellow frame appeared around white words on a black background:

WARNING

YOU ARE NOT AUTHORIZED ACCESS TO THIS LAPTOP.

DISCONNECT NOW.

All attempts to access and use this laptop are subject to keystroke monitoring and recording that can reveal evidence of criminal activity. Unauthorized use may subject you to criminal prosecution or other adverse action.

Falcone closed the laptop and called Sprague's private line. Sprague answered on the first ring.

"I'm home," Falcone said. "Please come here right away."

"What now?" Sprague asked.

"Just come here. We need to talk."

16

Barely fifteen minutes had passed before Sprague was dropped off in his chauffeured limousine in front of Falcone's residence. The tall building and its adjacent twin were marvels of Greco-Roman architecture. They wrapped the Navy Memorial fountain and the statue of the Lone Sailor in a graceful stone embrace.

As Sprague entered the building, he was greeted by a large uniformed man standing behind a concierge's mahogany desk.

"I'm Paul Sprague and I'm here to see —"

"Mr. Falcone is expecting you. He's on the penthouse floor. Turn left off the elevators and proceed to the end of the hall."

Sprague was a bit surprised when he realized that he had never been to Falcone's place before. They saw each other on the squash court and at a reception now and then. But, as far as Sprague knew, Falcone did not entertain very often.

The elevator whisked him quickly to the top floor and opened to a long hallway. Sprague's heels clicked loudly on the polished marble floor. At the end of the hall, Sprague saw Falcone standing in the open doorway of his apartment, waiting to greet him.

As Falcone extended his right hand and thanked Sprague for coming, he noticed that Sprague's eyes had drifted to a place above the doorway.

"Jesus, Sean. What happened here? Those look like bullet holes."

"Nothing nearly so dramatic, Paul," Falcone said. "The Secret Service pulled the security cameras off the day I left office."

"Well, it would have been real nice of the Secret Service to patch it up."

"Uncle Sam is quicker digging holes than filling them up. They will eventually. Probably bill me for the work, too."

"And what in hell happened to your eye? I didn't see that at the office. Did —"

"I ran into a little problem on the way home. Nothing serious," Falcone said, not wanting to discuss how he had nearly choked a homeless veteran.

Falcone escorted Sprague into his

expansive living room. A glass wall offered a view through that encompassed the majestic dome of the Capitol, the Washington Monument, the National Archives, and the large gray building that housed the Justice Department.

"Nice place, Sean."

"It's not the Ritz," Falcone said lightly.

"Great view, though. Besides, the Ritz isn't what it's always cracked up to be."

Falcone took Sprague's retort as a weak attempt at modesty. He'd read a *Post* gossip item that said Sprague had recently paid $8 million for an apartment at the Ritz in Georgetown. And that was just Sprague's city home. He also owned a huge estate in Middleburg, Virginia, and a place in Palm Springs that had been featured in *Architectural Digest* last year. Falcone had been around this town for a long time, but he'd never realized that a Washington law practice could possibly be so lucrative.

"Paul," Falcone said, pointing to the sofa, "why don't you take a seat over there," Falcone moved to a well-stocked bar situated in a corner next to a faux fireplace.

"How about a drink?"

"Pretty early in the day, isn't it?"

"Today is a little different."

"Sure. I'll have what you're having."

"Vodka okay?"

Sprague nodded. Falcone poured vodka into two glasses filled with ice. He handed one to Sprague and then slipped into an Eames Lounge chair. Both men raised their glasses in a silent toast and drank deeply.

"What's so urgent, Sean? Why couldn't you have just told me over the phone?"

"I needed to clarify a few things about what happened today and what you said about the need to protect the firm."

"I thought I was pretty clear that, depending on how we handle this mess, we have a lot to lose," Sprague said with a hint of impatience.

"Paul, a serious crime, no, a horrific crime, was committed and we have an obligation to fully cooperate and share whatever information we can with the police."

"Of course. But I don't understand. What's the problem?"

"This was no random act of violence. Our friend Hal Davidson was a target of an assassination. The others were killed just to make it look like an act of terrorism."

"And how did you come to this conclusion?"

Falcone took a sip before he said, "If it was intended as a massacre, the men would have started the killing spree as soon as they got off the elevators. Hal would have been the last person hit, not the first. Remember the sequence: Hal, then back down the corridor to kill Ellen and the two victims on the couch. The killers were clearly targeting Hal. They were on a mission."

"You're in the realm of speculation, Sean. You . . . we don't know that."

"I know what I know. And I know what I saw. If, as the DC police detective — Emmetts — believed, the shooters were crazies planning to wipe out the tenth floor, they would have started with Ellen and the man and woman across from her. Then they would've gone down the west corridor, office by office. In fact, they passed two offices, walking directly from the elevator to Hal's office. They opened his door, killed him, grabbed his laptop, walked back to the express elevator, and *then* shot Ellen and the others on their way out."

"And if you hadn't seen them, hadn't attacked them, they probably would have gotten away."

"And if I hadn't seen what had happened, the sequence of the shootings would not have been known. The assumption would be that Hal Davidson, like the others, was a random victim of an all-too-typical mass killing in a workplace."

"Okay," Sprague said. "You may have something there."

"There's something more, Paul. I still don't know why you were so concerned when I started telling the police that the bag looked like it might have carried a laptop computer."

"The answer is pretty simple, Sean. If in fact a computer was in the bag, the police would have started searching through all of Hal's computerized records centrally filed in the office. And then the search would be broadened to all of the internal correspondence that Harold had with his clients and with all of the other members of our firm. Of course we're going to give the investigators everything we can. I just want to proceed carefully."

Remaining silent, Falcone stood and finished off his drink. He turned away from Sprague and abruptly moved to a small study that was lined with books. He reached behind a desk and lifted up a black coat that was wrapped about something inside the coat. Falcone carefully pulled away the coat and placed a laptop and the Glock on the cocktail table in front of Sprague.

"These belong to the killer."

"Sean, how in hell . . ."

"A hunch. The killer must've panicked when he ran from the building and saw the police setting up the roadblocks. He tried to hide everything in an alley. I just got them," Falcone said, without mentioning that he held a homeless man at gunpoint.

Staring at the computer, Sprague said, "It doesn't look like anything that we authorize for the firm. It might be Hal's personal one."

"It can't be opened without special knowledge. Not just a password. Some kind of sophisticated protection."

"I'm sure the police have experts that can get into it. Let me check with some of the attorneys in the firm. Joe Kelly was closest to Hal. He may recognize this or know how to get in."

"Okay," Falcone said. "That makes sense. But you need to get everything over to Detective Emmetts right away. Tell him that a guy in the homeless shelter — the name is Thomas Crawford — found the computer and the coat — with a gun in the pocket — and gave them to me. He's a drunk and he didn't want to give up what he found until I . . . persuaded him. I think he saw the guy trying to hide this stuff."

"Got it, Sean. Absolutely. I'll take care of everything. Emmetts will want to talk to you about this again. But I'll do my best to handle as much as possible this afternoon."

Sprague wrapped the coat around the laptop and gun and headed for the door.

17

As soon as Sprague left, Falcone felt empty in an empty place. His apartment was not cold, but it lacked the softening touches of a woman's hand. The decor, in home-designer parlance, was "midcentury," an affected way of saying it was a throwback to the fifties. The living room's large gray sofa with brass nail-head buttons decorated a curved wooden base that paralleled a flat undecorated wall, against which rested a faux fireplace.

The fake logs contained a small blower that, when turned on, caused thin red and yellow ribbons to dance behind an unadorned metal screen. The eyes lied. The effect of burning logs was so real that Falcone, forgetting this deceit on more than one occasion, would pull his favorite chair closer to the fireplace and start to rub his hands to gather a warmth that it could not yield.

A classic Eames black leather chair that Falcone had acquired upon his return from Vietnam sat near a low, perfectly cylindrical brushed-steel table upon which lay a few copies of the *Economist* and *Bloomberg* newsmagazines. Near the floor-to-ceiling doors that opened to a sweeping terrace was a waist-high planter brimming with a cluster of orchids, his dead wife's favorite flowers.

Falcone could not make up his mind about the orchids. Keep them in the apartment? Why? To what end? Sure they were beautifully exquisite and required only a spray of water once a week. But their grace ripped open old wounds. In solitary moments, which were damn near most of the time, he would look at them and feel sentimentality flow through his veins as if it were a lethal poison. Karen's pure joy in selecting the flowers and appropriate bowls for special occasions infused the apartment with a palpable pride. She had not lived to see these rooms, but there were always orchids, and they sometimes seemed to come alive, as if they had just bathed and put on their best clothes. The walls were virtually singing their own praises, announcing to the evening's guests that they had prettied up just for them. Now the wall offered only sadness for a remembrance of joy.

Falcone kept one photograph. It was on a sleek mahogany table. In a moment that seemed so natural and unposed, the camera had captured the very essence of Karen, a striking blond woman in her early twenties with the high cheekbones and slim body of a *Vogue* model. She had her arms draped around a young, freckle-cheeked boy, who wore an embarrassed lopsided grin. That was Kyle, born while Falcone was enduring the ministrations of Hanoi's finest torturers. He never got to meet his only son.

Falcone couldn't count the times he wanted to smash the glass picture frame and burn the photograph. The memory of fleeting happy moments weighed like heavy, sharp-edged stones on the margins of his mind, severing any sense of meaning to his life, undercutting the will to live out what days or years were his to complete.

Guilt alone prevented him from carrying out an act of rage against the photograph or himself. Surely, he reasoned, he would roast in a phantasmagoric Hell — which he did not believe existed — if he were to exact vengeance against a universe he couldn't fathom by taking his own life. His Catholic education had really fucked up his mind.

There were only two books in the room, and Falcone kept them near his favorite chair. Both were about his war heroes, Oliver Wendell Holmes, Jr., and Joshua Chamberlain. Both had fought in the Civil War. Both had been wounded. Chamberlain had saved the Union from a disastrous defeat at Gettysburg, and Holmes had dazzled the nation with his intellect while serving as a justice on the Supreme Court.

There was a replica of Picasso's *Guernica,* which portrayed the horrors and destruction of war. Nothing else adorned the apartment walls or shelves. No mementos of Falcone's service in the Army, his career in the Senate or as national security advisor to President Oxley.

He felt what Churchill had called "the black dog" coming on as he went into his office, looked up a number on a slim, leather-bound address book, and called Tommy Goodman, an assistant secretary of the Department of Veterans Affairs. Goodman had not yet heard about the shooting. So the conversation was short, ending with a vague promise to get together for lunch and a firm promise to get somebody to check on the vets at the homeless shelter on Mitch Snyder Place.

Falcone went back to the living room.

There was a darkness that hung in the room even though it was filled with light. Loneliness was masquerading as simplicity, as if joy could be spun like cotton candy or the past erased by refusing to see or harbor its ghosts.

Falcone felt a wave of fatigue sweep over him. It wasn't from the fight that he had that morning. The punishing daily workouts in the gym kept him physically strong. And the fact that he killed a man — an enemy — was not a novel experience.

No, what weighed him down was the fact that violence seemed to be his constant companion, a dark angel that hovered somewhere above or just behind him.

As a young boy living on the mean streets of Little Italy in North Boston, he met taunts of being a "wop" and "mick" with flying fists. On college football fields and in boxing rings, he rejoiced when he leveled an opponent with a crunching block or devastating left hook.

After he married his sweetheart Karen, many of his friends thought that he would ease into a professional and less combative life.

It was not to be.

Impulsively, and without even consulting Karen, Falcone had joined the Army. Within months, he was the expectant father of a child conceived on his last leave before heading for Vietnam and war. He was leading men in battle while Karen gave birth to Kyle, alone. He had rationalized that he was simply answering the call to duty, inspired by the words of a young, charismatic president.

Falcone loved his country, to be sure. But it was not patriotism that was the driving force in his life. It was more than that. He was destined from the very beginning to run along the knife's edge of existence, to see how far he could go without falling, or, falling, how far he could drop without dying. Death was the sentence we all received, so why not defy it if he could, mock it, dare it to take him? He was going to plunge full-speed right into the heart of mortality and not wait, like his father, to be chewed up by cancer and just wither away.

He had gotten all that he had bargained for in Vietnam. And more.

18

Summoning darkness to a day of gunfire and death, old memories of gunfire and death flared again and again.

During his first major engagement as an Army Ranger, he killed more than a dozen Vietcong. Afterward, when he examined each of the men he had killed, he discovered that one of the black-clad soldiers was a boy, no more than fifteen years old. And he was surprised by his reaction. There was no sorrow or guilt. No empathy. Nothing. After all, he was just a few years older at the time, and in war, the calendar doesn't offer anyone bulletproof protection. One moonless night, while leading his unit on a patrol, he and his men were caught in a savage crossfire unleashed by the North Vietnamese. Falcone, though severely wounded, managed to survive the surprise attack. He was taken prisoner and moved to a POW site, dubbed the Hanoi Hilton. Almost everyone there was an Air Force pilot who had been shot down.

There were many days when he wished that he could have joined his dead comrades. For four years he was confined to a twelve-by-twelve cell. Each day he would be interrogated and tortured. Sometimes the torture was psychological, the sultry voice of Hanoi Hannah coaxing him to sign a confession so he could be released to join his family and enjoy moments of pleasure once again. But mostly, the punishment came at the hands of two particularly sadistic men that Falcone and the other prisoners called Bug and Prick. Their names fit their methods.

Without waiting for Falcone to recover from his wounds, the two men proceeded to hang Falcone by his arms from the ceiling of a torture chamber. They would hoist Falcone close to the ceiling and then let him drop several feet before stopping his fall. His shoulders were pulled from their sockets. Another favorite technique was to tie Falcone's arms behind his back and then tie his head between his legs. He would be left in this position all day and relieved of the pressure only for a few minutes two or three times a day.

During his third year of imprisonment,

Falcone was offered an early release for "humanitarian reasons." He was told that his wife and son had been killed in an auto accident. He simply needed to sign a confession admitting that he had committed war crimes on behalf of his imperialist country and he would be free to return to America.

Falcone suspected it was a trick and that both Karen and Kyle were alive. If he agreed to sign the statement he would be seen as a traitor by his fellow captives and by his countrymen at home. There were other prisoners who had been in prison far longer than he had. It would be unfair to jump to the front of the line. It was a bluff. It had to be. But even if it was true, Falcone was never going to leave before the others. It was a matter of honor. Honor to his country, to his fellow prisoners. Honor even above his family.

In fact, Karen and Kyle were dead. Killed by a drunken driver while returning home from grocery shopping.

When the war finally ended, Falcone was heralded at home as a hero. But Falcone knew he was anything but a hero. He had broken his marriage vow to love and protect Karen. She and Kyle never would have died if he had been home. If he had not responded to the bloodlust in his veins, if he had not left them for the rice paddies and prisons of another land. . . . He would carry the guilt of his decision like a watermark on his mind: one that only he could see and only when he held it up to the light of self-reflection.

He tried to obliterate the pain with a career in the law. He prosecuted Mafia dons and murderers. He went after corrupt public officials and corporate CEOs, sometimes wondering whether he was seeking revenge or redemption. Either way, it helped him to forget the emptiness inside, the hollowness he felt when he allowed himself a moment of reflection. He used to say that he was alone but never lonely. It was a lie that he constructed to keep others away from him, a wall that insulated him from the world of public adoration. Ironically, he was shielding himself from the very world that he was seeking to enter.

And when he was elected to the U.S. Senate, Falcone thought that just maybe his luck would change. It didn't. Senator Joshua Stock, his best friend, had his throat sliced by a Russian assassin. . . . Death just continued to stalk him. Tens of thousands died from a nuclear-bomb detonation in Savannah, Georgia. It was not his fault, but it was on his watch as President Blake Oxley's national security advisor.

And now, one of his law partners had been killed, nearly cut in two by the bullets of an assault weapon.

Was he so hated by the gods? For what? Was it because he abandoned his faith in that North Vietnam chamber of horrors or because God had abandoned him? Was it the melancholy of the Irish? Or the fatalism of the Italians?

He was never sure. But in the darkness of his soul he sometimes saw his fate: He was destined to lose those whom he loved or knew.

In the drawer of the end table next to his bed was a printout of an anonymous document he had come across one night when he was searching on Google for a poem that had dimly appeared in his mind and then disappeared. He did not find the poem. But he did find that anonymous document and had read it again and again. He had not quite committed it to memory. He did not want it in his mind, but it was there, confronting him.

How deep is the color black? Deep as a starless sky? Dark as Death's dank breath? How silent is silence before it becomes a sound? In here, where time does not exist, I spin through the night, screaming in a pain that no one hears. I cut through tissue that bleeds invisibly. I am neither myth nor the imaginary. I am the truth told too late.

He had read a recent study that said scientists were able to plant false memories in the minds of mice. Some predicted they would soon be able to apply this medical technique to people and block or erase bad memories by substituting false ones.

Falcone silently vowed that he would be the first in line to volunteer. Anything to forget. . . .

He returned to the bar, poured another slug of vodka into his empty glass, and knocked it down in one long gulp. Setting the glass down, he picked up the remote control to his Sonos Sound System and tapped the button that keyed into his favorite radio stations, a source of memories from earlier, better days.

He pulled off his slip-on shoes and stretched out on the living room sofa. The alcohol had started to ease the stress that he felt in his neck and soften the sounds of the traffic in the streets below.

Closing his eyes, Falcone listened to the lyrics and melody of an old song, the strings of the artist's guitar and timbre of his voice floating in the darkness in primary colors, like burnished leaves on a stream that wends its way to a cold and familiar destination.

19

Sergeant Clarence Reed watched the monitor as the image of the town car's muddied license plate enlarged until it was a mass of colors that looked like an amateur's attempt at an impressionist painting. Reed slowly brought the upper right-hand corner of the plate into focus. The orange color, topped by a blue band established that it was an Empire Gold plate, of the kind issued by New York State to replace blue-and-white plates.

The fake mud — a combination of water-based brown paint and silicone polymers — covered all but the tops of the plate's last two numbers. Reed split the monitor, leaving the plate on one side and pulling up a series of images of New York plates. Comparing the tops of the numbers, Reed came up with 4 and 8.

Assuming that the town car was registered in New York City and would be of interest to the NYPD Intelligence Division, he sent an urgent e-mail request for a search for the registered owner of a black Mercedes with plates ending in 4 and 8. Because any information about the Sullivan & Ford shootings was to be copied to Assistant Chief Louise Mosley, she saw the request e-mail within minutes. She immediately called Mike Simon, a former CIA officer who was deputy director of the New York Joint Terrorism Task Force, with whom she had worked closely on several clandestine intelligence cases.

The task force, a domestic intelligence organization formed by the New York Police Department in 1980, ran a network of undercover officers and informants to track suspected terrorists. It was frequently criticized for its profiling of Muslims and for its often unfriendly relationship with the FBI. But its relationship with the Washington police was quiet and friendly.

"Your guys just got an urgent request from us," she told Simon. "I'm calling you to tell you what's behind it. We believe the car contains one of the shooters who killed four people here. They may be heading to New York."

"I'm on it personally, Lou," Simon assured her.

Half an hour later he called her back to say, "This is a great lead, Lou. Thanks much."

"What have you got?"

"I can't tell you everything on the phone. But we traced the Mercedes with those last numbers. It's registered to a town-car company with Russian mob connections and maybe some deals that we're looking at. The task force has been keeping an eye on those guys. The guy who runs this is into some bad stuff. We've got an all-points out on the car, emphasis on East Coast, big emphasis on Washington–New York corridor. And, lest I forget, the FBI."

"Keep me posted, Mike. These are bad guys."

"Don't worry, Lou. We'll find that car and the bastards in it."

20

When Yazov turned the town car onto Pennsylvania Avenue, a red, two-tier Washington tour bus was in front of him. Ordinarily he would have swung around the bus. But the hulking concrete J. Edgar Hoover Building, headquarters of the FBI at 935 Pennsylvania Avenue, was coming into view on his left, and he decided to remain as inconspicuous as possible. On the GPS, the blinking red light showed the laptop was two blocks farther up, at 701 Pennsylvania Avenue.

Yazov was still behind the red bus when he pulled up to the curb opposite the Navy Memorial's granite sea.

"Any ideas what we do?" Yazov asked.

"Too much traffic," Kurpanov said. "We gotta get movin'. There's a cop car in the next block."

"Where's laptop?" Yazov said, pointing to the GPS. Kurpanov leaned forward and squinted at the image.

"Looks like seven hundred one," Kurpanov said. He opened the window, stuck his head out, and craned for a look at the tall semicircular buildings encircling the Navy Memorial. "It could be anywhere in these goddamned buildings."

"You are right. And now?"

"Somebody must've found it."

"Yes, Ahmed," Yazov said, laughing. "That is a true idea."

Yazov pulled away from the curb. His eyes shifting back and forth from the windshield to the moving arrow on the GPS, he turned left at the signal light onto Seventh Street. He made his way through knots of traffic to New York Avenue and turned in to the entrance of the Horizon Motel, which had an underground garage.

They did not speak to each other as they climbed the stairway to their second-story room. Yazov did not like talking on a job. And he did not like elevators, where you might meet a potential witness.

He was not used to taking charge. All he usually did was drive and wait, then drive again after the job. Now, Viktor Yazov decided, he had to take charge.

He slid the keycard into the lock and entered. He threw the keycard and car keys on the top of the cabinet containing the minibar. He opened the door and took out a miniature bottle of vodka and a Diet Coke. Sitting on the edge of one of the twin beds, he handed the Coke to Kurpanov, opened and drained the vodka, then motioned for Kurpanov to sit opposite him on the other bed.

Speaking in Russian, he said, "When we were at the parking lot at the airport, that guy —"

"Cole Perenchio," Kurpanov interrupted.

"Yes. That guy. When we were at the parking lot, the tracker was on, the tracker on the laptop."

"Correct," Kurpanov said, also speaking in Russian, which made talking to Viktor much easier than when he spoke in halting, "fucking"-laden English.

"We followed his taxi to the hotel, correct?"

"Correct."

"So we know where he is. Tonight we go there and we kill him."

"Viktor, we have no instructions to kill him."

"Correct. But we cannot go back to Basayev saying we lost Dukka. Lost the laptop! Kill Perenchio and we can tell Basayev we have done something."

132

"My gun —"

"Your gun," Yazov said, frowning. "Your fuckin' gun. Yes. And you also lost that. So we use my gun. We find him and maybe we find the laptop. Maybe he has it now."

"It is worth trying, Viktor. I agree."

"All right. Here is my plan. We lay low today, tonight. We eat in that Chinese place down the street. Hang out, watch TV. Tomorrow we wait for darkness. We drive to Perenchio's hotel, check in. You do your hit, like that one Dukka and you did in that hotel in Newark. We will do it like that. You call Perenchio's room, tell him he's got a pizza delivery. He knows he did not order it and gets frightened. He leaves the hotel to go to some safe place — maybe to that friend he met at the airport place — and you follow him and you kill him. Then I pick you up and we come back to this place and next day we pay our bill and —"

"And Dukka's room. He's . . ." Kurpanov said, his voice trailing off.

"Yes. We muss the bed and make it look like it should."

"Maybe he —"

Yazov, feeling like an uncle again, patted Kurpanov on the knee and said, "My father told me the proverb 'Maybe and somehow never make anything happen.' No maybe,

133

no somehow. We have a good plan. We will make it happen."

21

Paul Sprague had always prided himself on his ability to remain completely calm, his emotions under iron control, however dire the circumstances. But self-doubts now fluttered about in his mind like trapped bats as he approached the police barricade at the Sullivan & Ford Building. Asked for photo identification, he showed his driver's license. An officer checked his name against a list, and he was admitted. An officer in the lobby advised that the elevators had been "cleared," meaning probably that the body was gone. He slipped his S&F entry card into the express elevator slot and ascended.

Questions roiled through his mind: *What have you gotten yourself into? How could you have let your ambitions go unchecked?* His answers were hazy. He first tried to rationalize that it was his wife, Sarah. The Middleburg estate. The home in Palm Beach. It was her desire to play among the elite, to be the glamorous hostess who entertained the rich and famous. But that was a lie. *He* wanted the prestige, the associations, the reputation to be the man to see, to be the first name on the Rolodex of the corporate giants who were intent upon gobbling up their competitors.

And the Ritz condo in Georgetown? That was his idea. He could have rented a unit in the building that housed the Newseum on Pennsylvania Avenue for a fraction of what he paid at the Ritz. But he wanted the strange kind of notoriety that came from owning one of the most expensive apartments in Washington. His success — or perceived success — could only embellish the image of Sullivan & Ford as being the indispensable law firm in Washington. At least, that was why he had seen to it that the firm picked up some of the condo expenses.

His mind kept drifting back to that first day of law school at Yale. Dean Suskind issued a warning: "Just remember, don't ever sell your integrity to a client no matter how much he offers to pay you because you'll never become rich enough to buy it back." Well, he was certainly rich, but . . . Suskind's words haunted him as he reached his corner office.

Ursula appeared, and he told her, "I need to make a few calls. Please make sure that I'm not interrupted."

"Yes, sir. Can I get you coffee in the meantime?"

Stroking his temples, Sprague said, "That would be great. I have a bit of a headache. The coffee will help."

Ursula dutifully retreated to a small room that contained a large softdrink machine and a metallic marvel that brewed espresso, cappuccino, and drip coffee from a selection of the finest brands of coffee beans from Kenya, Colombia, and Jamaica. Ursula selected a dark French roast that was strong, her boss's favorite. She set a paper cup under the brewing nozzle rather than one of the law firm's branded ceramic ones. She had read somewhere that these paper cups and their plastic linings posed a long-term hazard to one's health. But the coffee stayed hot longer in them, and Sprague preferred heat more than health.

After setting the coffee on Sprague's desk, she asked, "Can I bring you anything else?"

"Thank you, Ursula. No. Nothing more. Just remember, no interruptions until I finish my calls."

"Shall I place them for you, sir?"

"No, I'll make them."

Unusual, Ursula thought. Sprague had almost always asked her to place his calls. Her soft voice, with just the right tone of Southern gentility and Germanic efficiency, broke through the barriers of the most unreachable CEOs. *Well, he probably wants to convey his deepest grief to the bereaved relatives and that would be signified by a call dialed by him personally.*

As soon as Ursula departed, Sprague unlocked the middle drawer of his desk and took out what looked like an ordinary landline phone and dialed a number. After a moment of silence, a series of beeps danced in his ear. And then an annoying buzz signaled that he was connecting to his designated recipient.

On the third ring, a man answered in a voice that was high-pitched and abrupt: "Yes? What is it?" The telephone's security-system electronics produced the high pitch; the hasty words conveyed the intended perception that the caller had interrupted important business.

" *'Yes? What is it?'* That's all you have to say?" Sprague asked, the words tumbling out with rage and without thought. He had been instructed to never use the client's name on the phone and to call the client only on this security system, which had been installed in Sprague's office by a silent young man who did not give a name, merely identifying himself as Hamilton's personal communications-security supervisor.

"Excuse me?" the voice asked.

"What in hell have you done?" Sprague shouted, momentarily losing control of his storied calmness.

"I have no idea what you're talking about."

"Turn on GNN, for Christ's sake! There's been a shooting, a goddamn massacre."

"I'm truly sorry to hear that," Hamilton said. "But I still don't understand why you're calling me."

"Stop bullshitting me! We spoke two nights ago. I told you —"

"Yes, and I said I would handle everything."

"Well, I guess somebody else decided they were going to handle it. . . ."

"Paul," Hamilton said, adding a calming tone. "Seriously, I have nothing to do with whatever happened today. So why don't —"

"Because I have something that may belong to you. And —"

"You have it?"

"Yes, and I'm about to turn it over to certain authorities."

"But it's my property, Paul."

"That may be so, Robert. But it's potential

evidence in a crime investigation."

"But, please do me a favor and be discreet. First of all, have you tried to open it?"

"Yes. But I couldn't. All I got was a warning that I had no right to open it."

"Paul, listen carefully." The man's voice suddenly turned solicitous — *insincerely solicitous,* Sprague easily sensed. "Turn the computer on. . . . Incidentally, did you type anything on the keyboard when you attempted to open it?"

"A couple of keystrokes. I didn't know whether it belonged to my partner, and I tried to enter the law firm's code numbers. Others may have tried. I don't know —"

"Okay, it's important to get this right. Type in —"

"Is this going to be complicated?" Sprague asked, suddenly sounding nervous.

"Well, it's just a series of strokes. Nothing complicated."

Sprague hesitated, saying, "Hold on. I need to get it and put it on my desk."

He put the phone down, opened the door, and gestured for Ursula. "I think I'm going to need some help," he said softly. "But don't speak."

Ursula nodded. This had happened before. It began when a client on the telephone or a client wanting an immediate e-mail response assumed that Sprague could at least operate a computer. Then she had to be a stand-in because her boss was computer-illiterate. She entered his office, saw the laptop, and signaled to Sprague to speak into the phone.

"Okay. I'm ready," Sprague said, moving to allow Ursula to sit before the laptop.

Following a routine she had for this situation, she pushed the speaker button on the phone as the unknown caller said, "First, type the word 'oracle,' followed, without space, by a dash and then the numeral two. That should lift the initial barrier."

Ursula followed the directions and looked at Sprague, who said, "Right. It did."

"Now enter the following numbers: zero, eight, two, eight, four, zero, one, two, two, two, two, four, one."

Ursula nodded and Sprague spoke, sounding convincingly surprised: "Okay. Got it. . . . There's a blank screen."

"Good. Now, this is very, very important. Strike the Microsoft symbol key at the bottom left."

Ursula did so, and Sprague said, "Okay," while looking at a string of symbols and a list of words that he did not understand.

"Next, hit Default Programs and choose Change AutoPlay Settings. Got it?"

Ursula nodded her head vigorously and Sprague said, "Got it."

"Now, type this," Hamilton said, speaking slowly: "lowercase 'f,' lowercase 'r,' six, eight, four, nine."

"Done," Sprague said when Ursula finished.

"Now, insert a thumb drive and strike the Caps Lock key."

"What?" Sprague said inadvertently. Ursula smothered a laugh.

"For heaven's sake, Paul. This isn't rocket science. Strike the Caps Lock key and insert a thumb drive."

"Wait. I need to get one," Sprague said, his headache pounding, his voice wavering. Ursula hit the mute button, went to her desk, and swiftly returned with a small box containing several thumb drives. She took the top off a black thumb drive labeled *DataTraveler,* inserted it, and struck the Caps Lock key. PRIVATEDATA.DOC appeared on the screen for an instant and then vanished. A green light blinked in the thumb drive.

"I don't see anything," Sprague said, as much to Ursula as to Hamilton.

"Good Lord," Hamilton said, "that's why it's called *private.* It's going directly from the computer hard drive to the thumb drive."

"Oh, no, I can't get the top off the thumb thing," Sprague moaned, scrawling a note and holding it in front of Ursula's spectacled eyes: *Make copy.*

She nodded, swiftly removed the thumb drive, plucked a white one out of the box, removed the top, and, smiling at Sprague, held it at the ready.

"Paul! You're acting like an idiot. This is very important to me. Okay. Just do it again. The system allows one bad try."

"Great. Here goes," Sprague said.

"Come on, Paul. I haven't got all day."

"Okay. Done," Sprague said, giving Ursula the "OK" hand signal as soon as Ursula removed the second thumb drive.

"Okay. Now turn the computer off and then restart it again. This time, when you get the warning, just type in any six random numbers. Anything but the ones I gave you previously. Then hit Enter."

Ursula followed the instructions and the laptop screen went completely blank. Then a long, thin oblong window opened at the bottom of the screen. After the empty window filled, it quickly became empty again, indicating that all of the data in the computer was being deleted.

22

As Sprague watched the screen go blank, a sudden thought came from the deepest brain cells, the ones that had to do with survival: *If Davidson was taken out, what about me?*

Sprague motioned Ursula to leave the room and switched off the speaker. She closed the door silently behind her.

"Jesus!" he exclaimed. "You've just destroyed evidence in a —"

"*I* didn't destroy anything. I simply — with your assistance — retrieved information that was illegally taken from me. You're free to turn over the computer to whomever you think has a right to my property."

"I'm going to turn it over to the police. And what am I supposed to say when they see that everything is gone?"

"You can explain that you simply wanted to see if this was your firm's computer and when you tried to log in, whatever was in it was deleted. Someone must have programmed the computer to self-destruct."

"Jesus . . . Okay."

"Please, Paul, do not blaspheme."

"Yes, sorry. But . . ."

"Now just hold on to that thumb drive. A messenger will pick it up."

For a long moment, Sprague stared at the screen. *What have I done?* He took a deep breath. "No," he said. "Security is needed. I will deliver it to you in person."

There was a short pause.

"You're the one with the passion for security," Sprague said. "Remember what I told you about government eavesdropping on face-to-face conversations? Government interceptions of those oral conversations are in violation of the Wiretap Act and cannot be used against you as evidence in a criminal trial."

"What about those NSA data sweeps?"

"Another issue. Court orders for bugs or telephone taps run to more than one hundred to one over face-to-face conversations. If you're feeling the government is tracking you, it's highly unlikely that you are actually being followed and having your oral conversations bugged."

The man on the phone waited a second before he said, "As you know, I have been summoned —"

"Asked," Sprague said, "you have been asked — not summoned or subpoenaed, asked — to appear at Collinsworth's hearing on NASA's budget on the twelfth. The boys out at Goddard are trying to get back into the business of setting up a little colony on the moon. Next thing, it'll be asteroid mining. You need to be there."

"Right, we could have our face-to-face then. And besides there'd be a client-lawyer privilege, right?"

"That's nearly three weeks off," Sprague said. "What if —"

"I don't deal in 'if's. A face-to-face hand-off is the absolute best choice."

Sprague smiled at a familiar maneuver: taking someone else's idea and making it sound as if it had originated in the mighty brain of Robert Wentworth Hamilton.

"At that fancy place you have in Georgetown," Hamilton said, pausing to check his cell-phone calendar. "Three p.m."

"And in the meantime?"

"I'm sure that Sullivan and Ford — or, I mean, *you* — have a way to keep a thumb drive safe."

"Are you sure?"

Another pause, then: "I am always sure about my decisions. This object has no time aspect. I merely want to have it for what you might call assurance. There is no need to move quickly. Or to panic." A click and the call was over.

Sprague put the white thumb drive into his shirt pocket and leaned back, his head still pounding.

23

The day after the shooting, Dr. Benjamin Franklin Taylor stepped into a taxi at Reagan National Airport and was taken directly to the Air and Space Museum, on the Washington Mall. He had been away on a tour to publicize his latest book, *It's Your Universe,* based on his popular PBS show, *Your Universe.* Taylor seemed always to be in a hurry, but today he was even more so. His wheeled suitcase bounding along behind him, he took the broad museum steps two at a time, nodded to a security guard, and sprinted across the entrance gallery to the staff elevator.

The elevator opened on the top floor, above the museum's two floors of immense galleries — "Exploring the Planets" directly below him, and Otto Lilienthal's 1894 hang glider ("Early Flight") directly below that. Taylor sometimes thought of himself as a gallery, for he was full of information that he dispensed about space, flight, and the universe. Besides being assistant director of the museum, he ran the new state-of-the-art Albert Einstein Planetarium on the museum's first floor. And there was the monthly television show *Your Universe,* which combined Taylor's easy-going, fact-filled commentary with dazzling images of Earth, the solar system, and the Great Cosmic Beyond.

Traditionally, astrophysicists treat the operators of planetariums as entertainers rather than astronomers. But Taylor's MIT doctorate and his postdoc work at the MIT Center for Theoretical Physics earned him the acceptance of scientists, just as his television fans applauded his approach to astronomy — "a down-to-earth approach," he called it with a punster's smile. He maintained a solid reputation with scientists, many of whom vied for guest appearances on his prize-winning television show.

"We all know he has the brainpower of a rocket scientist. And we can see that he still has the physique of a running back," the secretary of the Smithsonian said eight years before, when he introduced Taylor as the new director of the planetarium. "He was a Heisman Trophy nominee at Michigan. And after graduating at the top of his class, he had a choice: go pro or go for a PhD. We can all be thankful that he chose the Massachusetts Institute of Technology and a doctorate in astrophysics. But he still plays a mean game of touch football on the Mall when Air and Space takes on our other museums."

Taylor was proud of his ability to compartmentalize his mind and control the time he doled out to his various projects. Thanks to his on-time flight home, he had arrived at the museum earlier than usual, and he looked forward to a time of relative quiet, when he could arrange the day ahead.

But the shootings flared in his mind, and he realized that some days are rearranged by violence and madness. The first he knew about the shootings was a text message he received from his daughter Darlene — SHOOTING AT SEAN'S FIRM. 4 OR 5 DEAD. HE'S OK — while he was waiting to speak at Powell's Bookstore in Chicago. He hit the app for the *Washington Post* Web page and saw an account of the shootings.

Two gunmen armed with semi-automatic weapons terrorized the landmark Sullivan & Ford Building near Capitol Hill today, killing four people. One gunman plunged to his death during a desperate struggle with former Senator Sean Falcone, a partner in the firm. "Mr. Falcone risked his life and stopped a massacre," Detective Lieutenant Tyrone Emmetts said. "Those guys were planning to wipe out the tenth floor." The second man, who shot at Falcone and missed, fled the scene and apparently escaped.

Police said two men entered the lobby of the ten-story glass building around 11 a.m. and told a lobby security guard they were from a local television station, which police did not identify, and had an appointment to interview a partner on the tenth floor. The partner was identified by police sources as Harold Davidson, a senior partner. He followed procedure by sending a receptionist to the lobby to escort the men to the tenth floor, the so-called senior partner floor. The three got into a private express elevator, which could only be entered via the receptionist's keycard. One of the men carried a duffel bag supposedly containing a television camera.

Once on the tenth floor, the two men began their rampage, killing the receptionist

Sean Falcone? Hal Davidson? Taylor was stunned. He had been to Falcone's office a few times and could envision the site of the killings. He remembered the cheery receptionist, and now, from the *Post* story, he learned her name. Ellen Franklin. In his mind's eye he saw her lying in her own blood. *And Hal.* Taylor had known Harold Davidson since they were both in Cambridge, two black strivers getting by on their brains. They lost each other for a while, when Hal finished his studies at Harvard Law, but they had renewed their friendship when Taylor moved to Washington and looked up his old friend.

and a man and a woman believed to be clients. As one of the gunmen was about to claim other victims, he was tackled by Falcone. In the struggle, one of the gunmen plunged down the atrium of the glass-sheathed building. The other shot at Falcone, entered the elevator and reached the lobby. He fled on foot as police, including SWAT teams, responded to panicky 911 calls.

Detective Lieutenant Emmetts said that the crime was being handled as "an interrupted mass shooting with one shooter still at large." A spokeswoman for Paul Sprague, the managing partner of Sullivan & Ford, referred all inquiries to the police.

The story went on, noting Falcone's Vietnam record and Senate years, along with Davidson's career, which began when he became one of the first African Americans to be made a clerk to a justice of the Supreme Court. The story ended with a paragraph recalling other mass murders, noting that four was "usually considered the minimum number for a crime to qualify as a mass murder."

Hal's dead, Taylor thought, a wave of guilt flowing through his mind, the guilt of the living when death claims a neglected friend. *We just didn't keep up with each other.* Davidson had been one of those old friends that somehow slip away, he with one life, you with another. The last time he had seen Hal, Taylor remembered, was at the memorial service for a mutual friend; they had both been surprised and found little to say to each other. *We just didn't keep up with each other.*

Now, in the sanctuary of his office, Taylor pushed all thoughts about the shootings deep into his mind, text-messaged his safe arrival to Darlene, decided he would call Falcone later, took his laptop out of his suitcase, and walked from his desk to a high-legged table in a corner of the office.

He spent far more time at that table, where he could stand and pound away at a keyboard, than he did seated at his desk. He had rigged computer cables and connections so that he could choose to work on one of four widescreen desktop monitors, which he called his Four-Eyed Monster. He plugged the laptop into the system's central dock, downloaded its latest contents onto his hard drive, and clicked on the four monitors.

One monitor displayed a page in an overdue quarterly report on museum attendance (up twenty-three percent over the previous year). On the second monitor was a video of a new program that was scheduled to be premiered next week in the planetarium theater: "Are We Alone? Discovering Planets That May Support Life." On the third were rough cuts of scenes from a show about asteroids that he was proposing to *NOVA*. On the fourth monitor he brought up a recording of the GNN's *SpaceMine Special*.

He was soon lost in the special. He nodded when Molly Tobias stuck her head in, saw he was at the table, and closed the door without a word. A widow in her sixties, she had kept charge of him and his office since his first day at the museum. Molly never expected more than a good-morning — or even that when he was at the table, fixated on his computers. Chatter time would inevitably come at eleven o'clock, when Taylor brought them coffee from the nearby staff cafeteria and sat down at a chair alongside her desk.

During the book tour, switching to GNN on hotel-room television sets at the end of long days, Taylor had seen forecasts of an important SpaceMine announcement and, knowing he would be on the road, told Molly to tape it. In every city, at every Q&A session that followed his book talk, he had fielded questions inspired by the announcement about Asteroid USA. Now he had his first chance to see the entire show and decide how to integrate Hamilton's surprising announcement into the script and storyboard he had been working on in the months leading up to the Asteroid USA announcement. The storyboard had already been approved by his *NOVA* coproducer.

Taylor had seen, saved, and studied every GNN *SpaceMine Special,* but he had still not grown accustomed to seeing Robert Wentworth Hamilton at the head of a venture into space. Taylor knew Hamilton, not as an abstract personification of fabulous wealth, but as a personal opponent and an opponent of honest science.

24

Around the time that Hamilton was secretly founding SpaceMine, Taylor had joined nearly one hundred other scientists who had signed an open letter deploring Hamilton's latest million-dollar "scientific achievement award." Hamilton annually bestowed the award, selecting a scientist whose work matched what Hamilton called Christian science. One award, for example, went to a "young-earth creationist" who claimed to have scientifically proved — through geology and zoology — that God had created the universe in six twenty-four-hour days less than ten thousand years ago.

The scientific community essentially ignored the Hamilton Award as a billionaire's bauble; a way to give a boost to the right-wing zealots whose beliefs came from the pages of the Bible. But, to Taylor and the other protesters, the latest award had been a million-dollar attack on climate change. The award had gone to an evangelical minister who qualified as a scientist, in Hamilton's opinion, because he was an ex-astronaut who had written a best-seller about his encounter with God in space.

When he announced the award, Hamilton focused on climate change, which he called "the despicable anti-Bible campaign of atheists who claim that man can alter our world for good or for bad. But the future of the Earth is in the hands of a loving God. The fate of the human race will be determined by God, not by the foibles of mankind."

Hamilton did not treat his critics kindly. He was a man who held grudges. Many signers of the protest letter soon lost research grants without explanation. And Taylor had been told by the then-new secretary of the Smithsonian, Stephanie Sinclair-Hardy, that his signature had cost the Smithsonian the substantial annual donation from the Robert Wentworth Hamilton Foundation.

All this passed through the Hamilton compartment in Taylor's mind as Hamilton appeared in his hologram. *What a silly goddamn display of meaningless pop technology,* Taylor thought. And then Hamilton stepped out of his hologram and made his announcement about Asteroid USA. *Which asteroid is that? What's its astronomical name?* Taylor hit the replay button to hear the announcement again and again. "Payload . . . Asteroid USA . . . commercial property . . . free enterprise." *My God! He's playing with an asteroid — making it his branch office.*

Ned Winslow ended the show with NASA-produced animation scenes portraying what robot mining might look like on the moon — not on an asteroid. Taylor knew that NASA scientists who studied near-Earth asteroids were not enthusiastic about the unregulated mining of them. Mining of the moon would not nudge the moon out of orbit. But mining an asteroid might change its orbit and put it on a collision with Earth.

Taylor sent an e-mail to the *NOVA* producer: "SpaceMine's Asteroid USA gives us a natural peg. Will get update to you by tomorrow morning." He then turned to the monitor showing scenes from the proposed asteroid show. He was adding his notions on "impact avoidance" when a phone buzzed. He had rigged a speakerphone extension so that when that happened while he was at the table, he could answer without taking his eyes off the monitors or his hands off the keyboard. He saved the file and spoke into the speakerphone: "What's up, Molly?"

"Cole Perenchio," Molly answered. "He sounds a little . . . off." She insisted that Taylor never pick up the phone himself to shield him from what she called the people in the tinfoil hats.

"He sometimes sounds that way. Put him on. . . . Cole! Where have you been, man?" Taylor boomed. He envisioned a tall man whose arms jutted out of a white lab coat, a man of long silences. "Haven't seen you in — what — a year? And . . . I guess you've heard about Hal."

Cole Perenchio. The sportswriters called him King Cole of the Court. The MIT Engineers' highest scorer. The black guy who could have passed, with that name and with that shade of brown. . . .

"Yeah, I heard about Hal," Perenchio said, speaking so low that Taylor could barely hear him. "Maybe it was my fault."

"What? What are you saying?"

"Never mind. I've got to talk to you, Ben. You're the only guy I can trust."

"Where have you been? You left NASA?" Taylor asked.

"I can't talk right now," Perenchio said. "I've got to see you. Right away."

"You're in town? How about my house?

Tonight. It's on Capitol Hill. We could have a bite."

"*No,*" Perenchio insisted. "It'll be bugged. Everything's bugged."

Taylor was beginning to think Molly was right. But Perenchio was a brilliant engineer and had been a great coworker back in the days when they both worked for NASA. "Okay, Cole. There's a place near my house, an outside place. It's on Capitol Hill." He gave Perenchio directions and his cell-phone number. "How about eight o'clock?"

"Too early," Perenchio said in a hoarse whisper. "Probably still people around. Make it eleven. Eleven o'clock. And make sure you're not followed."

Before Taylor could respond, Perenchio hung up.

25

When Frederick Law Olmsted designed the grounds of the U.S. Capitol in the late nineteenth century, he included a small, red brick structure on Capitol Hill, a short distance down from the Senate wing of the Capitol. The Summerhouse, as it is known, is built as a hexagon open to the sky, with three arched doorways leading to a small grotto and a whispering stream of water flowing over the rocks. Around a central fountain are stone benches with stone armrests marking off seats, shielded by a ceiling of red tiles.

Dr. Benjamin Taylor jogged down Constitution Avenue to the Capitol Grounds at Northwest Drive. He looked at his watch's digital dial. *22:55. Five minutes early.* A light rain had just entered the crisp October night, and Taylor, without stopping, pulled up the hood of his gray sweatshirt. At the end of the path he pushed open a wrought-iron gate and entered the Summerhouse. He thought he saw someone sitting on one of the benches.

Turning his cell phone's flashlight toward the bench, he said, "Hello, Cole," and took a step closer. A man was slumped forward, his gray hair darkened by blood. Taylor leaned down and saw staring eyes and a ragged head wound. Stepping back, he punched 911 on the phone. The call was answered on the third ring.

"I have just found a body on Capitol Hill," Taylor said. "He is —"

"Hold on. I'm switching you to USCP."

Before Taylor could say another word, he heard, "U.S. Capitol Police. Where are you?"

"I'm at the Summerhouse off Northwest Drive."

"Summerhouse? There's no *house* there."

"It's a little brick building. That's its name. And there's a man in it. A man who looks dead. Shot."

"Stay where you are. Do not move," the voice said, ending the call.

In less than a minute he heard sirens. Two Capitol Police cars — white with blue side stripes — sped down Constitution and screeched into Northwest Drive. Farther down Constitution he could see the flashing lights of an ambulance.

Police-car doors opened and four police officers sprinted toward the Summerhouse. The first one to reach Taylor aimed his Glock pistol at him. Taylor, who was returning his cell phone into his sweatshirt pocket, looked down to see the white circle on his chest. His eyes traced the beam back to a flashlight mounted on the bottom of the Glock's magazine.

"Take your hands out of your pocket and get down," the officer with the Glock said.

Taylor knelt on one knee and then stretched his six feet, two inches onto the wet stone floor.

A second officer appeared. While the first one held his gun on Taylor, she said, "Hands behind your back." She grabbed his right arm.

Taylor saw a white police van and another police car pull up on the lawn flanking the path to the Summerhouse. Two of the new arrivals donned yellow raincoats and strung yellow crime-scene tapes among the shrubs and trees. Other cops set up three tripods holding lights whose rays cut through the night, sparkling in the rain. Suddenly, the Summerhouse was bathed in light.

The officer with the Glock aimed its beam toward the benches across from the body, and the two of them sheltered under the

164

tiles, now fringed with dripping rain. Taylor saw the three stripes of a sergeant and his nameplate, Malcolm, and asked, "Am I under arrest, Sergeant? I'm the one who —"

"Shut up," Malcolm said, jamming a hand into Taylor's sweatshirt pocket and taking out the cell phone. He next went through the sweatpants pockets, which were empty.

"What are you doing here? You and the deceased." He jerked his head toward the body.

"Am I under arrest?" Taylor repeated.

"Where's your identification? Your wallet?"

"My name is Dr. Benjamin Taylor. I live on Maryland Avenue. Near the Folger. I am the assistant director of the Smithsonian's Air and Space Museum and director of —"

The first notes of "Thus Spake Zarathustra," the musical theme from *2001: A Space Odyssey,* flowed from Taylor's cell phone.

Malcolm, seeming to be startled that he held a cell phone in his hand, stared at it for a moment and then pressed a button, saying, "Who is this?"

"Well, who are *you*?" The voice was female and surprised.

"I am a Capitol Police officer speaking into a cell phone held by a jogger in a hooded sweatshirt."

"Hold on, mister. I know where you're coming from. I'm taping this." Malcolm heard a faint click.

"I refuse to allow it."

"Well, then, you can just hang up."

"Lady, I'm black, just like this suspect here."

"Well, I'm black, too. And you are using my daddy's cell phone."

Malcolm pressed a button, ending the call. In an instant, Zarathustra spake again. Malcolm turned off the phone.

"That was my daughter, Darlene," Taylor said. "And that *is* my cell phone. She was calling to —"

A man in a brown suit and a red baseball cap appeared out of the darkness and ducked under the tiles. "I'll take that, Sergeant," he said, reaching out his left hand to grab the phone and pocket it. He aimed his right hand at Taylor and flipped open a black leather case bearing a Capitol Police badge. "Detective Willard Seymour," he said. "Is the number of that cell phone 202-345-6998?"

"Yes," Taylor said.

"The victim had a piece of paper in his pocket with that number written on it. So you knew the victim?"

"Yes. We were —"

"You were the one who called 911."

"Yes."

"We're taking you to headquarters," Seymour said, grasping Taylor by the right arm and motioning him to stand. The detective led him down the path to an unmarked car. The cop who had cuffed him followed the two men. She opened a back door of the unmarked car and stood on her tiptoes to push down Taylor's head and ease him into the backseat. She sat down next to him, slammed the door, and Seymour drove off for the short drive down Capitol Hill to the headquarters of the U.S. Capitol Police.

Taylor had walked past the plain gray building countless times without thinking that he was passing a police station. This block of D Street was better known for the Monocle Restaurant, a power-lunch Capitol Hill palace for members of Congress and their lobbying hosts. He had eaten there himself about a month ago with the chairman of the Committee on House Administration, which had jurisdiction over Smithsonian museums.

Like all other Capitol Hill residents, Taylor knew that his neighborhood was extraordinarily well policed and that the police belonged to Congress, not the District of Columbia. Congress had given the Capitol Police exclusive jurisdiction over the Capitol and about two hundred blocks in the Hill neighborhood, which radiated from the Capitol in all directions.

On his walking and jogging around the Hill, Taylor almost invariably saw police officers, in cars or on foot patrol. There were some 1,700 of them, about the number found in midsize American cities. When Taylor dialed 911, he had reached the District of Columbia Metropolitan Police, which had switched him over to the U.S. Capitol Police. Taylor was pondering that fact, wondering what a federal arrest might mean to him, when Seymour parked and led him into the building, followed by the officer who had handcuffed him.

They filed through a hall to an elevator that took them to the third floor. Seymour punched the number lock on an interrogation room, switched on the light, and nodded to the uniformed officer. She uncuffed Taylor, who pushed back his hood and said, "Thanks." Without responding, she punched the numbers on the inside lock of the door and left the room. The door closed behind her.

Seymour took a seat on one side of a metal table and motioned Taylor to a chair opposite him. The table and the chairs were bolted to the floor. Seymour touched a button under the table. On the wall behind Seymour, Taylor could see the aperture for a video camera that began silently recording.

"This is a custodial interrogation," Seymour said in his flat, slow speech. "You have the right to remain silent. Anything you say —"

"Hold on, Detective," Taylor said. "I want —"

Ignoring the interruption, Seymour continued, ". . . can be used against you in a court of law."

He paused long enough for Taylor to say, "I have the right to have an attorney present and —"

Seymour leaned forward and spread his hairy hands on the table. "Okay. Okay. You'll get a lawyer. So I'm not asking you any questions. I just want to tell you how it all looks to us. We don't get many murders on the Hill. So I'm just thinking out loud. There's a guy dead in an odd place, a place where gay guys sometimes meet each other. And there's another guy there with a cell phone whose number is in the dead guy's pocket. First on the scene, right? Well, lots of times — from what I know and what I read — lots of times the first on the scene is

169

the guy who did it. When that happens, well, that guy explains what happened, and then the crime is solved and nobody has any need to prolong the proceedings."

Seymour smiled and made an invitational gesture with his right hand.

"Oh, I see," Taylor said, smiling back. "This is not a custodial interrogation anymore. It's just someone asking me to tell him a story, give him a narrative."

"That's right," Seymour said, pulling a notebook out of an inside pocket. He opened it, turned a page, and glanced at it. "That's right, Doctor. What kind of a doctor?"

"That's a question, Detective. But I won't count that as interrogation. I hold a doctorate in astrophysics from the Massachusetts Institute of Technology. I am assistant director of the Smithsonian's Air and Space Museum and director of the Albert Einstein Planetarium there. If someone behind that two-way mirror on the wall there goes to a computer and logs on to the museum Internet site and searches my name, he'll see my face and get positive identity."

Seymour nodded, and Taylor continued. "Cole Perenchio called me this afternoon. I've known him since we both went to MIT. And we later worked at Goddard and NASA

170

Headquarters over on E Street in Washington. We hadn't seen each other for . . . I don't know. About a year."

"The NASA place up in Greenbelt," Seymour said, nodding again. "I've escorted members who went up there for congressional tours. Yeah, Cole Perenchio. That was the name on his driver's license. A Virginia license. Expired."

Taylor ignored the interruption and continued speaking: "Cole said he had something to tell me, but he was very . . . very, well, I guess I could say paranoid. But he's — he was — kind of religious, and I think that colors the way he looks at — looked at — things. Anyway, he said it was urgent and could we meet in some quiet place. I suggested my house — on the Hill, Maryland Avenue. Cole said, No, someplace private. Where there won't be any wiretaps or bugs."

"Wiretaps? Bugs? What was he talking about?"

"More questions, Detective. The answer is, I don't know."

"Tell me more. That's not a question."

"We agreed to meet tonight. I thought of the Summerhouse. It's quiet. I didn't expect rain. Anyway, I got there, saw he was shot, and dialed 911. That's the story."

"I still have questions," Seymour said, switching off the video.

"Then I need a lawyer. And when do I get my cell phone back? I need to call my daughter. She —"

Both men looked toward the sound of the door opening. Seymour rose and seemed to stand at attention. A short, rotund officer entered. His uniform sleeves had two stripes and his epaulets bore two stars. He introduced himself as Deputy Chief Barnett, the watch commander.

"You are free to go, Dr. Taylor," Barnett said. "Great Web site. Took my granddaughter to the planetarium a couple of months ago. You are not a suspect."

"But, we're not through here," Seymour said plaintively. He was stunned that his suspect was being given a get-out-of-jail-free card. "We need to have Mr. . . . or Dr. Taylor here . . . sign a statement. We need to take some DNA samples. Jesus, boss, Congress, the press will be all over us if we . . ."

Barnett turned and pointed toward the detective. "Seymour," he said, "give Dr. Taylor his cell phone."

Nodding to Taylor, Barnett said, "A car will take you home."

Taylor stood and walked toward the door.

Barnett, standing before the open door, shook hands with Taylor and stood there a moment, looking up. "Sorry for the temporary misunderstanding," he said. "As Detective Seymour told you, we don't get many homicides to deal with. If what happened was a street crime — your friend was in the wrong place at the wrong time and maybe you, too, if you had got there earlier — we could handle it. But from what you said — yep, I was behind the mirror — it sounds like maybe there's more to it. So we'll probably have to call in the FBI. You are a material witness. So you'll be part of the investigation. But, of course, you're free to go."

Taylor nodded, thanked Deputy Chief Barnett, and moved quickly out the door.

Detective Seymour was not happy. "So tell me how this goes down. We have a guy in custody who's found at the scene of a murder, and you spring him in less than an hour just because he's a big shot?"

"Watch your mouth, Detective," Barnett cautioned. "I released him because I listened to his statement and I believe him. And I don't want to have a story in tomorrow's *Post* that as far as the Capitol Police, the gang that can't shoot straight, are concerned, 'No good deed should go unpunished'!

"Dr. Taylor could have walked away from the crime scene and all you would have found was a piece of paper with Taylor's number on it. So you would have gone to the Smithsonian tomorrow and arrested him on that?"

"Yeah, well all I know is that in this town, money talks . . ."

"And bullshit walks, Detective," Barnett shot back. "Don't slam the door on your way out."

26

Darlene Taylor was standing in the doorway of a three-story brick house. A hall light silhouetted her, the shadow of her slim body streaming onto a small lawn. Beyond was a low wrought-iron fence that bore a bronze historical marker showing the house had been built in 1877. A rainy breeze sent a shower of orange leaves flying down Maryland Avenue toward the lighted dome of the Capitol, a few blocks away.

When the police car pulled up, Darlene ran to the opening gate in four quick steps and threw her arms around Taylor. She was nearly as tall as her father, even now, in bare feet. She wore gray jeans and a sweatshirt bearing the faded blue letters "USAF." In a moment she stepped back and said, "Well, thanks for finally calling me . . . and from a cop car. What the hell was that all about? I was worried sick."

"Let me in the house and I'll try to tell

you," Taylor said. "I'm still sorting it out."

They walked directly through the entry-hall door to the kitchen. Darlene went to the refrigerator. "There's chicken salad," she said.

"Thanks, sweetie," Taylor said, uttering a word that always pleased and mildly exasperated her. She served a helping onto a plate already set, with knife, fork, and napkin at one end of the table in the middle of the kitchen. "Eat and go to bed," she said, taking her usual chair across from him.

"This is very good chicken salad."

"Mom's recipe," Darlene said softly.

A sudden flash of memory. A neighbor had brought chicken salad to the house after Caroline died. He had taken only a bite of that salad. *Now it's going on six years, and Caroline is sort of still here.*

"It's the curry," he said. "Exactly enough curry."

After finishing the salad, Taylor rose, went to the refrigerator, and took out a beer. As he twisted off the cap, Darlene frowned. "A glass of milk would be better for you at this hour," she said. "It's nearly one o'clock."

He sat down again. "A teetotaler like you," he said, "would not understand that after you've been accused of murder, a glass of milk is not quite enough."

"Murder?"

"Hold on. I told you I was still sorting it out," he said in a slow, steady voice that she recognized as his lecturing voice. "Yesterday I got a phone call from an old friend, and —"

"Who?" Darlene asked.

"Cole Perenchio. You wouldn't know him."

"And he's the dead man, the murdered guy?"

"Yes. I haven't seen him in about a year. He was still at Goddard when I left. He told me he needed to speak to me, privately. He —"

"What did he want to tell you?"

"I don't know."

"You must have some idea," she persisted.

"Sweetie, this is a long night. A lot of questions. I told the cops and now I tell you: I didn't have any idea about what he wanted to tell. I suggested that we meet at the Summerhouse. From there, I thought I could convince him to walk home with me. Where we'd be more comfortable."

"The Summerhouse? I know you admire Olmsted and the Capitol grounds. So do I. Still, a funny place for some kind of secret meeting. But okay. So you —"

"When I got there, he was on a bench. Dead. Shot in the back of the head."

"My God! If you had . . ."

"No. Somehow I feel he was targeted, followed. I don't think anyone wanted to kill *me.* But the Summerhouse. I'll never think of it the way I always have."

"Neither will I," Darlene said. "And I do remember him."

"What? You never would have met him. I never really knew him socially, never invited him home. We were colleagues, guys who worked together. After he left Goddard we kept in touch. Lunch, maybe a beer — well, for me, not him. Anyway, you never met him."

"Yes, I did. You took me to Goddard on one of those stupid take-your-daughter-to-work days. It was *so* embarrassing. I'll never forget it. Here I was, a thirteen-year-old, starting high school, and you were treating me like I was an eight-year-old, holding my hand, bragging about my marks, my cross-country running. Oh, I'll never forget it. We were in that room with the big centrifuge they used for spinning astronauts, and they were doing a job for the Department of Transportation, seeing what it would take to make a car roll over, spinning a big SUV around and around. That was terrific, but of course I couldn't tell you that because I was sulking."

"The centrifuge. That's right," Taylor said, amazed at her uncanny ability to recall minor events. "What else do you remember?"

"I had said something about not seeing many black scientists. I was just beginning to go big into civil rights. And you said something about NASA was working on it — you always did have a good word for NASA. And —"

"Well, for good reason," Taylor interrupted. "It was a good place. And they were always working on increasing their racial diversity."

"Right," Darlene said. "And I'm sure things are different now. But I'm talking about my memories. I remember saying something like, 'Then where are the black experts besides you?' And you said, 'Well, I'll show you a black guy that I sometimes work with.' And you took me off to the place where they did Earth observations with satellites, and you introduced me to Cole Perenchio. He had an odd name for a black man. I wanted to ask him about it. He was polite but . . . I don't know . . . uneasy. It struck me that he was the kind of person who was a loner and isn't comfortable around kids."

"What else do you remember?"

"Not much. Just that I felt sort of sorry for him?"

"Why?"

"Well — you're going to like this — I think because he didn't seem to be fatherly. Like he didn't know how to deal with kids, with people." She smiled and paused to reach across the table to break off a bite of cheese.

"I *do* like that 'fatherly.' "

Taylor paused, lost in memories that Darlene's memories summoned. *The first year without Caroline, the first year as a lonely, solitary father.* He had a mind that he tried to keep compartmentalized. But sometimes, that mind blurred then and now.

"You're right about Cole," Taylor said. "He was a bachelor, and lots of times instead of going to the cafeteria for lunch he'd just wander off somewhere. Yes, that was the way he was. . . . Strange."

27

The GPS on the Mercedes dashboard said that it was 125 miles to the New Jersey Turnpike. By being a cautious driver who happened to have a police radar detector in his car, Viktor Yazov figured he would beat the GPS estimate of two hours and fifty-one minutes by at least twenty minutes, even though he had to stop at all the tolls; E-ZPass gave out too much information.

He paid the toll for Baltimore's Harbor Tunnel forty-two minutes after leaving Washington, and now the rest of the trip was a no-brainer. Cross the Delaware Memorial Bridge and hit that first stop on the Jersey Turnpike and get that hamburger. Back to home grounds.

Most cars, showing E-ZPasses, whizzed through the entrance to the New Jersey Turnpike. Yazov inched his way up a non-E-Z lane and was handed a toll ticket. A few miles down the turnpike, Yazov turned in to the first service stop, the John Fenwick, named after a seventeenth-century Quaker. Yazov pulled up to a Sunoco pump and ordered an attendant to fill the tank, as usual paying cash, adding a five-dollar tip that earned him a clean windshield. He drove to the parking area and parked in the first row, in a space facing the food court. They hurried inside, visited the men's room, guardedly avoiding eye contact, and headed for the lines strung out at the counters for the brand of your choice.

Yazov ordered two Burger King combos, fries, and coffee. Kurpanov fidgeted in the Nathan's line, stammering when he ordered two hot dogs and a chocolate milkshake. They had agreed to take their food to the car rather than linger inside. But Kurpanov insisted on dousing his hot dogs with mustard and ketchup. He was several steps behind Yazov when he hit the button to unlock the car. At that moment Yazov saw two New Jersey State Police cruisers enter the parking lot.

He hit the button again, said something in Russian, and abruptly turned around. He nearly bumped into Kurpanov, who followed Yazov into the food court. He sat at a table near the door and motioned for Kurpanov to sit next to him so both could look through the front window and watch the cruisers as they parked side by side at the edge of the lot. An officer got out of each car.

Yazov leaned forward and spoke in Russian again.

"Speak English, for God's sake," Kurpanov said.

"I think they look at our car. These fuckin' cops, they never get out of car unless they want to ask questions or give ticket."

"Maybe they're just coming in for eats," Kurpanov said. He was unwrapping one of the hot dogs.

"I know turnpike, turnpike cops. You don't. We go right now. Put down food. Need hands," Yazov said, standing up. "We drive to next exit, get off fuckin' turnpike."

Yazov's cell phone rang. "Dimitri," he said. He nodded, spoke a few muted words in Russian, and pocketed the phone. "Dimitri on cop scanner. Car hot. We can't drive."

"What? How —"

"I go to car to get gun. You wait a little, then come. Follow me, like you walk to car in back, where cars come in. We hijack car, take to next exit. Dimitri send car there."

"Hijack? Jesus, Viktor! I —"

"Shut up. I do it. Easy. Scare shit out of

183

driver, make him drive."

Yazov walked rapidly to the food court's glass doors. As he neared the car, the radios in the cruisers crackled. One of the troopers opened the driver's door and leaned in to listen.

"We go," Yazov told Kurpanov, who meekly followed a few steps behind.

Yazov hit the unlock button, got in, and sat in the driver's seat. He reached out to the door and pressed a switch under the armrest. Nothing happened. Then he remembered that he had to turn the ignition key to power the access door to the hidden compartment. He inserted the key and turned it. A section of the door lining opened and he grabbed the silver-and-black Sig Sauer P226 with its thirty-round magazine, minus the round that had entered Cole Perenchio's brain.

Kurpanov stood by the driver's door. Yazov stepped out of the car, jammed the gun in his waistband under his jacket, and angrily repeated, "We go."

As Yazov got out of the car, one of the troopers approached, walking along the parking spaces' white line, toward the driver's side of the Mercedes. He unlocked his holster, closed his hand around the grip of the gun, but did not draw.

The second trooper did the same and walked parallel to the first along another white line, nearing the car on the passenger's side.

"Raise your hands," the first trooper ordered, drawing his gun and aiming at Yazov.

Simultaneously, Yazov moved his hand toward his waistband and the trooper fired. Yazov slumped against the car and tossed the gun across the hood to Kurpanov, who raised it toward the trooper. He shot Kurpanov twice in the chest. As he fell dying, the last sound he heard was a toddler screaming in the Volvo parked alongside his body.

28

Boris Lebed, the President of the Russian Federation, had succeeded Vladimir Putin, who had died from what the Kremlin said was "a rare blood disease." Eloquent and charismatic, Lebed had convinced the voters and the kingmakers that a forty-six-year-old mayor of Volgograd, with a business degree from the London School of Economics, could lead Russia into a truly prosperous era — while keeping the Motherland strong and vigilant.

Lebed had managed to weather an outburst of fury when word leaked that Kuri Basayev was Lebed's major financial supporter. How could he associate with a man named Basayev, people asked, recalling a horror indelibly recorded in national memory? In 2004, Chechen terrorists, led by a warlord named Shamil Basayev, had seized a Russian school near the border with Chechnya and held more than 1,100 people

— including 777 children — hostage for three days. The siege ended with firefights and explosions that killed more than 300 hostages, including 186 children.

Lebed responded with an emotional press conference and survived the criticism. He called Basayev a friend and a patriot "suffering for his name and not for his deeds." Condemning Kuri Basayev "because of the crimes of a distant relative," Lebed said, "brings back the dark says of Stalin, when innocent Russians suffered because their names were on lists written by secret informers." Lebed also revealed that Basayev had served in the FSB, Russia's Federal Security Service, under its then-director Vladimir Putin. "And if Kuri Basayev was good enough for a future and beloved President of Russia, then he is good enough for me."

Lebed was in what he called his work office, an oak-paneled Kremlin room with a large square desk, when an aide brought in a sealed envelope from Colonel Nikita Komov. Lebed smiled at Komov's usual form of communication. But when he opened the envelope and read the handwritten note, he frowned and sighed. Komov wanted a meeting, not here in the work office but in the so-called safe room on the top floor. Lebed buzzed for his security detail and said he was going to the Deaf Room, as it was called.

In the 1980s, Komov, then a KGB colonel, had urged the creation of the room to foil CIA laser-beam eavesdropping that had been revealed by a defecting CIA officer. "There is reason, Comrade President, for extreme secrecy," the Komov note said.

Lebed had heard about Komov long before the transition period following President Putin's death. Komov had been the prime instructor in the KGB counterintelligence school when he first met the new KGB officer named Vladimir Putin. When the Soviet Union collapsed and the KGB was replaced by the Federal Security Service, Putin had been appointed its director. He overruled regulations and ordered Komov kept on well beyond retirement age. He was made director emeritus of the Archive of the President of the Russian Federation, which gave him access to any secret document.

Putin had always treated Lebed like a nephew, giving him numerous insights, such as why he kept Komov as an advisor on intelligence issues. Putin lavishly praised Komov for his truth-to-power honesty and his institutional memory, which went back to the beginning of the Cold War.

Putin credited Komov with a sixth sense for detecting defectors. His counterintelligence colleagues called him Comrade X-ray for his ability to see through the façade of anyone contemplating defection. But Komov, looking back on his long career, remembered most of all the two times when he had detected a defector only to have his suspicions ignored by his superiors.

While Lebed understood the importance of Komov's experience and counsel on intelligence matters, he distrusted Komov and feared that his loyalty ran to his friends in the old KGB.

Lebed had been surprised by Komov's capacity for total recall and had learned to respect him despite suspicion about his link to former KGB officers and security zealots known collectively as the *siloviki* — "the people of power." Their ever-suspicious, xenophobic views aroused the liberal left and threatened Lebed's promise to pursue a more moderate and less authoritarian form of governance. Anyway, he already had a well-connected advisor in the *siloviki:* his principal fund-raiser, Kuri Basayev.

President Lebed and Nikita Komov sat

across from each other at a narrow table in the Deaf Room. Komov, at ninety-one, was lean and sat ramrod-straight. His narrow, sharp-chinned face was thatched with wrinkles. His white hair was short-cropped. He wore the formal blue gold-belted uniform and black boots of a KGB colonel, a fashion statement frowned on by the civilian-attired employees of the Security Service.

"Now, Colonel, you said that this had to be an extremely secret meeting," Lebed said as soon as Komov had taken his seat. "What is it about?"

"It is, sir, about Kuri Basayev."

Lebed frowned, took off his wire-rimmed glasses, and rubbed the bridge of his nose. Without commenting, he replaced the glasses.

"A middle manager in our counterintelligence directorate opened a case file on Basayev and was censured by his superior — a rather brash, inexperienced analyst," Komov said in his crisp baritone. "He ordered that the file be erased. But I was alerted and, before the file was cast into digital oblivion, I saw it and preserved it. This preservation is not known to the manager of the directorate — I mean 'department,' the modern term that is deemed less sinister than 'directorate.' "

"What was the basis of opening a file on one of my trusted advisors, a man who himself is a veteran of the Security Service?" Lebed asked, glaring at Komov.

"I well know, sir, that he served briefly in the service when Comrade Putin was the director. I met him briefly after a lecture I gave to new recruits. He soon left the service and began making his fortune."

"I am well aware of his biography, Colonel."

Komov nodded and went on: "During the financial crisis caused by the greed of Wall Street, Basayev lost a great deal of his fortune. He then enlarged his criminal activity — drugs, money laundering, and some bloodshed; the details are not important. What is important is that American surveillance sharply increased, and —"

"He's no angel," Lebed said, shrugging. "I have been aware of what you call his criminal activity. Drugs? Not into Russia, correct? Money laundering? Of concern to America, not of much concern to us. And bloodshed? Well, he *is* Chechen."

"What you say, sir, is only partially true. Basayev's drugs *are* finding their way into Russia. But it is not the crimes that inspired the opening of a counterintelligence case

191

file. It is the shift in the structure of the surveillance."

"Meaning?"

"He has been under total surveillance by America. Total surveillance is very expensive and reserved for important targets."

"Well, as a known advisor to me, he would *be* important."

"Yes, sir. He would get the full menu: CIA, NSA, FBI."

"And so? Please, Colonel, get to the point."

"The FBI continues a surveillance operation that is highly visible for anyone looking for it. But the CIA has changed its pattern — and, I believe, has not informed the FBI, much as the KGB would not inform the GRU about a shift in surveillance. I have seen this before."

"You have seen *everything* before, Colonel," Lebed said with a condescending smile.

"Yes, counterintelligence is more art than science, sir. A CIA counter-intelligence chief named James Jesus Angleton called it 'a wilderness of mirrors' — and took credit for the phrase. In fact, the phrase is incomplete and was from a poem by a modern poet, T. S. Eliot."

"I am aware of T. S. Eliot," Lebed said.

"He stopped being modern a while ago. What are you getting at, Colonel?"

"Eliot wrote, 'In a wilderness of mirrors, what will the spider do? Suspend its operations?' The point for counterintelligence was: Do not be bothered by the mirrors; just keep watch on the operation. Our analyst noticed that the CIA has changed the operation. They are no longer giving Basayev the kind of surveillance designed to see — and hear — what he is doing. They have subtly modified the operation to see if he's being followed by *us* and to see whether he's doing what *they* told them to do. Your valuable advisor, sir, is a mole, working for the CIA."

Lebed stood, his face contorted in rage. "Get out!" he shouted.

Komov sprang to his feet. "Sir, no one else in your Security Service had the courage to tell you about the Basayev file. And no one knows that I have seen it." Komov reached into his tunic and took out four sheets of lined paper bearing handwriting. "I have written a report containing what is known and suspected. After you read it, you can decide whether to accept my facts or accept my resignation."

29

On the day after Cole Perenchio's murder, Taylor arrived in his office, as usual, at precisely 8:30. "Good morning, Molly. I . . . Do you know if Cole Perenchio had any kin?"

"I don't really know anything about him, Ben. Is something wrong?"

"He's dead, Molly. Shot last night."

"My God! How —"

"Is there anything in the *Post*?" Taylor asked, pointing to the folded paper on Molly's desk. She handed it to him and he rapidly flipped through the front section, then to Metro. On page five of the Metro section he saw a two-paragraph story with a one-column headline, "Killing on Capitol Hill." "Here it is," he said, folding back the page and handing it to Molly.

"Unidentified man?" she asked. "But . . ."

"That's Cole. Unidentified."

"Did you —"

Without answering her, he went into his office and directly to the Four-Eyed Monster.

At the worktable he checked his e-mail and then plunged into outlining the PBS-special idea. He had been at work for about fifteen minutes when his phone buzzed.

"What's up, Molly?" he said.

"It's a Mr. Sarsfield," she said, pausing to add, "That is, *Agent* Sarsfield. I will send him in."

Taylor stood as the door opened and the prototype of an FBI agent — fit-looking white male in his forties, wearing a black suit, white shirt, blue tie, and shoelaced black shoes — stood for a moment in front of Taylor and flashed his badge and identification card. "Special Agent Patrick Sarsfield," he said, swiftly pocketing a black leather case that looked like Detective Seymour's. Taylor idly wondered if there was one stockpile for all government ID cases. He put out his hand, as did Sarsfield.

"There are usually two of you," Taylor said.

"Like Mormon missionaries," Sarsfield said with a quick smile. "Budget cuts. And we are obliged to help out the dear old Capitol Hill coppers who don't have much detecting to do." As Taylor motioned Sarsfield to a chair next to his desk, the agent added, "Don't quote me about the Mormons. I can see my flippancy surprises you."

Taylor responded with a smile of his own. "Well, it is engaging. I'm sure you're a pro and know how to use your flippancy as a way to loosen up your . . . what? Suspects? So what can I do for you?"

Sarsfield already had his black notebook open and his silvery pen poised. "I think I know the basics. Detective Seymour e-mailed his report to the field office, and the FBI people in charge of things like dealing with cooperation between federal cop outfits set up the deal. We — that is, the bureau — cleared its jurisdiction with the U.S. attorney's office. So it's an FBI case . . . my case, with Detective Seymour as consultant."

Taylor slowly went to his desk, stood behind it for a moment, and then sat down, trying to use that moment to assume a calm air. Sarsfield took a few notes as Taylor again recounted the phone call from Cole Perenchio and the discovery of his body. After a short pause, he tapped his pencil on the open notebook and, nodding his head toward the monitors, said, "I was a bit surprised to see you in your office."

"Why?"

"Your friend Cole Perenchio was killed last night."

"We live in violent times," Taylor said.

"Yes, violent times indeed," Sarsfield said. He nodded toward the worktable. "What are you working on?"

"A *NOVA* show on asteroids."

"Inspired by the SpaceMine announcement about the asteroid?"

"Well, that and other things," Taylor responded, trying to keep himself from blurting out, *What the hell is this all about?*

"I heard about the asteroid from my ten-year-old son. Mind if I tell him that you're planning a show about asteroids?"

"Well, no date's been set yet," Taylor said, feeling himself relax. "But, sure."

"He's a big fan of yours. We tape every episode of *Your Universe*. Danny replays them a lot. And we've been to the planetarium a million times."

"Well, I'll be sure to invite him to the show. There's usually a preview. I'd like to invite you *and* Danny," Taylor said, paused, and then added, "Now, what's going on?"

"Dr. Taylor," Sarsfield said, "you're a person of interest, not a suspect. But we — the FBI — don't know as much about the victim as we'd like."

The calm in the room vaporized as Taylor loudly asked, "And what does 'person of interest' mean?"

"There's no legal definition of it. It's just a term that we use."

"Seems to me I heard that term before. It was used on that poor guy the FBI accused of setting off a bomb at the Olympics in Atlanta a while back, and the guy you accused of sending anthrax through the mail? Bruce Ivins. He . . ."

"Committed suicide before we could formally charge him. . . . Look, we're talking to you because we want to know certain things."

"What things?"

"General information about Cole Perenchio. Specifically, what he was going to tell you."

"I told Seymour and I've told you, I don't know what he was going to tell me."

Sarsfield flipped some pages on his notebook and asked, "Do you know a man named Peter Darrow? Or Daniel Bruce?"

"Look, Agent Sarsfield, I don't know anyone by those names. And I believe you're on some kind of fishing expedition, rather than an investigation. And, from what I know, when the FBI has a real case, *two* agents do the questioning. I'm ending the fishing expedition right now."

"Please, Dr. Taylor," Sarsfield said in a tone that was neither friendly nor pleading. "No need to get excited. I can assure you that those names are pertinent to a homicide. And they came out of what we believe to be a concurrent or related case involving the shooting at Sullivan and Ford.

"And, as to the late Mr. Perenchio, we think that if you put your mind to it, you'll figure out, at least in a general way, what it was he was hoping to tell you."

Taylor sat down. Again shaking his head and speaking slowly, he said, "So. Let me get this straight. You — the FBI — believe that Cole — and maybe me? — might be involved in a mass shooting. And you want me to be the mind reader of a dead man. Right?"

Sarsfield did not answer.

"Obviously," Taylor continued, "the FBI has some ideas about Cole. But you're not going to share them with this person of interest."

"Dr. Taylor, there is something we both know," Sarsfield said, his voice sharpening. "It involves you and the White House. The way you handle my — the FBI's — request for information in this case will have a direct effect on the matter involving the White

House. Goodbye." He closed his notebook, rose, and walked out of the office.

A moment later Molly came in and said, "I think we both need our morning coffee. Oh, and by mistake I left your phone open. And I accidentally recorded your interview with Agent Sarsfield."

30

Several weeks before, Ray Quinlan, President Oxley's chief of staff, had informed Taylor that he was under consideration to be the President's science advisor. If he was appointed, Taylor would want to put SpaceMine and asteroids high on his advice list. He would also be running the Office of Science and Technology Policy, where billion-dollar, politically thorny decisions about energy and environment issues would undoubtedly get priority over far-future ventures in space.

Quinlan had ordered Taylor not to tell anyone about the possible appointment. But he had told his old friend Sean Falcone. He did not seem surprised by the news, and Taylor wondered if Sean had had something to do with the appointment.

Taylor and Falcone went back a long ways, to the start of Taylor's career, when he was working at NASA's Ames Research

Center in California. Ames was NASA headquarters for SETI, the search for extraterrestrial intelligence in the universe. NASA officials put Taylor on the team that was sent to Washington to testify before a Senate subcommittee chaired by Senator Sean Falcone of Massachusetts, a champion of NASA and SETI. Falcone had also been vainly trying to get the Senate to restore the old Senate Committee on Aeronautical and Space Sciences, created by Senator Lyndon B. Johnson. The committee had been abolished in 1977. By then, NASA was already suffering budget cuts, even though the Apollo program was still going on.

Congress cut off the SETI funds, but Falcone continued his interest in space and kept in touch with Taylor. Falcone was still in the Senate when Taylor was transferred to NASA's Goddard Space Flight Center in Maryland, about fifteen miles north of Washington. NASA, sensitive to political winds, had kept a low profile about the UN-sponsored Outer Space Treaty (officially, in long-winded UN prose, the Treaty on Principles Governing the Activities of States in the Exploration and Use of Outer Space, Including the Moon and Other Celestial Bodies). But Taylor had taken the risk of losing his job by testifying before Falcone's committee and openly ridiculing the mind-set of anyone who were suggesting that a way be found to opt out of the treaty. No senators were prepared at the hearing to openly gut the treaty or declare that it no longer served America's security interests, but Taylor came off as too arrogant and sarcastic during his appearance. Scientists were supposed to keep their heads down and remain completely deferential to those who controlled their agency's budgets.

As the President's national security advisor, Falcone discovered that the treaty needed to be amended to deal with commercial activities in space and to clarify the ownership and property rights of all celestial bodies. President Oxley, however, did not want to rouse the fury of anti-UN voters and stoke their visions of black helicopters shooting down America's sovereignty. But Falcone stubbornly kept the treaty on his wish list. And Taylor's energetic support of the treaty helped win Falcone's influential backing when Taylor was a candidate for the Air and Space Museum post and now for his nomination as the President's science advisor.

Taylor had thought he should give Falcone more time to recover from the shootings before calling him. But the visit from Agent Sarsfield changed his mind. He needed the immediate advice of a friend and a lawyer. Usually he called Falcone at his office number, but, imagining the chaos there, he tried Falcone's cell phone.

Falcone answered on the second ring and, before Taylor could speak, said, "Ben, we need to talk."

Taylor for an instant was surprised to hear Falcone identify him. Taylor had never got used to caller ID and the fact that phones made "Smithsonian" his ID.

"We certainly do," Taylor said. "How about the club at twelve thirty?"

"See you then," Falcone said, knowing that Taylor's club was not the Metropolitan. His voice was tense, and it was obvious that he did not want to talk on the phone.

They would meet in the elegant old Massachusetts Avenue mansion that housed the Cosmos Club. There was an old Washington saying: "The Metropolitan Club is for people with money; the Cosmos Club is for people with brains; and the National Press Club is for people with neither."

Falcone belonged to the Metropolitan and the Cosmos. Taylor was a member only of the Cosmos. Someone had once described it as the perfect place for Mycroft Holmes to have met his brother, Sherlock — quiet, Victorian, a place where power dined with power, where intellect toasted intellect.

Included among the Cosmos Club members had been three presidents, two vice presidents, a dozen Supreme Court justices, thirty-two Nobel Prize winners, fifty-six Pulitzer Prize winners, forty-five recipients of the Presidential Medal of Freedom. And Sean Falcone and Ben Taylor.

Several men and women said hello to Falcone as he wended his way past their tables to his favorite, which was alongside a window that looked out upon a small garden. Ordinarily he would have stopped for a few words, but today he looked grim and merely nodded. At one of the tables, everyone stood. That idea spread throughout the room. Then, in a rare breach of decorum, the quiet of a Cosmos lunch was shattered by a wave of applause. Falcone, uncharacteristically taken aback, waved and nodded in acceptance.

As he was about to take his seat, Ben Taylor appeared. "A hero's welcome," he said, shaking Falcone's hand.

Falcone shook his head. " 'Being a hero,' Will Rogers said, 'is the shortest-lived profession on Earth.' Glad — *very* glad —

to see you, Ben."

By long tradition no one can do business at the Cosmos Club. No one may open a briefcase and spread papers on the immaculate linen tablecloths. And certainly no one may make or receive a cell-phone call or consult any other electronic device. But business and the promise of business flows through the quiet talk, and meetings are noted by members and guests who casually glance around the room to pick up clues to deals in the making.

There was a *National Geographic* editor talking to his guest, a bearded photographer who wore a flowery tie and an ill-fitting suit jacket supplied by the club. There were a pharmaceutical lobbyist and a fellow member, a potential Nobelist from the National Institutes of Health. And, Falcone wryly thought, *Enough lawyers to fill a couple of jury boxes.*

In an exercise that took him back to his days as national security advisor, Falcone had been deciding what to say and what, if necessary, he should withhold, temporarily or permanently. After they ordered — skewered fried shrimp for Falcone, butternut squash soup for Taylor — Falcone said, "I heard from the White House. Ray Quinlan called it a courtesy call. Sometimes he thinks he's an assistant president instead of chief of staff. He told me that the science advisor job is on hold."

"I'm not surprised," Taylor said. "I think I also heard from the White House. Well, indirectly." He told Falcone about finding Cole Perenchio's body, about the Capitol Police session, about the Sarsfield interview and the agent's parting remark. Falcone asked only a couple of questions, not wanting to interrupt Taylor's smooth-flowing narrative.

When Taylor finished, Falcone said, "So, I killed a gunman and you found a guy with a bullet hole in his head. It's a brutal time, a city and a country full of guns. These are just shootings that just happened to happen within a few hours of each other."

"One big difference, though," Taylor said, tightly smiling. "Your guys were on the front page. My guy was on the bottom of an inside page in the *Post*'s Metro section. A two-paragraph story with a one-column headline, 'Killing on Capitol Hill.' No mention of me or the FBI."

"I never read Metro," Falcone said. "There's usually nothing much there that interests me. Even the obituaries. I don't need the *Post* to tell me if someone I know dies. To the *Post,* murders in Metro are just happenings in the invisible black city of Prince George's County or Anacostia. This one gets two paragraphs even though it's on the Hill because the Hill cops told a reporter it looks like nothing more than a black-on-black street crime. Did the story identify Cole Perenchio?"

"No. Just said 'a Virginia man.' I remember that Detective Seymour had Cole's wallet in his hands. That's probably where 'Virginia' came from."

"But why didn't Cole's name appear in the *Post* story? Why just 'Virginia man'?" Falcone asked.

"The story said that police were withholding his name until next of kin are notified."

"That's bullshit. Police put out victims' names all the time, hoping to get witnesses or information about the crime."

"So why didn't the *Post* name him?"

"Because, I bet, the cops asked the reporter not to. And the reporter did it to stay on the right side of the cops. So the question is why withhold his name? And why no further information about him? Or even a short obituary? He's from the area. Used to work at Goddard, right? He told you he was consulting, like just about everybody in this town. Was he consulting for NASA?"

"NASA is like the Pentagon," Taylor replied. "Loves consultants. I haven't seen Cole for a while, but I think if he were consulting for NASA he would have said so. My instinct tells me SpaceMine. Asteroids were among his interests at Goddard, and, from what I know, SpaceMine demands pretty tough confidentiality agreements. And it's pretty secretive. I'll try to track down Cole's activities in the space community."

"Good," Falcone said. "But don't call me about that information or any other information. No e-mails either."

"Oh, God, Sean. So you've become one of those guys who are paranoid about cyberwar."

"You bet I am. And about the nosy NSA and its vacuum-cleaner sweeps of phones, e-mails, the Internet — and God knows what else. Our firm has a guy who does nothing else but try to keep our computers from getting hit or snooped. And until I get a better grasp about what's going on, I want to keep in touch this way, face-to-face. Not here. Too many know us. You live near the Folger. Let's plan to meet there at, say, three o'clock on Monday. Okay?"

"Okay," Taylor said. "If you want to play it this way, I'll go along. But I'm a guy who is a 'person of interest.' All I want to know is why the FBI stepped in and connected the shootings."

"I don't know what to make of it, Ben. Obviously they think they've found something. What were those names Sarsfield asked about?"

"Peter Darrow and Daniel Bruce. I don't have any idea who they are," Taylor said. "It gets me hopping just thinking about it. Where did they get those names? And what's the FBI doing in this anyway?"

Falcone paused to memorize the names; he did not want to pull out a paper and pen and violate the Cosmos rules. "The most probable answer," he said, "is that the Capitol cops are not capable of handling a murder case but can claim that the FBI was called in because it's Capitol Hill — federal property. However, Sarsfield's questioning of you sounds like something deeper. An agent investigating a shooting on Capitol Hill shouldn't know about your being in line for a White House job. Unless —"

"Unless what?"

"Well, he mentioned budget cuts. It's true that the FBI is feeling the pinch and agents are getting bigger caseloads. Maybe it was just a coincidence, getting the same agent doing a background check on you. That could mean that you were very close to becoming science advisor."

" 'Coincidence'? Come on, Sean. This is Washington."

"Let's stay with what we know," Falcone said. A waiter appeared and both men ordered coffee. As soon as the waiter glided away, Falcone continued. "Sarsfield interviews you. And I get a call saying the science advisor job is on hold. The Capitol cops and Sarsfield should have accepted your story. Something brought in the FBI, and I don't think it was just because the Capitol cops don't do murders."

"Then what was it?"

"I don't know. Let me do some sniffing around. See you Monday. Meanwhile, you keep busy."

"Oh, don't worry. Between you and Darlene I won't get a chance to brood about my fate."

The lunch ended with Taylor's mention of the PBS show he was working on. "I want to ride on the SpaceMine publicity and the curiosity about asteroids. A *NOVA* producer has okayed it and found funding. If I'm lucky, I can get it finished in two or three weeks."

They said goodbye on the steps of the entrance. Taylor headed for Dupont Circle

211

to board a Metro subway train and return to the museum. Falcone hailed a taxi and gave the Sullivan & Ford address.

"Where that shooting was," the driver said.

"Right," Falcone answered. He pulled out one of the three-by-five cards he always carried and scribbled "Peter Darrow" and "Daniel Bruce." He also wrote "S&F/Ben," envisioning lists for what he had to find out for his inquiry and what he had to find out for Ben Taylor. He knew he had to keep the two investigations separate. Then, remembering Sprague and the yellow pad, he wrote "Hamilton" and "laptop," reminding himself that there was a third investigation: his own, which might contain information he would keep to himself until he knew what to do with it.

On impulse, Falcone told the driver to stop two blocks from the Sullivan & Ford Building. He walked into a Best Buy, where he bought a cheap noncontract cell phone for cash and had it activated in the name of Fergus Quinn, a character he remembered from a le Carré novel.

31

A few minutes after Falcone entered his office, Sprague knocked, opened the door, and stuck his head in, as was his habit. "Some news," he said. "Can you please drop by my office?"

Falcone turned quickly, hiding with his body the bag emblazoned *Best Buy.* "Be right with you," he said, dropping the bag into a desk drawer as Sprague withdrew his head and closed the door. Falcone fished in the drawer for a rarely used key, turned the lock, and pocketed the key. He realized he was acting paranoid, and he did not want his new obsession to be noticeable. But here he was hiding a package and locking a drawer.

Outside Sprague's door, Falcone nodded to Ursula Breitsprecher, who was leaving her small office. Sprague opened his door and pointed Falcone toward one of the three leather armchairs arranged around a knee-high glass table. *Ursula just set up the recording device in the planter next to the table,* Falcone thought, angrily trying to push the thought away.

Sprague sat across from Falcone. The latest issue of the *Economist* was lying open on the table, next to a pile of file holders, the top two or three red, which was the law firm's code color for files that were to be handled with particular care.

"I've just been notified," Sprague said, "that the investigation of the shooting is now in the hands of the FBI."

"FBI?" Falcone exclaimed. "On what grounds?"

"Elementary, my dear Falcone," Sprague said. "All crimes committed in the District of Columbia are technically federal crimes and are prosecuted by a U.S. attorney."

"Sure. But these are *local* murders. DC cops got the case."

"I don't have any idea about why the FBI is coming into this," Sprague said. "But I do know that the FBI can get far more intrusive than local police. National security letters, for instance."

"I don't see any national-security involvement in the shootings," Falcone said.

"Well, perhaps the FBI does. That's all they need. Suspicion. I just looked it up.

USA Patriot Act Section five oh five. The letters are served like subpoenas on phone companies and communications systems providers. But, of course, they aren't subpoenas. There's no judicial review."

"I know," Falcone said, sounding irritable at being forced to listen to a Sprague law lecture. "I have no idea how the hell it's been held up in the courts. It's patently unconstitutional."

"Perhaps so. But we're not going to test it. We can't afford to antagonize the FBI. So be careful with your inquiry."

"I'm always careful, Paul."

Sprague turned, gazing toward the window, although all he could see was a vista of buildings full of offices and people like him. As he slowly swiveled around to face Falcone again, he replied, "Of course, of course. But I want you to think less of it as an 'inquiry' and something more like a piece of corporate history. You like history, Sean. So do I. The kind of history based on facts, not theories. I want a . . . narrative from you. Let's not call it an 'inquiry.' Leave sleuthing to the professionals."

"But I *have* a theory, as I told you. Hal was targeted," Falcone said. He waited a moment for Sprague's response. When there was none, Falcone continued. "Those guys

215

had an agenda."

"As I said when you first mentioned this, you may have something here," Sprague said, stroking his chin. He stood and added, "Apparently the FBI has a similar theory. They've put in a request for Harold's client list and recent billings."

"Jesus! What the hell is the FBI fishing for? Did you demand a subpoena?"

"I saw no reason not to simply cooperate. Cooperation defangs them. And you know that a subpoena often generates leaks and publicity. Anyway, Sean, we're talking about the inquiry. I want you to simply lay out what happened. On a practical level, we do need to think about . . . liability."

"Like those two people who were killed on the couch," Falcone said, standing. "You're worried about a suit."

"Yes. Their . . . deaths could obviously lead to civil actions against the firm. Also, if the FBI begins looking around, it frightens clients. We could even lose some."

"Well, we already lost two."

Sprague winced. "Yes. Mr. and Mrs. Pritchard. I doubt that they were targets of anyone." Sprague handed the red folder to Falcone, stood up, and said, "Take a look. You'll see they were here on a routine legal matter."

"What about the stolen laptop? Did you tell the FBI about that?"

"Let's table that for right now, Sean."

"Table it? You tell me that we don't want to scare off clients and you don't give a damn if a laptop full of confidential information was stolen?" Falcone pointed to the red folders. "I get the impression that you're trying to figure out what was in Harold's missing laptop." Falcone refrained from making a remark about Sprague keeping Robert Wentworth Hamilton's name out of the conversation.

"Sean, calm down," Sprague said with a theatrical sigh. "Yes, I am taking a potential damage assessment. I hope all goes well with the laptop investigation. But it is out of our hands."

In his office, Falcone took his personal computer out of a drawer, started it, and typed in his password. The screen remained blank until he took a cigarette-lighter-size device out of his pocket and pressed a button, generating a five-digit number that appeared on a small screen on the device. He typed in the numbers, which changed every twenty seconds. The computer's security system accepted the numbers. The next image on the monitor was a request for his fingerprint. A scanner approved his right thumb, and finally the laptop was ready for use.

Falcone next cut off the computer from the wireless network. Theoretically, the computer was now utterly secure and hacker-proof, but he knew that even disconnecting from a network could be an illusion. He read every book and article he could find about hacking and computer security. What it all came down to, he realized, was that you can never achieve complete security, but you have to keep trying.

With the red folder open on his desk, he began reading and taking notes, which he typed into an outline template. Until he started working in the White House, he had taken notes and composed on his lawyerly yellow pads. But in the high-speed, memo-prone Oxley White House, a yellow pad was as out of date as a mimeograph machine. Falcone switched from yellow pad to gray computer and slowly became an early acquirer. He was the possessor of a cell phone, an iPad, an iPod, a smartphone, two laptops (firm's and private), a desktop computer (firm's), and an electronic notebook.

He went through the red file, document by document, and then typed

"Stranger" Victims (based on copies of contents of purse and wallet, respectively)

Mary Ann Pritchard
- 28 years old, Bethesda, MD
- Purse contents: driver's license, VISA card, $97, cell phone

Walter R. Pritchard
- 63 years old, same Bethesda address
- Wallet and pocket contents: driver's license, VISA card, $32, cell phone, key chain, eyeglass case, receipt for the basement parking, pocket calendar containing entry for 11 a.m. appointment with George Crittenden

Falcone dialed Crittenden's number. His office assistant answered and said Crittenden would not be coming in today. Falcone knew that Crittenden, a senior partner in his seventies, more or less specialized in wills and estates. He represented some of the firm's longest-served clients. And Crittenden had taken the Pritchard deaths very hard. He had not been in the office since the shootings. There were rumors that he intended to retire shortly.

Falcone was convinced that the Pritchards were innocent bystanders, props for a staged mass killing. So their deaths were, to use a Pentagon term, collateral damage. His next move was a talk with Gabe, the firm's finance director, who never missed a day's work.

Gabe's real name was Hugh Berger, but the name of his father, Gabe, seemed to go with the job and Hugh accepted Gabe as an honorific. The first Gabe had retired a few years back and had been succeeded by Hugh, who had been with the firm since the day he became a CPA and, after his father retired, accepted the practice of being called Gabe. He skillfully and quietly managed a finance staff whose cubicles and offices occupied most of the fifth floor.

Gabe always answered on the first ring. Falcone asked to make an appointment to talk to him. "I'm having an easy day, Senator," Gabe said, observing the Washington protocol that preserves rank unto death. "I'll be up right away."

"What can I do for you, Senator?" Gabe said when he entered Falcone's office. He was slim and balding, black strands striping his shiny pate. He wore a gray suit complete with vest. His tightly knotted tie was light blue. Gabe put his unopened iPad in his lap and used it as a platform for his folded hands. He looked up in surprise when

Falcone told him he needed Harold Davidson's client list and billing records for the past year.

"I'm already preparing a memo for the FBI. Mr. Sprague approved," he said.

"What about billing? Will you include billings?" Falcone asked.

Billing, Falcone knew, was the heart of the multimillion-dollar, finance-managing department that Gabe ran. Lawyers accounted for their time in billable hours, which varied from a typical $800 an hour to variations somewhat above and somewhat below that. At the end of each day, lawyers, paralegals, and billing managers all submitted data about their billable time: hours spent on researching, analyzing, preparing, and producing legal documents; expenses for travel and commissioning consultants; court appearances, phone calls, appointments, conferences, e-mails — all the work that had been performed that day on specific matters for specific clients.

The exception was Falcone, who billed clients by straightforward memos that he sent to Gabe with copies to Sprague. The information flowed daily into Gabe's databases. Ultimately, complex algorithms transformed the data into invoices that were sent to clients. Incoming payments from the

221

clients were then recorded and deposited into the firm's bank and stock accounts. From that income pool came the distributions to everyone who worked for Sullivan & Ford.

"Billings, as you know, are highly confidential," Gabe said, a trace of shock in his voice. "The memo for the FBI will be along the lines that we have always followed in responding to such requests from law enforcement. The idea is to respond with just enough information to hold off a subpoena and to have it signed by Mr. Sprague, who adds a stern but polite note about client-attorney privilege."

"Yes," Falcone said. "Mr. Sprague can write a great note, I'm sure."

"All the FBI gets is a list of names and addresses. No e-mail addresses, no phone numbers. But you, as a senior partner, get whatever you want," Gabe said with a quick grin. "A useful client list — the kind I believe you need — has to be annotated. For instance, many of Mr. Davidson's clients are relatively inactive, kept on the list because they pay retainers. The *real* key to his work is billable hours. The more hours, the more appointments, the more consecutive days, the more likely that you're looking at an important client, one of the heavyweights."

"Exactly. Those are what I want."

"Are you investigating Mr. Davidson's murder?" Gabe asked. "Looking for motives? That sort of thing?"

"Mr. Sprague has asked me to write a report on the shootings, Gabe. I'm not looking for motives," Falcone said. "I'm trying to understand what happened. For instance, I have no idea why the Pritchards were killed."

"That would be the *second* Mrs. Pritchard," Gabe said. "There's a lot going on with those two. Mr. Crittenden needs all his skills to handle her."

Falcone knew that Gabe was a great gossip. He never spread it to outsiders, but he did provide his bosses with chitchat and rumors of scandals that he picked up on the Washington after-hours circuit. He was a middle-aged bachelor with a busy social life, primarily produced by invitations — to embassy receptions, new-book parties, cocktails on Capitol Hill, lectures, charity events — that partners declined to attend. Gossip never appeared on his Facebook page, which celebrated his evening rounds: *Enjoyed the celebration of Brunei Independence Day at the Brunei Embassy* or *Had a good chat with the Indonesian Embas-*

sy's military attaché at the National Defense University reception.

"Mostly I'm interested in Mr. Davidson's murder, Gabe," Falcone replied. "In going over his billing hours, did you get any sense that he was spending a lot of time with any clients lately?"

"That's the oddity, Senator. For the past six months his billing shows that he was doing pro bono work for the same client. It was taking so much of his time that he was getting complaints from his paying clients."

Falcone well knew that pro bono work — from the Latin *"pro bono publico,"* "for the public good" — was a contentious issue at most law firms. But Sullivan & Ford, operating under the American Bar Association's recommended ethical rules, required its lawyers to contribute at least fifty hours of pro bono service each year. And many exceeded the minimum, including Falcone, who focused his pro bono work on the legal issues of veterans and government workers.

"Who was the pro bono client," Falcone asked.

"That's another oddity, Senator. The pro bono client is not identified on our standard document: name, address, point person of client, and so forth. All that Mr. Davidson wrote was quote 'client requires anonymity' unquote. When I politely questioned this, Mr. Davidson referred me to Mr. Sprague. And he allowed this . . . irregularity."

"Did you get any clues about the anonymous client?"

"Well, one," Gabe said, and, when Falcone nodded, went on. "As you know, we — that is, our databases — keep track of partners' whereabouts."

"Oh, yes," Falcone said. "You're better than the White House switchboard."

"Thank you, Senator. Well, as you know, if you are not in your office, the firm wants to know where you are and whether to direct your absence to billable time for a specific client. All it takes is a few words into your desk phone or smartphone and the words are transcribed. Your presence or absence can also be indicated by the security system, which keeps track of the keypad that locks and unlocks your office door. Everyone has a pattern, and if that pattern changes, the system notes it."

"I never realized that," Falcone said. "But I'm not surprised. A lot goes on these days in the name of security. So, about the clue?"

"Well, Mr. Davidson stopped noting his whereabouts just about six months ago. His comings and goings were not recorded — except for the security system. Incidentally, we have our share of absentminded types. But this was unusual. Mr. Davidson was a meticulous man."

"So you attribute this change to his anonymous pro bono client?"

"Yes. The two seem to coincide. And I believe there is a clue," Gabe said, putting a special emphasis on "clue." "On four occasions in the past six months, our town-car database showed Mr. Davidson was being taken to and from Dulles."

"That doesn't sound like a clue to me. We all use the town-car service for the airports."

"Well, yes. But . . . I suppose I am not violating any confidentiality, since Mr. Sprague has commissioned you . . . and you are asking me . . ."

"Okay, Gabe, okay. Just tell me," Falcone said.

"Mr. Sprague had some concern about Mr. Davidson's absences and asked me to get some routine information from the town-car service. The drivers, of course, keep a precise record of where and when they take clients. All of the trips were for boarding or departing on South African Airways. And all were reported billable to the pro bono client."

"Complete with flight numbers?"

"Yes. I assume you want them. I'll prepare

a memo with all we have on this, including absences over the past six months."

"Thanks, Gabe. As soon as possible. And one more thing, if you don't mind."

Gabe had his iPad open, fingers jabbing the spectral keyboard.

"Two names. See if they show up anywhere in your databases. Peter Darrow and Daniel Bruce. And I'd like to see whether there has been any recent billable work for Robert Wentworth Hamilton."

Gabe looked up and stopped typing. "Mr. Hamilton is not in our regular databases, Senator."

"How do you know?"

"His name has come up occasionally in the past. He does not appear anywhere. Except . . ."

"Except what, Gabe?" Falcone asked, irritation tightening his voice, as it had with Sprague.

"There is a highly confidential database that I cannot enter. I thought . . . assumed . . . you would know about it. That database is controlled by Mr. Sprague. Highly encrypted. Mr. Hamilton's name may be in that database."

When Gabe said "may be," Falcone heard "is" and said, "Thanks, Gabe. You've been a great help."

"Anytime, Senator. Anytime."

32

Falcone deleted the outline he had begun. He decided that an outline was too orderly a way to envision the web that had begun — where? He tracked back in time, imagining himself sitting in the office, watching GNN. He wrote down the time sequence: *SpaceMine. Robert Wentworth Hamilton. Shootings. Emmetts. Sprague. Davidson's laptop. Cole Perenchio. FBI takeover.*

The FBI. Maybe he could at least find out something about that.

Falcone took the Best Buy phone out of his pocket and punched ten numbers to reach J. B. Patterson, director of the FBI. Falcone knew that all of Patterson's other numbers were answered by someone deep in his labyrinthine organization and then slowly transported upward. The direct line to the console on Patterson's desk was a number unchanged since the time when Falcone was the President's national security advisor.

J. B. Patterson answered. There was a split second of silence as he noted with surprise that the small ID display showed Fergus Quinn. Then Falcone said, "Hello, J.B."

"Sean! Or should I say Fergus? How are you? Glad the bad guy missed."

"Me, too," Falcone said, pausing before adding, "I'm wondering if you could drop by my place after work."

"Like the old days. Sure, Sean. See you around seven."

Falcone's apartment was just two blocks up Pennsylvania Avenue from FBI headquarters — the big, buff-colored concrete monolith called the J. Edgar Hoover Building. During Falcone's tenure as advisor, he had used his apartment as a discreet place to meet with Patterson for extremely off-the-record sessions that would not be chronicled in the visitor logs of either the West Wing or the FBI. Since going into private practice, Falcone had called Patterson a few times, always requesting nothing more than information or leads that would ordinarily have taken him weeks to obtain through channels. This would be their first meeting since Falcone left the White House.

Under the law, the director of the FBI

could serve a single term of no longer than ten years, unless the President asked Congress for a special extension. Patterson was midway through his term. At this point, Falcone realized, Patterson probably was not looking beyond his term, but people in high places in Washington always needed friends, and Falcone was a good, proven friend.

Patterson had been known as J.B. ever since his girlfriend (and future wife) noted that his initials were the name of her favorite play, *J.B.,* by Archibald MacLeish. When Patterson joined the FBI, J. Edgar Hoover insisted on a first-name-plus-initial identification. Agent James B. Patterson finally got his initials when he became Director J. B. Patterson.

At 6:49, Patterson took the elevator from his twelfth-floor office to the basement garage, where his security men were waiting at a black SUV. He was tall and slim, and rarely smiled. But Falcone knew the man who walked within the FBI armor. Patterson had a sly sense of humor and an inner happiness about wife and family that the widower Falcone envied.

The SUV pulled up in front of 701 Pennsylvania Avenue and Patterson stepped out. Two members of the security detail followed. As Patterson headed toward the open penthouse elevator awaiting him, he waved them away. They sat in comfortable chairs in a small alcove reserved for guests of the residents. "Just like old times," one of them said to the other, who had just joined the security detail.

Falcone met Patterson as he emerged from the elevator, and the two of them walked down the corridor to the foyer of Falcone's apartment. Following precedent, they walked into the living room. Falcone motioned Patterson to a leather chair that resembled the one off the lobby.

"Or we could go out on the terrace," Falcone said, handing Patterson a glass of Balblair single-malt Scotch. Falcone had poured himself a Grey Goose vodka. Carrying a tray with the glasses and bottles, he nodded to Patterson to open the door and they walked out to one of those Washington October nights when summery moments return.

"So," Patterson said, his arm sweeping across the terrace, across the Washington view, "this is the reward for a career of faithful service to the nation."

"The *thanks* of a grateful nation," Falcone said, sitting at one of the wrought-iron chairs at a round, similarly fashioned table.

Patterson sat opposite him.

"First, I wanted you to know that the other shooter — the one who fled — is dead," Patterson said. "So is the getaway driver. Killed by New Jersey troopers on the turnpike."

"How did —"

"It's sketchy and, as I said, Sean, it's complicated. The bureau wasn't in it, at least directly. But you know about the Joint Terrorism Task Force. Those guys got involved. A lot of solid police work here in DC and New York nailed the car. The driver made the mistake of pulling one gun on two troopers."

"Troopers okay?"

"Yes."

"Nice work," Falcone said, hoisting his glass. As he lowered it, he asked with a smirk, "So was the other shooter Peter Darrow or Daniel Bruce?"

Patterson put down his glass and said, "I see you've heard of Agent Sarsfield's interview of Dr. Taylor. The reason Sarsfield tried out those names on Dr. Taylor was because those were two names we were tracking down until we found that their California licenses were very good fakes. Prints from the body show the real name of the guy you wrestled with is Dukka Sadu-layev."

"Russian?"

"No. Chechen. The guy has quite a record. You did a public service. He was a pro, the trigger man on probably twelve hits in New York and New Jersey."

"And the guy killed in New Jersey?"

"That was Ahmed Kurpanov, Dukka's cousin, according to immigration ID prints. No police record yet. But NYPD thinks he was a hit man in training. Both of them were naturalized American citizens. Came here with Kurpanov's uncle from Chechnya as political refugees. The driver was Russian, worked for Kuri Basayev whenever he needed a driver in New York. The driver was clean enough to have a chauffeur license, but he was probably the driver on a lot of hits."

"Basayev?" Falcone said, surprised. "What the hell is he doing with hit men? He's a multibillionaire, big with the hedge-fund crowd and, I've heard, close to Boris Lebed."

"He's the classic Russian oligarch, even though he's Chechen," Patterson said. "High politics and big-time crime — everything from stock manipulation to murder. And untouchable. My guys keep an eye on him when he steps off his yacht in New York. Manhattan Pier Ninety. We don't have anything on him. He pops up here and there. But mostly he keeps on the run by staying at sea."

"I've certainly heard of him," Falcone said. "And I just assumed he was Russian."

"No. He's a Chechen, distantly related to a dead terrorist."

"I just can't see him mixed up in a hit on a law firm," Falcone said. "But you know an awful lot about him." He pointed to the empty glass. "Another?"

"Got to go," Patterson said, rising. "Thanks for the visit."

"There's one more thing, J.B."

"Try me."

"Why in hell did Ben Taylor get FBI interest? Why was he questioned by an agent?"

"Agent Sarsfield," J.B. said with a sigh. "He's very enterprising, very gung-ho. He was doing a background check on Dr. Taylor — I guess you know about the science-advisor job. Then the field office suddenly got two new cases. The Capitol cops, who don't do murders, handed us a shooting on the Hill. Sarsfield saw Dr. Taylor's name in the paperwork. Then we took over the shootings at your law firm, as I just told you. And Sarsfield wondered if the cases were related. He connected the dots — God, how I hate that phrase, as if a criminal or terrorist investigation is like moving from one to two to three — and he sent out national security letters. Then he —"

"National security letters!" Falcone exclaimed. "Of all the snooping, searching without a warrant, and —"

"All legal under the Patriot Act, Sean, as you know, and, believe me, I keep an eye on those letters. Well, anyway, Sarsfield got records of the phone calls that Taylor got and made that day, and —"

"Cole Perenchio," Falcone said.

"Right," Patterson said. "Look, I've got —"

"Well, what about Hal Davidson? Why is the FBI interested in the shooting at the law firm?"

Patterson sighed, sat down, and held out his glass for a refill. "This is, of course, for you," he said. "Not for other ears. Usual rules."

"Right," Falcone said, pouring. "I just need to know so I can know some other things."

"Well, the complications start with the weapon used. Remember Fast and Furious?" Patterson asked.

"Hell, yes. The crazy gun-tracking operation that backfired. ATF guys had the bright idea of allowing guns illegally bought in America to cross the border, hoping to trace the guns to the Mexican bad guys."

"Correct."

"And," Falcone continued, "the ATF geniuses thought they'd get points from Mexico's cops for nailing those guys, along with the Americans who bought them and sent them into Mexico. But all they found out was that guns kill people, including a Border Patrol agent. And Congress had a field day. The attorney general barely escaped alive."

"Very good memory," Patterson said, putting down his glass. "Well, just when Justice and the ATF thought Operation Fast and Furious was behind them, the issue rises again. The guy you . . . the guy who went over the railing . . . was carrying an M16, complete with serial number. The DC cops routinely sent the number into ATF — and, guess what. It was a Fast and Furious gun that had somehow *returned* to the United States.

"Well, that bit of news passed up the line pretty damn fast. I got a call from the director of the ATF. I decided for the good of everybody that we take over. One Department of Justice bureau helping out another

Department of Justice bureau. We get points for that. I called the DC chief of police and took a mass killing off his hands. He sounded very, very grateful."

"You make it seem so simple. But on what grounds did you take over?"

"The District of Columbia is federal property. Every crime committed there is a potential FBI case," Patterson said, holding up a hand to stop the comment that Falcone was about to start. "I know what you want to say. Abuse of federal power and so forth. But, as a matter of fact, we have reason to believe there is a national-security matter here."

"Mexico–U.S. relations? Slim reed, J.B."

"It's a little more than that, Sean. We believe that the gun came back to the United States not from Mexico but from Idaho."

"Idaho?"

"Check the map. Idaho has a narrow border — about forty-five miles — with Canada. There are small Islamic communities in Idaho — immigrants from Central Asia, places like Chechnya, with ties to Muslim terrorists. We think that the gun came in that way."

"So the shooters were Chechens and had a Fast and Furious gun that came in from

238

Canada? Jesus!"

"Right. . . . A complicated case. . . . Look, I've got to go," Patterson said, rising again.

"One more question," Falcone said, walking Patterson down the hallway to the foyer. Before pressing the elevator button, he asked, "Was Harold Davidson a deliberate hit, not random?"

"I can't say anything about that, Sean."

"National security?"

"Can't say," Patterson replied, pressing the elevator button. "But I will tell you this. We're retrieving the getaway car from the New Jersey police and we expect it will give us some answers. Stay tuned."

33

By Monday, when Falcone was to meet Taylor, the shootings had passed from media view. The memory remained only in the circle of people directly touched. At Sullivan & Ford, the FBI crime-scene technicians had been replaced by the crime-scene-repair technicians — the carpenters, the glaziers, the plasterers, the people who specialize in removing bloodstains and signs of death. Blood gone, bullet holes erased, windows restored, pierced and splattered books gone.

Falcone was the first to enter the Great Hall of the Folger Library, the block-long Capitol Hill home of the world's largest collection of Shakespeare documents and artifacts. He watched Taylor enter from the farther entrance, his steps echoing as he walked past the gift store and the first of a dozen glass display cases containing an exhibit on the writing and history of the

King James Bible, beginning with Anglo-Saxon biblical poems of the tenth century.

Taylor stopped at the Folger's first edition of the Bible, and opened to Genesis 8:22: "While the earth remaineth, seedtime and harvest, and cold and heat, and summer and winter, and day and night shall not cease."

Falcone was seated on one of the high-backed chairs drawn up in front of an audio display. As Taylor approached, Falcone stood and pressed a button. They listened for a few moments to the voices of the Apollo 8 astronauts reading verses from Genesis on Christmas Eve, 1968, as they orbited the moon.

"Sometimes, Sean, you amaze me," Taylor said softly, sitting down next to Falcone. "I was ten years old when I heard that and decided to be an astronaut."

"Coincidence, Ben. Absolute coincidence. I had no idea this was here."

"One of my fellow grad students was a Jesuit," Taylor said. "And he told me once that every coincidence traces back to an inevitability. I've seen enough coincidences to believe that Jesuit was right. Did you see the verse the Bible is open to? Genesis. The life of the Earth."

"I haven't looked at the exhibit," Falcone

241

said. "It just seemed like a quiet place to talk."

"Well, I'd like to start with a hypothetical question — as a client," Taylor said. Falcone, looking surprised, nodded. "If someone happens to have a copy of an accidentally recorded phone conversation, can he listen to it?"

"Well, I guess if someone handed him a tape and as he listened he realized it was a phone conversation that he took part in, he — the listener — would not be breaking any phone-privacy laws. But I'm sure you know that nothing from that recording can be used in court. I assume you're talking about your telephone conversation with that FBI agent, Sarsfield."

"Right."

"I assume that your loyal office mate — Molly is it? — thought she was doing the right thing. Delete the recording and tell her to forget about the accident. The good thing is we know the names he asked you about. And I have some information about those names."

After Falcone recounted what he had learned from Patterson, Taylor asked, "How the hell do you know all that?"

"I'm a good lawyer. I have open ears and a closed mouth, especially the names of confidential sources."

"Okay. I'll leave it at that. But what does it mean to me?"

"I'm not sure what it means to you. But I can guess. Once a national security letter gets into the picture, you have to accept the reality that the FBI knows just about all there is to know about you — and probably some of your friends."

"Like what?"

"I had a State Department employee as a pro bono client. She blew a whistle about corruption in Afghanistan and was demoted. She fought it. The FBI got her credit record, her bank records, her Internet provider, the address of every Web server she communicated with, the identities of people she e-mailed and got e-mails from — and, it turned out, some of those people got calls from the FBI. I finally got her reinstated, but my attempt to stop national security letters went nowhere."

"Whatever they know is okay with me," Taylor said. "It's what they *think* about me that bothers me right now. 'Person of interest.' What can I do about that?"

"Don't worry. Sarsfield was just poking, just looking for some way to connect the shootings at my law firm with the shooting of Cole Perenchio."

"What? How the hell can he do that? Except that they're both black. Who knows, maybe I'll be the third dead black guy."

"Keep your paranoia to yourself, Ben," Falcone said, smiling. "I've got enough for both of us. Right now, all the FBI has is a theory. Nothing more. But I do feel a little like Sarsfield. I'd also like to know what you think Cole wanted to tell you."

Taylor did not immediately respond. He shook his head and said, "He did not tell me anything. But I have a hunch that he wanted to tell me something about Janus."

"About *what*?"

"Janus. It's a big asteroid. And an attractive site for Hamilton because it appears to be a heavyweight full of ore."

"And it has a name?"

"When an asteroid is discovered, it's given a temporary label based on the order of its discovery. So asteroid 2014 AB would be the second — B — asteroid discovered during the first half month — A — of 2014. Later, when astronomers feel it has had enough observations, it gets a permanent number. And then the discoverer can add a name that is approved by the International Astronomical Union. The asteroid's name is Janus. In Roman mythology, Janus is the double-faced god of gates and doors, beginnings and endings. It's the ending that worries me."

"Any other candidate?"

"Dozens. Every day the asteroid-watchers find a new one and record it, putting it in the catalogue, giving it its anonymity. But, as I said, sometimes astronomers can't resist giving one a name. There's even one named after Thomas Pynchon."

"Gravity's Rainbow," Falcone said. "It gave me one of my favorite quotations: 'If they can get you asking the wrong questions, they don't have to worry about answers. . . .' Janus . . . How did Janus get that name?"

"Because it has an odd shape. Well, odd even for an asteroid," Taylor said. "Some radar images of it look like two profiles joined together — one looking to the past and the other to the future. It may have had a little moon once and they merged."

"What makes you concerned about Janus?"

"A lot," Taylor said, nodding toward an image of Earth taken from a spaceship. Below were the words of Archibald MacLeish: *To see the earth as it truly is, small and blue and beautiful in that eternal silence where it floats, is to see ourselves as riders on the earth together. . . .*

"Some scientists — and I'm one of them

245

— believe that Janus's orbit makes it a possible threat to Earth. I say possible, because I think it's a threat in the remote future. But I think it was one of those inevitability coincidences that Cole called me so soon after that SpaceMine announcement about their rocket reaching an asteroid that Hamilton named USA. I went to the star charts, to that spot where Hamilton pointed the laser beam toward Cassiopeia, and I got this hunch. I think Cole was going to tell me that SpaceMine had selected Janus as its mining site."

"So you think someone killed the messenger?"

"Maybe. But, anyway, I'm going public with Janus."

"How?"

"Ever watch *Street Speak*?"

"Occasionally," Falcone replied. He had appeared several times on Bloomberg's premarket morning news and talk show, giving his opinions, especially about Wall Street and government regulations.

After a moment Falcone added, "Are you sure going on *Street Speak* is a good idea?"

"I got invited, and I see no reason not to go on. Television is what I do a lot of. As for Janus, I figure I'll throw out the name and see what happens."

"Be careful, Ben. Take my advice. Don't mention Janus. You'd only be speculating, and, if you're wrong, you'll lose credibility."

"Don't worry, Sean. I'm always careful. And I have a mind that keeps things compartmentalized. You won't see me for a while. I have to put the finishing touches on my show. When I'm working on a show, Darlene calls it going into space. Well, that's where I'm going."

34

Jerry Quentin, the *Street Speak* anchor, made his show popular by linking the financial world to everyday life. Through his wisecracks and irreverent observations, viewers got a perspective that went far beyond the daily litany of Wall Street numbers. To him, SpaceMine was not about rocketing into the cosmos but was simply an earthly venture that like so many ventures involved not just dollars but also risk.

Quentin began his interview by noting that Taylor was the first astrophysicist to appear on the show. "Usually," he said, "we talk to people who handle really difficult subjects, like greed and staying out of jail. Space exploration ought to be easy. But let's start with greed anyway. What are the chances of making a lot of money by mining an asteroid?"

"Well, we didn't get many details from that SpaceMine announcement," Taylor said. "We don't know the location of the so-called Asteroid USA."

" 'So-called'? Why do you say that?" Quentin asked.

"You can't just pull a name out of a hat. There are rules about astronomical names."

"Well, those miners are going to need a name for the place they go to work, right?"

"I think we can assume that there won't be any human miners involved, Jerry."

"Robot mining?"

"Right. SpaceMine won't have to worry about the kind of miners' strikes that have been closing mines in Africa. But I worry that there are no regulations to establish rules for all of the commercial activity that's under way these days in space."

"What kind of rules are you talking about?"

"The United States is a signatory to an outer-space treaty that specifically says space should not be 'subject to national appropriation.' "

"Meaning what?" Quentin asked.

"Meaning no country can claim sovereignty over any heavenly bodies or asteroids. And if a country can't do that, I don't see how anybody can just plant a corporate flag in a large space rock and say you own it."

Quentin was stunned. "You mean private enterprise puts up all the money, takes all the risk, and they don't own what's in it or on it? Whoa! Isn't this socialism at its worst?"

"All I'm saying is that it's unclear. I think the treaty needs to be amended to take into account all of the scientific progress we've seen since it was ratified back in 1967. There are other issues that need to be examined. If something goes wrong up there, according to the treaty, the private companies — or their government sponsors — could be held liable for any damage they cause to other countries or companies."

"What do you mean 'if something goes wrong'?" Quentin pressed, clearly unhappy with the thought that Taylor was calling for international regulations in the very area where American enterprise had a technological lead.

"Hypothetically, if the mining involves changing an asteroid's orbit without proper controls in place, there could be problems."

"Such as?" Quentin asked.

"We don't know precisely what the unintended consequences might be. The worst result could be setting up a collision course with Earth."

"Oh, so we just get hit by an asteroid.

Nothing to lose sleep about," Quentin said with an uneasy laugh.

"I'm not suggesting that the sky is falling. I just want us to learn about asteroids."

"Okay. Let's start off by learning this: What are the chances of an asteroid hitting Earth?"

"There's no way to accurately calculate those chances. But an asteroid about, say, fifty meters in diameter, hits about once every thousand years or so on average. An asteroid large enough to cause global problems — one that's bigger than a kilometer in diameter — well, one like that hits about every seven hundred thousand years."

" 'Global problems'? Like, 'goodbye planet'?"

Taylor did not respond. Quentin waited a beat and asked, "So, is this the thousandth year or the seven hundred thousandth?"

"I didn't mean to post odds, Jerry. Don't tell your viewers to rush out and buy any asteroid insurance just yet," Taylor answered with a laugh, his eyes dancing with playful mischief. "I'm no expert on just what scares investors. But I think we're safe for another few years." Taylor couldn't contain a wide smile from breaking like a wave across his face.

"So there's nothing to worry about," Quentin said.

"I didn't say that," Taylor responded, losing the grin. "There are dangers."

"Yeah, every thousand years."

"No. Right now," Taylor responded. "The danger involves what asteroids are selected for mining."

"Oh, Ben, you are such a gloomy one!" Quentin said.

"It's not gloom, Jerry," Taylor said. "It's common sense."

"Let's get back to the financial angle," Quentin said, taking control of the interview. "The SpaceMine guys mentioned one asteroid that is supposed to contain eight trillion dollars' worth of platinum. Any idea what asteroid that would be?"

"Robert Wentworth Hamilton gave some asteroid his commercial name — the so-called Asteroid USA. But he didn't give us a clue about what astronomically recorded asteroid it actually is. There are more than one million near-Earth objects that are big enough to destroy a city. And we only know where about one percent of them are at any given time. Those near-Earth objects — NEOs — that have been studied appear to contain a lot of different metals. Tons of platinum is certainly possible, even on a

252

very small asteroid."

"Right now," Quentin said, "platinum is trading close to the same rate as gold. But what happens if you dump eight trillion dollars' worth of platinum onto the Earth market?"

"You're the business expert, Jerry," Taylor said. "Think about it. We're going to keep adding people to the planet, and they'll likely be making bigger demands for platinum, palladium, and other metals. Especially for hydrogen fuel cells to power cars. Right now, the bulk of the platinum and palladium comes from Russia and from mines in South Africa where rotten conditions cause some bloody strikes. So it looks to me that SpaceMine would break up the Russian and South African duopoly and own a piece of real estate worth eight trillion dollars. No wonder so many people seem eager to sign up for the IPO when it's announced. It looks like another gold rush, just as Hamilton says."

"It doesn't take much to get people to flock to an IPO these days," Quentin said.

"There's something else, Jerry. IPOs get regulated — maybe not as much as some people would want. But they get watched over by the SEC. There's nobody watching over space. Imagine what oil prospecting in the Gulf of Mexico would be like with absolutely no regulations. I just hope that the SpaceMine hoopla will get our politicians to start thinking about space law and the UN space treaty that's been around for years."

"A lot of people would chip in to send the UN into outer space," Quentin said. "Thanks, Dr. Taylor, for taking us out of the world."

35

Taylor's *Street Speak* appearance produced a flurry of e-mails — requests from Jon Stewart's *Daily Show* and other first-tier television shows, colleagues congratulating him for raising the dangers of unregulated asteroid mining, and the inevitable zealots who feared or welcomed the end of the world. He left them all unanswered because he was deep in space, day and night, plugging away at his *NOVA* show.

Two days after his Folger meeting with Falcone, Ben Taylor was driven to the Virginia studios of WETA, Washington's flagship public broadcasting station. He knew the place well, because this was where his monthly *Your Universe* show was produced. Now he was here to watch over a final run-through of "An Asteroid Closely Watched."

Near the end of the day, his *NOVA* coproducer convinced him to shave off one minute and nineteen seconds. When that was done, they then pronounced the show ready for prime time, and Taylor, carrying a digital copy of the show, was driven back to the Air and Space Museum. He had returned to Earth.

He went directly to the planetarium, handed the show disks to the operations manager, and then took the elevator to his office. As he left, his booming voice could be faintly heard on the recording of the day's final scheduled museum show, "Reaching for the Stars: A Trip to Our Nearest Neighbor." As soon as the show ended and the audience exited, staffers began transforming the planetarium into a theater. There a select audience would see a preview of the *NOVA* show.

When Taylor entered his office, Molly greeted him with the news that he was to call Agent Sarsfield.

"When did he call?" Taylor asked.

"About twenty minutes ago?"

Taylor looked at his watch and said, half to himself, "Just about when I got to the museum."

"You think they're following you?" Molly asked, instinctively looking toward the door.

"Maybe, Molly. Maybe. I'm going to call him. And," he added, "as I told you, no more accidents."

Taylor went to his desk, took a deep breath, let it out slowly, and then called Sarsfield, who answered on the second ring.

"Taylor here, responding to your call. How may I help you?" He spoke calmly, proud of his voice control.

"Just one question, Dr. Taylor. Are you familiar with Robert Wentworth Hamilton?"

"Familiar? No. But of course I know the name."

"In what context?"

"You said 'one question.' "

"Just following up, sir."

After a short pause, Taylor felt a surprisingly cautious tone seep into his voice as he said, "I suppose that, for me, the context is SpaceMine. Mr. Hamilton is the CEO of SpaceMine."

"Yes. That's correct. And, regarding Space-Mine, you may recall that, on a televised news show, you suggested that if SpaceMine were to mine a certain asteroid, the mining might put the Earth in jeopardy."

"Oh, for Christ's sake!" Taylor exploded. "What does this have to do with the murders you're supposed to be investigating?"

"I am not at liberty to say, Dr. Taylor. But it is a fact, according to the transcript of that show, *Street Speak,* you did discuss SpaceMine and asteroid mining dangers."

"Look, Agent Sarsfield. This happens to be a very busy day for me. If you want to know what I think I know about asteroids, I suggest that you see the show, which will be shown a week from tonight on all PBS stations. And then call me."

"I hope to do that, Doctor. Thank you for your call."

36

Taylor stood near the Touchable Moon Rock display in the museum's grand entry hall on the Mall, greeting guests as they passed through the "Milestones of Flight" gallery and headed toward the reception's wine and hors d'oeuvres. Many of them touched the lunar sample before shaking his hand. The gesture reminded him of the hand-dip into the holy-water fount at St. Sebastian's Church in his Bronx boyhood.

Among the first to arrive were Darlene and Major Sam Bancroft. Taylor leaned down to give Darlene a cheek-kiss and then gave Bancroft the full Dr. Benjamin Taylor handshake — right hand pumping, left hand reaching around to pat Bancroft's broad back. Darlene and Sam had met a few months ago, and Taylor believed that their romance was on the brink of serious.

"Looking forward to the show, Doc— . . . Ben," Bancroft said, slipping past the honorific to the recently bestowed first name. Bancroft was as tall as Taylor, a blue-eyed, buzz-cut blond Midwesterner in the blue uniform of an Air Force officer. *He could be on a recruiting poster,* Taylor thought.

Bancroft had met Darlene at the library of American University, where she worked while juggling graduate school courses on the long road to a doctorate in international affairs. He had been taking an accelerated summer language course in Arabic. He was now stationed at the Pentagon, doing something he did not talk about.

Darlene walked away to intercept another arrival, Sean Falcone, before he had a chance to reach Taylor. She hugged Falcone and said, "Sean! It's been too long."

"My God, how long it has been! And how beautiful you are!" Falcone said.

"You are very good for my morale, Sean. Come over and meet my . . . friend," Darlene said, pulling Falcone by the arm toward Bancroft and Taylor. When Falcone was introduced, he glanced at the rows of ribbons under Bancroft's silver wings. He recognized the bits of color that meant service in Afghanistan and Iraq, the distinctive color of the bar signifying a Purple Heart, and the red-white-and-blue for a

Silver Star. "Gallantry in action, wounded in action," Falcone said, looking up from the ribbons. "An honor to shake your hand, Major. Afghanistan?"

"Yes, sir," Bancroft said, looking embarrassed at the sudden attention.

"He won't tell you about that medal," Darlene said, touching the Silver Star ribbon. "I had to look up the citation. They're all online if you know where to look. It was a combat search-and-rescue mission. Landed a helicopter to pick up a couple of our guys who were in the wrong place at the wrong time. He shot some bad guys and took a round himself. But he stayed at the controls and got our guys out of there. Did I say controls? He's a regular control freak."

"A Pave Hawk?" Falcone asked.

"Yes, sir. A beautiful helicopter. May I ask, sir, are you retired military?"

"Well, I was military a long while back. Vietnam. But I was a civilian when I first heard about the Pave Hawk."

"Sean was a senator," Taylor said. "And President Oxley's national security advisor during the President's first term."

"Sorry, sir. I didn't recognize —"

"No need. Advisors are low-profile. There were people in the White House who didn't recognize me. And the Senate, like Vietnam,

261

was a while back. But I remember that the Air Force needed some money to upgrade the Black Hawks, and I was one of the senators who thought that was a good idea. Glad to hear yours did its job."

"Still have Black Hawks for jobs like the one on Osama Bin Laden," Bancroft said, suddenly losing his shyness. "Special Forces still call theirs Black Hawks. We — search-and-rescue — called 'em Pave Hawks for its avionics package. Anyway, I guess I should thank you, sir."

"Save your 'sir's for the Pentagon," Darlene said. "He's *Sean.*"

"You're at the Pentagon?" Falcone asked.

"Yes, sir."

When Bancroft did not elaborate, Falcone knew there would be no point in asking questions about his Pentagon duties. And, realizing that Taylor needed to circulate among his guests, Falcone steered Darlene and Bancroft toward the wine and hors d'oeuvres.

Taylor spied a man and woman stepping through one of the tall glass doors and strode toward them. *Rare to see them together,* Taylor thought as he extended his hand to Stephanie Sinclair-Hardy, the secretary of the Smithsonian. He next shook hands with Conrad LaSalle, chairman of

262

the board of the Corporation for Public Broadcasting. Neither got the full Dr. Ben Taylor handshake.

"I'm very pleased you both could come," Taylor said, looking toward Sinclair-Hardy first. She was a stunning woman in a fitted black jacket, black blouse, black pants, and black spike-heeled shoes. Shoulder-length white hair framed her impassive face. She gave Taylor a tight smile and silently moved on. He noticed that she did not touch the moon rock.

LaSalle looked up at Taylor through the lenses of rimless glasses, his face displaying the perpetual frown of an ulcer-prone worrier. He was in the black tie and black dinner jacket that was the fading dress code for evening social occasions in Washington. *Has another event tonight,* Taylor thought. *Busy man.*

"I'm looking forward to your presentation," LaSalle said.

"Good turnout," Taylor said, looking around. The cost of the reception had come out of his entertainment fund, and he never shortchanged Air and Space, which drew far more visitors than all other Smithsonian museums combined. Taylor shook LaSalle's limp hand, expecting a short, quick exchange of bland remarks. But LaSalle hurried on to catch up with Sinclair-Hardy. He also did not touch the moon rock.

As the stream of arriving guests thinned, Taylor made his way toward the reception, walking beneath a Viking lander like the one that touched down on Mars and Space-ShipOne, the first manned private spacecraft — a reminder, if he needed one, that entrepreneurs like Hamilton were moving into space. Nearby were other miletones: the Wright Brothers' spindly flying machine . . . the *Spirit of St. Louis* that had carried Charles Lindbergh across the Atlantic . . . *Columbia,* the command module used on the Apollo 11 mission . . . a Predator drone.

Taylor stopped frequently to shake a hand, get a hug, and have a short chat, all the time weaving through the growing crowd of tray-bearing waiters and jugglers of food and drink. Among the sixty-odd guests, Taylor spotted two senators, three House members, and the stand-ins for several other lawmakers: clusters of young Hill staffers who were transforming their bosses' invitations into plates full of free meals.

Precisely at 7:30, the lights in the vast gallery dimmed, signaling the opening of the doors to the planetarium. Usually the rows of seats were arranged in concentric circles surrounding a dark hub that contained the heart of the planetarium, a projection apparatus that bathed the domed ceiling in images of constellations and planets. Tonight a segment of seats was realigned so that the rows faced a small stage and a theater-size screen that rose from the hub. In the front row were the senators and House members, flanked by Darlene, Bancroft, Falcone, Stephanie Sinclair-Hardy, and Conrad LaSalle.

The lights dimmed and Taylor strode to the center of the stage. After thanking Sinclair-Hardy and LaSalle and their organizations, Taylor turned toward Falcone's seat.

"Before taking you into space," Taylor continued, "I want to thank somebody right here on Earth: former senator Sean Falcone, who, in his recent post as national security advisor to President Oxley, began the process of getting law into the heavens." Pointing to Falcone, Taylor continued, "I joined him in calling for a Senate hearing on updating the Outer Space Treaty of 1967. And on the day of that hearing is called, I hope I will be given the opportunity to testify about my particular concern: the dangerous exploitation of asteroids."

As Taylor stepped off the stage and took

the empty seat next to Darlene, he noticed Sinclair-Hardy and LaSalle glancing toward each other. LaSalle was frowning, and Sinclair-Hardy coolly nodded. At the back of the room, Taylor saw a door open and a planetarium staffer escort a latecomer to a back-row seat. Taylor recognized someone he had decided not to invite: Agent Sarsfield. *This is an invitation-only event,* Taylor thought. *He's using his FBI badge to get in and watch his person of interest.*

The show began.

37

A Texas-size asteroid is tumbling toward Earth. Zoom to a NASA installation near Washington. An official says, "We're going to fly to that asteroid with a nuclear device, implant it, and get off before it blows." Bruce Willis, leading a crew wearing bright-orange astronaut-style outfits, heads for a spacecraft, which rockets off to land on the asteroid.

Willis, sweating and puffing through a few more scenes from the movie *Armageddon,* directs the drilling of a shaft deep into the asteroid. The crewmen drop a nuclear bomb into the shaft. After some bits of drama about Willis's acceptance of martyrdom, he triggers the bomb. The asteroid explodes and splits in two. Fragments fly off and zip past the rescued Earth, ending the outer-space special effects of the movie.

"Sorry, Bruce. That might not work," Taylor says from the screen. He wears his familiar television attire: red sweater over a white shirt, khaki slacks, and big brown boots. Running along the bottom of the screen are the words LOS ALAMOS NATIONAL LABORATORY.

He begins narrating in a deep voice that sounds like Darth Vader's: "We've done a lot of research on asteroids since that movie came out in 1998. In fact, as we learned not long ago, with the creation of the corporation SpaceMine, asteroids are potential sources of riches rather than objects of terror.

"Some scientists here at Los Alamos accept the Bruce Willis Solution. Using a supercomputer, they produced a three-dimensional vision of what they think would happen when a one-megaton nuclear weapon explodes on a good-sized asteroid."

An enormous splash of red and orange fills the screen as the bomb explodes. The bomb's shock wave surges through the potato-shaped asteroid, which disintegrates into a stream of rocks.

The explosion fades and Taylor reappears before a sky full of stars and says, "The Los Alamos scientists believe that a nuclear bomb would, in their tidy words, 'mitigate the hazard.' Well, frankly I think they're prejudiced. After all, they design nuclear weapons at Los Alamos, and since we haven't used any nuclear bombs since 1945, this scenario was an interesting way to show how a nuclear bomb could be put to peaceful, lifesaving use. And that supercomputer? It belongs to the National Nuclear Security Administration, which also naturally favors the use of a nuclear bomb to rescue Earth. But let's take another look at those rocks."

The stream of rocks reassemble in slow motion and the asteroid takes shape again as Taylor continues: "That is a possible structure of some asteroids: countless rocks of many shapes and sizes, drawn to each other as the core of the asteroid first began traveling through space, its gravity field acting like a magnet. The nuclear-bomb theory is based on the bunch-of-rocks theory, which holds that the asteroid would be blown to smithereens and those smithereens would vaporize and burn away in the atmosphere, never reaching Earth.

"Another theory, which *I* endorse, says that this may not be the structure of most asteroids. And even if it were, some of the rocks produced by the explosion would be large and dangerous. And *all* or *most of* those big ones would strike the Earth — meaning that we would have to cope with many impacts instead of just one. A dubious kind of rescue.

"Now let's move from Bruce Willis and Hollywood and nuclear bombs to the real stewards of an asteroid-endangered Earth, the NASA experts who were directed by Congress in 2005 to find, identify, and track ninety percent of asteroids larger than one hundred and forty meters — four hundred and fifty-nine feet — across. Scientists believe there are about twenty thousand asteroids that are labeled 'city destroyers.' NASA has identified and tracked about thirty percent of them.

"NASA defines 'near-Earth objects' as asteroids and comets with orbits that come within twenty-eight million miles of Earth's orbit around the sun. Asteroids are dark rocks that roughly show their size by reflecting light. We've worked out formulas for guessing the size of an object by the amount of light it reflects. Trouble is, a small, light-colored space rock can look the same as a big, dark one. As a result, data collected with optical telescopes using visible light can be deceiving. An asteroid labeled small may really be big. And big may be bigger.

"Here's the main outpost of NASA's Deep Space Network at Goldstone, California." An image of several huge, bowl-shaped antenna structures appears. "And here is an actual asteroid, Toutatis — it's named after a Celtic god." A gray object that looks like a huge, jagged rock slowly tumbles on the screen. "What you are looking at was formed of images generated from radar data collected at Goldstone.

"Toutatis is an asteroid about three miles wide. It passed four point three million miles from Earth in December 2012, only seventeen times the distance between Earth and the moon. That's close by astronomical standards, but not a threat. NASA described its movement as that of a wobbly football that was poorly thrown. So imagine trying to tame Toutatis as it erratically spins across the sky.

"What is also significant about Toutatis is that it was first discovered in 1934 and was then lost. Lost! It was rediscovered in 1989, and NASA has been keeping an eye on it since. This once-lost asteroid reminds us how little we know about these odd neighbors of ours. There are about one thousand seven hundred heavenly bodies classified as potentially hazardous asteroids by NASA's Near-Earth Object Program. Toutatis is one of them.

"If Toutatis had struck the Earth, the force of the collision would have produced more energy than all the nuclear weapons on the planet. But even a small asteroid could cause a catastrophe. If it exploded at the right altitude, spewing a ring of debris, it could cause climate shifts that would be sufficient to drastically cut crop yields, perhaps for several years.

"Our lack of knowledge about asteroids is amazing — and dangerous. Remember that fireball that lit up the skies of Russia a while back? It was called a comet, a meteorite. . . . Well, now we know that it was a tiny asteroid, only about fifteen feet long! That's right. Tiny, but able to scare us — and explode with a shock wave that shattered windows, loosened bricks, and injured twelve hundred people."

The scene shifts to NASA's Near-Earth Object Program office at the Jet Propulsion Laboratory in Pasadena, California. Taylor and a NASA scientist are talking about the Impact Hazard Scale. A copy of the multicolored scale, in chart form, hangs on a white wall. The chart rates the potential peril of asteroids that scientists have spotted and are tracking.

Taylor, pointing to the chart, says, "The hazard scale ranges from zero for an asteroid that has virtually no chance of colliding with the Earth, to ten, which signifies a certain hit — a certain catastrophe. Alongside the numbered scale is a color code that reminds me of the warning system that Homeland Security once used."

Taylor's hand runs down the chart, showing how the colors range from an unthreatening white through cautionary yellow to threatening orange — and finally to several shades of red. Taylor reads from the gravest of the red warnings: " 'A collision is certain. It can produce a global climatic catastrophe that may threaten the future of civilization as we know it.' "

Taylor turns toward the camera and says, "Scary, no? Here's something scarier: Congress has stopped funding research into how best to deflect or destroy asteroids believed to be on a collision course with Earth. That's right. The same Congress that ignores the climate changes threatening the future of our planet also has chosen to ignore another planetary threat that is just as real.

"Don't just listen to me. Here's what I learned from a visit to the Armagh Observatory in Northern Ireland, founded in 1789."

As Taylor walks along a sidewalk that courses through a greensward, from an old brick tower to a modern gleaming sky telescope, he talks to an astronomer, who says, "It's a question of *when,* not *if,* a near-

Earth object collides with Earth." She leads him into the observatory and says, "We're used to earthquakes, floods, volcanoes, great storms. Believe me, all those disasters are trumped by objects that reach Earth from outer space. The density of threatening objects is incredible. Here's a map we created, showing the terrestrial planets — Mercury, Venus, Earth, and Mars — with their asteroids. Our solar system is full of asteroids."

The dense population of asteroids fades away as Taylor reappears in NASA's Near-Earth Objects Program office. "We discover new asteroids nearly every day," he says. "The other day, I received my regular NASA report on near-Earth objects. It showed that in the previous month NASA spotters had found more than two hundred. The total number of known asteroids in Earth's neighborhood is heading toward one million, a number that grows daily.

"NASA classifies more than one thousand four hundred near-Earth objects as potentially hazardous asteroids because they are large and because they follow orbits that pass close to the Earth's orbit. Despite that 'potentially hazardous' label and despite our ability to keep increasingly close watch on those big hazards, no country on our threatened Earth has an official warning system.

"We once had one, run by the U.S. Air Force. It was called the Space Surveillance System, which the Air Force described as a 'fence' of radar energy projected into space to detect objects intersecting that fence. I quote from the Air Force's unclassified description of the system. 'The operational advantage of the AFSSS is its ability to detect objects in an un-cued fashion, rather than tracking objects based on previous information.'

"Well, it's not tracking objects, because it has been shut down for budgetary reasons. To run it costs about fourteen million dollars a year. According to recent figures, the U.S. Air Force spends thirty-five million dollars a year on 'civic outreach,' such as the Thunderbirds flying team."

As the Thunderbirds whiz by in a clip superimposed over an image of the Impact Hazard Scale, Taylor continues: "Yes, there are copies of that Impact Hazard Scale hanging on astronomers' walls. But you won't find it in the Pentagon or in the White House. Neither the President nor any other leader in any other country knows what to do if an asteroid threatens to strike the Earth. And nobody knows the best way to get the public ready for a possible impact."

In a realistic animation, a close-encounter asteroid bears down on Earth. Taylor fades away, but his voice lingers:

"Astronomers sometimes give asteroids names. They call this one Janus, after the two-faced Roman god, because of its odd, double-profile shape. It's been out there for millions of years. But we did not discover Janus until 2009. Astronomers are not really sure about its orbit. We can try to keep watch on an asteroid long enough to figure out its orbit. But it can suddenly shift. If it swerves into a collision path to Earth, we can detect that, and all we can do is pray. It would be coming at us at seventy-five times the speed of sound. There would be a warning time measured in days. A lot of scientists worry about that today. But what they worry about the most is that they aren't able to get any attention from any government on Earth."

The image freezes on screen and Taylor reappears, standing in front of the image. "There is, in fact, no government out there in space. If people want to mine Janus — or any other asteroids — all they have to do is figure a way to get there and start mining.

"Janus is handy for mining. It is expected to pass closer to Earth than any asteroid recorded in human history. But if its orbit were to take it through a precise region in space, known as a gravitational keyhole, Janus could be on a collision course on its next visit, on the seventh of April in 2035. 'The keyhole' is a way of describing what happens when Earth's gravity alters an asteroid's orbit in such a way that the asteroid will collide with Earth at some future pass."

The show ends in a simulation of Janus's two journeys. In the first, it passes so close that backyard astronomers can see it through ordinary telescopes. Its orbit, as scientists hypothesize, takes it through the gravitational keyhole. On its second pass, in 2035, it heads toward Earth.

The simulation suddenly fades.

On screen, Taylor stands before a huge photograph of felled and blackened trees — a Siberian forest leveled by an object that fell from the sky. "The unnamed asteroid that hurtled down here at Tunguska in 1908," he solemnly says, "weighed 220 million pounds and entered Earth's atmosphere at a speed of about 33,500 miles per hour. The air around it heated to a temperature of 44,500 degrees Fahrenheit, consuming the asteroid in a gigantic fireball and releasing energy equivalent to about 185

Hiroshima-size nuclear bombs.

"There was no warning in 1908. For Janus we have a warning."

The red zone of the impact hazard scale reappears. "This was a warning that we must heed. We have enough time for all the nations of Earth to find a way to defend Earth."

When the show ended, many people headed for Taylor to congratulate him. As they gathered, he looked beyond and saw Stephanie Sinclair-Hardy and Conrad LaSalle walking toward the exit. And a few paces behind them was Agent Sarsfield.

38

The next day, Taylor decided that it was time for him to make the trek out to Goddard Space Flight Center to see if he could find out what Cole Perenchio had been working on and why he left NASA. Rather than hire a limo or taxi to take him to Goddard, Taylor was determined to drive his own car. To hell with Washington's infamous traffic snarls. He wanted to get behind the wheel of what Darlene called his outrageously expensive midlife-crisis car, an Audi A8 L W12, and feel that he was in control. He simply couldn't stand being at the mercy of other people — especially cabdrivers for whom English was the verbal equivalent of a Rubik's Cube.

Through someone he knew in Human Resources, he learned that Perenchio's last assignment had been to a night shift at the Laser Ranging Facility. Taylor decided to talk his way into Goddard and go to the range at night in hope of finding someone who would tell him about Cole.

After Molly left, he spent an hour at the Four-Eyed Monster, visited a vending machine for two packages of peanut-buttered crackers, and went down to the museum's underground parking garage. He had gone scarcely a block before he ran into a snarl owing to a detour that herded traffic away from his chosen route.

Pushed left and right by big orange detour signs, he wound up crawling north on Connecticut Avenue. Seething over the delay, he swung over to Wisconsin Avenue in the hope that there would be a breakthrough, but he found only another long line of cars and trucks puffing out exhaust fumes as far ahead as he could see.

After sitting for almost twenty minutes at an intersection that had been blocked by a major fender bender, Taylor decided he had had enough. He resented the wasting of time, and frustration finally ignited his rage. Running a red light was no capital offense in his mind, and tonight he did just that without the slightest remorse.

He shot through a light on Wisconsin Avenue, then through another one and found himself on a twisting suburban road. A sudden rain etched the darkness ahead.

Unfamiliar with the Maryland roads, he peered through his sloshing windshield wipers and realized he was completely lost. A green light ahead changed to red and he shot through it. This ignored red light was at the south end of a single-lane Civil War–era stone bridge controlled by a traffic light at each end.

Halfway across the bridge, Taylor, unaware there was only one lane, saw headlights coming toward him. He twisted the wheel to the right, mounted a low curb, and struck the stone wall of the bridge. The on-coming pickup truck braked, swerved, and slammed into Taylor's prize Audi. Air bags popped all around Taylor, knocking his chest and head back violently. The driver in the other vehicle dialed 911.

A dazed Taylor managed to open the front passenger door. He stumbled out, stunned and confused. As he stood in the chill rain, all the recent days flowed jaggedly through his mind — Hal, Cole, Sarsfield, murder, death, fear. The horn on the pickup truck blared nonstop. The driver, a young man wearing a camouflage jacket and cap, stepped out and glared at Taylor, adding to his confusion and stoking his paranoia. The pickup driver, cell phone in hand, stared vacantly at it in the glare of a single headlight.

Two Montgomery County police officers arrived. When one approached Taylor, he pointed to the pickup driver and shouted, "He's trying to kill me!" Taylor was still convinced that he had been on a two-lane road and been hit by a killer driver who had deliberately swung over from another lane.

The officers helped the two drivers off the bridge, where an ambulance and police cars were parked, lights flashing. Both drivers were uninjured except for bruises caused by the air bags.

"I am in danger, real danger!" Taylor insisted to the officer who was trying to question him.

The other police officer briefly questioned the pickup driver, handcuffed him, and took him away.

Taylor became more agitated. "See? See? He did it!" he yelled. "He tried to kill me!"

A medic tried to soothe Taylor and finally convinced him to get into the ambulance, which took him to a hospital a short distance away.

Two more police cars arrived to handle the jams caused by the ever-growing lines of cars at each end of the bridge.

Taylor, his mind clearing, called Darlene from the hospital. As soon as she was sure he was not injured, she said, "You ran a red light, right?"

"Right," he replied. He did not tell her that while he was being questioned about the accident, those questions in the rain seemed to run into other questions at the Summerhouse with Cole's body lying nearby. His bewilderment was so profound that the officer knew this was not a driver who had been drunk or reckless. This was a driver who had been confused by an unfamiliar road and a peculiar bridge, perhaps even by some of his own demons. And he had been hit by a driver who was high. The officer did not charge Taylor with running a red light.

39

Philip Dake, who had been in the audience during Taylor's show at the museum, filed a story about the show for the *Post*'s Style section, calling it "a fascinating and sobering look at the big lumps of rock that hang over Earth." Dake praised Taylor for "warning us Earthlings that we must be careful when we treasure-hunt in space."

Three days after Dake's story appeared, he called Falcone on his private line. Without any preliminaries, Dake said, "Sean, there's a *Grudge Report* in the works on Ben Taylor — and you're mentioned."

"About the asteroid show?" Falcone asked. "Another one? I meant to call you to thank . . ."

"This is a long and rotten story," Dake answered. "A real tough one, goddamn it. A hatchet job, aimed mostly at Ben Taylor. Full of innuendos. Amateur stuff. No sources, of course."

"When does it hit the Internet?" Falcone asked.

"I'm told that *Grudge* will put it out around eleven tonight. Will you be home? I'd like to see your reaction."

"Sure. You still a wino?" Falcone joked. Dake owned an interest in a Virginia wine firm.

"You still pour fifty-year-old brandy?" Dake said, anger gone. "See you around eleven."

Falcone and Dake sat on a couch in Falcone's home office. On a remote control he connected his computer to a television wall screen. Before them was the *Grudge Report*, which Falcone's TiVo was recording while they watched it. THE THREE BLACK MUSKETEERS ran across the top of the screen. Below were three photographs with these captions:

Dr. Benjamin Franklin Taylor
The Scientist

Harold Davidson
The Attorney

Cole Perenchio
The Engineer

Next came a full screen presented as if it was in a report appearing in a newspaper or magazine:

Cambridge, Massachusetts, 1988: Benjamin Franklin Taylor is working on his PhD thesis, "Formation of Galaxies and Clusters of Galaxies," at the Massachusetts Institute of Technology. Cole Perenchio is in his senior year at MIT and is top scorer for the MIT Engineers basketball team. Harold Davidson, a graduate of the University of Massachusetts in Amherst, is in his first year at Harvard Law School. When black students at U of M take over a university building to protest campus racism, Davidson goes to Amherst and runs into Taylor and Perenchio, who made the 90-mile trip to Amherst to show solidarity with fellow African-American students. They all get arrested for trespassing, call themselves the Three Black Musketeers, and vow lifelong friendship.

Washington, D. C., now: Harold Davidson and Cole Perenchio are dead. Benjamin Franklin Taylor, who found Perenchio's body and was briefly held by Capitol Hill police, is a "person of interest" to the FBI — while also being considered for appointment by President Oxley as his Science Advisor.

"Jesus!" Falcone exclaimed. He froze the image and, rising from the couch, pointed at the wall as if it was warning about something dangerous or loathsome. "Where the hell did this come from?"

"Scroll down. Scroll down, Sean," Dake said calmly, a snifter of brandy warming in his hand.

Falcone unfroze the image and slowly scrolled farther down the story.

Davidson was one of four people shot to death on October 4 in the mass shooting at the Sullivan & Ford Building. Taylor was reportedly out of town on that day. Late the next night, Taylor called police to report finding a body in the "Summerhouse," a small 19th-century structure on Capitol grounds. The shelter has long been known as a rendezvous for gay trysts. The body was identified as Cole Perenchio, who at one time worked with Taylor at NASA's Goddard Space Flight Center in Greenbelt, Maryland.

"Gay trysts! God damn! They're practically accusing him of killing his gay lover!

How the hell does this crap get on the Internet?"

"Keep viewing and scrolling," Dake said. "When you're finished, I'll give you my theory."

Falcone gripped the remote and scrolled down. The story went on to say that Taylor had been taken to Capitol Police headquarters and questioned by Detective Willard Seymour and released by Deputy Chief Walter Barnett.

Falcone began reading out loud: " 'Until now, Taylor's questioning by police — and his designation as "a person of interest" — have not been revealed. The *Grudge Report* discovered this possible cover-up from interviews with law-enforcement personnel. Coincidentally, attorney Sean Falcone, hero of the Sullivan and Ford shooting, is representing Taylor. Law-enforcement sources suggested that Falcone, former national security advisor to President Oxley, may have called on powerful friends to keep information about Taylor secret.' "

Falcone sat down and pounded the arm of the couch. " 'Coincidentally'? What the hell does that mean? That Ben is in trouble and needs a lawyer? And how the hell does *Grudge* know that I'm Ben's attorney?"

"Keep on reading and scrolling," Dake said.

Falcone did, silently fuming:

Taylor's nomination as Presidential Science Adviser — officially, director of the Office of Science and Technology Policy — had been a well-kept White House secret. Falcone, who still maintains ties with the Oxley White House, allegedly put Taylor's name forward. When Taylor had his encounter with police, Falcone and his powerful friends are believed to have managed to convince police to keep Taylor's case unpublicized.

However, FBI agents, doing a confidential background check on Taylor, learned of the alleged Capitol Hill cover-up, questioned Taylor and made him "a person of interest." Word of this reached the White House, where, a spokesman said yesterday, Taylor's nomination is "under review."

Falcone kept scrolling down and reading silently. He was barely able to keep from exploding.

Two paragraphs were devoted to the time when Perenchio and Taylor worked together at Goddard, quoting an unnamed former

NASA employee as saying, "Cole was an engineer and Ben was a scientist. Scientists like Ben told us what they want, and engineers like Cole worked until the scientists were happy. Sure, there would be disagreements between an engineer and a scientist. But those two guys, they got along okay most of the time."

The story concluded with a description of Taylor's "sensational and fear-inducing" show, noting that Falcone was in the audience. He resumed reading aloud:

" 'PBS officials told the *Grudge Report* that they are "discussing the scheduled *NOVA* broadcast of Taylor's show." ' "

"And you know what that means," Falcone said. "No show. And I'll bet that Smithsonian officials are discussing Ben's museum job. Jesus! This is character assassination."

Falcone picked up his snifter for his first swallow. "I've got to call Ben," he said. "But first tell me your theory."

"First of all," Dake said, "there's no indication of sources or of its provenance. It probably went through a hell of a lot of writers and edits — and undoubtedly a few lawyers. Also, I get the feeling that there was someone powerful hovering over this, pushing for information, exploiting sources."

"And who could that be?" Falcone asked.

"Somebody who is very pissed off at Taylor. My guess is that it starts with the Capitol Hill Police. Note that you get the name of the cop who questioned Taylor and brought him in. What's his name?"

"Willard Seymour."

"Yeah. Seymour. And then you get the name of the high-ranking cop who let him go. My bet is that Seymour had what could be a big-publicity pinch and the perp gets snatched away."

"That's good for a start," Falcone said. "But the 'person of interest' had to come from the FBI. That bothers me a lot."

"Why?"

"I knew about it, Taylor of course knew about it, and the FBI knew about it. The FBI has to be the source that gave the *Grudge* that 'person of interest' label. Nobody else — unless Taylor told somebody, which doesn't make sense."

"Okay," Dake said. "So the FBI leaked something. For God's sake how long have you been in this town? When the FBI wants something known, it leaks it."

"Yeah. You're talking about more or less authorized leaks, the kind you get sometimes," Falcone said. "But I think this is deeper, bigger. Take a look at the span of

291

the story — a mass shooting, three black guys, FBI, and the White House. It's a hatchet-job story. Somebody obviously is out to get him."

"I think I know who," Dake said.

"Who?" Falcone asked. He stood, pressed a button, and the screen went blank.

"Come on, Sean. It's got to be Hamilton. And get this: For a little while when the Three Black Musketeers were in Cambridge, Hamilton was, too. Funny the story didn't mention it."

"You're kidding."

"I never kid about stories. For about two years, while Ben and Cole were in MIT and Harold Davidson was in Harvard Law School, Hamilton was in the Harvard Business School. The business boys and girls — many boys, few girls — divide into sections for studying. Hamilton's was called Section X, composed of very wealthy students who were there mostly to study how to manage their family fortunes. I doubt if he spent much time making friends at MIT or Harvard Law. The Section X students stuck together, went on spring-break trips together, like to Dubai or Hong Kong."

"Fascinating," Falcone said. "Sounds like your Hamilton book is progressing. I'd like to hear more. But right now I have to talk to my client. And so, good night," Falcone said, motioning in the direction of the entrance-hall door.

40

Darlene sleepily looked at the clock beside her bed. *A 1:27 a.m. call never brings happy news.* Her heart was pounding when she picked up the phone, which was oddly heavy in a hand used to speaking into a cell phone.

"I've got to talk to your father," Sean said flatly.

"Oh, Sean. What's —"

"Is he up?"

"I'll wake him."

"Okay. Tell him I'll be there in about ten minutes. I've got to talk to him right away. And, please, Darlene, make some coffee."

Falcone hung up, pressed a button on the phone console, asked the night watchman to call a cab, and walked into his bedroom to exchange slippers for sneaks. He grabbed a windbreaker out of the closet and put it on over his sweatpants and Celtics sweatshirt. He picked up his wallet and keys from the top of his bureau and walked out the hall door.

Falcone could hear the phone ringing in Taylor's home as he closed the taxi door and sprinted up the front walk. At the edge of his vision he saw a white truck with a satellite dish coming up the street. *I'm not the only one who saw the* Grudge Report *tonight.*

Darlene stood in the lighted doorway.

"Don't answer that phone," Falcone said as he entered. "And don't answer the doorbell."

Darlene nodded and closed the door.

"Where's your dad?" Falcone asked.

"He's still upstairs. It's been a rough couple of days."

"What happened?"

"You know how impatient he is. . . ."

"I think you mean what a hothead he can be."

"Well, he decided to drive out to Goddard to find out about what Cole Perenchio had been doing there."

"And?" Falcone asked, worry in his voice.

"He was on the Cabin John Bridge. You know, the one where only one line of traffic can pass at one time."

"Know it well."

"It was dark. Raining. And he saw headlights coming toward him. And he thought someone was trying to run him off the road. And he saw it was a pickup truck barreling right at him. There was no place he could move to. Nothing he could do."

"So what happened?" Falcone was getting impatient and he was not known for having a very long fuse.

"The truck hit Dad's car dead-on . . . well, head-on."

"Was he hurt? Is he okay?"

"He's fine. Just a little banged up from the air bag that went off."

"Was it . . . ?"

"Intentional?" Darlene finished Falcone's question. "Police don't think so. The kid driving was from Hicksville and high on weed. Jesus, I hope they never legalize that stuff around here. They arrested him for DWI."

"Your dad get medical treatment?"

"Sean, are you kidding? He's scared to death of doctors. Figures they'll always find something wrong with him."

Ben Taylor slowly came down the stairs a bit unsteadily and stood behind Darlene. He wore a red and gray bathrobe over blue pajamas. His feet were bare.

"Christ, Ben, you look like hell. Darlene told me what happened. The accident. You okay?"

"Yeah. Headache and sore arm from those damn air bags."

"You're sure it was an accident?"

Taylor nodded and said, "Pretty sure. At first I thought I was about to become the next man on the hit list. But no. The kid was a stoner. Had one too many bongs. Nothing more sinister. . . . So tell me, Sean. What the hell's going on?"

"Bad stuff, rotten stuff, Ben. Where's your iPad?"

Darlene picked up her iPad from a kitchen counter. "He never knows where his is," she said. "What's up?"

"Bring up the *Grudge Report.*"

"What? I never look at . . ."

On the iPad appeared the three photos and the headline "Three Black Musketeers." Darlene clicked the headline and the story came up, surrounded by advertisements and pointers to other stories.

Taylor stared at the iPad on the kitchen table and silently began reading, with Darlene looking over his shoulder, now and then exclaiming "My God!" and "Good Lord!" The doorbell rang three times, followed by heavy pounding. They heard the sound of a vehicle starting and moving away.

Falcone walked over to the coffeemaker. When the light went on, he poured three

297

cups, added milk to Darlene's coffee, brought them to the table, and sat down. Neither Taylor nor Darlene said a word until Taylor finished reading and switched off the iPad.

"Quite a piece," he said quietly. "Three Black Musketeers. Brings back memories. Actually, we just called ourselves the Three Musketeers. Anyone could see we were black."

"That's all you've got to say?" Darlene exclaimed. "The goddamn *Grudge Report* is crucifying you. You've got to sue him."

" 'Crucifying' is a bit strong, Darlene," Taylor said. "But it certainly doesn't make me look good."

"There's really nothing to sue over, Darlene," Falcone said. "No libel suit. No defamation of character suit. Not on my advice anyway. There's a lot of nasty stuff, but as far as I can see, there's no absolutely false statement — and sometimes even that's not enough. Anybody who tries to sue over anything like this gets hit between the eyes by the First Amendment. But, if the Smithsonian or PBS moves against your father, we have a lot of choices."

"Like what?" Taylor asked.

"Like breach of contract for starters."

"You think they'll fire me?"

"I think PBS will cave by taking something like the White House line and saying the show is 'under review' and is no longer on the schedule. The Smithsonian will probably choose putting you on 'administrative leave' with pay."

"Like they do with cops who shoot somebody," Darlene said. " 'Administrative leave' gives people the idea that maybe you're guilty of something. Guilty until proven innocent."

"So be it," Falcone said. "We've got a bigger issue: Who set this up? My candidate is Robert Wentworth Hamilton. But why is he going after you? And what will he do next? Get serious, Ben. Two of the Musketeers are dead."

"Well, I told you I did have that run-in with Hamilton," Taylor replied, speaking calmly, as if nothing serious had happened. "It was over the letter from scientists. We were protesting his selection of an anti-global-warming guy for a scientist award. But I'd think that was ancient history by now."

"Not ancient, Dad," Darlene said. "You're exasperating! Don't you know what happened yesterday? Somebody at PBS got all excited about the show and put out a tweet that used the words 'asteroid' and 'collision.'

The *Huffington Post* picked it up and, of course, mentioned the SpaceMine announcement about Asteroid USA. Then the tweet went viral and —"

"What?" Falcone interrupted. "I did see *Street Speak* mention something about what this might mean for SpaceMine. But I didn't know that a PBS tweet was involved."

"There's a big new Twitter world out there, Sean. Just like the wild Internet world and its *Grudge Report* world," Darlene said. "And the old world doesn't know anything about it."

"Look, Sean. I agree that this is serious," Taylor said. "And there's a lot that the old world doesn't know. A lot."

Outrageous as it was, the *Grudge Report* on the Musketeers stirred a sudden memory for Taylor. Back in 1967, an MIT professor had lectured about a mile-wide asteroid named Icarus, after the mythological daredevil who flew too close to the sun. Asteroid Icarus would pass relatively close to Earth in 1968. The professor told his students to assume that Icarus was on a collision course with Earth — and they had to save the planet. They decided to pummel Icarus with thermonuclear bombs borne on Saturn V rockets.

The Icarus project inspired the 1979 science-fiction film *Meteor,* which Taylor saw as a teenager. He came out of the theater determined to learn all he could about asteroids, not realizing that he was putting himself on the path to MIT.

41

Besides being chairman of the Senate Committee on Appropriations, Senator Kenneth Collinsworth was also a member of the Senate Committee on Commerce, Science, and Transportation (CST), which had jurisdiction over highway safety, inland waterways, ocean navigation, marine fisheries, weather and atmospheric activities, the Merchant Marine, the Panama Canal, and space sciences, among other matters. After several hysterical calls from Hamilton, in a rage about Taylor, Collinsworth decided to place a call to Senator Frank Anderson, the Oklahoman who chaired CST.

After an exchange of pleasantries, Collinsworth plunged into his reason for the call: "Frank, it seems that this guy Dr. Taylor has stirred up a firestorm with his TV appearances and documentary about the need to change the Outer Space Treaty and get the damn feds involved in a place where it has no business to be. I think I'll need a little help to put this fella in his place."

"Talk on, Ken. I'm with you so far," Anderson said.

"I already have a public hearing scheduled for next week on NASA trying to get back into the game of setting up a moon colony," Collinsworth continued. "They're afraid the Chinese are going to build some of their megacities up there. What say we make it a joint committee hearing so we can round up some votes? I've got some folks on my committee who are pretty wobbly when it comes to taking on NASA and President Oxley. Their states used to get quite a bit of business out of NASA before we cut NASA's budget, and their governors are putting pressure on them to start the printing presses rolling again."

"Absolutely! I'm with you, Ken," Anderson replied. "We got a goddamn nineteen-trillion-dollar train wreck coming at us and we've got to hold Oxley's feet to the fire on our national debt or he's going to take us all the way to Greece and back before he leaves office. I'll get my press guy to work with your man on a release. How about something like, Senators Kenneth Collinsworth and Frank Anderson announce a joint hearing to examine 'Federal

303

Waste in Space'? We can fold the issue of asteroid mining in, along with hammering Taylor for scaring the hell out of the American people so he can get the so-called international community into Uncle Sam's knickers."

"Spoken like a true patriot, Frank," Collinsworth said, a half smile racing across his lips. "You have a way with words, my friend. Let's move on it."

When Senator Sarah Lawrence, the senior senator from Maine and chairwoman of the Armed Services Committee, learned of the joint hearing, she cornered Collinsworth on the Senate floor following a recorded vote.

"Frank, I saw the notice of your hearing next week," she said, placing herself directly in front of Collinsworth, stopping him in midstride. She was a foot shorter than Collinsworth, but long ago she had learned if she stood back far enough, she did not have to look up at a man's face. She was in her early fifties, with a figure little changed since her cheerleader days at the University of Maine. She wore a black skirt and a white blouse under a dark blue jacket. Her black pumps had sensible one-inch heels.

Although a space treaty sounded like a subject beyond the jurisdiction of the

Armed Services Committee, she was powerful enough to have her way. Collinsworth knew that she also was popular enough with the media to grab some attention. But, with a broad smile and nod, he asked what he could do for her.

"I'd like to sit in on your hearing with your permission," she went on. "It'll give me an opportunity to see where all of this asteroid talk is heading."

Collinsworth held Lawrence with barely concealed contempt. She was just too damn liberal to suit him. To him, she represented a bunch of liberal bastards trying to pass themselves off as "responsible" conservatives who believed the art of compromise. *Horseshit,* he thought. He was not one to follow Senate protocol or courtesy, but he decided that someday she might become an ally, as unlikely as that might seem at the moment.

"Well, it's going to be a little crowded up on the dais, but sure, Sarah, I'll see that you get a seat." *Jesus,* he thought to himself, *and I'll have to listen to her pontificating.*

A "little crowded" was an understatement. Originally, the hearing had been scheduled to be held in the Dirksen Senate Office Building. But so many senators planned to attend the hearing that a larger room was

305

required. Collinsworth called Charlie Napolitano, the architect of the Capitol, and tasked him to come up with the best way to accommodate as many as twenty-five or more members.

Napolitano, a short, wiry man who wore large horn-rimmed glasses and a poor comb-over, said, "Not a problem, Mr. Chairman. We'll set everything up in the Caucus Room of the Russell Senate Office Building. Just a matter of marshaling lumber, carpenters, and a small amount of money which I can take from the contingency fund."

"Excellent, Charlie. I'll need to have it ready by next Wednesday."

"Done."

And it was. The construction crew carried out the project quickly and without a hitch. The workmanship was excellent. The dais had the appearance of a permanent structure with all senators having an assigned seat where they could see — and be seen.

A lot of history had been made in the Caucus Room. It had been the site of the hearings held on the sinking of the *Titanic,* the Teapot Dome scandal, and the Army-McCarthy, Watergate, and Iran-Contra hearings. It was in that very room that

Supreme Court Justice Clarence Thomas accused tormenting senators of conducting an "electronic lynching" during his confirmation hearing.

There were likely to be a lot of histrionics displayed on Wednesday, and just maybe a little history made as well.

42

When Falcone, a veteran of countless
congressional hearings as both inquirer and
responder, heard about the announcement,
he knew what to expect, especially from
Collinsworth. He knew Collinsworth and
his reputation. He would produce his own
little play, with himself as hero and Taylor
as villain. Falcone quickly called Collinsworth's office to say that Taylor would appear voluntarily. But a subpoena was already
on its way to Taylor, creating the false appearance of his being a reluctant witness
being dragged to the hearing. Falcone tried
in vain to meet with Collinsworth or his
chief of staff to lay out ground rules. That
made it inevitable that the hearing would
be a kangaroo court.

Assuming that Ben Taylor would be
sandbagged by aggressive questioning,
Falcone called for a prehearing strategy session. A few minutes after he, Ben, and

Darlene gathered around the table in the Taylor kitchen, Sam Bancroft appeared. He wore jeans, sneakers, and a blue polo shirt bearing the image of USAF wings instead of a polo player. He carried a briefcase.

"First order of business is our pizza order," Falcone said. "You can't make strategy without pizza." He and Sam quickly agreed on a chorizo and pepperoni pizza. Darlene chose broccoli and mushrooms. Ben Taylor did not make an additional choice, accepting whatever had been chosen.

Bancroft took a thick loose-leaf binder out of his briefcase and placed it on the kitchen table. "I've been thinking about your opening statement, Ben," Bancroft said. "I figured that Collinsworth and Anderson's strategy will be to belittle you, build up Hamilton and SpaceMine, and stop you from saying anything about the dangers of mining satellites. So I thought we should have a counterstrategy."

"Looks like you have a secret weapon," Falcone said, pointing to the binder.

Bancroft nodded, opened the binder, and began talking. His voice had the soft accent of South Carolina mountain country.

"Ben, I guess you know that the Pentagon, with much cooperation from NASA, runs a quiet little outfit called the Operationally Responsive Space Office," Bancroft said.

"Sure, I remember it, the place was always spoken about in initials," Taylor said. "The ultimate idea of the ORS, as I got it, was to develop a way to have standby space vehicles that could react to some vague, unstated need. Most people in NASA shied away from it. Sounded like space warfare."

"Well, yes. Some classified stuff. I've been working for the office for about a year, but spending most of my time at the Pentagon instead of NASA headquarters. Mostly, I've been churning out unclassified reports full of empty phrases," he said, pointing to the binder and flipping through pages. "You know, 'the military's need for responsive, flexible, and affordable systems operating in space' or there is 'a critical need for improved space situational awareness.' "

He flipped to a page and looked up to say, "But I've also seen some solid stuff about how an asteroid could kill millions and maybe wipe out civilization. It made me wonder why we aren't spending more time and money setting up a warning system. We have systems like that for floods and tornadoes and hurricanes — maybe not perfect systems. But they exist and they improve. A warning system for asteroids seems like a no-brainer."

He read from the page: " 'The impact of a relatively small asteroid would, in all likelihood, cause catastrophic damage and loss of life — even the possible extinction of the human race!' That sentence, by the way, ends in the only exclamation point I have ever seen in a Pentagon document."

"Pentagon?" Falcone said. "You mean that you're reading from an official DOD document?"

"Yes. Don't worry. It's unclassified." Bancroft said. "It's a report issued by an Air Force study group a long time ago."

"The title, believe it or not, is *Planetary Defense: Catastrophic Health Insurance for Planet Earth.* And, get this: It was written in 1996. It was produced by a group of brilliant, forward-looking military officers who were concerned about an overlooked threat, not just to the United States but to the whole world. They imagined a planet defense system that would be operated by spacefaring nations and — get this — controlled by the UN."

He opened to another page and read: " 'Concern exists among an increasing number of scientists throughout the world regarding the possibility of a catastrophic event caused by an impact of a large earth-crossing object (ECO) on the Earth-Moon System (EMS), be it an asteroid or comet.'

"And listen to this: 'Due to a lack of awareness and emphasis, the world is not socially, economically, or politically prepared to deal with' the asteroid threat. And this: 'Collectively as a global community, no current viable capability exists to defend the EMS' against a good-sized asteroid. The report goes on to say that a good-sized asteroid could wipe out the human race. What the endangered world needs, these officers wrote, is a planetary defense system. Then they tell how to develop the system and deploy it."

"How long is this document?" Falcone asked.

Bancroft turned a tagged page and said, "Sixty-seven pages."

"Ben, this is terrific," Falcone said. "I suggest you read through Sam's document and, if you think it's as good as it sounds, take pertinent statements from it for your opening statement and then make the whole thing an appendix to the statement."

Taylor agreed, and talk about his statement went on until the pizzas arrived and they moved to the dining room. As the pizza interlude ended, Taylor and Falcone began rehearsing possible questions and lining up possible answers.

Falcone didn't have to tell Taylor to be polite; he was naturally genial. But Falcone did warn him about Hamilton's connection to Collinsworth and predicted that he would try to rattle Taylor or goad him into losing his temper.

"It'll be an uneven match, Ben," Falcone said. "Anderson and Collinsworth will be giving Hamilton a televised platform to tell the world what he — not you — has to say about asteroids. They have home-field advantage. Much as you might want to, don't try to fight back. Collinsworth and Anderson will not be friendly. They both get bagfuls of Hamilton's campaign contributions. Just be humble. Be responsive. For God's sake, don't say 'No comment.' And don't forget that I'll be sitting next to you."

Taylor spent the next day writing his opening statement, using some material from the asteroid-show preview and some from the report that Bancroft found.

"In 2001, I was one of seventy scientists and engineers from around the world who attended a workshop on Hazardous Comets and Asteroids," the statement began. "It was clear then and is clear today that we are not doing enough research on this potential hazard to Earth and that the prime impediment to that research is the lack of any international or national governmental organization dedicated to the defense of Earth."

Taylor e-mailed copies to Falcone, Sam, and Darlene for comment, adding the U.S. Air Force Defense of Earth document as an appendix. After accepting and rejecting their comments, he polished it and sent it to Falcone.

Two days before the scheduled hearing, Falcone sent copies of the statement to Anderson and Collinsworth for them and members of their staff to read. This was a routine practice for congressional witnesses. Although Falcone expected aggressive questions from Collinsworth and Anderson, he did not expect what they would manage to do with Ben's opening statement.

43

At precisely 9:00 a.m., with a friendly nod
to his "esteemed colleague and cochairman
of this hearing, Senator Frank Anderson,"
Collinsworth banged his gavel and announced that the hearing had begun. In
fact, it had begun when he realized what a
chance it would be to please Hamilton and
at the same time to ride the publicity that
had made asteroids a major media subject
ever since Hamilton announced the existence of Asteroid USA and his promise of
its Morse code signal — *U-S-A, U-S-A,
U-S-A.* "Diggin' Our USA" made the Top
10 Songs. Ex-astronauts and their past
flashes of fame appeared on talk shows.
NASA-produced images of asteroids, looking like tumbling gray potatoes, zoomed
across YouTube videos.

But Collinsworth had to balance his
constituency against his largest donor. Back
home, his voters wanted a return to the

moon more than they wanted to help a billionaire to make more billions. He had been told at town meetings that the United States needed to go back to the moon and claim it for the United States. But, as he proudly told his constituents, he had suggested to Hamilton the name Asteroid USA rather than SpaceMine I. And, from what he was now hearing, his connection with Asteroid USA greatly helped to placate voters and donors who were yearning for the moon.

Ten minutes before the hearing was to begin, Falcone and Ben Taylor were standing at the door to the Caucus Room that had become Collinsworth's theater.

Down the marble hall, Falcone saw Sprague leading three other Sullivan & Ford lawyers. Walking alongside Sprague was the lawyer entourage's client, Robert Wentworth Hamilton. Although Hamilton was not scheduled to testify until the following day, his principal lobbyist had convinced him to appear at the opening day of the hearing. From a publicity point of view, it was a sensible move. And Hamilton, tipped off to the script for the hearing, wanted to be there when Collinsworth and Anderson flayed Taylor.

Hamilton wore a dark gray suit and white shirt with a spread collar that flattered his narrow face. Falcone, noticing Hamilton's star-spangled, red-white-and-blue tie, recalled a *Wall Street Journal* profile that said, "Hamilton has a tendency, in both private and business life, to go a bit beyond the necessary." As the thought flitted through Falcone's mind, Hamilton caught his eye, frowned, and spoke to Sprague. The group stopped while the two conversed for less than a minute.

Sprague speeded his stride, pulling away from Hamilton and the others. When he reached Falcone and Taylor, he ignored Taylor and, face flushed in anger, said to Falcone, "What the hell are you doing here?"

"I'm obviously here to represent my client," Falcone said quietly.

"Are you aware that Robert Wentworth Hamilton is a client of our firm?" Sprague asked, eye-to-eye close to Falcone.

"Of course."

"And you are aware of the firm's rules about conflict of interests?"

"Yes. But I don't see how it applies here."

"Don't be foolish, Sean. It is obvious that you must drop Dr. Taylor as a client," Sprague said, speaking as if Taylor were not standing next to him and Falcone.

Falcone pointed to the *Légion d'honneur*

rosette in Sprague's lapel, without quite touching it. "No worse than representing the United States and New Zealand and France at the same time," Falcone said. "Exceptions are made to every rule."

Sprague hesitated before replying. He was proud of the decoration from France but rarely explained why he got it.

As a young U.S. Foreign Service officer, he had secretly negotiated, on his own, a settlement between France and New Zealand, ending a crisis for France but leaving New Zealand unhappy. Two French intelligence agents had been sentenced to prison for the 1985 sinking of the Greenpeace ship *Rainbow Warrior* in a New Zealand harbor during a campaign protesting French nuclear-weapon testing in the Pacific. Without the knowledge of his State Department superiors, Sprague had come forth with a settlement that allowed the agents to serve a lesser sentence on French soil. Shortly after producing the audacious settlement, Sprague left the Foreign Service and went into private practice in Washington with several French clients, putting himself on the path that led to Sullivan & Ford.

"My work was classified," Sprague said. "Your representation of Taylor is highly public. A televised Senate hearing no less.

318

You must resign this client right now. I will not allow you to appear on television as Taylor's lawyer."

"Ben Taylor *is* my client," Falcone said, putting a hand on the doorknob. "I will resign from Sullivan and Ford, not from him."

"Resign?" Sprague asked incredulously. "Resign from the firm?"

"That's right," Falcone said, turning his head to smile at Sprague's astonished face. "I resign from the firm." He opened the door and led Taylor into the hearing room.

44

Senators Collinsworth and Anderson settled into their side-by-side seats as on a double throne. They reigned from the center of the stage set where their morality play would be presented, looking down at the long witness table with a cardboard name card, DR. BENJAMIN FRANKLIN TAYLOR, in the center.

As Falcone and Taylor took their seat at the table, Falcone quickly scanned the long array of television cameras, cables, wires, and floodlights. The room had been stripped of its rich luster in the glare of the klieg lights. The thick Corinthian columns and classical chandeliers seemed violated by the cables that curled along the marble floors like dark snakes about to strike.

The room had the ambience of a crowded mall. Tourists, photographers, journalist, and staff members were all moving about, walking, talking, whispering, and snickering. Some were wide-eyed. Others wore expressions of deep cynicism.

What struck Falcone as he and Taylor moved to the witness table was how the hearing room had been transformed into a mini-Colosseum, with senators peering disdainfully down upon the two of them. They might have been Roman potentates eager to turn thumbs up or down on the poor Christians who had been dragged before them.

The script instructions put Taylor at the witness chair, with Falcone at his right. Directly behind him, in the first row of witness chairs, sat Darlene Taylor, blue skirt chastely covering her knees, iPad at the ready. Seated next to her, in uniform, was Major Sam Bancroft. One row back, almost directly behind Darlene and Sam, were Sprague and Hamilton, flanked by other Sullivan & Ford lawyers.

"Before we call the first witness to appear before this joint committee," Collinsworth began in his sonorous voice, "I feel it my duty to state that I am gravely concerned about the use of fear and panic as a way to present a case — whether it be global warming, climate change, or the quest for resources, whether on Earth or in distant space. All too often, prophets of the God's honest truth are not heard because of the

321

constant drone of fearmongering."

Collinsworth paused and slightly moved his head to look directly at Falcone.

"Mr. Taylor, before you proceed with your testimony, I note the presence of President Oakley's *former* national security advisor with you at the witness table. According to my records, he is not scheduled to testify before our joint committee hearing. Mr. Falcone, may I ask why you are here?"

"Since I served in this great body for twelve years, I think you can address me as Senator," Falcone said. At the corner of his right eye he saw the blinking red light of a television camera and realized that C-SPAN was in Ping-Pong mode, switching from one protagonist to the other.

"Ah, well, *Senator* Falcone. My oversight. No slight intended. But can you answer the question? Why are you here?"

"I represent Dr. Taylor."

"Indeed? But this is congressional inquiry, not a criminal proceeding. I've not been advised that Mr. Taylor intends to invoke his Fifth Amendment right not to incriminate himself."

"I don't anticipate that he will feel compelled to do so," Falcone countered. "But I would like the record to show that he reserves the right to do so, depending on the nature of the questions he's asked to respond to."

"You're not suggesting that there are other investigations pending, involving Mr. Taylor that might be compromised or complicated by his testimony today, are you?"

Sly bastard, Falcone thought. Everyone was aware of the Three Black Musketeers article that had appeared in the *Grudge Report.* It had gone viral on the net less than an hour after it first appeared. Falcone realized that Collinsworth was trying to trap Falcone into citing the FBI's murder investigation that was under way and thereby undermine Ben even before he began to testify.

"I'm suggesting that Dr. Taylor has been quite willing to appear before this committee . . . these committees . . . without the need for a subpoena and that he intends to be responsive to the members' questions while preserving his constitutionally guaranteed rights."

"Very well, Mr. . . . Senator Falcone. Perhaps under the circumstances, I should just address you as 'counselor'?"

"As you wish, Mr. Cochairman. Oh, is that the proper title?"

"Yes, counselor, it is. Now, I will call as a witness Benjamin Franklin Taylor. Will you please take an oath?"

Taylor stood and raised his hand.

Before leading him in the oath, Collinsworth said, "Do you have any objections to taking an oath? Are you aware that if a witness is sworn in and lies to a congressional committee, he may be prosecuted for perjury? Any hesitation about waiving your Fifth Amendment rights by refusing to testify before this committee?"

"No, Senator. In fact, I welcome the —"

"I'm sure you welcome the chance to have this forum as a way to spread your personal views, Mr. Taylor."

After taking the oath and sitting down, Taylor nodded. Although Taylor had appeared before congressional committees numerous times, he had never before faced a hostile inquisitor. NASA scientists called before Congress usually were treated gently, catchers of soft questions thrown by sympathetic inquisitors, many of whom had NASA facilities or contractors in their states.

Taylor glanced over to Falcone with a grim look that said *this is about to go south sooner than we thought.* Then Taylor turned back to Collinsworth.

"The question I have," Collinsworth said,

"is this: Do you believe in God, Mr. Taylor?"

45

Taylor was stunned by the question and not eager to get into an explanation of his shaky religious beliefs, which zigzagged from Baptist to Methodist to Unitarian to . . . what? *How do I describe spiritual ideas outside any religion?* In his softest voice, he said, "Can I ask what concern my personal beliefs are and how they're relevant to this hearing?"

"So," Collinsworth retorted, arching an eyebrow at Taylor's challenge, "you are answering my question with a question? It's very simple, Mr. Taylor. Moments ago you took an oath and swore to tell the truth, 'So help me, God.' I think the committee needs to know whether you believe in God so we may properly judge the credibility of your testimony."

Falcone reached in front of Taylor and brought the microphone close to his lips. "With all due respect, Senator Collinsworth, Dr. Taylor's personal beliefs are just that — personal. I don't have to remind you that they're protected under the Constitution."

"And I shouldn't have to remind you, counselor, that you are out of order. I'm not trying to suppress Mr. Taylor's free exercise of religion. I am trying to determine if he has one. . . . Mr. Taylor?"

"I do not believe in a personal or anthropomorphic God, if that's what you mean by your question."

"So," Collinsworth said, pursing his lips and nodding as a professor might to a recalcitrant student, "you're in the company of the atheists Sam Harris, Richard Dawkins, and — now the thankfully departed — Christopher Hitchens."

"No, Senator. More in the company of Albert Einstein, who believed that there's a harmony in natural law that reveals an intelligence that is so superior that it's beyond man's comprehension."

"You're comparing yourself to Einstein? That's rather large of you."

"Not at all. Just that I share his sentiments."

"I see," Collinsworth said, making it clear by his tone that he did not see at all.

During this quick exchange, Falcone

noticed one of Collinsworth's eager staffers tapping away on an iPad. Not having the time to print out whatever he was searching for, he simply handed the iPad to Collinsworth, who seemed annoyed to be so openly dependent upon staff assistance for his questions.

"But didn't Einstein . . ." Collinsworth said, and paused to put on his black-rimmed reading glasses. "Didn't he also write that, quote, 'the word God is for me nothing more than the expression and product of human weaknesses, the Bible a collection of honorable but still primitive legends which are nevertheless pretty childish,' unquote? So those of us who believe that the Bible is the Word of God, are primitive and childish? Is that your testimony, Mr. Taylor?"

"He may have written that," Taylor responded. "But I believe if you have your very competent staff check, you'll also find that Einstein held no tolerance for atheists and criticized their absolutist views for lacking any sense of humility in the face of the unknowable. Einstein himself was not an atheist. But, if anything, he was a pantheist who saw the hand of a superior intelligence in every facet of life on this planet and beyond. He famously noted that, quote, 'God does not play dice with the universe,' unquote, a statement that reflects his acknowledgment of a higher force or being."

"Excuse me, Mr. Chairman," Senator Lawrence said, raising her hand to seek recognition. Lawrence was sitting at the very end of the dais's front row, signifying her junior status at this hearing. "I came to learn more about asteroids, and I want to see how SpaceMine deals with the space treaty," she said. "I'm not here to listen to some irrelevant discussion about Einstein."

Collinsworth tapped his gavel to silence muffled laughter that had spread through the room. "I would remind my esteemed colleague from Maine that, while she does not serve on either of the two committees meeting here today, she will, as I promised, be afforded an opportunity to question the witness at an appropriate time."

Before any congressional theologians could join in the dialogue, Anderson upstaged Collinsworth and declared a five-minute recess.

In the silence of the interval, Falcone leaned toward Taylor, squeezed his arm, and said, "Hang in there, Ben. This can't get any worse."

When Anderson called the end of the recess, Collinsworth took a sip of water, and said in a soothing tone, "Now, Mr. Taylor, if you will bear with me for another question, could you explain to me your economic philosophy?

"In what sense?"

"Another question for a question?" Collinsworth said with feigned exasperation. "I'm interested in knowing whether you subscribe to free-market capitalism where people are rewarded for their labor. Where people who take risks with their capital and, indeed, in many cases, their lives, should be forced to share the rewards they reap with others who have risked or contributed nothing?"

Taylor turned toward Falcone, who looked ready to launch another objection or quite possibly storm the dais and slug Collinsworth.

"I like to think that I'm a product of the free-market system, Senator. I've been allowed to pursue and achieve a measure of professional success well beyond my dreams, and surely those of my parents. But I had a helping hand along the way with great teachers, scholarships, grants, and loans. In other words, like the frog sitting on a lamppost, I didn't get there all on my own."

"This isn't about frogs or lampposts, Mr.

Taylor, but about your belief that the U.S. government and its citizens should not be allowed to claim title or ownership to any real estate or resource in international waters or outer space. That we must share the fruits of our labor and capital with other nations under a treaty drawn up by the United Nations, which boldly questions American sovereignty. That is not capitalism, Mr. Taylor. Not as I understand it. That's unadulterated socialism."

Falcone knew that Collinsworth was going to play hardball, but this was a brass-knuckle assault on Taylor. First, Collinsworth accused Taylor of being an atheist, and then a socialist — which was just a Texas taco short of being labeled a communist. Collinsworth was a throwback to Joe McCarthy's headline-making anticommunist crusade that ruined the reputations and professional lives of scores of innocent people.

Collinsworth, however, was smarter than McCarthy, more telegenic, and wise to the ways of the new social media, which operated without filters for either truth or decency.

Falcone ignored the advice he had given Taylor to remain calm. "Senator Collinsworth," he shouted, not bothering to speak into Taylor's microphone. "I object to what can only be described as outrageous and reprehensible —"

"I warned you, counselor," Collinsworth barked back, repeatedly slamming his gavel. "Any more interruptions or outburst and I'll have the sergeant-at-arms remove you from this hearing."

"It's all right, Sean," Taylor said. This time it was his steel-like grip on Falcone's arm. "I can handle this.

"Senator Collinsworth," he continued, sweeping his gaze along the dais, "as you know, and most if not all of you know, through my writings and public appearances, I strongly support NASA's space programs. The exploration of space is in my DNA. I am incurably curious about the creation of our planet, our galaxy, and those that exist in the unbounded universe. Many find their curiosity and questions about our beginning in their religious faiths. I respect those that find such solace there. But the pursuit of scientific knowledge, of trying to comprehend the mysteries of the unknown, has been the driving and uplifting force in my life.

"And there is another reason that explains my passion — a sadder, darker, and less noble reason. I believe that humankind will one day destroy life on this planet. That we will continue to overpopulate, to desecrate and despoil our fragile ecosystem through the mindless denial of our contribution to climate change — yes, global warming — and —"

Collinsworth was pounding the gavel, but Taylor spoke on, his voice strong and sure, the voice of a scientist and a skilled showman. "And, I say to all members of these committees, I fear that nuclear weapons will continue to be proliferated and that they will one day be unleashed and result in a nuclear winter that may leave insects as the only animate life on Earth. I further —"

"My, my, Mr. Taylor," Collinsworth sneered, putting down his gavel and deciding to engage. "From Einstein to Malthus! Oh, ye of little faith."

"Ironically, Senator, I know your vision of the future. I share your view — and that of so many of your Texan supporters — that we should be sending explorers to the moon, to Mars, and eventually to other galaxies. Not just for the wonder and the miracle of space travel, but so we can have the chance to save our species, to start over, to build a more humane and peaceful civilization — having destroyed the many opportunities we've had to do so here."

"I'm astonished at the depth of your pessimism about God's children and our ability to be redeemed by God's grace," Collinsworth said, affecting a tone intended to express sadness rather than anger. "But based on what I've heard today, I don't think you're exactly a role model for the younger generation who might be looking to you and your fellow scientists for leadership. That's my personal opinion and others on these committees may differ.

"But just one final question from me before I yield to others. I have been told by my staff that in public and private conversations you have advocated that the United States should lead a crusade to change the UN space treaty so that commercial activities in space — such as the mining of asteroids — are regulated or restricted or even banned. Is that correct? If so, why do you take this anticapitalist position?"

"Because greed is going to kill us all," Taylor calmly answered. "You may think that since America has a lead in technology at the moment that we are always going to enjoy the high ground on the new frontier of space. But others have the same goal in mind. The Chinese are planning to set up a colony on the moon. If they arrive first and claim title to all of that cratered land, are you willing to say that the first ones to plant a flag, create a village, and draw territorial boundaries become the owner of the property? And if they get to Mars before we do, will we have to buy or rent a piece of the desert from them? Or will you start banging the drum to go to war to challenge their ownership claims?"

"As I understand the Outer Space Treaty — which you have supported with such gusto — you might recall that states, nations, governments, can exercise no claim of ownership of heavenly bodies."

"Indeed, Mr. Chairman, I recall it well, and I recall that you and some of your colleagues over the years have tried to find a way to circumvent the treaty's provision against land — or should I say — space grabs?"

Taylor paused for Collinworth's retort. When none came, Taylor went on: "It's not my area of expertise, but I feel the same way about the need for the United States to ratify the Law of the Sea Treaty — we being one of the few nations on the planet who've refused to do so. What if the Russians or the Chinese lay claim to the resources under what remains of the ice cap in the Arctic, which is melting at an alarming speed? What if —"

Before Taylor could finish his question, Collinsworth slammed his gavel down and said, "You are here to answer questions, not ask them. And it may come as a surprise to you, but we don't need to wave a piece of paper at the Russians and Chinese. We need to stick a missile right in their gazoos if they ever try to interfere or stop us . . ."

"So you think shooting off some missiles is a better choice than —" Taylor parried, before he was cut off again.

"Yes, sir. Rather than raising a white flag and turning everything over to the UN. You bet. A few years ago, the Chinese up and destroyed one of their own satellite systems. No notice to anyone. Just damn well did it. They spread debris all over the place, putting our assets and manned missions in jeopardy. They didn't give a flying French fry if they hurt or killed anyone. They wanted to make a point. Show the world. And what about the Russians invading Ukraine, an independent and sovereign country?

"What did the U.S. do about it? Complain to the Yu Nited Naations?" Collinsworth asked, looking theatrically over his pair of half-rim reading glasses at his fellow senators on the dais, sarcasm dripping with every stretched-out vowel.

"Hello, anybody home there? No answer? Doorbell didn't work? Next stop the International Court at The Hague with all of those wigged European judges? Well I'll tell you where I come from, possession pretty much determines ownership, and if we get our hands on one of those ore-rich rocks, well game over and the Chinese and Russians can —"

"Go to . . . war?" Taylor asked, forcing a smile, hoping he didn't appear as contemptuous as he felt right then.

"We've heard just about enough from you. As I said at the very outset, Mr. Taylor, you pander in fear. And it's clear that your science has been shaded by your liberal, socialist agenda —"

"You insisted that I come here today, Senator," Taylor broke in, stunning Collinsworth. "I thought you wanted an honest discussion of the issues that affect our economic and national-security interests. But it's apparent that you have other motivations. I know you want the federal government, and especially NASA, to fold up and disappear. Just step away and allow the private sector to explore and exploit space, including the mining of asteroids.

"My word of caution to you and your colleagues is that space is no place for Lone

Rangers. No place where finders-keepers cowboys ride asteroids to the promised land of wealth. If there are no rules, no regulations, there are going to be mistakes and miscalculations made. And when that happens, you are going to see calamity come rushing at us with the power of a thousand suns."

Taylor felt a curious mixture of anger and adrenaline welling up inside him. Then his voice trailed off as he took a deep breath and exhaled. He had said enough.

For the first time that morning, the low-level buzz and chatter stopped completely. A few seconds passed, and then several members in the audience stood up and started applauding.

Hamilton, fuming, looked around, then turned to Sprague and said, "That stupid jerk has lost control. What the hell is going on?"

"It's over. Anderson's taking charge," Sprague said, nodding toward the dais. Collinsworth was slumping in his chair, as if battered by Taylor's stream of words. Anderson took the gavel from his hand. He banged down once and, aiming his stare at the witness, said, "Mr. Taylor, I would advise you to cease the outbursts and answer my questions with direct and responsive answers."

"Certainly, Senator. As you know, I have a statement that I would like to have entered into the record. The gist of my statement is the necessity to —"

"I'm afraid that your statement cannot be entered into the record of this hearing," Anderson said, conjuring a frown on his broad brow.

Falcone grabbed Taylor's microphone and said, "My understanding, Senator Anderson, is that my client would have the opportunity to make a short opening statement. Obviously —"

"I'm afraid that is not possible, counselor. I've had the chief counsel of my Committee on Commerce, Science, and Transportation examine your statement, and she advises us that it contains classified information that, if disclosed, would institute a serious breach of national security."

Taylor at first clamped his jaw shut and fought to control his rage. But in a moment it erupted: "That is flat-out false, Senator, and I say that with all due respect."

"Take care, Mr. Taylor, before you call this senator a liar."

"I repeat that —"

Slamming his gavel loud and hard, Anderson cut Taylor off and said, "I have referred your statement to the Department of Justice for investigation as to how you obtained this classified information and whether prosecution is warranted. You hereby are properly advised not to attempt to disclose this information to anyone."

"That's bull . . . feathers," Taylor said. "I used open-sources information for my statement. The public deserves to know the dangers posed and —"

"You're out of order," Anderson fairly shouted. "I'm in charge of this hearing now. And I will not tolerate any insolence. And I'm not going to permit you to say anything more. This witness is dismissed for now. The hearing is adjourned until two o'clock this afternoon, when, Mr. Taylor, you will get some questions from me."

Falcone and Taylor looked at each other. They both expected that the worst was yet to come.

46

Falcone, Taylor, Darlene, and Sam Bancroft headed for Hunan Dynasty, a Capitol Hill restaurant that was a short walk down Pennsylvania Avenue. As soon as they were seated around a window table, Taylor turned to Falcone and asked, "What was that business in the hallway? Did you really quit?"

"You heard it right, Ben. No big deal," Falcone said.

"What are you two talking about?" Darlene asked. Taylor told her what he heard when Sprague confronted Falcone.

"You quit? Just like that? Why the hell did you do *that*?" she exclaimed. An approaching waiter, hearing a raised female voice, turned away.

"Let's not make a big deal of this, Darlene," Falcone said. "I'm your father's lawyer. And that's all there is to it. I don't think much of Hamilton anyway. Or of Sprague, for that matter. This was bound to happen."

"I don't know about that, Sean," Taylor said, reaching out to pat Falcone's hand. "I thank you. But I feel guilty and —"

"My clients are never guilty, Ben."

"Okay, Sean. Thanks. But I worry —"

"And my clients never worry, either, Ben. I'm in fine shape. That's what's important — for you and for me."

"Okay, Sean, if you say so. But . . . it's more than worry. It's disgust at the way they acted in there this morning. . . . Was it like that when you were here, Sean?"

Falcone did not speak immediately. He was at a loss for words. He couldn't believe how far the Senate had fallen in the years since he left. No longer was there any respect for tradition, for Rules or Protocol or Grace. *Now it was just throw everything and everyone into the meat grinder and churn out the gross-smelling sausage on prime time. Hell, at anytime.*

"No," he answered. "It wasn't this bad. But by the time I decided to leave, it was headed toward the gutter."

"They ever treat a former member like they did today?"

"No. Well, maybe if he had been tossed out of the Senate or been convicted of something."

"Sad," Taylor said. "Used to be a lot of respect and prestige that went with the title Senator."

"Hell. Some of them quit halfway into their terms to take high-paying jobs with political action groups masquerading as think tanks. . . . But, you know, Ben, it's not just the Senate. The deterioration is happening everywhere."

Everywhere. No matter where Falcone turned, he saw the loss of quality. In the people who served, the bridges that were falling, the roads that were crumbling. And the financial marketplace, where the rules were there to be broken and the people in charge, the people with power, were never charged for breaking them.

"And crude, mean language in messages and tweets," Darlene injected. "We're the fattest nation on the planet, and we don't seem to give a damn! There's no middle class any longer. Just the rich, super rich . . ."

"And the poor bastards at the bottom of the pyramid," Falcone said. "All true. But at the moment, it does us little good to complain about it. We need to try to get back on what we came here for."

"What's going to happen next back there?" Taylor asked, pointing a thumb over his shoulder in the direction of the Capitol.

"You all saw what Collinsworth and Anderson were up to — belittle you, build up SpaceMine, give Hamilton a platform for spouting his private-enterprise gospel, and ignore worries about mining satellites," Falcone replied. "You'll get another session on the hot seat this afternoon. And then will come Hamilton for the finale. If you think of this as reality television instead of a congressional hearing, you'll understand it better. It's staged for drama, not truth."

"What about the opening statement?" Bancroft asked. "They suppressed the Air Force report. It's not classified. It has never been classified."

"I know. I know," Falcone said. "There's nothing we can do about it right now. In a while we can petition the White House for a declassification order. Eventually, we'll get that report made public. It will take time. Right now we've got the hearing to deal with."

"But how could Collinsworth say it's classified? . . . That's a lie."

"I've seen it done before, Sam," Falcone said. "A powerful congressman decides to bag something that is not classified. He takes it to a friendly intelligence bigfoot and gets it provisionally classified."

"He can do that?" Bancroft asked. "I thought only the President can classify and declassify. Or am I being naive?"

"No, under the law, you're absolutely right. The law says only the President can classify and declassify. But he can also deputize the job. And so some secrets are artificially classified without the President's notice."

"But Ben needs to get it out, needs to tell the public. Can't we get President Oxley to simply order it declassified?"

Falcone reflected on his dealings with Oxley. The President was single-minded in the pursuit of his own agenda. He was not inclined to take any risks, not even for friends.

"He could," Falcone replied. "But he won't. Not at this point at least. He's trying to make a budget deal with Congress, and crossing Collinsworth would be a deal-breaker. Think how it would look to the press."

"You're ahead of me. I'm just a flyboy. Tell me how it would look."

"The CIA has classified a report that an astrophysicist wants to release so that the information can be used by our enemies against us. And, by the way, few people know what in hell it is that an astrophysicist does, other than he's some egghead who is trying to discover the origins of our planet and deny that it was God's handiwork. And —"

"Come on, Sean. That would be bullshit."

"Sure. But lots of times news *is* bullshit, and with the CIA and Collinsworth in the story, it's big news. And there's more. This particular atheist is involved in a murder that's being investigated by the FBI. . . . So you tell me, what do you think Oxley will do?" Falcone turned to Taylor. "Okay, Ben. It's back into the Colosseum."

47

Senator Frank Anderson of Oklahoma, chair of the Commerce, Science, and Transportation Committee, was a slight man in a rumpled brown suit, checkered shirt, and yellow and black bowtie. He sat at Collinsworth's right. As soon as the room settled down for the afternoon session, he took up his part in the script that he and Collinsworth had laid out days before over a two-martini lunch at the Monocle.

A member of Anderson's staff led Taylor to the witness chair and reminded him that he was still under oath. Then Anderson rapped the gavel and said, "I believe you realize, Mr. Taylor, that, although you describe yourself as assistant director of the Smithsonian's Air and Space Museum, you no longer are actively carrying out your duties."

Falcone turned first to Taylor and then toward Anderson. Falcone was angry but not surprised. Anderson was part of the tag team.

"In point of fact, Senator," Taylor said calmly, "I am on administrative leave, which is a temporary leave from a job assignment, with pay and benefits intact."

"So, Doctor, does that mean you are ill?" Anderson asked with a mean grin.

"I am very well, thank you, Senator. My status is a personnel matter. And I am obviously able to carry out the assignment I have today, which is to testify about asteroids."

Before Anderson could respond, Taylor continued to speak: "Natural disasters — such as volcanoes and tornadoes and earthquakes — are difficult to predict, but we know a lot about them. That knowledge leads us toward understanding them and developing ideas about how to predict the seemingly unpredictable. That is what we need about asteroids and other near-Earth objects. We've —"

"Hold on there, Mr. Taylor. I haven't asked a question."

"I'm simply responding to what the hearing was supposed to be about — 'activities regarding asteroids.' I tried this morning to read —"

"And you were warned that the material

you were attempting to reveal is classified. Now, I —"

Taylor, acting as if he had not noticed Anderson's sputtering, continued to speak, rapidly and emotionally: "With increasing regularity, we are discovering asteroids and comets with unusual orbits that take them close to Earth. We have made a start on gaining knowledge — scientific knowledge — about asteroids. Today, with what we know, we can say that the possible collision of an asteroid with Earth is the one potential catastrophic natural disaster that we believe we can do something about. I call it defense of the Earth. That is —"

"*Collision.* That is exactly what I am talking about," Anderson said, his voice rising. "You seem to automatically connect the word 'asteroid' with the word 'collision.'"

"I beg to differ, Senator. In lectures I have given and, indeed, in testimony three years ago before your committee, I —"

"At which time I was not the chairman, and —"

"Yes, but you were a *member.* And I said then, and as I say again this afternoon, NASA has done an excellent job in finding and tracking asteroids and near-Earth objects. Today, we know the location and orbits of about ten thousand NEOs, as they are labeled. About one thousand of them are about one-half mile in diameter, or larger. The unofficial, unscientific name for them is 'civilization killers,' and —"

Anderson, banging down his gavel, loudly proclaimed, "The witness is flouting this committee! 'Killers'! I instruct you, Mr. Taylor, not to test our patience any longer. You will confine yourself to answering statements, not issuing manifestos."

Falcone whispered to Taylor, then glared at Anderson. Taylor leaned back in his chair, his face expressionless.

As a florid-faced Anderson looked as if he was about to speak, Senator Lawrence bent her head toward her microphone and said, "Mr. Chairman, a point of order."

The camera swung to her, drawn as much by her words as by her telegenic face, which could shift in a moment from serene to appalled, from cover-girl pretty to dragon-lady fury.

Anderson, without looking at Lawrence, said, "And what may that point of order be, under Senate rules?"

"Mr. Chairman, according to the call for this hearing, witnesses were to begin their testimony by reading initial statements," she began, her voice primly stern. "Since Senator Collinsworth this morning unilaterally decreed the opening statement classified, I believe, as a matter of fairness, that *Doctor* Taylor should be allowed to tell us what he, as an expert witness, believes to be a matter of national security."

Anderson, with a glance and a nod toward Collinsworth, said, "With all due respect, Senator Lawrence, we have a lot of ground to cover, and I believe that our needs would be best served through an ordinary question-and-answer procedure."

Anderson turned to look directly at Taylor and said, "You have testified that you are on administrative leave in regards to your position at the Air and Space Museum. I would like to ask you about a television show that you produced with taxpayers' money. Would you please state the title of the show?"

"The title is 'An Asteroid Closely Watched,' Senator. I am a coproducer with *NOVA*. And I would like to note that almost the entire budget for shows like this comes from viewers' contributions."

"Forgetting for a moment the annual congressional appropriation for public television, Doctor, is it not true that the show is in fact *not* going to be broadcast? That it has been essentially scrapped?"

Falcone and Taylor both looked stunned, as did Darlene and Bancroft. Falcone turned and whispered, "Jesus! What the hell is this?"

"I am unaware of any change, Senator," Taylor said, looking puzzled.

"Well, I am," Anderson said, holding up a sheet of paper. "I have here a joint statement from Stephanie Sinclair-Hardy, secretary of the Smithsonian Institution, and Conrad LaSalle, chairman of the board of the Corporation for Public Broadcasting, announcing that your show, 'An Asteroid Closely Watched,' has been indefinitely postponed."

Taylor did not respond. Falcone leaned into the microphone and said, "Dr. Taylor has no knowledge of this cancellation, Senator. May we see the document?"

"You are interrupting this hearing, counselor. If you persist in such interruptions, you risk the possibility of being held in contempt of Congress," Anderson said. He paused. An aide handed him a note. He glanced at it, and said, "I've just been advised that the majority leader has scheduled six consecutive votes that begin in five minutes. Accordingly, this hearing will now stand in recess until nine a.m. tomorrow. And, counselor, your client will not be recalled. But he must remain under subpoena to this committee."

48

As soon as the hearing ended, Falcone led Ben, Darlene, and Sam Bancroft to a side door into an anteroom. One of its walls was lined with chairs, which Falcone arranged in a circle. Darlene smiled, remembering how, in the third grade, Miss Templeton arranged the chairs in fours.

"Tomorrow is your call, Ben," Falcone said when all four were seated. "There's no real need for you to be here. It's going to be another act in the senators' circus. They'll be giving Hamilton a televised platform to tell the world what he has to say about asteroids."

Falcone turned to Bancroft. "It was gutsy for you to show up in uniform today. But please take my advice and don't appear tomorrow. There's no need for backup then."

"It's a free country," Bancroft said. "It sounds like it will be a good show, and I want to be there."

Through the closed door they could hear the scuffles and muffled sounds of the hearing room closing down for the day. Taylor looked at Bancroft and nodded. "I agree with Sean. But, like you said, it's a free country."

Darlene leaned forward and touched her father's folded hands. "And what about you?" she asked.

"I wouldn't miss it for a million dollars," Taylor said.

"Great. I give good advice and nobody takes it," Falcone said. "I'll meet you at the entrance tomorrow morning. As for you two" — he nodded to Darlene and Sam — "I suppose you're both as stubborn as he is." He stood, adding, "You've seen enough of me today. I'm off to clean out my office. Then home for a tall drink and a long night's sleep. See you all tomorrow."

Falcone kissed Darlene, patted Ben on the shoulder, shook hands with Bancroft, and left via the door to the marble hallway.

The Taylors and Bancroft sat in silence for nearly a minute. Then, as she had been doing since childhood, Darlene asked a question that seemed to come from nowhere. "Dad," she said, "how come you know Sean so well?"

"Well," Taylor said, "we met when I was at Goddard and he was a senator on the Science Committee. I filled him in on NASA projects. He was always hungry for solid information. That's how we met. I mean it could have been one of those Washington things where people become, you know, contacts for each other's business. But, somehow, right from the beginning, we had a friendship."

"You mean you both just hit it off? That's *it*?" She sounded exasperated.

"I've never thought about how we became close friends. I guess, when I look back now, it was Vietnam. He never told me about what had happened to him there. But I read about it one day, and he became a real hero to me, and, I guess, that was part of it. Being a hero." He looked toward Bancroft, who remained a witness to what had suddenly become a father-daughter dialogue.

"Vietnam," Darlene said. "It's not part of our generation. But heroes? Show me the hero and I'll —"

"I know," Taylor interrupted, smiling. 'write you a tragedy.' "

"Hey, I thought you had your head stuck in physics books! You know Fitzgerald?" Darlene asked.

"MIT did have some English courses, you

know. And an art and literature journal. I wrote an essay for it contrasting the writings of Stephen Vincent Benét and Fitzgerald." He smiled at her dumbfounded response. "You've always underestimated me."

He looked at her, his smile waning, and said, "Sean . . . Yeah, Fitzgerald would understand Sean Falcone. There's tragedy in him. And heroism seems to come easy to him — Vietnam, taking on that gunman."

"And, Dad, the way he quit today. You know: Bam! He makes a decision in a second. I had a psychology prof who lectured us once about what we know from hero studies."

"About *what* studies?" Bancroft asked. He spoke instinctively, then seemed embarrassed that he had injected himself into the dialogue.

"Heroes. They intrigue some psychiatrists," Darlene said, looking at Bancroft for the first time. "The consensus seems to be that heroes are born, not made. They instinctively act in an instant. You know that awful shooting at the movie theater in Colorado a couple of years ago? Three women who survived the shooting said they had been saved by their boyfriends. The men had shielded their girlfriends with their own bodies. And they were shot to death."

Taylor paused to let several thoughts sink in and then asked, "Is that what attracted you to Sam?"

Bancroft squirmed in his chair, hands in his lap, the fingers of one hand nervously running around the rim of his uniform cap.

Darlene looked away from Bancroft and, after a moment, said, "I . . . I never thought of that. Hero? If I had to pick a word about you, Sam, it would be 'integrity.' But that sounds so pompous. I don't know. I just think . . . that" — she reached for Sam's hand — "that you're a wonderful man. And, well, that sounds silly. . . ."

" 'Integrity,' " Taylor said. "That's a good word for Sam. Fine word. And Falcone sure has that, too. Maybe your hero studies will show that to be a hero you have to have integrity," Taylor said.

"I . . . I had never heard that Fitzgerald quote before," Sam said, hesitantly. "Tragedy. I guess that, for me, anyway, tragedy is when you want to save somebody . . . and . . . I just don't know, Ben. Tragedy is big, impersonal. When I think about . . . about loss in combat, I think heartbreak."

"What's that song?" Taylor asked. " 'The

hurt doesn't show but the pain still grows.' "

"I have no idea," Darlene said and, deciding she had heard enough about tragedy, added, "Must be on one of your seventy-eight-rpm albums."

Taylor went on as if he had not heard her: "He got beaten up pretty bad in Vietnam. Lost his wife and kid while he was in prison."

"My God! I never knew that," Darlene said.

"He's a great guy, a wonderful guy. But he's uptight about himself, his life. I think he's always blamed himself for not being home to protect his family."

"Loved his country more than his family? That kind of guilt?" Bancroft asked.

"That's part of it, I think."

"There's more?" Darlene asked.

"Yeah, the torture part of it."

"I don't understand."

"The pain he suffered was pretty intense. One day it got to be too much. He signed a confession, admitting that he had committed war crimes against the Vietnamese people. They broke his body and then his will."

"Doesn't everyone break under torture? Everyone would understand the confession was made under duress," Bancroft said.

"True. But you don't know just how proud and stubborn a man Sean is. He was angry with himself and started to cause so much trouble for his 'interrogators' that they kept him in solitary confinement for most of the time. They told him that Karen and Kyle had been killed. They told him that they'd let him out — an early release — so he could attend their funeral. He refused. More to be guilty about."

"Why would he do that?" Darlene asked.

"I guess he didn't believe they had died, and he didn't want to be a pawn in the Vietcong propaganda plans. But I think it was more than that. A code of honor. No cutting in line no matter what the reason. He'd leave when his turn came up. Not before."

"And that's what he did? Refused to leave?"

"He was among the last to be released at the very end of the war. He came home on crutches with a shattered hip and broken arm that had gone untreated for four years."

"So," Darlene said in her pupil-with-the-answer voice, "he feels guilty for not being home to protect his family and not being there to bury them."

"Exactly."

"Sounds like he *did* open up for you. How come?"

"Well, we were talking one night — a couple of drinks at his big empty place on Pennsylvania Avenue," Taylor said, looking first at Darlene, then at Bancroft, hesitating and then deciding to plunge on. "And I mentioned . . . your mother . . . and how I missed her still. And all of a sudden it all came tumbling out."

"Guilt . . . Is that why he's never remarried?" Darlene asked. She instantly touched a hand to her face, feeling guilt herself for asking a question she had often wanted to ask her father.

"Who knows? Maybe. . . . Maybe he just doesn't want anyone to enter the prison that he's never really left."

Tears were glistening in Darlene's eyes and on her cheeks. "It's the same for you, isn't it, Dad? I mean in some way something stopped. Mom's death. Something stopped."

"Maybe it did — *something*. But I have a fine life. There's, most of all, you. And my work. Anyway, I stick to exploring space and all its mysteries. It's less complicated than what's down here on Earth. I think we'd better go before they turn off the lights."

Bancroft was the first to the door. He

opened it and stood back to let father and daughter exit, holding hands.

49

Senator Anderson banged his gavel and paused for the silence that slowly descended over the room. He cleared his throat, and said, "Before resuming this hearing today, I wish to give my distinguished colleague, Senator Kenneth Collinsworth, the opportunity to say a few words." Anderson turned his head and beamed at Collinsworth.

He began his opening statement by praising SpaceMine for its "trailblazing venture that brought American free enterprise to space." He also called on the U.S. Air Force to return to its 1958 proposal for an underground base on the moon. In his rambling speech he chided NASA for scrapping an old plan for the Neil A. Armstrong Lunar Outpost, which he called a prelude to American colonization of the moon. Obviously, his heart wanted to go back to the moon and claim it as U.S. territory. But his campaign treasury wanted the contributions that came from Hamilton.

Collinsworth concluded his statement by beaming back at Anderson and saying, "Thank you, Senator Anderson, for this opportunity to speak."

"It is now my privilege," Anderson said, going on without a break, "to welcome America's great visionary, Robert Wentworth Hamilton."

A slight frown swiftly came to and disappeared from Collinsworth's round pale face. *Privilege? Goddamn it. I thought we agreed that I would do the welcoming.* But Anderson was chairman today and got his way. He, too, was a beneficiary of Hamilton's campaign-fund largesse.

Hamilton slid into the witness-table chair, with Sprague at his left. Both had that poised look of witnesses called before a friendly committee.

Before Anderson could continue his scene-stealing, Collinsworth leaned into his microphone and said loudly, "And may I add my warm welcome? Many distinguished Americans have appeared in his historic room, and all of them came here to give witness to accomplishments on Earth. In Mr. Hamilton we have the first witness of achievement beyond Earth to the Heavens."

Before Anderson could interrupt this rapturous paean to Hamilton's genius, Collinsworth went on: "Perhaps you could tell us about the inspired events that led up to SpaceMine's rocket roaring off to Asteroid USA."

Hamilton's usual proud bearing seemed to melt away as he somehow created an illusion, making himself look modest and unassuming.

"That rocket did not reach Asteroid USA because of the efforts of SpaceMine alone, Senator," he began. "We had, first and foremost, the help of God, Almighty God, who has blessed our work. We also had the help of top-layer scientists. They came from NASA, from the Jet Propulsion Laboratory, and from several private corporations that wanted to join this pioneering utilization of space resources."

"Could you give us an example of the research that led to this historic milestone?" Collinsworth asked.

Hamilton theatrically frowned and said, "I must respond carefully, Senator, because there are certain proprietary matters that are covered by non-disclosure agreements."

"Understood, Mr. Hamilton," Collinsworth nodded benevolently. "I image that if pioneers like Alexander Graham Bell and

Tom Edison were testifying about commercial applications of their inventions, they would have made a similar remark."

"Thank you, Senator," Hamilton said. "While I certainly do not want to compare myself to those titans, there is some similarity."

"And what would that similarity be?"

"Well, Senator, back in the golden age of American genius, those inventions moved quickly from laboratory demonstrations to commercial applications. Free enterprise was the highway to the future. And now we are on a skyway. We are leaving the era of government-sponsored footprints and flags on the moon and moving to a free-enterprise era of liberty and prosperity, an era that begins with asteroid mining and continues to the colonization of Mars."

"And the moon," Collinsworth added.

"Yes, certainly the moon, Senator."

And so it went, Hamilton flying high in answer to Collinsworth's gentle questions. Regularly, one of the other senators would make a perfunctory remark, nod to Anderson, and steal away from the Here's Hamilton Show. After a while there were only three senators in the chairs on the dais: Anderson, Collinsworth, and Sarah Lawrence. There was no way Anderson could snub her. He finally had to acknowledge her.

She looked up from a small stack of documents and asked, "Isn't it true, Mr. Hamilton, that SpaceMine did not reveal the launch site of the rocket that reached Asteroid USA?"

"Yes, Senator Lawrence. We simply saw no particular need to go into the technical matters that led to our reaching our goal, Asteroid USA," Hamilton replied, his tone cold.

"And wasn't the launch site, in fact, Russia's Plesetsk Cosmodrome, designed originally for launching ICBMs aimed at America?"

Collinsworth and Anderson exchanged puzzled glances, as did Ben and Darlene Taylor. The audience stirred.

"Yes, Senator, although that is a rather melodramatic way to put it."

"And wasn't the launch supervised by the Khrunichev State Research and Production Center?"

"Yes, Senator," Hamilton repeated. Anticipating the next question, he glanced anxiously at Collinsworth.

"And did not the Russians suffer five major launch failures — resulting in tremendous explosions when the rockets struck the Earth?"

"The ground damage was minimal, Senator. The explosions were exaggerated on unauthorized YouTube videos taken by Russian dissidents."

"Did the Russians show you any *authorized* videos of these massive explosions?" Lawrence asked.

Before Hamilton had a chance to answer, Anderson banged his gavel and said with a trace of anger, "We are not here to discuss methods, Senator. We are looking at results."

Lawrence ignored Anderson and said, "You mentioned NASA, Mr. Hamilton. Did you consult their extensive asteroid studies?"

"I'm glad you asked that question, Senator," Hamilton said, a trace of relief in his voice. "We found NASA's asteroid studies to be hesitant and inconclusive. Instead, we turned to privately sponsored research that looked at the feasibility of asteroid mining. Those studies showed that there was no doubt that the best way to mine an asteroid was to put it into a lunar orbit."

"You mean *move* the asteroid, right?"

"Precisely, Senator. And we found that the best cost-analysis approach came down to picking one of the biggest, closest asteroids."

"Incidentally, does that asteroid have a

number or name?"

"Of course, as I've testified. Asteroid USA."

"No, Mr. Hamilton. The name given by the scientific community?"

"I believe some had referred to it in the past by other names, but —"

"Such as Janus?"

"I'm not familiar with all the mythological names some in the scientific community use, and as a Christian I prefer good Biblical names or in this case good American ones. But if you'll allow me to continue without interruption . . ."

Anderson, tapping his gavel, and glowering at Senator Lawrence, said, "The chair agrees that the witness should be allowed to complete his thoughts without interruption."

"Thank you, Mr. Chairman. I was about to say that as I understand the law, possession is pretty close to ownership. Since our team is now controlling the asteroid, I believe we are entitled to bestow its title."

"So you are in the process of moving what you call 'Asteroid USA'?"

"Indeed, Senator Lawrence. That's what I announced almost two weeks ago on GNN. It's no secret."

"And can you describe with greater

particularity exactly where you intend to place it?" Lawrence persisted.

"Actually, this is not the appropriate time. But I plan to do so within the next thirty days."

"Rumor has it that you intend to issue an IPO for SpaceMine soon."

"It's a long process, Senator. My attorneys and bankers have been working diligently on this question and hope that we might be able to move forward in the reasonably near future. But no final decision has been made and no date set."

While Hamilton continued projecting an air of nonchalance, Sprague knew that Lawrence was starting to irritate his client.

"With all due respect, Mr. Chairman," Sprague said, "I think we're drifting pretty far afield with this line of questioning. The financial aspects of Mr. Hamilton's venture are very complex and currently under considerable review in preparation for any public offering of stock which may or may not materialize. This is hardly the forum for such analysis."

Senator Anderson was quick to respond. "Your point is well taken, counselor. This line of inquiry goes well beyond the scope of this joint committee's inquiry —"

Not ready to yield the issue, Senator

Lawrence retorted, "Mr. Chairman, there is all too much secrecy, too much ambiguity surrounding this 'venture,' as you describe it. There are serious national-security implications involved in moving asteroids around in space, and we need to —"

"We need to desist, Senator Lawrence. Perhaps you can take your concerns up in your own committee. We need to move on and the clerk advises me that your time has expired."

"My God!" Taylor whispered to Darlene. "I think that Hamilton's messing with Janus! He wouldn't answer her question. If he's not familiar with mythology, how did he know Janus was a mythical figure? Janus! That's what Cole must have wanted to tell me! It's Janus!"

With one pound of his gavel, Anderson ignored Lawrence's attempt to raise a final question. "This hearing," he declared, "is hereby adjourned."

50

Sprague and Hamilton slipped out of the hearing room through a side door, avoiding a scrum of reporters and cameras at the main door. They hurried down the corridor, Sprague leading the way, the phalanx of lawyers trailing behind. Atop the broad stairs at the entrance to the Russell Building, the lawyers went off on their own. Sprague and Hamilton walked down the steps into a shadowy Capitol Hill bathed in the warm light of a lowering sun.

Sprague's Lincoln Town Car was the first in a line of black limousines parked along the curb. The driver pulled up directly in front of Sprague and stepped out to open the passenger door. Sprague motioned Hamilton to enter, then followed. At luxurious moments like this he secretly relished the idea that a boy who had been so poor could become a man who was so rich.

The car cut smoothly through Capitol Hill

traffic, heading down Constitution Avenue. As the car passed the National Art Gallery, Hamilton said, "Fusty old place full of fusty old masters." He looked at the black face of his Rolex and asked, "How long will this take?"

"Not long," Sprague said, too quickly, too defensively. He had never found a way to get to a comfortable level with Hamilton. Sprague knew that Hamilton regarded him as just another person paid to help get Hamilton through life.

"I think things went well today. Taylor discredited. Your firm presentation. Glad that's behind us."

"I want to call my pilot as soon as possible and give him an estimated time," Hamilton said in the weary tone he sometimes affected. "It has been a long and tiring day. Yes, I thought it went well."

They made the rest of the trip to Georgetown in silence. When the car pulled into the driveway of the Ritz-Carlton, a doorman in blue livery opened the door and said, "Fine day, Mr. Sprague." He nodded and stepped back for Hamilton to enter first. Inside, Sprague awkwardly passed Hamilton so he could lead him to the elevator, which took them to the fourth floor.

Sprague punched the buttons on the

number pad, opened the door, and stepped back, allowing Hamilton to enter first into the marble-floored entrance to a starkly white room — white walls, white high ceiling, white carpet, long white sofa, and white armchairs. Through white sheer curtains could be seen a terrace and a view of the Potomac, gray under darkening clouds. Sprague paused to share the view with Hamilton. But he looked toward a hallway. "I've got to hit the head," he said. "Is there one down here?"

"Yes, second door to the left."

Sprague was still standing on the spot when Hamilton returned. "Clouding up," Sprague said, walking to the fireplace, an oblong slot in a marble wall, under a wide inset television screen. With a flick of a switch, two rows of gas flames rose. Sprague pointed Hamilton to an armchair at the left of the fireplace.

On the wall to his right were shelves containing mementos of Sprague's Foreign Service days — a dozen Japanese netsukes, most of them mildly pornographic; two Javanese shadow puppets; miniature Taiwanese paintings full of eerie, brightly colored faces; a piece of jadeite carved into the shape of a Chinese cabbage with a locust within its leaves.

"It's . . . how shall I say it . . . curiously interesting, but I give little notice to non-Christian art," Hamilton said, turning away from the artifacts. "I prefer Biblical art, particularly paintings and sculptures that attempt to lead the viewer toward God's word, such as Gustave Doré's illustrations for the Book of Revelation. Are you familiar with those works?"

"I know who Doré is. But I don't know much about the Book of Revelation."

"It is more than a book, far more than a book," Hamilton said. " 'Revelation' means exactly that. Its words show us 'things which must shortly come to pass.' It is a guide to direct us to the Final Days.' "

"Hmm. Interesting," Sprague said awkwardly, at a loss for an honest response.

"Some of my collection is in the Getty Villa in Los Angeles. I assume you've been there."

"I'll make it a stop on my next trip to LA," Sprague said. Knowing Hamilton did not drink alcohol or soft drinks of any kind, he asked, "Can I make you a cup of tea?"

"I'd like a glass of water — tap water — and no ice cubes. Where is it?"

Heading toward the kitchen, Sprague stopped and asked, "Where is what?"

"The thumb drive. I assume it's here or

we would have gone to your office."

"I think this place is safer than my office," Sprague said. "I have a wall safe in my — in the master — bedroom. I'll get it."

Sprague detoured to a bar in the library, poured himself a Scotch, and carried it into a large bedroom with off-white walls and ceiling and a television screen positioned for viewing from the oversized bed. He finished the Scotch and put the glass on a table near the bed. Then he removed from the wall a high-grade print of a Winslow Homer landscape, opened the safe that it had concealed, and took out a small lacquered wooden box. It was decorated in pale red and yellow stripes. On the top was a copy of an eighteenth-century portrait of a long-faced Japanese courtesan.

Detouring to the kitchen and filling a glass, he walked back to the living room with the glass in one hand and the box in the other. He proffered both to Hamilton, who was back in the chair. Sprague took the chair opposite Hamilton, who drank the water and put the glass on the table between them. Hamilton examined the box, which did not appear to have a lid.

"How the hell do I open this?" he asked.

"It's a Japanese puzzle box. A curiosity. To open it, turn it over and press the fourth red stripe from your left."

Hamilton tried to follow directions, said, "I hate puzzles," and tossed it to Sprague. He quickly opened it, took out the thumb drive, and handed it to Hamilton, who put it in his suit coat's inner pocket.

"It's yours," Sprague said, pointing to the box he had placed on the table. "I have one that takes seventy-eight moves to open."

"Thank you, Paul. But it's not my type of thing. . . . I guess it's more like your type of thing: complicated, tricky."

"That doesn't sound like a compliment."

"Wasn't meant to be, Paul. I'm still angry about your tone in that nutty phone call you made after the shooting."

"Maybe my tone wasn't to your liking, Robert. Sorry about the tone. But don't forget: That was your lawyer talking. This is serious."

"How serious?"

"I hate to admit that I don't know. All I know is that I got a call from Hal Davidson, late on the night of October second. He said he had to speak to me the next morning. When I asked him why he was sounding so excited and why was this so urgent, he said it involved the firm's most important client. That, of course, would be you."

"Yes, that would be me."

"I believed him. He was a sound attorney, very precise. But I felt I had to stall so I could call you and get an idea about what was going on."

"Yes, yes. I remember the call. And I remember saying that I thought I knew what this was about and would take care of it."

"I must know, Robert. Exactly *how* did you take care of it?"

"I called Basayev."

"Basayev? What in hell . . . Robert. Why call him? I have warned you that —"

"You are my lawyer, Paul. Not my nanny. I called him and told him that a disgruntled employee had walked out and had taken information that could be embarrassing to him, to me, and to SpaceMine. I think that is exactly the way I put it."

"And then did you —"

"You're straining my patience, Paul. I'm not going to submit to a deposition."

"I must know, Robert. For my own understanding, as your lawyer. Our conversations are protected by —"

"Oh, come off it, Paul. When I mentioned that this employee had turned a computer over to Hal Davidson, Basayev cursed in Russian. I don't know exactly the words he used, but he seemed to know about Hal. And just from his tone, it was clear he didn't like him.

"Then Basayev said — these are the exact words — he said, 'Don't worry, little bushkin. I'll take care of everything. There will be no loose ends.' I was surprised when he said this that he had only a slight accent."

"Loose ends?" Sprague repeated, his face paling.

Hamilton took his smartphone out of his pocket and hit a button. Looking at Sprague, he said, "Excuse me." He then spoke into the phone and said, "Mike. Hold on."

He looked at Sprague again. "I assume I can take your car to Dulles?"

Sprague nodded slowly, as if in a trance, and said, "I'll call. It will be here when you want it."

"Okay, Mike," Hamilton said. "I figure I'll be leaving for Dulles in less than half an hour." He pocketed the phone and turned back to face Sprague.

"Yes, you said you'd take care of it," Sprague said. "Loose ends. And then Hal Davidson was shot to death, along with three innocent —"

"Paul!" Hamilton shouted, leaning closer to Sprague. "Shut up! Shut up about that shooting."

Sprague's heart began pounding. He felt

light-headed. Hamilton had that look in his eyes that was stone-cold and threatening, sending a chill right through him. He had never seen eyes quite like Hamilton's. They were eyes that never seemed to blink.

Sprague shifted in his chair, then, getting face-to-face to Hamilton, said, "I *can't* shut up. I am your attorney. The police have Hal's cell phone. They will —"

"The police do not have the case. It's in the hands of the FBI," Hamilton said, leaning back.

"For God's sake, Robert. That obviously makes it worse. The FBI is going to find Hal called me and —"

"And was shot? So what? Where is the connection to me?" Hamilton said. He leaned back, paused, and resumed speaking calmly. "Let me tell you something, counselor. Collinsworth and Anderson are my connections. They are powerful senators, even more powerful than the FBI. They control the bureau's budget! They're both up for reelection next year. And my money and my resources will reelect them. That's *connections.*"

"I wouldn't count on controlling the Justice Department or the FBI if I were you. Your 'connections' just might one day find themselves on the other side of a subpoena."

"Meaning what?"

"Meaning that you'd better walk a little more humbly. I know that you and some private investigators on your payroll can make life tough for Ben Taylor. And you can get his show canceled, maybe even get him fired. All that is politics, political power. This is *crime,* a crime being investigated by the FBI. Don't you realize the FBI will track your connection with your Russian partner? Don't you realize that the NSA has to be eavesdropping on him — and, as a result, on you?"

"Again, so what? He's always being investigated. He and I have a legitimate business relationship."

"You realize I have to take your word for that. You have never let me see your contracts with him."

"You know all you have to know, Paul. I needed a Russian partner — associate, really — to get a launch of Asteroid USA."

"You can't keep up this secrecy, Robert. When SpaceMine announces its IPO it has to make a regulatory filing. You'll have to open your books. The SEC will be looking at your dealings with your Russian associate."

"There's something called a stealthy IPO, Paul. I take it you know that! Lots of high-tech companies are doing it. In any event Basayev and I are soon to have a meeting, Paul. We'll discuss the IPO. As I said when you called me about — what's his name? Davidson? — I will take care of it."

"And that item in your pocket?"

"It's like your artifacts," Hamilton said, gesturing toward the shelves next to him. "It is interesting and it is now mine." He seemed lost in thought for a moment. Then he looked at his Rolex and said, "You'd better call for the car."

51

When Falcone walked into the lobby of the Sullivan & Ford Building, for an instant he thought that he saw blood on the floor. *A trick of the shadows,* he thought. He inserted his keycard into the express elevator slot. The card was spat out, and DENIED flashed in a narrow window above the slot. Falcone tried a second time, got the same message, and realized that Sprague had transformed his resignation into a firing, complete with the humiliating ritual that was the modern corporation's version of giving an employee the bum's rush.

He took the regular elevator, got off at the top floor, and stepped onto the new carpeting in front of an eerie restoration of Ellen's cubicle, complete with a new blue ceramic vase containing a spray of yellow flowers that he could not identify. At the reception desk sat a young woman he vaguely recognized. She looked up, embarrassed and confused.

"Mr. . . . Mr. Falcone . . ."

"Good afternoon," he said, turning toward his office and trying to look as if he did not know what was going on.

"Mr. Falcone," she said in a pleading voice. "I . . . you . . . should . . . see Dr. Breitspecher before . . ."

"I understand," Falcone said, turning the other way. *Doctor?* Then he remembered that Ursula had a doctorate in political science. *From Cornell, I think. Have to look up her thesis. Probably something involving her homeland, East Germany.*

Sprague's office door opened and Ursula walked out with her usual Brunhilde stride and pointed toward his office. They arrived simultaneously at his door, which no longer bore his name. She punched the keypad numbers, which, Falcone noted, had already been changed, and motioned for him to enter.

On the top of his desk were three white file boxes and his rarely used Sullivan & Ford laptop. The two photographs of Falcone with President Blake Oxley — one in the Oval Office, the other in the Situation Room — were off the wall, as was a pencil sketch of a Vietnam village, which he had drawn while a prisoner. He had never been interested in doing much decorating in his office. Now, though, its bleakness saddened him. He had spent many hours here, and now those hours had shrunk to three white file boxes.

"You can take these with you," she said. "Or you can have them delivered, of course at your expense. If you want this desk," Ursula said, nodding toward it, "you must pay what the firm paid for it plus shipping charges."

"I'll buy it. Ship it to my address and send me the bill. Anything else?"

She opened the folder she was carrying and, reading from a paper in it, said, "You will leave on this desk the firm's cell phone and laptop, your identification badge, your elevator card key, your Sullivan and Ford credit card, your —"

"I never used that credit card," Falcone said, opening an unlocked drawer and tossing the card on the desk. "And look, Ursula, there's no need to make this a drumming-out-of-the-regiment ceremony. I'll take what I want right now and leave the rest for you to deliver — of course at my expense. I'll put all the stuff belonging to the firm on the desk and walk out. You can go back to your office and do something useful and —"

"Don't patronize me, Falcone," she said,

looking up and glaring. She looked down and kept reading. "Your health insurance will continue through the end of the month. You will then be required to obtain your own insurance under the Affordable Care Act. The firm will no longer make payments to your life insurance policy, which will remain in place if you continue the premiums. Regarding your e-mail account here, your access to the system is locked. An automatic e-mail notification will alert senders that you are no longer affiliated with the firm. If you have any pending matters that will need the attention of another member of the firm, send an e-mail to me. You will notify clients that you are no longer with the firm. I have drafted such a notification letter. I have also compiled a final compensation payment."

She handed him two pieces of paper. "The final compensation will be deposited in your account and the account will then be terminated." She handed him another piece of paper. "Also sign this."

Falcone glanced at it. "Termination notice? Come on, Ursula. We're friends. Don't make this so . . . nasty. Your boss didn't terminate me. I quit, goddamn it." He handed back the paper. "I'll write a letter of resignation that will be short and polite and send it to you via registered mail. And I'll write my clients without any help from you." He crumpled her draft of the letter and tossed it on the desk.

She handed him another paper and, in her coldest, most official voice, said, "You are hereby reminded that the confidentiality and proprietary-information agreement you signed upon joining the firm will remain in effect indefinitely."

Falcone accepted the paper, folded it, and put it in his pocket. "Okay, Ursula. You have done your duty. Now go back to work with my fond goodbye. At heart you are a fine person doing her job."

"I am instructed to escort you out."

Falcone turned his back and put the law firm's cell phone and keycards on the desk. He lifted the covers on the boxes, examined their contents, transferred the photos and pencil drawing to the box containing his personal laptop, and hefted the box off the desk.

They silently descended in the public elevator. Ursula followed him to the entrance door and said, "I will not miss you."

"Goodbye, Ursula," Falcone said. "Tell Paul I left smiling."

52

By word of mouth and from an item in *Washington Lawyer* magazine, the legal community learned that one of Washington's Super Lawyers was at large. "Super Lawyer" is a title awarded by a rating service of outstanding lawyers, and it added to Falcone's luster as a prospective recruit into one of Sullivan & Ford's rivals. But the most attractive attribute of all was his connection with the White House.

The reason for his resignation was vaguely smoothed over by Sprague as differences over the strategic future of the firm. Whatever the real issue, a dozen firms and two premier law schools sent him cordial greetings and invitations. Falcone, however, decided to try lawyering on his own for a while.

With the aid of an interior decorator and an old friend who was a contractor, he expanded his apartment's home office to accommodate the great mahogany desk he kept at the law office. *I'm hanging out my shingle again,* he thought, reminiscing about that first day in a little Massachusetts town when he slipped a bronze nameplate into the stack of nameplates arranged in the lobby of the office building near the courthouse.

He was celebrating the arrival of the desk when his house phone rang. He picked up the phone and saw the ID panel: US GOVERNMENT. A woman's voice said, "Please hold on for FBI director Patterson."

The formality surprised Falcone, who was used to direct calls from Patterson. "Sean? This is J. B. Patterson," said the next voice. "I would like you to come to headquarters to answer some questions."

Falcone paused before responding. The wording and the tone of Patterson's voice added to the surprise. "Sure, J.B. When?"

"As soon as possible." The voice sounded official.

"Sounds serious," Falcone said.

"It is."

"I can get there in twenty minutes."

"Fine. An agent will meet you at the entrance and escort you."

"Escort." That's not a friendly word, Falcone thought, running through events since the

last time he talked with, and had a drink with, Patterson.

He changed from sweatshirt and jeans to suit and tie, took the elevator down to the lobby, and briskly walked up Pennsylvania Avenue to the hulking J. Edgar Hoover Building, which one architectural critic called Orwellian and another described as having "a rather intimidating, temple-like look vaguely reminiscent of an old Cecil B. DeMille set."

Falcone entered the courtyard and went through two typical security stops — empty-your-pockets-into-the-dish and walk-through-the-scanning-detector — and was ushered into the small entrance foyer by a member of the FBI's uniformed police force, who asked for his cell phone and handed him a visitor's laminated identification. She then took him to a set of waist-high turnstiles, where a man in a dark blue suit, white shirt, and blue-and-green striped tie was standing. He stepped forward, flashed his identity-and-badge holder, and then slapped it on an electronic pad that read his identity card.

"Put yours next to mine," he told Falcone. "We have to register your entrance together, and, when you leave, we have to register your exit together."

As Falcone touched his visitor tag to the reader, he saw the name on the agent's card: Patrick Sarsfield. Falcone stifled a remark about Sarsfield's peripatetic sleuthing and simply said "Right" as the turnstile barrier bar clicked.

Sarsfield nodded toward an elevator, which took them to the seventh floor. Falcone had never been in the director's top-floor suite. Protocol called for the FBI director to go to the White House for meetings, many of which were in the Situation Room. At a desk outside Patterson's corner office, a trim young man, whose quick movements and physique said security detail, rose, opened the door behind him, and motioned them to enter.

Patterson was standing beside his desk in a room that Falcone estimated to be almost the size of a squash singles court. On the paneled wall behind him were an enlarged copy of the FBI's seal and photos of agents who had been killed in the line of duty. Falcone did not have time to count them, for Patterson immediately stepped forward, shook his hand, and said, "I'm not in this, Sean. It's Agent Sarsfield's case."

Case? Again, Falcone stifled a remark, deciding that anything said about this odd little ceremony would not do him or his client any good.

Falcone did not take Patterson's arm's-length treatment personally. Patterson was profoundly scrupulous in a town that rarely heard the word. He was not a man of ceremony or puffery. He did not accept invitations to Sunday talk shows, embassy receptions, or other stops on the Washington social circuit. He gave few speeches, and those were usually to law-enforcement gatherings. He was rarely seen on television; when a major FBI investigation ended successfully, he let the persons who did the work stand in the spotlight.

Falcone nodded and smiled at Patterson and followed Sarsfield out a door leading to a conference room that had one large window overlooking Pennsylvania Avenue. Sarsfield pointed to a chair at one end of a highly polished table long enough to accommodate eight or so people. In the middle was a multidirectional microphone.

As Falcone sat down, he noticed an aperture, presumably for a video camera, on the wall nearest the table. Sarsfield took the chair to Falcone's left. Seated on his right were two people whom Sarsfield did not introduce.

Sarsfield gave the time and date and added, "This is an interview with Mr. Sean

Falcone in regards to case seven eight six four. I am Special Agent Patrick Sarsfield. At the table are forensic IT specialists Horace Poindexter and Sunithat Agrawal, both assigned to the FBI Laboratory in Quantico." Falcone noticed that a red light appeared on the microphone stand.

"This is an interview, Agent Sarsfield? And it is being recorded?" Falcone asked.

"Yes to both questions, Mr. Falcone. Do you agree that you have come to headquarters voluntarily at the direct request of Director Patterson?"

"Yes, but I am unaware —"

"On October fourth of this year were you in possession of a laptop that was the property of SpaceMine?"

"Yes," Falcone said, making up his mind to be the perfect interviewee by answering as briefly as possible.

The specialist, identified by Sarsfield as Sunithat Agrawal, reached down and took from a larger case next to her a laptop encased in transparent plastic. She had the dark-haired, dark-eyed beauty of a bright young immigrant from India. But, knowing FBI personnel rules, Falcone assumed she was the American-born daughter of immigrants. She wore a rose-red suit jacket over a white blouse.

"Is this the laptop that was in your possession on the day in question?" Sarsfield asked.

"It appears to be."

"Your fingerprints are on its cover and on the space bar and on several keys," Sarsfield said. "Also, records kept by the manufacturer, Dell, show that it was one of at least forty-five purchased by SpaceMine. So we have good reason to believe that this laptop was the one stolen from your law firm during the commission of multiple homicides on October fourth." He nodded to Agrawal. She pressed a button and a large screen on the nearest wall lit up with an image of the laptop.

"This is a somewhat unusual laptop," she said. An image of the open laptop appeared on the screen. Poised over the keyboard were two delicate, perfectly manicured hands without nail polish — hers, Falcone decided, after glancing at the real right hand that grasped a remote control.

After several keystrokes and repeated pressing of the power switch, the laptop's screen remained blank. "As you can see," she continued, "the laptop will not turn on."

"But when I had it," Falcone said, "I was able to turn it on. All I could see was a warning that I did not have access."

"We managed to reconstruct the commands," Agrawal said, touching a control on the remote. "Did the first lines look like this?"

On the computer wall screen appeared

WARNING
YOU ARE NOT AUTHORIZED ACCESS
TO THIS LAPTOP.
DISCONNECT NOW.

"Yes," Falcone said. "How —"

Agrawal looked across the table at Sarsfield. "Shall I explain?"

"Let the record show," Sarsfield droned, "that Technician Agrawal is authorized to explain the procedure in order to expedite this interview."

"This laptop was turned over to the bureau by the District of Columbia Metropolitan Police. It appeared to be inoperative. We thought at first we were dealing with a dead or cleaned-out hard drive. But I was able to pull some information out of it. We extracted the hard drive, which appeared to be normal for that type of Dell laptop."

Another click produced on screen an image of the disassembled laptop. She switched to a laser pointer and aimed its beam at the hard drive and a green card laced with wires and tiny components.

"I could see that the card was vastly different from the manufacturer's card. And the hard drive did not resemble any in our collection. But, by using Self-Monitoring Analysis and Reporting Technology, I was able —"

"Okay, Suni," Sarsfield said with a quick smile. "Easy with the technology."

"Oh, sorry," she said, smiling back. "Well, it all came down to this: Only someone who knew the password could turn it on. And if someone tried more than three times to open it, all data on the hard drive would be erased. That's a very high-risk security system, indicating high-value data. I also found a very interesting feature. The USB — universal serial bus — you know, where you stick in the thumb drive — was disabled."

"Meaning?" Sarsfield asked.

"Meaning that there was no way to steal data through the USB, the way that guy in the Pentagon did. And —"

"Watch it, Suni. That's classified," Sarsfield said. Turning to Falcone, he added, "I must warn you that willful communication of classified information —"

"I can assure you, Agent Sarsfield,"

Falcone said irritably, "that, first, I still hold very high clearance and, two, I know all about the case that Ms. Agrawal referred to. The Pentagon's temporary solution, by the way, was to glue all USB slots shut."

Sarsfield did not respond. He looked at Agrawal and nodded.

"There was a complex commands structure that enabled a witting operator to make the USB slot work," she said. "In other words, if you knew the command series, you could insert a thumb drive and download data from the hard drive."

"And did you find that happened?" Falcone asked.

"Yes," Agrawal said. "Twice."

"*Twice?*" Falcone asked.

"We will be discussing that in due time, Mr. Falcone," Sarsfield said. He nodded again to Agrawal.

"While we were examining that system to see if the slots had been activated," she continued, "we discovered another anomaly, a very sophisticated tracking device. That same unique chip card had a tiny chip that functioned like a GPS, recording the location of the laptop and saving the geographic data onto the hard drive. We were able to reconstruct that part of the hard drive. The drive's prime data area was another matter."

She looked at Sarsfield, who said, "That's of no interest here. From that tracking device you were able to develop a timeline, correct?"

"Yes, sir. However, in terms of chain of evidence —"

"Thank you, Suni. That will be all for now." Sarsfield pointed a finger at the other technician and said, "Okay, Poindexter, let's hear about the car."

"Excuse me, Agent Sarsfield," Falcone said. "I assume you're talking about the car the shooters used."

"That's right," Sarsfield said. "We got it from the New Jersey State Police and shipped it to the Quantico lab."

"I touched the laptop — but I didn't have a damn thing to do with that car. And I wonder about that 'chain of evidence' remark —"

"There's nothing to wonder about, Mr. Falcone. We are investigating a crime that you witnessed, a death that you caused, and an important piece of evidence that you had in your possession."

"I'm beginning to think I'm a 'person of interest.' "

"That's right. You are."

53

Falcone knew he should have ended the so-called interview right then and there, but he felt a surge of memories about his days as a trial lawyer and then as a prosecutor. He decided to stay in the game. *Of course, it's never a game. It's always* Les Misérables, *and you're either playing the role of Valjean or Inspector Javert. Only,* Falcone thought, *I'm a Valjean who did not commit a crime.*

Poindexter chose to stand rather than sit, as Agrawal had. He was a pudgy, balding young man in his midthirties. He wore a blue blazer with golden buttons over a white shirt and flowery tie, and he had that ineffable look of a man not used to wearing a tie. Agrawal handed him the remote. He brought up an image of a black Mercedes-Benz S600 on a lift in a garage that looked as sanitary as a surgical theater. A click on the remote changed the image to the inside driver's door and showed the opened pocket that had contained Viktor Yazor's gun.

"An extra accessory," Poindexter said.

The image shifted to focus on the navigation screen to the right of the steering wheel. "This car is a treasure for us. The navigation system produces what we call a bread-crumb trail that shows dates, time, routes, and destinations and saves it all on board. The user would undoubtedly like to encrypt or dump that data to keep it secret. But because the car's navigational electronics is so intertwined with the car's other suites of electronics, tampering is limited and encryption is weak, unlike the laptop. We attacked the car encryption with relative ease. We were able to download everything it had. One of the —"

"Results," Sarsfield cut in, "is that we can construct two timelines. Okay, Poindexter, put them on screen."

Onto the screen came what at first looked like two Google Maps pages, one labeled *Laptop Timeline,* the other *Car Timeline.*

Falcone leaned forward as, under *Laptop Timeline,* a blue, arrowheaded line appeared on a map of the Washington area.

"Okay," Sarsfield said. "The computer arrives at Reagan National Airport on the night of October second at a time coinciding with the time that an American Airlines

Los Angeles flight arrives. Cole Perenchio is on that flight."

"Under his own name?" Falcone asked.

"Yes," Sarsfield responded, frowning at the interruption. "Carrying a stolen laptop."

Agrawal's laser beam hit the blue arrow, which moved from the airport to the Rosemont neighborhood in Alexandria, Virginia.

"The laptop goes to Locust Lane in Alexandria. Investigation shows that it was carried in a Town Car, owned by Luxury Autos of Washington and hired by Harold Davidson, a partner in the law firm Sullivan and Ford, which maintains an account at Luxury Autos."

Falcone knew that FBI agents were extremely proficient at courtroom testimony, often embellished with charts and maps. Even the tone of an agent's voice was modulated so that it was flat, unemotional, thorough, and therefore trustworthy to a juror's ears. He was listening to a bravura performance of FBI testimonyspeak.

"The laptop spent the night at Davidson's home, and —"

"How do you know that?" Falcone asked.

"His wife — widow — was shown a photograph of the laptop," Sarsfield said, his voice turning from that of a testifier to that of an interrogator. "She says that

Davidson brought a Dell laptop, which she had not seen before, into the home on the night of October second. On the morning of October third he took it with him when another Luxury Autos vehicle picked him up and took him to the Sullivan and Ford Building, arriving at nine thirty-five, according to his elevator-entry card."

Sarsfield nodded to Poindexter, who aimed his laser at the car timeline and controlled the movement of a red, arrowed line as Sarsfield narrated its October 2 passage from the airport to a hotel at Thomas Circle — "following the taxi that Cole Perenchio took, because the driver of his taxi said in an interview that he dropped him at this site, the Washington Plaza Hotel, at ten fifty p.m. The car then drove to a motel at New York Avenue in Washington, where, earlier in the day, three men had registered for individual rooms."

Sarsfield continued his narrative, noting that the men spent October 3 in their rooms, except for venturing out to eat lunch and dinner at places that Sarsfield did not include in his narrative, probably because they left the motel on foot, separately or together. "The only use of the car, according to the GPS data," Sarsfield said, "was a drive to the area around the Sullivan and Ford Building, apparently to plan the attack."

"Does the car show up on security cameras on that day?" Falcone asked.

"I am confining these two timelines to data obtained from the computer and the car that pertain only to this interview."

"So far," Falcone said, "I have not seen any reason for this interview. May I ask why I am here?"

"Very well, Mr. Falcone. I am examining the chain of evidence regarding an exhibit from the crime, the SpaceMine laptop. Through the use of the laptop tracker and the car's GPS data, we have determined that there is a gap in the movement of the laptop from the crime scene at the law firm to the District of Columbia Metropolitan Police, prior to when that organization turned the laptop over to the bureau."

"Gap? Where's the gap?"

Sarsfield pointed to the car timeline and motioned to Poindexter. The red arrow point moved to Eleventh and D. "The car stops here," Sarsfield said. "We think the driver picked up the surviving shooter here." The arrow kept moving. "They pull into a public parking garage, where they spent nearly two hours — and then they stop at 701 Pennsylvania Avenue, where you happen to live."

Falcone said, "What the hell are you —"

"Switch to the laptop timeline," Falcone ordered, and Poindexter moved that map's blue arrow to accompany Sarsfield's narrative of the laptop's passage from the Sullivan & Ford Building to the homeless shelter and then to 701 Pennsylvania Avenue.

"Paul Sprague told me, in a sworn statement," Sarsfield continued, "that you, Mr. Falcone, called him at approximately three thirty p.m. and said you had the laptop. My question, Mr. Falcone, is how did you obtain the laptop?"

"I told Paul how I obtained it. I got it — along with a gun and a black jacket — from a homeless guy who had picked it up from behind a Dumpster near the Second Street shelter."

"That is not what Mr. Sprague told me. He merely said you handed him the laptop, gun, and jacket and asked him to give it to the DC police. But these two timelines indicate that the car stopped at the homeless shelter on Second Street Northwest, discovered that the laptop was no longer there, and then drove to your address, where the laptop next appears."

"I told Paul Sprague about getting the

items from the homeless man — his name was Thomas Crawford. I asked Sprague to give the laptop, gun, and jacket to Detective Emmetts, along with the name Thomas Crawford."

"Mr. Sprague *did* hand the laptop and other items to Detective Lieutenant Emmetts, but there was no mention of a Thomas Crawford," Sarsfield said. "The laptop tracker shows that the laptop was briefly in the Sullivan and Ford Building."

"This is ridiculous," Falcone said, raising his voice and staring at the laptop timeline. "Your timeline shows that Sprague had it for thirty-two minutes. The building is so close to DC police headquarters that Emmetts would be there in, at most, ten minutes after Sprague called him."

Before Sarsfield could respond, Agrawal said, "There's an explanation. The phone calls."

Sarsfield glared at her as Falcone asked her, "Phone calls?"

"Using a national security letter, we obtained records of the firm's phone calls on the day of the shootings," Sarsfield said. "Mr. Sprague appears to have made two phone calls during the time that he was in possession of the laptop."

"To whom?" Falcone asked.

"I am not at liberty to say," Sarsfield mumbled.

"And did Verizon get a national security letter from you to get a record of my home phone calls and Ben Taylor's calls?"

"Again, I am not at liberty to say."

Falcone turned to Agrawal and asked, "Does the tracker show that attempts were made to use the laptop's USB ports during the time that Sprague made those two calls?"

"Don't answer that," Sarsfield ordered. That was answer enough for Falcone, remembering his favorite Pynchon quotation.

"This is a farce, Sarsfield," Falcone said "I'm beginning to feel like that poor son of a bitch in Atlanta whom you guys called 'a person of interest.' "

"That's what your friend Dr. Taylor told me," Sarsfield said. "But neither one of you is charged with anything . . . yet."

"Well, then I'm through here."

"I thank you. And I know all we need to know . . . for now," Sarsfield said. "I'll make an appointment soon to obtain a formal statement."

Sarsfield stood up. He told Poindexter and Agrawal to stay while he escorted Falcone out of the building and added, "I'll be back.

We have a few things to tie up."

"Like who killed Cole Perenchio," Falcone said.

Sarsfield turned, pointed at the car timeline for October 5, and said, "At nine fourteen, they park near Perenchio's hotel. The night manager's log shows that at nine twenty he called for a cab. The cabbie who responded identifies Perenchio from a photo, and —"

"Excuse me," Falcone interrupted. "A photo?"

"Correct. Obtained from NASA Human Resources," Sarsfield said. "And the cabbie drops him off at Constitution Avenue near the Capitol Grounds. He remembers because there's nothing there, no bar, no restaurant, and he asked his passenger if he was sure this was the right spot. The cabbie figured maybe he was meeting someone. The car moves two minutes later, obviously following the cab to Capitol Hill. Nine minutes later, the car returns to the motel."

"And Cole Perenchio is dead."

"Correct," Sarsfield said. "Let's go."

54

Falcone stepped out onto Pennsylvania Avenue and took a cab to the Taylor home. When a surprised Ben Taylor answered the door, Falcone said, "Sorry I didn't call ahead." As he followed Ben to the entrance hall, he kept talking: "We both definitely have to watch what we say on the phone. Tell Darlene. And tell her to warn Sam. We all have to be very careful."

"Sit down, Sean," Ben said, pointing to the living room couch. "Can I get you anything?"

"No, thanks. I've just had an 'interview' with Agent Sarsfield. We have to move fast. Now we're *both* persons of interest."

"Welcome to the club. What's he after?"

"The shooters are dead. So the shootings case is closed. But he keeps working. I think he's obsessing to find out what's behind the shootings and the murder of Cole Perenchio. He knows there's a connection, but he doesn't know where to find it."

"What are they getting off the hard drive? Was it completely cleaned?"

"You know better than I do that a good tech can pull a lot out of a hard drive. They'll eventually get some bits and bytes."

"But it will take a long time and a lot of work to put them together and make sense," Taylor said. "They'd probably have to hand it off to NSA experts. They're the folks with very dark techniques unknown outside the NSA. From what I've heard, there's no such a thing as a cleaned hard drive."

After describing what had happened at FBI headquarters, Taylor said, "But I should thank Sarsfield for what he gave me."

"What's that?" Taylor asked, sinking into his favorite living room chair.

"All along I've wondered why Cole lugged a laptop around when he could have just put a thumb drive in his pocket."

"Right. I wondered that, too," Taylor said.

"Turns out the USB ports were disabled, locked — but they could be activated on command. And it looks as if Sprague did use them."

"Downloaded them before he gave the laptop to the DC police," Taylor said, leaning forward. "I guess he did that to give the data to Hamilton."

"Bull's-eye! Sprague made two phone calls while he had the laptop. One to the cops about turning it over and the other, I'll bet, to Hamilton, who gave him the commands to open the laptop and activate the port. So Hamilton would get what was on Cole's laptop — and the cops would get an empty laptop."

"The FBI will figure that all out," Taylor said. "They should be talking to Sprague, not you."

"I think their real person of interest is Sprague," Falcone said. "Sarsfield is incredibly thorough — and clever. He called me and set up his dog-and-pony show because he wanted to find out whether I was somehow involved with Sprague. Turns out Sprague didn't tell them what I had told him. It was a typical Sprague move: get me *into* trouble and keep himself *out of* trouble. But forget that. I know something that Sarsfield doesn't know."

"What's that?"

Falcone told him about Sprague's computer illiteracy. "Now stay tuned," Falcone said. He reached into his suit coat pocket and pulled out his Best Buy cell phone. "I don't think they've got me linked to this number yet." He tapped the number for Sullivan & Ford and asked for Ursula

Breitsprecher, knowing she never let her phone ring more than twice.

"Ursula? Sean. Don't hang up. You need to hear this," he said.

He could picture the frown rippling across her face, the good-sense part of her brain calculating.

"Make it fast," she said icily.

"I have just visited the USG organization on Pennsylvania Avenue," Falcone said, fearing that "FBI" would trigger an NSA keyword response. "I learned that on the afternoon of October fourth you provided your boss with your usual assistance. Twice. For your own good, you need to get that information to the correct USG officials," Falcone told her in his most persuading voice. Now he pictured her, pursing her lips and raising her head, as if the answer were on the ceiling. *She has to know she tampered with evidence,* he thought. *And "USG" will get to her German soul.*

"How?" she asked in a firm voice.

"Easy. Meet me at the Starbucks near you in an hour. Bring the thing. I'll bring my laptop, load it in, and give it back. You will have cooperated. Problem solved."

Seconds ticked by. Then, lowering her voice, she said, "Is this a client-lawyer conversation?"

"If you want it to be."

"I do."

"Agreed. As usual, Ursula, good thinking. See you in an hour."

Taylor's car was parked down the block. While he drove Falcone home, they planned their next moves. At 701 Pennsylvania Avenue, Taylor parked underground. Then they took the elevator to the penthouse, where Falcone picked up his laptop and put two cups of morning coffee into the microwave.

Sitting next to each other at the kitchen counter, they completed their plan.

"I used to hate heated-up coffee," Taylor said, extracting the cups and handing one to Falcone. "Not bad from a microwave, though."

Falcone nodded. He took a couple of sips and said, "Right. Not bad. But not good. I've got another reason for looking forward to Starbucks. What do you think we'll be getting?"

"We'll be getting something that Hamilton wanted real bad. That's for sure," Taylor said. "And remember Cole said to me that he blamed himself for Hal's death. He was scared. He thought he was in danger. And he was right. Hal dead. Cole dead."

"Don't brood, Ben. We're both still vertical," Falcone said. "See you soon with the goods."

He finished his coffee, put his laptop in its carrying case, and headed for the door.

55

Falcone's bespoke suit and cashmere topcoat did not blend into the Starbucks style, which favored jeans and hooded jackets with the hoods down. But his laptop certainly did fit in. He opened it and looked around. From his corner two-person table he counted twelve fellow patrons hunched over their laptops. He did not count the number of times he looked at his watch. Fifty-two minutes had passed since he said he would meet Ursula in an hour. He believed that she would be here in eight minutes or she would not come at all, because she did not know how to be late.

She swept into Starbucks with seven minutes to spare, her long blond hair and her crimson cape flowing around her trim figure. Several men looked up from their screens as she twisted through the tables to Falcone, who rose and extended his hand, which she did not take.

"Can I get you coffee — or tea. I nearly forgot, you prefer tea," Falcone said.

"No thanks," she said as she sat down opposite him and used her coldest voice. "Luckily Paul is in Middleburg for the day. But I'm jammed, as usual. Let's get to the business. I have what you want." She pulled the cover off a black thumb drive and inserted it into the side of his laptop.

"I did not know what to do. I knew . . . knew something was wrong," she said, her voice losing its frost. "Paul, always with secrets. I know he is doing something wrong and . . . pulling me in."

"You're doing the right thing, Ursula," Falcone said.

"But, Sean, what does it mean for me to do the right thing?"

"It means you are putting yourself on the right side of the law."

Falcone's eyes were locked on the laptop. When the thumb-drive download ended, he grasped the drive with one napkin and wiped it with another before handing it back to her.

She slipped the thumb drive into her small black handbag and asked, "What will you do with this?"

"Hold on to it for now. I guess you know that the laptop was taken from Hal's office during the shooting."

"Yes, although Paul did not tell me that."

"You probably know more law than most of the partners. So I'm sure you realize that one important element in the chain of evidence is who secured the evidence and who had control or possession of the evidence."

"So Paul was in possession — and tampered with the evidence," she said, lowering her voice and leaning across the table. "And . . . and I helped him."

"But you didn't know it was evidence, did you?"

"No. I walked into Paul's office and saw a laptop, and I did what he told me to do."

"The usual ballet?"

"Ballet? . . . Oh, yes. The system for when he had to act like he knew how to use a computer. Oh, yes!" She smiled. "Like a pas de deux. Very funny."

"I'll need you to give me a formal statement, giving all the details, such as how Paul got the passwords. I assume it was someone from SpaceMine."

"Yes, it was Mr. Hamilton."

"Wonderful! Then Hamilton himself literally gave Paul the key to tampering?"

"Yes. I see the need to give you a deposition as soon as possible. When and where?"

415

Falcone took a sip of coffee and then put the laptop in its case. Suddenly, he looked up and said, "I just had an idea, Ursula. Let's go to FBI headquarters."

He told her about his session with Sarsfield's timelines and how the double download made him realize what had probably happened.

"Exactly how. The pas de deux," she said, smiling. "I can see why going to the FBI is a good idea. I agree." She leaned back and said softly, "I feel relieved. Very relieved. It's like I am two persons. One who works there" — she tilted her head toward the Sullivan & Ford Building — "and one who . . . who has a life . . . who tries to have a life."

Falcone took out his cell phone and called Taylor to say, "I've got it. I'll be dropping it off shortly. Then I'll be going with my provider to where I was earlier. Can't say more."

He next called Patterson's private number. "J.B., I need a return visit with Agent Sarsfield. Right away."

"I would think you had enough of him for the day," Patterson said dryly.

"No. This is hot, J.B. I have someone who wants to make a statement. A big statement. I can be there in fifteen minutes."

"Okay, Sherlock. Sarsfield will meet you at the gate."

56

Falcone and Ursula jumped into a cab and took it to his apartment. Falcone handed the laptop to the doorman and asked him to deliver it to the penthouse, where there would be someone to take it. Then the pair sprinted two blocks to the J. Edgar Hoover Building.

Sarsfield was standing in front of the entrance to the courtyard. He checked Ursula's identification and swiftly ushered them through the security path to the elevator. On the seventh floor, they bypassed Patterson's office and entered the conference room. Falcone nodded to Agrawal and Poindexter, who were in the same seats. At the far end of the table, Falcone was surprised to see Director Patterson. Seated at his left was a woman in her fifties wearing a dark-blue blazer and holding an iPad. Sarsfield took the chair to Patterson's right.

"This is our general counsel, Marjorie

Humphreys," Patterson said, nodding toward her. "She'll handle any legal issues that may come up."

Falcone, standing behind the chair he had recently occupied, said, "This is my client, Ursula Breitsprecher" — he spelled out her name and then went on. "She is the executive assistant to Paul Sprague, to whom I gave the laptop we had been discussing. She wishes to describe what happened on October fourth."

Humphreys ducked and came up from her briefcase with a Bible, which was passed down the table to Ursula, who, under the general counsel's direction, swore to tell the truth.

As Ursula began describing the speakerphone system that she and Sprague had worked out, the door opened and a man slipped into the room. He took a chair next to Humphreys, who introduced him as Assistant Attorney General James Cosgrove.

After Humphreys gave Cosgrove a whispered summary of the deposition thus far, she signaled for Ursula to continue, step by step, describing the downloading and disabling on October 4. When she mentioned the phone call, she identified the other person on the line as Robert Wentworth Hamilton.

"What is the basis for your identification?" Humphreys asked.

"No other client of Mr. Sprague uses a telephone encryption system. It distorts the voices of both parties. I know his voice through that distortion. It makes him sound like one of those children on *South Park*."

Humphreys smiled. Falcone was the only person in the room who laughed.

Finally, at Humphreys's request, Ursula handed the thumb drive to Poindexter, who accepted it with a gloved hand and placed it in a transparent evidence bag.

"Don't we get to read it?" Falcone asked the end of the table.

"It's evidence," Sarsfield said. "It must be processed and analyzed."

"What about a video of this deposition?"

After a long silence, Patterson had a whispered conversation with Humphreys and Cosgrove and finally said, "You will receive a copy for your client. Thank you both for coming here today."

Sarsfield led Falcone and Ursula back through the security gauntlet and left them with a wave on Pennsylvania Avenue.

"There's a restaurant, D'Acqua, just a block from here," Falcone said. "It's an Italian and seafood place, but you can get tea there, too, I know."

"Come on, Sean, give me a break! Already it's been a full day. I'm going right home and . . ."

"Please, Ursula. This is something that I need to know. You liked Hal Davidson. He had never done anyone any harm. But he was shot to death."

"Yes, a fine man. But, Sean, he just happened to be in the wrong place at the wrong time."

"I don't think so, Ursula," Falcone said, pointing to the Starbucks on Seventh Street, half a block away. "I think he was murdered because somebody wanted him killed. Please, five minutes."

"All right. You have my attention. I want to know why you think that."

They entered from the side door. Ursula sat at a table along the far wall while Falcone ordered his coffee and her chai tea latte.

When he returned carrying the cups, she looked up and said, "I . . . I am grateful that you had me go to the FBI. Next, Paul will be hearing from Sarsfield. And I will be without a job."

"He'd be a fool to fire you. And . . . there's your friend."

"Ralph. He spends half of his time back in South Carolina. But, you're right. Having a member of Congress as a boy . . . as a friend, will help," she said, smiling and pausing. "Maybe he could get me a job on the Hill. . . . Well, okay, what is it you want to know?"

"Hal Davidson made several recent trips to South Africa on a pro bono case of some kind. I have a hunch that whatever he was doing is somehow connected with his murder."

"Murder?" Ursula asked. "I can't believe that."

"I know it seems incredible, but I'm convinced that Hal was the target, and there had to be a motive."

"All I know is that he had been helping South African miners for a couple of years when we took on Hamilton as a client," Ursula said. "Helping those miners was like a crusade, a cause, for Hal. There was one day when the police and miners fought. Hal was there. The miners had clubs and machetes. The police had guns and killed a lot of the miners. Hal told me how horrible it was. He knew I was . . . dating . . . a congressman. Hal asked me to talk to Ralph and have Congress investigate the terrible conditions the miners worked under. But Ralph ran into a brick wall. He couldn't find any cosponsor for a congressional hearing. The word was out that big money — big donors — didn't want anything to do with the African miners."

"What did Hal have to say?"

"He wasn't surprised. He said that something funny was going on. 'Something funny.' That's what he said."

"Do you have any idea what he meant?"

"The strike should have ended. I think he thought that the strike leader acted like he didn't really want the strike to end. He was working with people in South Africa, trying to figure out what was happening."

"Was this when Hamilton became a client?"

"I really can't say definitely. I think so. Anyway, Paul said Hal had to drop the miners. And, Hal told me, Paul gave no reason. But Hal was suspicious."

"How? What was he suspicious about?"

"He knew who Hamilton was, of course. Then he heard something on a TV show — I don't remember its name — something about a monopoly of something. He was angry, very angry. There was a big scene. I heard Hamilton's name."

Falcone thought for a moment. "Was it *Street Speak,* the show about Wall Street?" he asked.

"Perhaps. That sounds familiar. Paul

watches it. He has a large portfolio. . . . Wait. He had me get a transcript of a show. Now I remember. Yes. It was *Street Speak.*"

"And did the transcript have Ben Taylor talking about SpaceMine?"

"Yes. That's right."

"I watched, too," Falcone said. "Taylor was talking about how most of the world's platinum and palladium comes from Russia and South Africa and that SpaceMine would drastically change the market for them. It's beginning to fall into place."

Ursula looked puzzled and said, "What is?"

"The whole damn thing. How was it when Hal was killed? Was he was still working for the miners?"

Ursula put down her nearly empty cup. "Yes. Hal even threatened to resign and talk publicly about being fired because of the miners if Paul forced him to drop them. He was a stubborn man."

As she and Falcone neared the door, he said, "Do you think Hamilton was behind this?"

"Paul never said so. He just said that Hamilton was our most important client. Anything he wanted, we had to do," Ursula said. "Like firing you."

"You, forget, Ursula. He never fired me. I had already quit."

57

After flagging down a taxi for Ursula, Falcone strode across the Navy Memorial toward the door of his apartment building. But the ring of his cell phone stopped him: "This is Ben. I'm at my house. Needed to drive here. Will explain when you get here, which I hope is right away." Falcone blessed his luck for getting a taxi in minutes and headed for Taylor's Capitol Hill home.

Ben had left the front door unlocked. Falcone walked in and found Taylor at the kitchen table, hunched over Falcone's laptop. Next to it was an open dictionary and a notepad. In Taylor's left hand were a black ballpoint pen and a notebook. To the right of the laptop was a bottle of beer and a half-eaten sandwich on a paper towel.

"Sean, I'm so glad to see you," Taylor said, rising and hugging Sean, who was surprised by Taylor's rare emotional display. "This really shook me up. It was like Cole reached out and touched me."

"You okay?"

"Yeah, I'm fine," he said, sitting down again. "Real glad you're here. Darlene's out somewhere with Sam. Reading this, I didn't want to be alone. Grab a beer and make yourself a cheese sandwich," he said.

Falcone went to the refrigerator, took out a beer, and opened it while looking at the laptop screen over Taylor's shoulder. "Why did you come here?" Falcone asked.

"I came here for a dictionary," Taylor replied. "I needed this one" — he pointed to a Webster's dictionary with its fading red cover case half attached and bearing coffee-cup ring stains. "It's the one I need for decryption."

"Decryption? I don't get it," Falcone said.

"It's from Cole. Encrypted. I'm not surprised. It's Cole protecting himself."

"How's it going?"

"Just fine. Just fine," Taylor answered, tapping out two words. *God* and *dare* appeared on the screen.

"What the hell?"

"It means 'Goddard,' " Taylor said. " 'Goddard' doesn't make this edition of Webster's. But 'Hamilton' does. Both those words show up several times in the message. When I find a frequently used word, I jot it down with its coded form in the notebook." Looking closely at the computer screen, Falcone saw what he assumed was Cole Perenchio's encrypted message, line by line, with Taylor's decryptions between the lines.

"I can't believe you cracked it this quick," Falcone said. "You're a goddamn genius."

"That may be true. But in fact I knew the code system the minute I saw it," Taylor said. "It's an encryption system — called a dictionary code. Cole developed it for the three of us while we were in college. For it to work, all three of us had to have exactly the same dictionary. Each word in a message contains the page number, column number, and the sequential number of the word on that page and in that column. So theoretically this would be 'Hamilton.' " He scrawled "604233" on the notepad.

"But to make it a little harder, we put in a simple superencryption." He pointed to "9H7566" on the screen. "We added 'three' — Musketeers, get it? oh, how clever! — to each digit. So 'six' becomes 'nine' and 'four' becomes 'seven.' And 'zero' becomes H— Hal; 'one' becomes B— Ben; and 'two' becomes C— Cole. That's how those numbers and the letter" — he pointed to the screen again — "become 'Hamilton.' "

"Whose idea was it for the Three Musketeers to communicate in code?"

"Cole started it because he thought that someone had named us as members of the Black Panthers. He was always a touch paranoid."

"*Were* you guys Black Panthers?"

"Hell, no! We were too busy keeping our scholarships and getting four-point-oh GPAs. But Cole at the time was sort of the leader and we went along. The code came in handy when we were rating girls and we wanted to keep the ratings confidential."

"How long will it take Sarsfield and his chums to crack it?"

"They'll probably hand off the problem to the NSA. Any cryptographer there would quickly see it's a dictionary code. But what dictionary? What edition? That'll slow them down for a while. There isn't any punctuation. And spacing is arbitrary, so at first it looks like the message is in code words four or five characters long. Also, Cole drops words like 'an,' 'the,' 'of,' the idea being that the cryptographer doesn't get a chance to have any easy way into the encryption through those little words. And then there are the anomalies, like this one."

In the notebook list of frequently used words, Taylor drew a line under "Kuri

Basayev" and said, "Boy, what a name to decrypt! Cole produced Basayev's name by encrypting 'Cure,' then 'I,' 'B.A.,' 'say,' and 'ev' — that's the abbreviation for 'electron-volt.' See? 'Cure-I-BA-say-ev.' Took me a while to nail all those words as one name."

"Kuri Basayev?" Falcone exclaimed. "How the hell does he get in here?"

"It looks like he's Hamilton's silent partner. You'll see. What's the deal about him?"

"Basayev is a crime boss. And one of the richest, most powerful men in Russia," Falcone said. "We know from Senator Lawrence's research that the rocket to Asteroid USA was launched from that Russian site."

"Khrunichev State Research and Production Center," Taylor said. "And from what I know about that place, the Russians had to do some work there to accommodate the rocket they used to launch the SpaceMine spacecraft."

"Okay," Falcone said. He felt his old prosecutor instincts kicking in. He leaned toward the screen. "Just give me what you've got on that son of a bitch."

"Slow down, Sean. Slow down. Let me finish. Then we can see the whole message from Cole."

430

"How far along are you?"

Taylor stood, stretched his arms, and said, "Well more than halfway through. I've worked out a couple of algorithms. Applying them speeded things up. And there's a sharp learning curve."

"Can I start reading?"

"I'd prefer finishing it, giving it a read-through, and then printing it out. You want to start reading? Why not go into the living room and start reading that exciting new book, *It's Your Universe*?"

58

Three hours later, Taylor walked into the living room and found Falcone writing on a yellow pad. *It's Your Universe* lay open next to him on the couch. Taylor handed him a cup of coffee and a stapled document entitled "Cole's Message." Taylor had another copy. Without exchanging a word, they sat side by side and began reading.

The following is a faithful decryption of an untitled memorandum written by Cole Perenchio, my friend and a true friend of Earth. As is the typical practice in decryption, I have added only punctuation and minor words, such as "the," "a," and "of," which do not appear in the encryption. — Dr. Benjamin F. Taylor

First of all, I want to say that I believe in God. I am saying this right out in case someone comes along and accuses me of

432

theism and says that my belief in God, not scientific reality, is driving me. I can't tell you how many times I have been in a group of scientists (or engineers) and found that I was not only the only black man but also the only theist. All of this you might call a prelude to what I am about to set down. I found myself in a place and time, a where and when, that held the fate of the world. I suddenly realized that I could save the world. And, because I believe in God, I believe that God put me in that place and time.

The place was NASA's Goddard Space Flight Center. The time was a little while after an explosion over Chelyabinsk, Russia. That was an asteroid only about 50 feet in diameter. It never touched Earth. But the atmospheric explosion injured more than 1,200 people and broke almost all the windows in the city.

Fatefully, the explosion was extensively photographed, particularly by windshield cameras that Russian drivers favor. We were given an unprecedented opportunity to collect and analyze data about an asteroid that menaced the Earth. We could further our knowledge of the laws of orbital mechanics, possibly making it possible to develop a way to predict the time and probable place of an impact of future asteroids.

The day after the explosion, I went to my superiors at Goddard and said I wanted to drop the work I was doing on Moon-Earth gravitational variations and set up a task force that would study the Chelyabinsk event to see how it affects our estimates of asteroid impact probabilities. I have always considered NASA's attitude toward asteroids was to treat them as space objects rather than possible hazards.

Preliminary data from Chelyabinsk indicated that the traditional estimates of risk of impact may be ten times greater than we had thought. In my memo, marked urgent, I quoted Dr. Qing-Zhu Yin of the University of California at Davis, who said, "If humanity does not want to go the way of the dinosaurs, we need to study an event like this in detail." He estimated that the energy of the Russian explosion was equal to the blast from about 500 kilotons of TNT. As a matter of comparisons, each of the nuclear bombs that wiped out Hiroshima and Nagasaki had the explosive energy of about 16 kilotons of TNT.

My memo was ignored — just as all my memos have been ignored in the past. I had already been exiled to Goddard's Laser Ranging Facility, where I shot laser beams at the Moon and at satellites in order to get accurate measurements of Moon-Earth gravitational effects. I'm sure that our measurements are imprecise and need to be continually sharpened so we can make accurate predictions of asteroid orbits.

Shortly after the Chelyabinsk event — and the rebuff of my memo — I left NASA and contacted a headhunter firm, gave my qualifications, and said I believed I would be a good recruit for SpaceMine. I was known as an authority on gravitational fields and their effects on the orbits of objects in space. I soon was approached, hired, and on a plane to SpaceMine's headquarters in Palo Alto, California.

My plan was to infiltrate SpaceMine and do what I could to stop any attempt to endanger Earth. I would perform criminal acts, if necessary. In fact, as soon as I got all the data that I could, I walked out of the building and went into hiding, to write this and pass it on to Hal. I realize that I am taking a risky course. And I realize that I might even be killed because of what I have learned. So, if that happens, I ask the person who reads this to act on it, by presenting it to President Oxley.

When Falcone got this far, he stopped reading. A moment later, so did Taylor. Falcone described what had happened at FBI headquarters. After going over the analysis of the car and computer timelines, he said, "It's pretty clear that Hal had the laptop — with this coded message — in his possession when he was killed. When Cole called you, he would have known about Hal's murder. The killers followed him to Capitol Hill and shot him there."

"Why didn't they kill me when they had the chance?"

"You were saved by the laptop's GPS signal, which showed that the laptop was in the possession of someone on Pennsylvania Avenue."

"So it was *you* who might have been killed," Taylor said.

"All the GPS told them was that the laptop was somewhere in a building at 701. They knew it would be crazy to try knocking on random apartment doors in a building that had to have tight security. So, I guess, they decided to kill Cole because he knew what was in the laptop."

"Poor, poor Cole," Taylor said. They both resumed reading Cole's message.

59

At SpaceMine headquarters, I worked night and day analyzing all the data that came from the Chelyabinsk explosion, adding it to the data I had developed while working at Goddard. My conclusion was that we simply do not know enough about Near-Earth Objects, especially asteroids, to carry out SpaceMine's plans to extract ore from asteroids. I also believe that there is a hidden side to SpaceMine involving a Russian silent partner named Kuri Basayev. He seemed to me to be a gangster. Initially, I wasn't able to determine his role.

"There it is!" Falcone exclaimed, reaching this point before Taylor.

"Keep on reading," Taylor said. "There's more."

When I began my work at SpaceMine, I soon deduced that the asteroid known to astronomers as Janus had been selected for mining and would be given the name Asteroid USA. I wrote an urgent report based on what is known about Janus and its hazardous, Earth-threatening orbit. After getting the usual run-around from a hierarchy of bosses, I slipped into the executive office wing and demanded to see Robert Wentworth Hamilton to show him my report.

He asked me to sit while he read the 26-page report. When he got to about the fourth page, he handed the report back to me and said, "Kind of long, Perenchio. You guessed right. We're aiming at Janus."

"Please, Mr. Hamilton. I implore you to at least read the summary of my findings," I said, referring to the following passage:

Investigation of the orbit of the asteroid known as Janus reveals a 20-minute interval in April 2035 when there is a high probability of the asteroid colliding with Earth. Trajectory knowledge remains accurate until then because of extensive astrometric data, an inclined orbit geometry that reduces in-plane perturbations, and an orbit uncertainty that is deepened by gravitational resonance. In 2035 this uncertainty will be further increased by accelerations arising from the thermal reradiation of solar energy absorbed by the asteroid. The accelerations depend on the spin axis, the composition, and the surface properties of the asteroid. So refining the collision probability may require direct inspection by a spacecraft long before 2035.

After reading this, Hamilton said, "You mean I should send up a spacecraft just to look at the asteroid? And have it come back empty? Look, Perenchio. I'm a businessman, not a scientist. When we send up a rocket, it's not going to come back empty."

"I cannot make it more clear, Mr. Hamilton," I said. "There is a high probability that this asteroid will strike the Earth in 2035. Attempts to mine Janus would raise the risk of putting it through a gravitational keyhole, a place in space created when the Earth's gravity's alters an asteroid's orbit in such a way that the asteroid will collide with Earth on a future orbital pass." I told him that he was running that very risk in his attempt to move Janus without more proper research and controls.

"Listen, Perenchio," Hamilton said, laughing. "If things go my way, there won't be much left of that asteroid by 2035.

Besides, if it should ever hit, it would only be the end of this world. That might be a blessing. A gift from God. End of discussion."

I didn't know what to make of his comment. It was bizarre, too cynical.

Then he said, dismissing me, "You were hired to give us credibility. We knew you were NASA's expert on extraterritorial gravitation. All you were supposed to do for your paycheck was provide NASA credentials for an imprimatur on Space-Mine's plans. If you can't do that, we'll find someone who will."

I was in the Future Projects Department, and I had access to just about any database I wanted. The moment I walked out of Mr. Hamilton's office I decided to gather as much information about Space-Mine as I could, with the intent of publicly warning that SpaceMine was putting Earth in danger. And I was determined to find a way to destroy SpaceMine.

Because I had Privileged EXEC, the highest security level at SpaceMine, I found it amazingly easy to insert my ID card into the proper computer slot and hack into SpaceMine's data files. I knew I could cause havoc by tampering with them. But I was in for the long game.

441

Hamilton is extraordinarily concerned about security at SpaceMine. He relies mostly on his security director, a former NSA official. He was responsible for the so-called tamper-proof laptops like the one I am writing on. The USB slots are disabled and they cannot be connected to the Internet. They are issued to workers who do not have Privileged EXEC clearance.

The laptops have live-surveillance chips through the webcam and microphone features. Supervisors can surreptitiously hear and photograph users through a standard piece of software called RAT for Remote Administration Tool. There's also a tracker that uses GPS data to trace any travels the laptop may make.

At the end of a work shift, the laptops are collected by the Security Office, emptied, and their contents distributed to the proper superiors with Privileged EXEC clearance. It was easy for me to obtain this laptop simply by forging an acquisition permit. I was able to disable RAT but decided to allow the tracker to function, figuring it might be useful.

All e-mail accounts must be sent and received through desktop computers that are monitored by the Security Office. But the e-mail accounts are amazingly easy to hack.

On the day I had my meeting with Hamilton, he sent an e-mail to his lawyer, a Paul Sprague at sullivanford.com, in Washington, telling him to check up on me through a private investigator that Hamilton apparently regularly uses. In the e-mail, he stressed the importance of Janus to SpaceMine: "It's worth around eight trillion dollars."

"Sprague!" Falcone said, thumping an index finger on the page and turning to Taylor. "He was on to Cole . . . and he was on to you right after the shootings."

After Falcone briefly recounted his conversation with Ursula, Taylor said, "So Sprague heard me on *Street Speak* and probably sent the transcript to Hamilton."

"And you began having your troubles. Hamilton started pulling his power levers: show canceled, administrative leave . . ."

"Right," Taylor said, looking shaken. He calmed quickly and said, "Read on."

I checked Sprague's name on the Internet and learned that he is in the same law firm that Hal Davidson is in. That made me cautious, lest Hal get in trouble. I did a name-search for Davidson in the e-mail accounts. I found that his name occurred once in a Sprague-Hamilton e-mail exchange that mentioned an interest in mineral mining in Africa.

Falcone looked up from the document and said, "As I remember, you said something about African mining on the *Street Speak* show."

Taylor thought for a moment and said, "I think I just said SpaceMine would be using robots and wouldn't have problems with miners' strikes. It was just an offhand remark."

"But I'm convinced that somehow Space-Mine and the miners are tied together," Falcone said. "Did you know that Hal Davidson was doing pro bono work on the African miners' strike?"

"I didn't see Hal that often — maybe lunch once in a while, a birthday party at his house. All we did when we were together was reminisce about the old days. He never talked shop. What are you getting at?"

"You know that I think Hal was a deliberate hit. Hamilton must know that."

"That's a stretch, Sean."

"I don't mean that Hamilton ordered it. I mean he *knows*. Read the next couple of paragraphs."

There is one e-mail account that goes through a highly secured router. Since I hope that this document will be presented to President Oxley, all I can do is list the clues I have and hope that the U.S. Government, with better resources, will be able to determine Hamilton's relationship with a Russian associate named Kuri Basayev.

I found one message, which came in from Basayev. After that date, a new layer of encryption was added because Basayev had become involved with SpaceMine and was shielded by its most effective safeguards.

Here is the message: "I have arranged to take over the Khrunichev State Research and Production Center, where expensive modifications had to be made to arrange for the launch of your Space-Mine rocket. If you want your rocket to reach Asteroid USA safely, you will agree to sell me 40 percent of your proposed Initial Public Offering at 2 percent below the opening price. Details can be worked out through your Mr. Sprague." It was signed K. Basayev.

As Hamilton has just announced, the

rocket did reach the asteroid. So I must conclude that Basayev's extortion worked.

Hamilton and Basayev seem to have exchanged some more e-mails because I came across several references to Basayev in Hamilton's e-mails to Paul Sprague. One of them complained about "Davidson's work in Africa." When I saw that, I felt I had to warn Hal. But things began tightening up here. I could see addressees and subject lines, but I was no longer able to read the messages themselves.

"Jesus! I'm starting to see it," Falcone said. "Hal probably suspected that someone was bribing the strike leader to continue shutting down mining operations. Now Cole sees Basayev's name. He was keeping supply low so that the price of palladium goes up. And when he and Hamilton start digging on Janus, they'll have a goddamn monopoly."

"Okay. Now you're the genius here, Sean. Finish up."

To enter SpaceMine's databases, I had an enable password — a random group of numbers and letters — that changes every twelve seconds. The entry device contains the user's right thumb print and is usable only on-site. That takes you into User EXEC. After using a second, frequently changing password, I gained Privileged EXEC status on a special router terminal that enables full use of all databases. I am sure that with this knowledge a skilled NSA operative can penetrate SpaceMine.

As soon as I got all the data that I could, I walked out of the building and went into hiding, to write this and pass it on to Hal.

"We need to get these printouts and your laptop into a safe-deposit box," Taylor said. "I feel as paranoid as Cole must have been."

"You're right to be scared," Falcone said. He stood and began pacing as he spoke. "What I'm seeing now is this: Cole contacts Hal and arranges to hand over the laptop on October second. That shows up on the computer and car timelines I told you about.

"Hal calls Sprague and says he has a laptop that belongs to Hamilton and will meet Sprague on October fourth. Sprague calls Hamilton. And Hamilton calls Basayev, who says he'll take care of the problem. Then that Russian motherfucker decides to send his goons to retrieve the computer and take out Hal. Two problems solved with one hit made to look like a random multi-shooting. Next day, you get the panic call from Cole. And —"

"And the goons kill Cole," Taylor said. He shook his head and added, "If we know this much, imagine what the pros know. The FBI, the NSA, the CIA —"

"You think, in other words, that the government knows all this, right? Government trial and judgment, as in Department of Justice and grand juries? I doubt that very much, Ben. For one thing, top officials at the FBI and the CIA still don't talk to each other, and that's also true of a lot of people who are in the White House. I think it's up to us right now."

"So what do we do next?"

"You go to Goddard — and Ben, for Christ's sake, don't drive yourself this time!"

"Okay. Okay."

"And try to find out all you can about Cole and what he was doing there. We need to know if he was loony or on to something big enough to be murdered for."

"And what about you?"

"I'm going to find out what I can about Basayev. And I won't be asking the FBI or the CIA."

60

The day after Ben Taylor decrypted Cole's message, he called Karen Thiessan at Goddard. Karen was the project manager of LOLA, the lunar orbiter laser altimeter that had been carried in NASA's lunar reconnaissance orbiter spacecraft. LOLA's job was to measure the shape of the moon by precisely measuring the distance from the spacecraft to the lunar surface. Cole Perenchio, in his encrypted message, said he had been exiled to Goddard's Laser Ranging Facility, as Taylor's earlier call to Human Resources had confirmed. And Taylor knew that the Laser Ranging Facility was involved with LOLA.

"I'm not surprised by your call, Ben," Thiessan said after Taylor told her he wanted to talk to her about Perenchio. "You knew Cole better than I did, and I'm sure his murder is even more of a shock to you than it was to me. And . . . it's been a while."

They arranged to meet the following night. That was the best time to be at the range, because that was when the place came to life.

As soon as Taylor got on the Baltimore–Washington Parkway in his rental car he felt he was on familiar ground. He had lied to Falcone about not driving out to Goddard, but it was only a white lie. Besides, he would be more careful this time. Six and a half miles north on the parkway was Greenbelt, Maryland, and the Goddard Space Flight Center, which brought together America's largest concentration of scientists and engineers.

Taylor the scientist and Perenchio the engineer. . . . That's the way it looked on the NASA payroll. But Taylor was remembering the unique atmosphere of Goddard, where the labels meant little when men and women of both persuasions plunged into a project.

Taylor and Perenchio had worked together in Goddard's Exoplanets and Stellar Astrophysics Laboratory, which studied the formation and evolution of stars and planets. Cole was especially fascinated by the thousands of exoplanets that existed far beyond our own solar system.

Engineers like Cole built such instruments as the Hubble Space Telescope and the imaging spectrograph; scientists like Ben tried to figure out what the devices were showing them. Cole designed and helped to build an instrument that identified the contents of the atmospheres of exoplanets when they were passing in front of their suns. One day the engineers and scientists cheered at the news that faint signs of water had been discovered on five exoplanets, raising the likelihood of life beyond the solar system. That was a day of great joy for Cole, Taylor remembered. "Life, Ben!" Cole had exclaimed. "Life is showing the power of God's universe!"

Taylor's memories brought back a Cole Perenchio who had never quite found the niche for his genius. He had been brilliant at MIT — "a credit to his race," a phrase that infuriated him but became a mocking line for the other Musketeers. After getting his doctorate, he was invited for a postdoc sojourn at the Institute for Advanced Study, in Princeton. But he had chosen NASA, drawn to its promise of an amazing future, built upon its man-on-the-moon triumph.

Cole had bounced around NASA: the space shuttle, the International Space Station, the early work on space telescopes and sensitive spectrographs. All that while he had been becoming more withdrawn and simultaneously more religious, beginning with Buddhism and finally ending with an embrace of a kind of Christianity that followed the thinking of the Jesuit paleontologist Pierre Teilhard de Chardin. He believed that the Earth, with an enlightened humanity, could evolve toward the noosphere, a mystic sphere of pure thought.

The last time he saw Cole, Ben remembered, they were sitting on a bench in Lafayette Park, across the street from the White House, and Cole was talking about de Chardin and his theory of complexity and consciousness. . . . Taylor could barely understand what Cole was saying, but his voice was soothing and he seemed happier than Ben had ever seen him. . . .

Taylor drove instinctively toward the employee gate and was politely directed to the visitors' entrance, where he parked and called Karen Thiessan. A few minutes later, he saw her leave the visitors' center and pass rapidly across the beam of his headlights. She was a large woman, "full-bodied," as she sometimes laughingly called herself. A long black coat gave her a rectangular figure. Her black hair was short and gray-streaked. She carried an immense handbag.

She opened the passenger door, slipped in gracefully, leaned across, and gave Taylor a kiss that touched his cheek and a corner of his lips. "Good evening, Ben," she said. "Where have you been keeping yourself?"

"Work, work, and more work," he said, instantly regretting his pathological inability to make small talk. "Well, not really," he added. "I think I'm becoming dull, dull, and more dull."

Thiessan laughed and touched his cheek with a soft, cool hand. "You still look good to me," she said, kindling his memory of the night two years before when, after a retirement party for a mutual friend, he had wound up in her bed. That had started something. They had dated a few times after that, but she had left for the Jet Propulsion Laboratory in California on a temporary assignment and had not found a way to start something again.

She directed him back to the highway and toward the gate that led to the Laser Ranging Facility, on the western edge of the campus, as employees usually called the center. He turned off the highway more than a mile from the cluster of buildings that was the heart of Goddard. The guard gave her a hearty hello, glanced at Taylor's visitor ID, and waved them down a two-lane road that could have been a country lane. Moonlight rippled through the dark trees flanking the road.

"You've been to the range before, haven't you?" she asked.

"No. The moon wasn't on my agenda much."

"Too bad. It's an interesting place."

"Cole, you know, said that being assigned to the Laser Ranging Facility was like being exiled."

"A lot of the moon rangers say that," Thiessan said, laughing. "But most of them wind up liking it out here, far from the chatter and the office politics." She was cheery and easygoing, a rare quality in a bureaucracy full of grim-faced men and women who managed Goddard through budget cuts, layoffs, sequesters, and government shutdowns.

She had once claimed that a good way to get a proposal started at Goddard was to come up with a snappy acronym, and LOLA was a fine example. The acronym had become famous at Goddard. And her project had been launched so smoothly that managers of other projects claimed it all had to do with its catchy name, and the inevitable claim that "Whatever LOLA wants, LOLA gets."

"So, Ben. What's this all about?" she asked.

Taylor told of how Cole had called and acted frightened. "But he was shot before he had a chance to tell me anything," Taylor said. He had decided not to mention Cole's encrypted message. "I had an idea . . . just an idea that it had something to do with what he was doing here."

"Do you think Cole's murder had anything to do with the shooting at that law firm?"

Surprised, Taylor said, "What do you mean?"

"Come on, Ben. I knew about the Black Musketeers long before that awful *Grudge Report* story. Certainly it must have occurred to you that there was a connection."

"God, Karen, you really know how to get right to the point. Yeah, I did think of that. I've been questioned by the FBI. They took over Cole's murder from the DC cops. But, honest, I don't know what the connection is — or if there is one."

"What makes you think there's some answer out here?" Thiessan asked with a sweeping motion of her hand. Before Taylor could respond, he could see the moonlit outlines of the trailers and sheds that jutted up along the outpost's narrow road.

"Pull up over here," she said, pointing to four cars and a pickup truck parked in a paved area alongside the road. She took a flashlight out of her handbag and pointed to a figure coming toward them. "Dick Gillespie," she said. "He's the manager. We're in luck." When they got out of the car, she did not turn on the flashlight. "They don't like lights out here."

She introduced Gillespie and said, "Ben was a friend of Cole's."

"It's a privilege to meet you, Dr. Taylor," Gillespie said, shaking hands. He led them into a windowless, unpainted concrete-block structure that looked as if it had started out as a garage. A dim, flickering fluorescent light fixture hung from the low ceiling over a wooden table with a scarred top. Three metal chairs had been unfolded and placed around the table. Gillespie sat on one side, Taylor and Thiessan opposite him.

"Welcome to the moon base," Gillespie said. He pointed to a wooden bookcase in a dark corner. "You go through the journals on those shelves and you'll find some of your publications. Like I said, Doctor, a privilege. Karen says you were a friend of Cole's." He paused, then lowered his voice and asked, "Do you know what happened?

Why it happened?"

"Call me Ben, Dick," Taylor said. He shook his head and repeated what he had told Karen Thiessan. "I had an idea that he may have said something out here that could give me a lead to what was . . . frightening him."

"Cole usually didn't have much to say," Gillespie replied. "Except once in a while he'd talk about de Chardin and the future of the human race. Heady stuff. But it seemed to come naturally to him."

Taylor smiled and nodded. "I got a couple of doses of de Chardin, too."

"Cole was here, you know, when that asteroid skimmed over that Russian city — the same day that another asteroid came close. That *really* got him going."

Taylor knew that the day had been a turning point for Cole, but he did not want to mention the encrypted Cole message. "What happened?" he asked. "What did he do?"

"He sat down at that computer over there," Gillespie said, pointing to a vintage PC on a table near the bookcase. "And he began pounding away at a memo to the director of Goddard with a copy to the administrator of NASA."

"What did the memo say?" Taylor asked.

"Essentially, he wanted an overnight change in NASA's missions. He wanted us to begin a major effort to start a defense of Earth. That's what he called it. A defense of Earth."

"What happened?" Thiessan asked. "I never heard anything about it."

"Nothing happened. Absolutely nothing," Gillespie answered. "So he sent another and another. He believed that the Russian air-burst was a sign — not from a divine source but from collective human consciousness, a warning that we must defend Earth against asteroids on collision orbits. Finally Human Resources sent him an invitation for a consultation. He ignored that and all of a sudden he focused all his energy right here."

"How?" Taylor asked. "What did he do?"

Gillespie looked at his watch and stood up and said, "Maybe if we walk around and you see what we do out here, you'd understand. . . ."

61

Gillespie led them up the road to two trailers that were attached together alongside a platform for what looked like the dome for a small telescope. As they mounted the steps to the platform, they heard a fusillade that sounded nearby. Taylor ducked and flattened himself against the platform.

"That's the Secret Service training center on a night exercise," Gillespie said. "They're our neighbors on this great big piece of federal real estate. They could give us warning when they start shooting. But it's hush-hush. They make believe we aren't here and we make believe that they aren't here."

Gillespie opened the trailer door and yelled to someone inside: "Okay, let her rip!"

The white dome swung around, a lid slid back, and from what looked like the tube of a telescope came a narrow green light that cut across the sky toward the moon. "That's a laser beam that is enclosed in a kind of radar envelope," Gillespie said. "If the radar detects an aircraft nearing the beam, the beam is automatically turned off so that it will not disturb or harm pilots."

"So the beam is aiming at the moon. Looks like an easy target tonight," Taylor said.

"But what we're aiming at, Ben, is a bit smaller," Gillespie said. "Our target is the lunar reconnaissance orbiter spacecraft that's zooming at nearly thirty-six hundred miles per hour in its orbit around the moon. And inside is Karen's wonderful LOLA, the lunar orbiter laser altimeter."

"She — of course, LOLA is a she — sends back distance measurements accurate to within about four inches," Thiessan said. "We need accuracy like that for the maps we'll need before we send anybody back to the moon."

"It's getting a little chilly down here on Earth," Gillespie said. "Let's go inside."

The joined trailers were crammed with electronic panels. Gillespie, Taylor, and Thiessan walked single-file, squeezing past shelves and narrow tables bearing computers whose screens displayed ever-changing lines that peaked and plunged across graphs or turned into squads of digits marching left to right, then right to left. Taylor could

460

infer what some of them were reporting. But there were so many displays of data that they became to his eyes pieces of a jigsaw puzzle that was undoubtedly interesting.

"Measurements. Measurements. Measurements. That's what we do," Gillespie said. He was pointing to one of the screens. "That's one of the measurements that Cole began obsessing on. Without going into detail, it's one of the data points he used in his gravitational studies. And it's what brought him down."

"I don't get it," Thiessan said.

"His defense of Earth," Gillespie said, "was defense against asteroids. Part of that defense was determining precise forecasting of near-Earth asteroids. And that involved knowing all there was to know about the gravitational interplay between the moon and the Earth."

Words in Cole's message popped into Taylor's mind. *Gravitation. Gravitational keyhole. Imprecise measurements.* "What happened?" he asked.

"When I was here, I could control him. Or thought I could. He was insisting on data that were not in our regular drill. Essentially, he was trying to run his numbers inside our numbers. He was a fanatic about it. I tried to humor him and at the same

461

time stay on our regular LOLA schedule. Then one night I wasn't here and all hell broke loose."

He paused, not for dramatic effect, Taylor believed, but because he was recalling a painful event.

"I told you that we don't fire a beam if radar indicates there's an aircraft in the airspace of the beam. Well, that night he was running the show, and the radar picked up an aircraft. Cole ordered the beam fired. The guys on duty refused. But Cole, he could be a tyrant, like those guys who think they're on the list for a Nobel. So he did it on his own. The aircraft was Air Force One."

"My God!" Karen said.

"It so happened that the Secret Service's number-two guy was next door. He got word as soon as the aircraft and its pissed-off pilot landed. A big black SUV roared up and Cole was whisked away. Next morning, the head of Human Resources and a couple of people from the director's staff are talking to Cole at a Secret Service office downtown. And Cole agrees to a leave of absence."

"But he went to work for SpaceMine," Taylor said. "How did —"

"I know. The whole thing was hushed up by the Secret Service. I guess so that nuts wouldn't get ideas. And the director himself signed off on a glowing recommendation. Cole was a genius, you know."

They followed him out of the trailer and back to Gillespie's moon base. "Those e-mails that Cole sent about the asteroid explosion," Taylor said, "could I see them?"

"I'm sorry," Gillespie said. "Those little gems were deleted from the system."

"By whom?" Thiessan asked.

"I have no idea," Gillespie said. "I just work here. But I do have this." He went over to the bookcase and from a wire basket on top of it he pulled out a sheet of paper. "Cole sent me this e-mail. It's from him at SpaceMine, asking for the latest LOLA measurements."

"When is it dated?" Taylor asked.

"September thirtieth," Gillespie answered.

"I think that was his last day at Space-Mine," Taylor said. "And five days later he was killed."

62

Falcone knew he had to move carefully when dealing with Philip Dake, who did not *give* information. He *traded* what he knew for what you knew. Falcone realized that the instant he asked, "What do you know about Kuri Basayev," Dake would start his what-have-you-got-to-trade game.

"You must be psychic," Philip Dake said when Falcone called him and asked about Basayev.

"No one has ever accused me of being psychic," Falcone said. "Where does that come from?"

"It's my project on Hamilton," Dake said. "I was just writing up some notes on Kuri Basayev when you called. Seems he appeared in Hamilton's radar a while back, just about the time Hamilton announced the startup of SpaceMine. I can't figure Hamilton mixing in with Basayev. So why all of a sudden are you wondering about

Basayev, too?"

"I want to talk about him with you," Falcone said. "Can you come over, have some phone-in food, and give me a bit of Basayev?"

"Glad to. Because I'm familiar with your phone-in cuisine, I'll bring some decent sandwiches. What's the rush?"

"Something has come up," Falcone answered. "I'll tell you when you get here." The game had begun. *How much can I tell him?*

"Okay. I'll pull together some bits on Basayev and drop by in an hour or so."

Falcone envisioned Dake's Georgetown home office. Filing cabinets lined the walls. In the cabinets were file folders bulging with information from precomputer days. And nearby were two or three computers, where Dake and his assistant typed away, putting facts into hard drives instead of filing cabinets.

Dake had a passion for finding information where nobody else could find it. And no one had ever successfully challenged him on any substantial fact, but his conclusions and accusations created controversies — and made his books into best sellers. In a book describing the administration that preceded Oxley's, for example, Dake once accused a high-ranking Pentagon official of getting kickbacks from defense contractors. Sued for libel, Dake triumphed, and the official went off to eight years in a federal prison.

While waiting for Dake, Falcone went into his office and turned on the PC standing on his mahogany desk and brought up Kuri Basayev on Wikipedia. He was described as the son of one of the few Chechens to reach the zenith of riches and power in postcommunist Russia. The Wikipedia entry, as usual, bristled with what appeared to be facts but refrained from analysis. *How the hell did a Chechen become an oligarch?*

Falcone went on to read that Kuri "was a brilliant student at the elite Moscow State Institute of International Relations, the diplomatic school for the Ministry of Foreign Affairs. An avid linguist, he became proficient in German, English, and Sesotho, three of the fifty-six languages taught at the institute. He spent three years as a cultural affairs officer at the Russian Embassy in Pretoria, South Africa.

"Kuri Basayev's diplomatic career ended after his father's death in an automobile accident in Moscow. He took over the family's holdings and added interests in mines in

South Africa. Basayev's immense wealth came from oil, natural gas, and the mining of palladium, a relatively rare metal that was becoming an important ingredient in electronics and catalytic converters."

Falcone was still wondering about Basayev's curious career when the concierge called to say that Dake had arrived. Falcone met him at the entrance hall. Dake was carrying a cloth bag containing sandwiches and wine. Slung over his shoulder was a laptop bag. *God! Another laptop,* Falcone thought as he stood at the doorway.

At the kitchen counter they unpacked the sandwiches and filled their wineglasses. After a sip and a smile of appreciation, Dake opened his laptop, turned it on, and said, "To talk about Kuri Basayev, you begin with his yacht. She's a target for the paparazzi whenever she finds a yacht basin that's big enough to accommodate her."

On the screen appeared a frozen-video image of a sleek white ship with layers of multiwindowed covered decks. "This is a video taken at Antibes on the French Riviera," Dake said. "The spot is known as the Millionaire Quay, a quaint name that ought to be updated to Billionaire Quay.

"Superrich guys seem to compete for who

has the biggest yacht. This is Basayev's entry. She's five hundred and thirty-two feet long, has four topside decks, and is second only to the five-hundred-and-ninety-footer owned by the president of U.A.E. Basayev's *Aglaya* — it means 'splendor' in Russian — has two helicopter pads, two swimming pools, and accommodations for a couple of dozen guests.

"Because Basayev has so many enemies he's rightfully paranoid. The yacht's bridge and his private suite are protected with armor plating and bulletproof glass. *Aglaya* also has a laser shield that detects and sizzles electronic devices, particularly cameras. Watch this."

Dake turned on the video. The image of *Aglaya* changed from bows-on to a starboard view as the video camera began circling the yacht. Suddenly there was a blast of light and the screen went blank.

"Bingo!" Dake exclaimed. "Basayev doesn't like being photographed. And he has teams of experts working to keep him as invisible as possible. For the past couple of years, he has mostly lived aboard *Aglaya*, rarely coming ashore. Folks trying to keep an eye on *Aglaya* — such as the NSA or Russia's Federal Security Service — find she's hard to track. I'm told that she sails a course based on handoffs from one communications satellite to another. Not going anywhere in particular, favoring areas where satellite signals are spotty."

Dake pulled up the image of Basayev and the bodyguard that had appeared in the *New York Post.* "He's usually surrounded by big, tough-looking Chechens," Dake went on. "And they flatten the photographer along with his camera." Then he noticed the credit: GOOGLE GLASS IMAGE. "Modern technology. No camera but he still gets a couple of kicks. I'll bet he is on his way to the *Aglaya,* which is —"

"Docked at Pier Ninety," Falcone said, laughing at Dake's surprise.

"Come on, Sean," Dake said. "You must know a lot about this guy already. What's up?"

"He looks younger than I thought he'd look," Falcone said.

"You didn't answer my question," Dake said, sounding irritated.

"I'll tell you what I can tell you in the fullness of time."

"Oh, God. Your favorite put-off phrase."

Falcone ignored the remark. "What puzzles me about Basayev is that he's Chechen," Falcone said, refilling their glasses. "Russians are supposed to hate

Chechens. The Chechen-Russian civil war. That horrible school massacre. Hundreds of kids killed by Chechen Islamists. The theater where the Chechens held the audience hostage, killing I don't know how many. The Moscow subway bomb. They're heartless bastards."

"The Russians hate the Chechens — and they fear them," Dake said. "You say 'Chechen' to Russians, and they get an image of that school or that theater. The monster behind both of those atrocities was a terrorist named Shamil Basayev. And in some cousin-of-cousin way, Kuri Basayev is related to Shamil Basayev."

"Shamil's dead, right?"

"Right. Targeted assassination by Russia's Federal Security Service. What the KGB used to call a wet job. In 2006, as I remember. So Shamil's dead. And Lebed is so popular, so good at being charismatic, that he convinced Russians that Kuri Basayev is a good guy, a Lebed guy. But, from what I'm told by people who watch Chechen-brand terrorists, Kuri is on a hit list."

"Russian?"

"Nope. Chechen."

"I don't get it."

"It's the yacht."

"What do you mean?"

"Basayev's father was a pal of Vladimir Putin, who reached out . . . carefully . . . to a few chosen Chechens, all sinfully rich. The elder Basayev was portrayed in Russian media as an okay Chechen. And he flaunted his wealth in an acceptable Russian way: beautiful women, night clubs, being driven around in big foreign cars. He was a flashy Muscovite, part of the city scene." Dake turned off the laptop and closed it. "Chechens took offense.

"Young Basayev," Dake continued, "hasn't set foot in Chechnya in a couple of years. But he's a member of Lebed's brain trust, and totally protected by him."

Falcone reported what he had read in the Wikipedia entries and said, "I didn't see any of that information in there."

"Those entries are all dry-cleaned," Dake said. "Basayev's says that, after getting all of his fancy college degrees, he was in the Russian Foreign Service. But he really was under diplomatic cover working for the Federal Security Service, the new and improved KGB. He was a Putin protégé. Then, he became one of the money men behind Boris Lebed's election. And that stuff about Kuri's father in an automobile accident? It was a hit-and-run in broad daylight in Moscow. The rumor is that the Chechen underground handed Kuri a warning by killing his father."

"Why? What was behind it?" Falcone asked. He began making coffee.

"They consider Kuri a traitor. He's not just making money through bribes and extortion in the accepted oligarch business model. He's stepped way over the line. He's been getting into big-time crime, taking over the Afghan heroin express to Russia and trying to get a piece of Mexico narcotics.

"He tried to take over the Chechen crime syndicate and killed a couple of their warlords. So the syndicate killed his father. Then he helped the Russian police find his father's killers.

"Now killing Kuri is a matter of Chechen honor."

63

Falcone's cell phone rang. He tried to
ignore it. But he never could avoid looking
at the ID panel. When he saw that the caller
was US GOVERNMENT, he went into the living room and answered with a crisp
"Falcone here."

"This is Agent Sarsfield. With the
resources available at this time, we are unable to decrypt the laptop contents."

"Why is that?"

Falcone could hear Sarsfield sigh and say,
"As you undoubtedly know, the file in question was encrypted. I am calling to
determine whether you have decrypted it.
This could save us time and —"

"No. I did not decrypt it. How could I?
The thumb drive is in the possession of the
FBI."

"Surely, Mr. Falcone, you have a copy."

"No. I do not."

"Are you aware, Mr. Falcone, it is a

federal crime to make a false statement to an FBI agent or any other federal investigator?"

"I am quite aware of that, Agent Sarsfield. I repeat: I do not have in my possession a copy of the thumb drive."

"Very well. It may become necessary for me to obtain a search warrant."

"Give my regards to the judge. Goodbye."

64

When Falcone returned to the kitchen, Dake asked, "What was that all about?"

"My favorite FBI agent. Let's go back to Basayev."

Dake looked wary, deciding whether to press Falcone about the call. Falcone smiled inwardly, realizing what was going on in Dake's brain.

As national security advisor, he had seen dozens of profiles like the one he was getting from Dake. The profiles came from CIA analysts whose job was to piece together bits of information about people the White House wanted to know about. The profiles were almost always highly readable and often provided insights that Falcone found useful. Dake's sketch of Basayev convinced Falcone that Dake had got most of his information directly from a top-secret CIA profile. The thought was not far-fetched, given the authoritative tone of

Dake's *Post* articles and books.

Dake finished his sandwich and poured himself another glass of wine. "Okay, Sean. Now tell me what the hell this is all about. Why the sudden interest in this guy?"

During Dake's commentary on Basayev, Falcone had been awaiting the inevitable question and was mentally framing an answer. He wanted Dake on his side, and so he had to tell him the truth, but it had to be a limited truth. Falcone's basic formula was Facts plus Opinion minus Sources.

"Basayev is a silent partner in Space-Mine," he began. "We — Ben Taylor and I — believe that Hal Davidson was essentially a Basayev-ordered mob hit, and the other Sullivan and Ford victims were killed as a coverup."

Dake nodded and did not seem surprised. "You get this from your old pal J. B. Patterson?"

"I'm not going to tell you who told me about anything that I'm going to tell you," Falcone said. He then described the way he got the SpaceMine laptop, how the FBI took over the case, and what happened when he and Ursula went to the FBI. He also sketched what Patterson told him, including the discovery of the Fast and Furious gun.

Now Dake did look surprised. He seemed to be wandering through some thoughts for a moment, and then he asked, "Why do you think the FBI was so eager to take over the shooting of Perenchio and the people at your former law firm? And why hasn't Director Patterson jumped all over the case and put Sprague in handcuffs?"

"Good questions. My answer: Because the Justice Department doesn't want to get roasted again over that stupid Fast and Furious operation."

"I don't think so," Dake said. "Patterson had an assistant attorney general at his side when you and Ursula were there. James Cosgrove, right?"

Falcone nodded and, with a hint of exasperation, said, "And I suppose you know him."

"As a matter of fact, I do. And I know he's a heavyweight. His specialty is keeping the AG out of trouble. He was not sitting there just because of the Fast and Furious angle, Basayev and the shootings. Serious as they are."

"You sound as if you already know some of this. So why didn't you write about it? Or write about it now? Saving it for a book?"

"Thanks for the vote of confidence. There's a rogue CIA cell that has been using Basayev to get into the Russian Defense Ministry, which has been supplying advanced rocket technology to Iran's Islamic Revolutionary Guard Corps."

"Basayev is an agent for us? Phil, you've got to be shitting me!"

"I wish I were. But it looks true, especially in light of what a couple of CIA analysts did in running that poor old retired FBI agent in Iran. None of the bosses knew about that one either, until his family blew a whistle. And my story sounds as if it comes from the same playbook."

"Jesus! Won't those by-the-book dicks ever learn?"

"Apparently not. The recruiter was also a former FBI agent. He had been stationed in Moscow as part of the bureau's counter-narcotics operation. Spoke fluent Russian. Son of Russian émigrés. Educated at Brandeis. Did graduate work at London School of Economics. Retired two years ago. He's been living in Dubai, where there are a lot of oligarchs playing in the sand."

"How the hell could they get away with it?

"Same way the other guys did. They came upon a juicy piece of intel and knew that the only way to keep it going was to keep their big boss totally in the dark. None of the big brass knows about the operation."

"So the DCI is blind on this?"

"Yep. So is the secretary of defense. And the director of national intelligence."

"How the hell could that happen?"

"The NSA kicked it off inadvertently by picking up calls between Hamilton and Basayev. Not just length and time, the so-called metadata, but actual conversations that they were able to decrypt."

"Conversations? For that the NSA needs a warrant."

"No warrant. The CIA is essentially blackmailing the NSA because if this got out, the NSA gets more trouble for breaking the law."

"But this is basically pointless," Falcone said, shaking his head. "The conversations would be fruit from a poison tree if the U.S. tried to prosecute on that evidence."

"Right. But in one conversation it looks like Basayev is trying to link up with Hamilton to take advantage of SpaceMine technology and ultimately gain control of the palladium market, which would cut into the Russian economy. The rogues think they can turn Basayev by threatening to reveal his back-office deal with Hamilton to his pal Lebed."

"But at this point neither Oxley nor Lebed

has a clue about what's going on. And that means if this comes out Oxley will be shown doing business with a billionaire mobster who's murdered at least five American citizens and has helped put our planet in jeopardy!"

"Well put. Looks like you jumped Oxley's ship at the right time," Dake said. He poured himself a cup of coffee and proffered the carafe to Falcone, who held up his cup to be filled.

"Christ, if I were still there I wouldn't have had any knowledge about this insane operation," Falcone said.

"No, but you might have been taken down just the same. That's the way fall-on-my-sword usually works."

"When do you think you'll be blowing this wide open?"

"Right now I have only one source. A good agency source. But, as with most good sources, this one has an ax to grind. I need at least two more sources before I can think about going with this. The public already knows that a U.S. immigration agent was killed by one of the guns the ATF allowed to be sold to Mexican drug gangs. Just think what the reaction will be that another ATF gun ended up in the hands of Chechens who killed all those folks at Sullivan and

Ford. Someone's head would be sure to roll. Maybe Patterson's. Maybe the attorney general's."

"Well, you've caused heads to roll before, Phil."

"Yeah. But this one scares me. The SpaceMine-Basayev connection could start a global panic. Suppose Basayev is using the cover of this joint project with Hamilton in order to take over the operational control of Asteroid USA? Maybe under the direction of someone in Moscow leading a coup."

"Come on, Phil! That's a stretch even for you."

"Maybe. But it certainly would be possible for Russia to have a monopoly on precious minerals well into the future and cause havoc all over the world. And just one tweet by a conspiracy nut — a claim, say, that the Russians are threatening to aim the asteroid toward us — would be all over the Internet in minutes. Run on the banks. Stock markets crashing. That's why I think I need to hold back on this."

"Okay. But if you do hold back, the thing still goes on," Falcone said. "There's only one way to stop Hamilton. I'm going to take it all directly to President Oxley, one-on-one. No one else in the Oval Office. No one taking notes. No one hiding in the corner."

"That might work. But then Oxley would have to turn to the CIA, the FBI, the whole apparatus that keeps lids on things. Would he want to lift the lid?"

"I'll find out," Falcone said. "And you will never know what I found out, maybe even when it happens."

65

As Falcone well knew, it was almost impossible to meet one-on-one with President Oxley. He was protected from assassins by a cordon of Secret Service agents and from outside influence by Ray Quinlan, the President's chief of staff and guardian of the presidential clock and calendar. Quinlan made it a firing offense if a White House staffer allowed someone to meet with the President without the presence or authorization of Quinlan.

When Falcone was national security advisor, he had often clashed with Quinlan over unrestrained access to the President, especially when President Oxley politely asked Quinlan to leave him alone with Falcone. Now, as a former advisor who was still loathed by Quinlan, Falcone knew there was no way he could directly reach President Oxley by any of the regular routes. But there was a place they could meet. As soon as Dake left, Falcone called Betty LeGarde, once a young staffer in his Senate office. She now held a job that Falcone had helped to arrange: the President's personal secretary.

"Thanks for the flowers, Sean," she said, noting the name on her phone console. "You never miss my birthday."

"You're welcome, Betty. It's been a while."

"What can I do for you?" she asked in a voice somehow both warm and efficient.

"You can call your boss and tell him that tomorrow would be a good day for golf."

"The President had planned to take the day off with the family. You know what Marcie will say."

Falcone also knew what the White House press corps would do with another presidential golf game. The reporters and pundits analyzed the President's every word and every move, focused on every minute that the President was not working, or, as the press corps called it, carrying out his official duties. Even a rare night out with his wife at the Kennedy Center counted as nonworking time. And golf was chalked up as recreation even if his foursome included the Speaker and the Senate minority leader. So suggesting a round of golf was setting up a chance for the media to review the number of the President's golf dates, inspiring dozens of snarky tweets, blogs, and TV commentaries.

"Tell him we'll just do nine holes," Falcone said. "Right after church. He can be home by four o'clock and have the rest of the day with Marcie and the kids. Tell him it's important to get some relaxation. He'll know what I mean."

"Relaxation" was a code word between them, dating back to a three a.m. call from Falcone about a flaring crisis in the Middle East. After giving the President the details, Falcone had said, "Just look upon this as a kind of relaxation. You can toss away the day's schedule of boring meetings and get down to real stuff in the Situation Room." After that, Oxley always responded to Falcone's crisis calls as a summons to "relaxation."

Falcone's call set in motion the machinery that delivers the President from the citadel of the White House to the perils of the outside world, which today was the Army Navy Country Club across the Potomac, a twelve-minute trip by presidential motorcade. The club is on a Virginia ridge where a Union fort stood during the Civil War. Golfers can still see the fort's parapets and ditches around one of the greens. But those bits of the past are usually noticed only by golfers who shank or hook an approach shot to that tricky green.

The club's three courses are for playing golf, not dwelling on history. But a kind of secret history is made here, woven from the conversations between golfers whose jobs, from the President on down, involve governing the nation. The club's members are retired and active-duty officers, along with civilians who are "bound together by the fraternal and patriotic spirit of serving the best interests and efficiency of the National Defense," and the industrial-military complex.

A Secret Service agent called Falcone and told him which of the courses had been selected, along with the tee time, and said that a car would pick him up in twenty minutes. When Falcone arrived at the first tee, he was assigned the presidential golf cart. "The President will be at the wheel," an agent told Falcone, grinning. Falcone knew that meant pedal-to-the-floor.

Standing alongside another cart and offering hearty handshakes to Falcone were the governor of Maryland and the secretary of commerce, the rest of the foursome. Falcone imagined the surprise White House phone calls that had informed them of the President's unexpected invitations.

The President teed off first, a powerful drive that landed on the edge of the green. Falcone and the others landed far from the green. The President finished off with two putts. The rest of the foursome proved themselves duffers, and Oxley was looking displeased, whether for the poor competition or for the delay in hearing Falcone's relaxation report.

At the second tee, Oxley whispered to Falcone, "Into the rough." His tee drive was weak and hooked into a long, wide stretch of brush and trees that appeared a third of the way to the green. Falcone followed with a similar drooping drive. The others managed to stay on the fairway. As they headed toward their balls, Oxley sped his cart toward the rough. One of the Secret Service carts tailed them but kept at a discreet distance.

Oxley and Falcone left the cart and plunged into the rough. "Mind the poison ivy," Oxley said, pointing to a patch between two pines. "This better be good. Marcie's barely speaking to me."

Falcone gave a SitRoom-style point-by-point summary of what he knew about Hamilton's connection to the shootings and his secret partnership with Kuri Basayev. He ended with, "As for the SpaceMine asteroid, if it's moved for mining, it puts the Earth in danger. And adding to the danger is Basayev, who . . ."

"Who is someone that your friend Dake has been talking about," Oxley interrupted. "He's calling it a rogue operation out at the agency, right?" Oxley said.

Falcone nodded.

"How long did you work with me?" Oxley said. "Do you really think I didn't know about or approve the plan to develop a Russian asset, one that is so close to the Russian president?"

"Wait!" Falcone exclaimed. "You're telling me that this is an authorized operation? That making it seem 'rogue' was a cover to give you deniability in case it became known?"

"It's a little more ambiguous than that," Oxley said, poking in the high grass with a seven iron.

"One who could turn out to be a double and turn the sword on you?"

"Come on, Sean. You still think I'm an intelligence ingenue? Don't know how to play chess with the big boys?"

Falcone did not reply.

"The NSA routinely intercepted and

488

decrypted the calls between Hamilton and Basayev," Oxley continued. "Basayev's been an intel target for a long time. We knew that Basayev had muscled his way into Space-Mine, and the agency believed he had a hand in the shootings."

"So that's why you ordered J.B. to have his FBI take over the hit on the firm?"

"I didn't order J.B. But after a conference — NSA, CIA, FBI, God, even Homeland Security — that's what we came up with."

"What about the Fast and Furious gun? Suppose it comes out that a gun blessed by the U.S. Department of Justice killed five Americans?"

"I'll handle it if Fast and Furious comes up. I'll worry about it when I have to."

"So let's say that temporarily stays under the rug. But why hasn't the FBI arrested Sprague and Hamilton?"

"On what charge? The evidence was too thin. Hard to show a direct murder link based on what was said over the phone. We needed time to let it play out. Hell, you were a prosecutor once. Think you could convict on circumstantial evidence?"

Falcone stooped and picked up his ball. "Mine. Where's yours?"

"I give up. I'll take the new-ball penalty."

"I will, too," Falcone said, pocketing his

ball. "But what about Hamilton's plan to move the asteroid? You haven't done anything to stop what Hamilton is doing."

"Come on, you know the answer. The Hill would see it as a phony excuse to burn the Silicon Valley boys. Lot of campaign money there, and not just Hamilton's. If Justice moves against Hamilton, it has to be airtight," Oxley said, looking toward the fairway. "We'd better get back." Oxley headed toward the cart.

Falcone did not move. "Sometimes, Mr. President, you have to hear the truth unvarnished," he said. "Isn't the real reason the White House — Quinlan, that is — is keeping this bottled up is so it doesn't get out that you — not your administration but you — have been running an operation with a Russian thug who murdered five Americans? A thug who just might take over control of an asteroid from Hamilton and put it on a collision course with Earth. Or use it as a weapon against us or against China. Did it occur to your team that Basayev could become one of the greatest extortionists in history?"

"What the hell are you talking about, Sean?"

"Basayev may be using a commercial activity as a cover for a covert operation of his own — controlling an asteroid that could be a weapon, using it to demand tribute from the U.S. or face annihilation . . . Or maybe it's Lebed who has been running Basayev all along. Maybe Lebed, Russia's new Vladimir Putin, is managing a new charm offensive while plotting to take advantage of U.S. technology and our stupid decision to slash our defense and space budgets."

Oxley climbed into the cart and started it up. "You were always good at seeing the things that aren't here yet," he said, smiling. "So what do you suggest I do?"

"Meet with Ben Taylor and me tomorrow."

"Taylor? The Air and Space guy? Quinlan dropped him as science advisor."

"As usual, Quinlan is being a horse's ass."

"I'll let that pass. What do you propose about the asteroid? I admit we're in the dark. There's some encrypted message that NSA's working on. I heard about that. Something about the asteroid. Yes, I want to know about that."

"Taylor decrypted that message. He'll tell you what Hamilton's been doing and why it's incredibly dangerous. Think Carl Sagan. And think the end of the world."

"Okay. I'll get Betty to set up a three-for-lunch without telling Quinlan. I like getting him mad. It makes him smarter." He gunned the cart and made a sharp turn. "Now let's get this awful game over with."

66

As soon as he returned to the White House, President Oxley called FBI director Patterson, reaching him at his home in McLean, Virginia. When the special phone rang, Patterson was reading a letter from his daughter, who was in her second year at Tufts. Like her mother, she preferred to write letters on paper and send the letters via the U.S. Postal Service.

The direct line from the White House to Patterson's home had been declared secure by the NSA. But both the President and Patterson were wary of NSA declarations. So the conversation was cryptic.

"J.B.," Oxley said. "Hope you're having a quiet Sunday. Talked to a very knowledge-able mutual friend you recently visited. Let's sweat the man with the thumb drive. Tell Sarsfield to invite him in for a talk and a look at Sarsfield's dog-and-pony show. See what that stirs up."

■ ■ ■ ■

Paul Sprague was in his study, looking westward toward the mountains. The sun had nearly set. A yellow band of clouds glowed in a sky yielding to the first stars of night. *We bought this place for moments like this,* Sprague thought, *Well, no longer. . . .* He was alone, as usual ending a weekend at Sprague Farm — his Shangri-la, as he called his house and fourteen acres in Middleburg, Virginia.

His wife, Sarah, preferred Washington. From the beginning she had despised the farm as feeling and looking like a B&B, and she despised Middleburg as horsy and snooty. Now she did not even feign an excuse for not coming here. Sprague had thought of selling the farm. But he cherished the feeling of landed gentry. *And besides, how can I sell? The place is mortgaged more than it's worth.* He poured himself another glass of bourbon. Sarah thought it was hilarious that his favorite bourbon was Virginia Gentleman.

The landline phone rang, startling him from his reverie. He had turned off his cell phone, and the landline number was known to few people. *Maybe Sarah.* He walked from the leather chair at the bay window to his reproduced-antique desk, which had a gold-toothed leather top and carved reeded corner posts. The phone looked out of place on that fine desk. He decided he would move it to the table next to the leather chair.

"Paul Sprague here," he answered briskly. "Who is this?"

"Special Agent Patrick Sarsfield of the Federal Bureau of Investigation," said a voice that instantly conjured up in Sprague's mind thoughts of phone taps, surveillance — and, suddenly topping the other fearful thoughts, a raging panic about Hamilton and Basayev. He suppressed a mad urge to shout their names.

"And what is the purpose of this Sunday phone call, Agent Sarsfield?" Sprague asked, confident that he sounded calm.

"Sir, I have been tasked by the director to ask you to come to headquarters on Monday morning to —"

"What . . . what is the reason?"

"I am sorry, sir. But I am unable to discuss this matter on the phone. I will meet you at the Pennsylvania Avenue entrance at ten a.m. Monday."

"And if I fail to appear?"

"I would not advise that, sir. There is a stigma associated with a subpoena, as you, a member of the bar, surely know. Director Patterson wishes to avoid that, sir. As you know, the bureau would be forced to apply in court for a subpoena, and that application would make certain matters public."

After a short pause, Sprague said. "I will appear tomorrow."

"Thank you, Mr. Sprague. Would you wish to be accompanied by your lawyer?"

"As you know, I *am* a lawyer. I will come alone."

"Very well, Mr. Sprague. Goodbye."

Sprague returned to the leather chair and stared into the twilight. *Bring a lawyer? With the shootings and Falcone's exit, the firm's in enough of a mess. There's no way I can shop for a criminal lawyer without the whole town knowing. . . .* He tried to come up with a plan. He could not call Hamilton from here. He had to leave for Washington immediately. He could not assume that the FBI or the NSA had not been able to not tap the special Hamilton phone locked in a drawer of his desk at Sullivan & Ford. But he had to call, had to take the chance.

"Tasked by the director . . ." He could not drive the phrase from his panicking mind. *"Tasked by the director . . ."*

67

"For God's sake, Paul. What now? Why a Sunday call? Sundays are special to me. A day of worship. What can't keep till Monday?" Hamilton said, his voice distorted as much by anger as by electronics. He had answered the phone in his apartment, which spread along a small arc of the second floor of the SpaceMine building. The two-story, glass-and-shiny-metal structure lay like a giant halo that had been tossed onto Palo Alto's greensward of lawns and walkways.

"It's the FBI," Sprague said. "I've been invited to talk to an agent there. There's good reason to believe they'll be wanting to talk to you next."

"*Invited?* What the hell kind of lawyer are you? And why would they call you?"

"I think . . . I think it's because they know about the deletion of data on the computer." Sprague's thin, halting voice revealed a panic that he fought to control.

"So what?" Hamilton said. "I simply retrieved my property, which was stolen."

"Yeah, and O. J. Simpson was simply retrieving his football memorabilia," Sprague said, surprised at his sudden flare-up of anger. "Well, O.J. is still doing hard time. What worries me is that you interfered with a criminal investigation. And now —"

"Let's end this conversation right here, Paul. The fact is I have also been asked by the FBI to pay a little visit to their shop. I received a call two days ago to appear Monday. I'm flying out tonight."

"What? Why didn't you tell me? Why —"

"I'm no fool, Paul. From what I have learned about Washington, if a lawyer gets in trouble, his clients are well advised to treat him as a leper."

"You were *told* I was summoned?"

" 'Invited,' Paul. That's your word, 'invited.' "

"We should talk," Sprague said desperately.

"I think not, Paul."

"But I'm your lawyer. You need —"

"You're not my lawyer anymore, Paul. Be sure to send me an e-mail *today*. I want you not to be my lawyer tomorrow."

"God damn it, Robert! Don't you see? You will *need* a lawyer."

"Do not take the Lord's name in vain, Paul. I *have* a lawyer. He's just not you. And he will be with me *if* it turns out that I must honor the invitation. I think there is no more to say, Paul. Goodbye."

Hamilton immediately called Senator Collinsworth, reaching him on the cell phone that Collinsworth reserved for calls to and from Hamilton and four other major contributors. After Hamilton told him about the invitation from the FBI, Collinsworth promised to join with Senator Anderson and demand a meeting with Director Patterson.

68

Sarsfield escorted Sprague to the same room where Falcone had viewed the car and laptop timelines. The only others in the room were the two forensic experts, who had arrived via helicopter from Quantico an hour before.

As soon as the image of the laptop appeared on the wall screen and the forensic expert began her technical narration, Sprague knew, beyond any doubt, that he had been betrayed by Ursula. He recalled, in exhaustive detail, the way she manipulated the two thumb drives, and could only nod when Sarsfield asked, "Is it true, Mr. Sprague, that you were not able to operate the computer under Mr. Hamilton's directions?"

After a pause, Sarsfield added, "Let the record show that Mr. Sprague nodded in assertion.

"And is it true, Mr. Sprague, that your

executive assistant, Miss Ursula Breitsprecher, aided in the transfer of data from the computer to two thumb drives?"

"Yes, but —"

"And is one of those thumb drives in your possession, Mr. Sprague?"

Sprague nodded again.

"Were you aware, Mr. Sprague, that you went tampering with evidence in a criminal investigation?"

"You have gone to the edge, Agent Sarsfield," Sprague replied sharply, feeling a defense-lawyer surge of confidence. "I will not answer any more questions."

"Very well, Mr. Sprague. This preliminary inquiry of Paul Sprague is completed," Sarsfield said. He turned to look at Sprague eye-to-eye. "As part of an investigation under way, I wish to obtain that thumb drive. With your agreement, I will accompany you to your office, obtain the thumb drive, and provide a receipt." He paused as Sprague nodded. "The U.S. Attorney's Office for the District of Columbia," Sarsfield continued, "is examining the probability of empaneling a grand jury to seek indictments in the matter of homicides at Sullivan and Ford. I urge you again to obtain legal counsel."

Sprague nodded and Sarsfield escorted him, in silence, from the building and walked Sprague to his office. There, with little conversation, Sarsfield obtained the thumb drive from Ursula, placed it in an evidence bag, signed a receipt for it, and left.

Sprague and Ursula stood for a moment, each looking at the other to begin the ceremony.

Sprague finally broke the silence, saying, "You will give me the firm's cell phone and laptop, your identification badge, your elevator card key, your Sullivan and Ford credit card. . . . Your health insurance will continue through the end of the month. You will then be required to obtain your own insurance under the Affordable Care Act. . . ."

An hour after Sprague walked out of the FBI conference room, Hamilton walked in, accompanied by Akis Christakos, whom Sarsfield recognized as one of Washington's most expensive and most successful criminal lawyers. Early in the presentation of the car and laptop timelines, Christakos interrupted. Soon, however, he merely sat next to Hamilton and scrawled notes on page after page of yellow-lined paper. After summaries of Ursula's and Sprague's statements were handed to Christakos, he whispered to his client.

Tight-lipped, Hamilton was escorted out of the room by Sarsfield. Christakos remained behind to spend a few minutes talking to Assistant Attorney General Cosgrove.

69

Patterson had expected that Sarsfield's call to Sprague would create a chain reaction. So he was not surprised on Monday when he received a call from Collinsworth, who ignored the protocol of the FBI's Office of Congressional Relations and used Patterson's private number to reach him directly "because this is an urgent security matter."

Patterson juggled his schedule to squeeze in a meeting that afternoon with Collinsworth and Anderson. At their request, the meeting would be held in the basement Hart Senate Office Building room assigned to the Senate Select Committee on Intelligence. Officially a "sensitive compartmented information facility" (SCIF, pronounced "skiff"), it was sealed off from the Washington tell-me-a-secret games. Under the committee's rules, no one could take notes in the room and no one could remove any document seen in the room.

Patterson sat at the room's principal piece of furniture, a long, highly polished table flanked with chairs. Collinsworth put him at one end of the table and took the chair to Patterson's left. Anderson sat at Patterson's right.

His entwined hands resting on the table, Patterson listened patiently as each senator made his request that the FBI drop its interest in Robert Wentworth Hamilton "and his great work for this nation."

"I fail to see where national security is involved, Senators," Patterson said. "That was your reason for meeting here."

"Well, Director Patterson," Collinsworth said, smiling, "I am sure you understand that Mr. Hamilton, as one of America's great innovators, is a national resource that deserves protection."

"No, Senator," Patterson said. "With all due respect I do not see any need to look upon Mr. Hamilton or his corporate doings as matters that would in any way influence bureau decisions regarding an important homicide case."

At the word "homicide," Anderson winced, turned toward Collinsworth, looking to him for further arguments. When Collinsworth failed to speak, Anderson leaned forward and said, "J.B., all we ask is that you step carefully when dealing with Mr. Hamilton."

"Step carefully, Senator?"

Collinsworth glared at Anderson for a moment. He did not like "J.B." and he did not like "step carefully."

"I believe," Patterson continued, "that it is you and your colleague who should be stepping carefully. Are you aware, Senators, that your request constitutes an interference with a criminal investigation into the murder of five innocent people?"

The two senators looked at each other, then at Patterson.

"What?" Collinsworth asked, as if an answer to that one word would somehow answer many of the questions that were roiling through his mind.

"I am sure you remember the Keating Five," Patterson said, pausing to let that remark sink in; even the most junior senator knew about the Keating Five. "It's necessary for me to file a report on this meeting to the Department of Justice. The report will be available to any reporter who files a Freedom of Information Act request. I will also file with the attorney general a recommendation that he consider filing criminal complaints against both of you.

"At the very least, once this meeting becomes the subject of public discussion, Senate leaders will want to refer the matter to the Senate Ethics Committee to determine what action should be taken to condemn your action or possibly even expel you from the Senate. Again, I refer you to the Keating Five. Thank you, I must now return to my office."

In 1987, during the nation's savings-and-loan-associations crisis, five senators met with federal banking regulators on behalf of banker Charles H. Keating, Jr. He had made a total of $1.3 million in campaign contributions to the senators. The connection between the meetings and the campaign funds triggered a scandal known as the Keating Five. A Senate ethics investigation produced twenty-six days of televised hearings and set off an FBI investigation into possible criminal actions by Keating and the five senators. Keating eventually spent five years in prison. The Senate censured one senator and reprimanded the others for their "poor judgment." The scandal, said the New York Times, was "an embarrassment for the entire Senate, shining a light onto the ways in which campaign donors sought and often received favors."

And now, Patterson had walked into what

could have become the "Hamilton Two." When he walked out of the Hart Building, he felt, for the first time in years, that he and his FBI were on the side of the angels.

70

Collinsworth and Anderson, too shaken to return to their offices, walked two blocks from the Hart Building to the Monocle Restaurant, their favorite spot for hatching plans. Unhatching a plan was much more difficult, they discovered after a few minutes over their first martinis. Finally, Anderson decided that it would not be prudent to call Hamilton. Collinsworth nodded assent, saying, "For his own good. We're doing him a favor not dragging him into this."

They agreed to tell their chiefs of staff to send carefully worded e-mails to Hamilton. "The e-mails shouldn't be identical, of course," Collinsworth said. "But they should politely advise him that the matter he raised — no need to be specific — is under Department of Justice review at this time."

"Exactly," Anderson agreed. He looked both ways and leaned in, half whispering, "Butner. In North Carolina. Know anything about the place?"

"It's a medium fed prison. Couple of congressmen sent there," Collinsworth replied. "And that's where Bernie Madoff went. Not so bad, I heard. Just white-collar inmates."

"Right. Well, I don't want to go there, Ken," Anderson said. "So you be sure that you get that goddamn e-mail off. No more contact with Hamilton. Period."

Collinsworth raised his glass. "Agreed."

Hamilton did not get many e-mails. He ran SpaceMine with the aid of a half-dozen subordinates, and he preferred to hear about solutions — not problems, solutions — directly from whomever was handling the operation. No need for paper trails. And none of his aides used e-mails. They communicated either directly through cell phones or through texting.

The two e-mails from Washington arrived within minutes of each other. They were handed to Hamilton by an administrator who acted as if he were holding pieces of papyrus bearing messages in hieroglyphics.

"Just got these, Mr. Hamilton," the aide said. "Odd ones. Looks like they're telling you they struck out about something."

"Can't seem to get good help these days,"

Hamilton said, grimly smiling. He put them into a recycling container next to the glass-topped table that served as his desk. "I've got to make a call." The aide left.

He dialed 1-877-555-4151 on his encrypting phone, waited thirty seconds, and hung up. In a few minutes the phone rang. The caller did not identify himself, but Hamilton knew it was Kuri Basayev. Hamilton had met him only once, at night, at a dock in New York, aboard *Aglaya*. Two big and taciturn men picked up Hamilton at his hotel, drove him to the dock, and took him up the gangway. The meeting had only lasted about twenty minutes. It ended with a champagne toast, celebrating the legal conversion of Basayev's extortion into a contract making him owner of a forty-percent share of SpaceMine. The men re-appeared and took Hamilton back to his hotel.

They had spoken on their theoretically secure phones a few times since then. Basayev had indicated that he was aboard the *Aglaya,* but he had not said where the yacht was. The private investigators hired by Hamilton tried to keep track of Basayev and the *Aglaya*. For the past couple of months the yacht was said to be in the Black Sea.

"My friend, Robert," Basayev said. "What

is the news?"

"The news is not good news, Kuri. Certain authorities — high authorities — are asking questions that do not have good answers. I think it is time that I buy you out of your forty percent."

After a short silence, Basayev spoke, hardening his voice. "Perhaps it is time for me to buy *you* out, Robert. I think it is time to talk. Your troubles have to go away. You will enjoy a few days on *Aglaya.*"

"I'm willing to meet you, willing to talk, willing to compromise. But 'a few days' is impossible."

"Very well. Two days. One day to talk, one day to enjoy *Aglaya.* All you have to do is fly to Moscow and wait there. Check into the Baltschug Kempinski. Beautiful hotel directly across the river from the Kremlin. Wait there until I make arrangements to have you flown to a port on the coast of Turkey. You will be contacted. I have a special aircraft that will take you to the *Aglaya,* where we can talk in comfort and security. Just let me know a few days in advance. I promise you an enjoyable visit."

71

A White House car picked up Falcone and Taylor and took them to the East Wing entrance, where an agent handed them visitor identification tags and escorted them to a small room off the Oval Office. President Oxley entered a couple of minutes after they did, and all three sat at a round table that looked big enough for no more than four people.

After a steward served them grilled chicken salad, cornbread, and coffee, Falcone formally introduced Ben Taylor as assistant director of the Air and Space Museum and added, "He's also a writer and a documentary producer."

"I don't need an introduction, Sean," Oxley said. "When I told my kids I was meeting with Ben Taylor, they were real exited. They're great fans. What's the documentary about?"

"Asteroids, Mr. President," Taylor replied.

"But somebody talked PBS into not showing it," Falcone interjected. Oxley looked up quizzically as Falcone added, "And I think I know who."

The three men began lunch in silence, Taylor and Falcone waiting for Oxley to speak first. He buttered a piece of cornbread, took a bite, and said, "Okay, Ben. Tell me about the asteroid that's worrying you."

"I'll try to make this fast, Mr. President. First of all, we have no idea where SpaceMine's asteroid is. Hamilton told us that his so-called Asteroid USA would send a message from space. That has not happened. He is tightly holding all information about that asteroid. Second, it's possible to change an asteroid's orbit, and if you change it in a reckless way — which many scientists believe SpaceMine is doing — you can put the Earth in danger. My murdered friend Cole Perenchio, a genius about gravity, using calculations gathered by NASA, calculated that the new orbit planned for Asteroid USA puts it on a collision course with Earth in 2035."

"Okay. Assuming what you're telling me is scientifically sound, what can we do about it? Blow it up with a nuclear bomb?"

"No, Mr. President. All a bomb would do

is create big chucks of rock that would hit the Earth in several places. I have a friend, a former astronaut, who put it this way: 'If you have a big rock on a hill above your house, you don't want to blow it up and just hope that one of the pieces doesn't hit you.' "

"So what *do* we do?" Oxley asked, showing more interest.

"The best idea, I think, is to use a spacecraft to nudge the asteroid off its collision course."

"And then what will happen?" Oxley asked. "Suppose it goes off on another orbit that's just as dangerous?"

"Good question, Mr. President. It would depend upon where the nudge were applied. If it were heading say, for the northern Atlantic, and the nudge struck the asteroid one way, it would move across the UK, northern Europe, and Russia and if it were hit another way, its pass would go across the United States and Canada."

"And suppose things didn't happen exactly the way the nudgers hoped?"

"Then some place on Earth would be hit," Taylor said.

"And somebody would be blamed."

"That's exactly it," Falcone blurted and getting a nod from Taylor. "We need global cooperation to save the Earth — and to accept responsibility on a global level. If something goes wrong, it would not be because one nation did something wrong."

"You're back to the UN space treaty," the President said, shaking his head wearily. He looked toward Taylor. "And you're talking about something that's going to face world leaders decades from now. You're both taking me down roads that haven't even been made yet, roads that cost a lot of money."

"Defense of the Earth is a good investment," Taylor said. "To build and launch an infrared, asteroid-hunting telescope would cost about three percent of NASA's budget."

"Is any of this in that documentary you made? What's its name?" Oxley asked.

" 'An Asteroid Closely Watched,' Mr. President."

"Please send me a CD of it, if that's possible," Oxley said to Taylor. "I'd very much like to see it." Then, turning to Falcone, he added, "Get me a memo, through Betty per usual, about how and why PBS didn't broadcast the show. After I see it I may try to see if those PBS folks will change their minds."

Oxley stood, signaling the lunch was over and bringing the others to their feet. He shook hands with both and said to Taylor, "Thanks for the eye-opener, Ben. I'll be thinking about asteroids and what we might be doing down the road."

"There's something that you can do right away," Falcone said. "You can talk to President Lebed about Kuri Basayev." At the mention of the name, Oxley and Falcone exchanged swift, furtive glances.

"About who?" Oxley asked, as if he had not heard the name before.

"Basayev is the silent partner in Space-Mine," Taylor said. "He made the arrangements for launching the SpaceMine spacecraft from Russia."

"And what could I tell President Lebed to do about Basayev, Sean?" Oxley asked, a glint in his eyes.

Falcone turned to Taylor. "Tell the President about Ivan's Hammer," Falcone said.

"It's pretty wild," Taylor said. "But Carl Sagan thought it was feasible. He wrote that in the nineteen-eighties the Soviet Union might use man-directed small asteroids as first-strike weapons. The Soviet plan, he said, was called Ivan's Hammer. RAND made a study of it for the U.S. government."

The President looked surprised, then frowned.

"Maybe Ivan's Hammer is reason enough to suggest that Lebed make sure Basayev doesn't get access to Russian space resources anymore," Falcone said. "It makes him a dangerous man. And you could get Lebed to join you in developing a United Nations system for defense of the Earth. It could make the two of you visionaries, maybe Nobel candidates."

"I'll be seeing Lebed at the G-20 Summit next week in Istanbul," Oxley said. "The Russians haven't been kicked out of the G-20 yet. Basayev might turn into an interesting topic, Sean. A very interesting topic."

President Oxley left the small room and entered the Oval Office. A moment later Ray Quinlan entered, his face red and tight with rage.

"What the hell was that about —" Quinlan asked, pausing a moment before sullenly adding, "Mr. President?"

"I wanted to have a private lunch to catch up with Falcone and Dr. Taylor to discuss some space issues," Oxley answered.

"It was not on your calendar." Again a pause before "Mr. President."

By now Oxley was seated behind the majesty of his desk. "You know, Ray," he said softly, "lately you've been wearing my stars, strutting around like a little 'Mr. President.' I'd like you to stop that."

Ray, his face still contorted, his breathing heavy, "Better still, Mr. President, maybe I should resign."

Oxley picked up a pen and held it as if he were about to hand it to Quinlan. Then he put it down and said, "I think you had better think about it overnight, Ray."

72

Under the six minarets of Istanbul's Blue Mosque, while craning his neck to look at thousands of coolly beautiful blue tiles, President Oxley was asked by the Turkish prime minister if there was any other treasure he would like to visit. Oxley said he wanted to walk in Mihrabat Grove, a hillside park with a spectacular view of the city.

A few hours later, while Oxley was in a heavily guarded villa being briefed on the G-20 summit's upcoming schedule, Russian president Boris Lebed was being shown the Blue Mosque. When he was asked the same question, he gave the same answer. The prime minister nodded; he had done his work for this particular little diplomatic matter.

In a few days of cables and phone calls, the U.S. ambassador to Moscow, the Russian ambassador to Washington, and the Turkish ambassadors to both countries had all worked together to make sure that the two presidents would be able to have a private, face-to-face meeting while they were in Istanbul for the G-20 summit. The annual meeting of the finance ministers and central bank governors of the world's twenty leading economies also drew many of the world's leaders.

The plan begun by Oxley put him and Lebed in Mihrabat Grove the day before the summit began. Protected by the U.S. Secret Service, Russia's Federal Security Service, Turkey's National Intelligence Organization, and the Turkish First Commando Brigade, the two presidents found themselves sitting at a table set on a park ridge that overlooked the city, glasses of tea in front of them.

They had met once before, at the annual opening session of the UN General Assembly, but they had not had much of a chance to talk. The U.S. was on a Cold War footing with Russia, after Vladimir Putin had conspired to grab Crimea from Ukraine and prevent Ukraine from ever considering a dalliance with the European Union or NATO. Neither man wanted to risk a political backlash by seeming to dine with their respective devils. From then on, they had kept up by following intelligence reports on each other.

"I'm told," Lebed said, "that this was your idea of our speaking man-to-man. I agreed. Good idea." His English had a slightly rough edge, which Russians never seemed to be able to lose.

"Somebody had to," Oxley said, adding, "How sure are you that this table isn't bugged?"

"Perhaps by NATO? By the Turks? By NSA? By us? I'm not sure at all," Lebed replied. "You?"

"I have given orders that we are not to be bugged."

"And you know that the NSA will obey?"

"Well, of course I hope so. But I do believe that if we walk about thirty feet — ten meters — from this table to an empty piece of lawn we can at least be sure we are not near any object that could have a bug."

"Very well," Lebed said, gulping down his tea. "What is it you wish to talk about?"

Oxley, who had only sipped at his tea, followed Lebed down a path that ran across the park hill and did not speak until he felt safely unobserved and unheard. They stood next to each other, their shoes sinking slightly into the freshly cut, freshly watered lawn.

"You seem very conscious of surveillance,"

Lebed said.

"Aren't we all?"

"You wish to talk about Basayev."

"Good guess."

"Not a guess," Lebed said, laughing. "You have to be careful of those balls lying around in the rough at the Army Navy Club."

"I'll be goddamned!" Oxley exclaimed. "Thanks for the warning. I'll be more careful. I guess you realize I'll have to ask for some better sweeping. But thanks."

"You are welcome. Call it a goodwill gesture."

"I'm surprised that you feel any goodwill. You must have got an immediate report on what Falcone and I discussed about Basayev."

"It's all bullshit," Lebed said. "Kuri Basayev would never be turned."

"Actually, it's a lot more sweet-smelling," Oxley laughed. "Our boys got a lot out of your friend. Such as what military equipment and advice Russia has been giving Iran's Islamic Revolutionary Guard Corps. He's been singing like Pavarotti."

"Impossible!" Lebed shouted, all semblance of calm leaving him in an instant.

"I have a report that contains transcripts of his conversations with his CIA handler,"

Oxley said, reaching into the inside pocket of his suit coat, taking out a thick envelope, and handing it to Lebed.

Lebed held the envelope in his right hand, striking it against his left for a few moments before he pocketed it and said, "There have been suspicions. Certain ports where his yacht docks, the same man boarding the yacht, staying only a few moments, not looking like a guest. One of my officers insisted that the visitor was CIA. I could not believe it. I was against putting him under deep surveillance. But there *is* a counterintelligence operation going on. When I got a report on your golf talk, I started thinking, started believing . . ." He pocketed the envelope and patted the pocket. "If this holds up under examination . . ."

"This is real, Boris, I assure you."

"That motherfucker!" Lebed muttered.

"Not quite," Oxley said. "He likes young men. Our folks caught him in a gay bar in Hong Kong. That's how the turning started. The photos are . . . well . . . interesting. . . . And given how your fellow Russians feel about such matters. They don't have the benefit of a London education and enlightenment. . . ."

Lebed quickly regained his self-control.

"So," he said with a smile. "Maybe I dangled him to see if you would bite and then I used him to feed you shit for information."

"Don't bullshit a bullshitter, Boris. We know what he is, and if we don't make this deal, the Russian people are going to find out about him — and start asking questions about why you have such a man so close to you. . . ."

Lebed looked away and did not respond.

"What you do about him is your business," Oxley continued. "But we don't want him involved in what we feel is a potential danger to our national security."

"National security? What the hell are you talking about?" Lebed asked.

Oxley told him about Ivan's Hammer and got an incredulous laugh in response.

"Oh, come now, Blake . . . I can call you that now. That's science fiction."

"Look it up in your archives. And I'll send you what our files have on asteroids as space weapons. We think Basayev may be going in that direction: take control of SpaceMine, make demands, and stir global panic. You may think Ivan's Hammer is amusing, but I'm sure your scientists will agree on the danger of changing a near-Earth asteroid's orbit. And I think we need to get the UN involved in . . . well, a scientist I admire has a name for it: 'defense of the Earth.' I think we could make it a good joint project."

"I'd like to know more," Lebed said cautiously. "As for Kuri Basayev, it appears that he is a problem." He patted the pocket. "I will take care of the problem."

Oxley saw a waiter emerge from the hilltop restaurant. Someone pulled him back in.

"There's no time to talk much more," Oxley said. "The security boys are getting nervous. This has been a good little session."

"I agree. It's good to get to a moment where there's no bullshit. . . . There's one more thing. I know you get those morning intelligence reports on what the vacuum cleaners picked up. So do I." Lebed looked down at the Bosporus glittering below. "We — and probably you, too — got a tap that showed your Mr. Hamilton is planning to visit Basayev. In fact, right now Basayev's off there somewhere." Lebed pointed toward the Black Sea. "And your Mr. Hamilton is in Moscow at this very moment, enjoying the hospitality of one of Russia's finest hotels. It would be unfortunate if his meeting with Basayev takes place."

"That's right," Oxley said. "We've been thinking about finding a technical way to stop Hamilton. He might try to become a fugitive. But at the moment he can legally travel."

"Like Snowden," Lebed said with a sharp laugh.

Oxley did not respond.

"Seriously," Lebed resumed, "We'll make sure Hamilton doesn't visit Basayev. It could make matters complicated."

"Okay," Oxley said, extending his hand, wondering what was going to happen to Basayev, yet knowing.

"This looks like it might be starting something good," Lebed said.

"I sure hope so. Putin saw everything as a zero-sum game. Russia wins, America loses. That's back-to-the-future thinking. It won't work. Not in the long run. But we both lose in the meantime."

"Perhaps when you recognize that Russia is a great country and more worthy of respect than you and your European friends have given us . . . But enough. Let's talk again another time."

They shook hands and began walking toward the top of the hill as Turkish commandos and men in suits began appearing.

Oxley began speaking rapidly: "Listen, Boris. This is an opportunity for Russia to finally be serious about wanting to play a leading role on the world stage again and assume the role of a real peacemaker."

"What kind of a deal are you talking about?" Lebed asked.

"We've got to come to terms about the asteroid that Basayev's involved with. He and Hamilton are putting us — all of us — in danger."

"What are you proposing?"

"A joint press conference announcing our plan to support asteroid research and bring the UN into space. After all, your country has had an asteroid skim over it."

"I have advisors. You have advisors. They don't want us to talk. They'll go crazy," Lebed said, his smile returning. "I assume that pocket of yours also has a draft of a statement about all this."

"It so happens that you're right," Oxley said, taking a sheet of paper from his pocket. "It has my cell phone number on it. Take a look, make whatever changes you want. We can bounce it back and forth and have a press conference later today."

"I'll take a look, as you put it," Lebed said. "Maybe show it to a couple of my people and get back to you. But there's something we haven't discussed . . . China."

"You want to bring the Chinese into this?"

"We don't have a choice. You know that they're working to set up shop on the moon and then use it as a launching pad to colonize Mars."

"They're a long way from doing either," Oxley said, a touch dismissively.

"Not so far away, I assure you. We've been talking to them. They are going to shock you. Believe me. . . . They're working on a solar sail to move asteroids as well. We need to meet this afternoon with President Zhang Xing. Otherwise, he'll think this is a plot to contain China's missions in space."

"But Zhang might tell the world what Hamilton and Basayev have been up to and claim that China's research is for science, peace, and harmony." Oxley made no attempt to conceal his growing frustration in dealing with an increasingly powerful and not-so-humble China. "And then denounce us as global terrorists!"

"If he does, we'll go public with what we've got on the Chinese military." Lebed chortled. "Your NSA doesn't know everything, well . . . at least not anymore. Our FSB may be a little old-school for you, but we still do intelligence the old-fashioned way." A smile spread across Lebed's broad face, revealing a set of teeth so perfect that Oxley found himself wondering if they were real. "We might even release documents showing how much he and his family have tucked away in Swiss bank accounts and London real estate. All that propaganda about antimaterialism and rooting out corruption . . . well, it might not play so well on Twitter."

"Tell me, Boris," Oxley said, leaning slightly into Lebed's shoulder. "Do you know what a 'Sabra' is?"

"Of course, it's a Hebrew word for Jews who are born in Israel."

"Yes, and it also refers to people who are like a desert cactus, a prickly pear, which is tough on the outside but soft and sweet on the inside."

"Your point being?"

"I know Sabras, Boris," Oxley said, jabbing Lebed's arm. "And you're no Sabra!"

Taking Oxley's joke as a compliment, Lebed said, "You're right. I am more like what one of your politicians once said about your political caucuses — the pricks are all on the inside."

With that, both presidents broke into unrestrained and infectious laughter and Lebed said, "It is good, Blake, that we have this talk. We should have more."

Two motorcades appeared at the top of the park, near the restaurant. Each president's official photographer had them pose for a handshake before they headed for their cars. When Oxley got into his limousine, he found Ray Quinlan awaiting him in the backseat. He was seething.

"First that goddamn golf course caper," Quinlan said. "Now this, Mr. President. What the hell are you doing? You could lose a secretary of state over this. She's back in the villa, boiling mad."

"So are you, Ray," Oxley said, laughing.

"Again, what the hell are you doing?"

"A walk in the woods. Like Reagan and Gorbachev."

"Get your facts right, Mr. President. The walkers in the woods were Paul Nitze and a Russian negotiator."

"Well, anyway, it will go into the memoir," Oxley said.

"Are you going to wait for the memoir before you tell me what you two talked about?"

"World peace, Ray. What in hell do you think we'd talk about?"

"Fine. But how about a few details? The press is going crazy and we've got to brief them before they start running totally false stories and crazy speculations. Was it a good meeting or a bad one? Nasty or nice? Lebed's a fucking dictator masquerading as a moderate. New bottle, old wine. Stone-

531

cold killer. Come on, Mr. President. Give me something."

"Okay, Ray, okay. Tell Jimmy to alert the press that Lebed and I will hold a press conference this afternoon to make a major announcement."

"Just the two of you?"

"Well, there's likely to be one more. President Zhang Xing."

"What? . . . What about the Indians, the Japanese . . ."

"I'm sure that all of them are going to support what we'll say," Oxley said, free of any self-doubt about what he was about to do. "Come on, Ray. Enough of the negative stuff. *'Doveryai, no proveryai.'* "

"Jesus, You really believe that 'trust but verify' shit?"

"Ray, I said to get on board. We're about to make some history."

73

Kuri Basayev rose from a night of lovemaking and slipped on a pair of swimming trunks. He moved swiftly from the master bedroom suite without disturbing his companion and climbed to the top deck of the *Aglaya*.

While not obsessively narcissistic, Basayev was proud of how his body looked. He was lean, muscular, and tanned. Worthy of an *Esquire* magazine cover, he mused. Well, only if he was a publicity-seeking hound, which he clearly was not.

Women were drawn magnetically to him. On occasion, he would be seen in the company of a beautiful woman, but his interests lay elsewhere. It wasn't that he didn't enjoy the company of women. Actually, he found them to be both interesting and entertaining. But whenever he sensed they were moving a bit too close to intimacy, he diplomatically eschewed their romantic advances by intimating that his heart belonged to others.

Those "others" required extreme discretion. He could not afford to have rumors floated about his sexuality. Not in today's Russia. Maybe not in any Russia.

Nikolay, his latest love, had been carefully vetted — and forewarned. His relationship with Basayev was to remain private. Failure to abide by the rules would have grave consequences. Nikolay had little trouble understanding the message.

Today was picture-perfect in every way. The sun had surfaced miraculously from behind the horizon, mystical in its illusion of cylindrical perfection. So close, you could dive into its very center and emerge as a god on fire.

The giant red ball had burned off the earlier morning haze, revealing a sky so blue that it convinced Basayev that there really was a heaven on Earth.

"Another shitty day in paradise," Basayev joked to his two steroid-buffed-up bodyguards.

"Right, boss," Andre Margelov, the taller of the two, responded. "Better enjoy it. Weather is supposed to shift tomorrow."

Basayev dove into the saltwater pool that

ran nearly the length of the *Aglaya*. He swam with long, leisurely strokes for nearly thirty minutes. Invigorated, he concluded a final lap and then hoisted himself out of the pool. An eager servant handed him a large Egyptian cotton towel emblazoned with the letters "KB" and placed a freshly brewed cup of coffee at a table nestled between two teakwood deck chairs.

As Basayev toweled off and slipped into one of the padded chairs, he picked up the book he had skimmed the previous evening before turning his attention to Nikolay.

The book had a clever title, which had caught Basayev's eye. The author of *The Geography of Bliss* had traveled to a number of countries in an effort to determine which people deemed themselves happy, and which did not — and the reasons that accounted for their state of mind.

In some countries where the people were dirt poor, the writer had found that the people were generally satisfied with their lives. Yet in other, more wealthy nations, he discovered palpable discontent and unhappiness. The answer seemed to be that those who were happy had trust in their leaders and fellow citizens. They believed that whatever their economic status, others saw them as people and truly cared for their

535

well-being.

"What horseshit! Pure psychobabble," Basayev laughed, and tossed the book into a large straw wastebasket. "I'm happy," he proclaimed to his two musclemen, who had no idea what prompted him to blurt out his feelings at that moment.

I'm about to dump that sniveling coward Hamilton, Basayev thought. *That loser who pissed his pants at the thought of having to meet with the FBI, a bunch of law-school rejects who think they can still ride on a reputation they no longer deserve — if they ever did. . . . Soon, I'll be one of the richest men in the world and I'll hold the keys to the future in my hands. And I won't have to worry about the law because in Russia, Boris Lebed is the law, and his law is all that matters!*

Basayev rose from his chair and started for the gym below, where he planned to lift weights and then spar with his black-belt martial-arts instructor.

A soft whine in the sky above caught his attention. He glanced up and saw what looked like a large bird, silhouetted against the sun, circling overhead. He surmised it was at least ten to fifteen thousand feet above them. It couldn't be a bird. He had never heard a bird make such a sound.

"Andre," Basayev shouted, "what in hell is

that . . . thing?"

Margelov, placing his left hand over the brow of his forehead, squinted at the object Basayev was pointing to. "Don't know, boss. Looks like some kind of small plane," he said, hitting the call button of his walkie-talkie.

"Captain, there's a plane circling above us. Can you get a call through and tell the pilot to fuck off? And I mean now!"

Several minutes passed as the plane continued to circle overhead. Finally, the *Aglaya*'s captain said, "Sorry, I can't get through to the pilot. I must have the wrong transmission code or he simply refuses to acknowledge the call."

Without further warning, Margelov whipped off the automatic rifle slung across his shoulder, slammed the bolt of his weapon back, and fired a burst of twenty rounds in the direction of the plane. It was a foolish and futile act. The bullets had no chance of hitting the aircraft.

Almost in anticipation of Margelov's action, the plane above peeled away to the right, and then swung behind the *Aglaya*'s stern, releasing two smoking arrows that headed straight for the boat.

"Holy fuck, boss. Get below. Quick! That son of a bitch is going to . . ." Margelov's warning died in his throat. The aircraft was Russia's latest entry into its drone arsenal.

It was the Altius-M, developed at, and operated out of, the Sokol design bureau in Tatarstan. It was patterned after the American-designed MQ-9 Reaper and was two years ahead of what the CIA had predicted for its production schedule.

Unlike the Reaper, it carried only two Hellfire-type missiles and not fourteen. But two missiles were more than enough to sink the *Aglaya*.

Each of the laser-guided missiles weighed over a hundred pounds, including a twenty-pound warhead, and traveled at a speed of 950 miles per hour. One of the missiles carried a thermobaric warhead, which penetrated the surface of the *Aglaya* and collapsed the lungs of all personnel on board before burning them to a crisp.

The second missile carried an armor-piercing warhead and locked on to the *Aglaya*'s large fuel tanks, which had been refilled the previous day.

In a matter of a few seconds, the *Aglaya* was shredded into a thousand pieces and reduced to a smoldering burnt-out carcass of a sea myth, bobbing on the surface of the Black Sea.

74

Two days after the G-20 summit, GNN's Ned Wilson, nearly hyperventilating, broke through an afternoon soap opera to make an unscheduled news announcement.

"This just in," he said, as an image of a white yacht came on screen. "Turkey is reporting the apparent sinking of the yacht *Aglaya,* owned by multibillionaire Kuri Basayev, the Russian financier who is one of the richest men in the world. He is believed to have been on board, along with an undisclosed number of friends and crew members."

In the right-hand corner of the screen appeared an officer in a white uniform, standing in front of a map of Turkey. A caption identified him as Captain Ömer Ozsecen of the Turkish navy.

As Ozsecen spoke, an interpreter translated: "A fisherman reported hearing a very loud explosion and seeing flames

twenty or thirty meters high this morning."
The officer pointed to the map, and the
interpreter continued. "The spot was about
sixty kilometers off Sinop. A destroyer sent
to the area discovered evidence of wreckage
identified as the *Aglaya*. No survivors were
found. . . ."

Upon learning of the sinking of the *Aglaya*,
Ray Quinlan quickly directed that all
members of President Oxley's national
security team meet with Oxley for a briefing
in the Situation Room. The greetings and
normal preliminaries were dispensed with
as President Oxley made it clear that he was
in no mood for business as usual.

"Frank," the President said, directing his
question to Frank Carlton, the director of
national intelligence. "How many goddamn
times does GNN have to beat the CIA to
the news when it involves something as
important as the sinking of Kuri Basayev's
boat? Jesus!"

"I don't have a good answer for you, Mr.
President," Carlton said sheepishly.

"And don't tell me it's because Congress
has crippled the NSA! We're supposed to
be tracking every movement, every
conversation that President Lebed and his
military chiefs have. When did that stop?"

"It hasn't stopped, but . . ."

"Never mind, just tell me what in hell happened. Was it an accident as GNN is reporting?"

Carlton shook his head. "No. It went down off Sinop. There used to be a Turkish naval base there. Now it's a university. But luckily, one of our destroyers happened to be in the area and picked up a radar trail. Here are several photos our boys took. Take a look."

Oxley did so, and saw a ghostly red trail arching across the Black Sea. In a corner of the photo was an inset photo of a drone.

"The Russians call it the Altius-M, their new long-range attack UAV. It looks to be a knockoff of our Reaper," Carlton said.

"I thought our intelligence people said the Russians were two years away from building drones," Oxley queried, clearly angry and worried about this revelation.

"Well, the Russians have been getting some help from the Israelis on design work and the Iranians gave them access to the RQ-170 that we lost over the border of Afghanistan, and the Russian scientists are no slouches when it comes to technology and the budget of ten billion dollars that President Lebed is pouring into their UAV program . . ."

"Okay. Okay," Oxley said, anxious to get on with the briefing, while signaling that it was anything but okay with him.

"But we shouldn't overstate what the Russians have," Carlton offered, trying to ease Oxley's concerns. "They're still at least ten years behind us on drone technology and their video jet jockeys are no match for our guys. . . ."

"Try telling that to Basayev," Oxley snapped. "Never mind. Just get on with what we know."

"We believe that the drone took off from a small Russian airport at Sochi, as the map shows. The Altius-M we believe was armed with only two Hellfire-type missiles, but those beauties roasted the *Aglaya* like it was a marshmallow."

"Reuters says the Turks call it an apparent accidental explosion," Oxley said.

"Yes, sir. The Turks figure it's none of their business."

"And the passengers on board?"

"Regular crew and bodyguard. About sixty, all Chechens. Basayev and a couple of relatives and friends. No Americans that we're aware of. We zeroed in on that, sir. NSA says Robert Hamilton was scheduled to meet Basayev, but we don't believe he ever made it to his yacht. He was last seen at a hotel in Moscow. Probably canceled a flight to Turkey after hearing the news."

"Coincidence, Frank?"

"My guess, sir — and it's a guess — is that Lebed's boys wanted to pull this off when our American friend was not on board. Courtesy gesture that can never be revealed or confirmed."

"Thanks, Frank. I agree. Hate to think that we owe any favors to the Russians, though. They'll double down on us at some point. But we need to get Hamilton back here. We've got to have an important discussion about what he's been up to with Basayev."

Oxley hesitated to say anything specific about the nature of that discussion. He had to get Hamilton back because one of Silicon Valley's golden boys was an accessory to the murder of five innocent Americans. And that was the least of it. He was the only one who knew where Asteroid USA was located.

But there was no immediate rush, Oxley reasoned. Even assuming that Cole Perenchio had been right about his calculations — and Oxley was not entirely convinced that he was — they still had twenty years to figure out a solution. It wasn't as if there was going to be a collision tomorrow.

"Yes, Sir, Mr. President. We'll find a way

to get him back even if the Russians grant him asylum like they did with Snowden."

"You think Lebed would do that?" Oxley asked, startled by the thought.

"I think Boris Lebed is a Russian and he'll do whatever he can get away with. Remember, Putin was his mentor."

Oxley simply nodded, his thoughts drifting back to his moments with Lebed at Mihrabat Grove in Turkey. The shoulder hugs, the repartee, the goodwill banter. *"Oh, come now, Blake, I can call you that now."* Perhaps he'd been a fool to think that Lebed would be a friend he could work with.

"Don't worry, we'll get him back. Right now, Mr. President," Carlton said solemnly, handing a folder marked TOP SECRET to Oxley, "the North Koreans are at it again, threatening to test another nuclear bomb and long-range missile, one that can hit our heartland. And the CIA confirmed this morning that Al Qaeda has had some of its recruits in Yemen infect themselves with a deadly virus they've developed and are arranging for them to travel throughout Europe and the United States."

"Ebola?"

"No, Sir. Something that CDC has never seen before."

"Jesus, Frank, now it's virus bombs? Is it

ever going to end?"

"I don't think so, Mr. President. No, Sir."

EPILOGUE

Two weeks after the sinking of the *Aglaya,* Falcone and Taylor were on Falcone's terrace, their suit jackets off, smoking Falcone's Cubano cigars, the tips of which had been dipped in cognac.

"Damn, Sean. What a spectacular day it's been." Although it was late November, the temperature in Washington had held steady at seventy degrees for nearly a week.

"Freak of nature or our doing?" Falcone asked.

"Now don't get me started on climate change or you're going to ruin a good night."

"Just curious," Falcone laughed, knowing how outraged Taylor was about the way Earthlings were plundering the planet.

"What a spectacular view out here," Taylor mused as he blew smoke into the night air.

"I have a Chinese friend who told me that

you can't eat a view, and that beauty outside a home was not nearly as important as the beauty inside."

"That's because your Chinese friend can't see through Beijing's smog and never stood out here. Just look at the sweep of history you can see standing here. The Capitol looks like a brilliant diamond set off against a sheet of black velvet tonight. . . . You know, Sean, whenever I look up and see that magnificent dome —"

"You think about some of the cretins running around under it," Falcone said to lighten the touch of melancholy that had made its way into Taylor's voice.

"No . . . well yes, that too. But they come and go. Some are bad, but I think most come here to do good. Then they get tied up in knots by all the lobbyists until they forget why they came in the first place. And then they keep running just to hold on to their jobs."

"So what were you thinking?"

"I look at that dome and I keep thinking how it was built mostly by my ancestors for little or no pay. It's probably the greatest symbol of liberty anywhere in the world, and it was built on the backs of my folks. And that Statue of Freedom? A slave helped make it, the first bronze statue ever cast in

547

America."

Falcone could see that Taylor's eyes were starting to tear up.

"And right down there," Taylor pointed with the tip of his cigar, to the corner of Seventh Street and Pennsylvania Avenue, "right near that Starbucks that you like so much, that was one of the most prominent slave markets in the city. Think about it. They were selling my shackled brothers and sisters to the highest bidders right under the gaze of the Statue of Freedom that stands on top of that dome."

"History has its cunning passages and contrived corridors," Falcone said, thinking how hollow the poet's words sounded when weighed against the enormity of past crimes.

"Yeah, and after it's illuminated for everyone to see, we're asked to forgive."

"Have you?" Falcone asked, knowing that a state of grace would never be his to enjoy. Out of an incurable habit, Falcone's eyes shifted downward and stared at the statue of the Lone Sailor, his collar upturned against an imagined wind, standing astride a large globe etched in the glazed stone plaza below. Falcone could never detect whether the sailor was about to ship off on a long voyage or was just returning from one. But always, the sailor seemed to be world-weary and sad. Maybe the sailor was just a one-way mirror inside Falcone's mind.

"Oh, I still see the dark side of our history," Taylor said. "But when I look at that dome, it still gives me hope. And when Blake Oxley was elected, I thought, man, the American Dream had just been ratified. Anything is possible in America. Anything. . . . But hey, this is getting way too serious. Here's to you," Taylor said.

The men raised their glasses to toast each other and hailed Falcone's birthday.

"So what's the magic number now, Sean?" Taylor asked.

"I stopped counting a long time ago. I just figure every day I'm on this side of the grass is a good day."

Pointing to the starry sky, Taylor said, "I've got to believe that there's something more out there."

"You? I thought you were a scientist who . . ."

"Who believes there's god in everything that's alive, that moves."

"Stars move," Falcone said, refilling the glasses.

"You know what I mean. Everything that's organic. Everything that breathes, grows, thinks, is . . ."

"So, you're coming back as a goat?"

"Man," Taylor said, "you're really dark."

"Just the Irish coming out," Falcone said, laughing, a touch sadly, picking up his glass. " 'Forgive, O Lord, my little jokes on Thee . . .' "

" 'And I'll forgive Thy great big joke on me.' "

"Jesus!" Falcone said. "Is there anything you don't know?"

"Not much, my brother from another mother," Taylor said, taking a long drag on the Cubano.

"Is it at this point where we fist-bump and I call you bro?"

Taylor broke into a belly laugh, then choked on the smoke that he had not meant to inhale.

"So, bro, how come you decided to walk away from being Oxley's science advisor?"

"Many reasons. I gave it a lot of thought," Taylor said. He leaned on the railing, again looking at the night sky. "The title's nice, but I'd have to go through the hassle of giving up my show, my wonderful job, and most of my personal investments. And pay a fortune to lawyers like you to make sure I haven't omitted anything that would get your boy, J. B. Patterson, on my ass. Not worth it, and Darlene agrees."

"You know I'd have covered you pro bono."

"Actually, I was counting on you to do just that," Taylor said, a smile sliding across his lips. "But, there was still the *Grudge Report* smear hanging over me, and I just couldn't bear the thought of having to deal with some of those . . . 'cretins,' as you called them, up on the Hill. The ones 'who refuse to look at the new moon out of loyalty to the old.' Don't know who said that, but half of the tea baggers insist the Earth was created in six days and that evolution is just a theory."

"Well, there'll be two less of them soon. You no doubt heard that Senators Collinsworth and Anderson have announced their retirement."

"Yeah. Two years before their terms are up. . . . Must be something pretty bad when two powerful chairmen decide to hang it up."

"I think J.B. gave them some friendly advice."

"They cut a deal?"

"I don't know the details. All I know is it's amazing how fast a house of cards collapses when there's a little wind."

"You mean Paul Sprague? Heard he has agreed to plead guilty to obstruction of justice."

"You must have good sources. It's not public yet."

"You're not the only one who's wired in this town," Taylor said, tipping the ash off his cigar.

"Yeah, well, he's getting off pretty easy, given what he did. Three years in a federal penitentiary, with time off for good behavior. Loses his license to practice law forever, of course. Sprague's wife's decided to divorce him. She's moving to New Mexico. And she gets what's left after he sells his estate in Middleburg, the place in Palm Beach, and the condo at the Ritz and pays off a settlement package he signed with the families of all who were killed at the firm."

"And what's the deal with Hamilton? What's going to happen to him?"

"Don't know. Last I heard he was still in Moscow."

"Doing what? Jesus, don't tell me he's defected!"

"No idea, Ben. Maybe he's insisting on a deal for immunity. No jail time like Sprague's getting."

"Why wouldn't Oxley give him whatever he wants? He may be in the best position to help avoid a global calamity."

"You'd think so," Falcone conceded, "but maybe Hamilton doesn't want any deal. He's a very strange dude. J.B. gave me a little briefing . . ."

"J.B.? I thought you were a 'person of interest,'" Taylor said, flexing his eyebrows in Groucho Marx fashion.

"FBI thinks I'm just an interesting person now. Just like . . ."

"I know. Just like you've always been," Taylor interjected, completing Falcone's flippant attempt at immodesty.

"In any event," Falcone continued, "it seems that while Hamilton was waiting for Basayev to transport him to the *Aglaya,* he took a tour of Saint Basil's museum."

"Nothing too strange about that. I did the same thing when I was in Moscow. It really is something special. Incredible architecture. You know the legend about Ivan the Terrible?"

"Doesn't everyone?" Falcone said, smiling and shrugging.

Taylor sighed theatrically and said, "Ivan had the architect blinded so he'd never be able to create anything so beautiful again."

"Just a myth from what I'm told. Russians love it, though. Tragic fuckers that they are." Falcone chuckled. "But that's not what I meant about Hamilton. Soon after he left the museum, he had a car drive him out to Krasnogorsk to visit a Russian Orthodox church."

"Why Krasnogorsk?" Taylor asked.

"I don't know. J.B. speculated that maybe he wanted to see the icon of Jesus on the brick wall of a chapel there. Son of God complex, maybe. Who the hell knows? But it turns out that he met with Bishop Nikoli Vosnesenski while he was there. The visit lasted more than an hour and when Hamilton left, he was carrying a Bible that was written in Russian, a gift from the bishop."

"I still don't get it, Sean. So Hamilton is a fundamentalist who still believes that you and I are going to roast in Hell. Maybe he just wanted to make sure that our fate didn't get lost in the Russian translation," Taylor quipped.

"What's interesting is that Hamilton specifically wanted to examine those passages in the Book of Revelation that contained predictions of the end of life on Earth."

"How do we know that, Sean?"

"Not at liberty to say, Ben," Falcone said. "But I'm told that what struck Vosnesenski the most were Hamilton's eyes. They were as cold and unblinking as a snake's. Apparently he had seen eyes like that only once before, in a Russian psychopath."

"Well, as you said, a strange dude. But who's to say that if we keep on with what we're doing, maybe the Bible has it about right?" Taylor drank deeply from his glass of cognac. "By the way, I heard you're going back to the law firm. How come?"

"By popular demand. Seems the partners still think I'm something of a hero."

"Boy, are those lawyers fucked up!" Taylor chuckled, clinking glasses with Falcone. "You giving any odds that this whole business about Janus and the possibility that someday we're going to get hit won't make it to GNN and the rest of the media?"

"I'm not a betting man, but I'd say the chances aren't great. We have a free press, remember. And . . ."

Before Falcone could finish, his cell phone's annoying buzz interrupted him.

"Senator Falcone . . . I'm sorry to call you at home. It's Philip Dake. He's been practically stalking me. Another call from him tonight. At home. He's says it's important, murderously important, he said to tell you."

"Ursula, you just call Mr. Dake and tell him your boss is away from the office. Better yet, whatever he's calling about, just say that I'll talk to him . . . in the fullness of time."

AUTHOR'S NOTE

This is a work of fiction. All of the people and events are imaginary. The fictional asteroids mentioned in the novel are, however, based on several real asteroids, including asteroid (29075) 1950 DA. The source of Cole Perenchio's smuggled report about Janus, beginning on page 432, is based in part on an article, "Asteroid 1950 DA's Encounter with Earth in 2880: Physical Limits of Collision Probability Prediction," published in *Science* on April 5, 2002.

Asteroid (29075) 1950 DA was discovered in February 1950 and observed for seventeen days. It was then lost. But on New Year's Eve in 2000, a newly discovered asteroid, after having been given the designation 2000 YK66, was found to be the long-lost 1950 DA.

Constantly updated information on near-Earth objects, including discovery statistics, close-to-Earth approaches, and impact probabilities, is available at http://neo.jpl.nasa.gov. For information about NASA's search for extraterrestrial life, see http://history.nasa.gov/garber.pdf.

ACKNOWLEDGMENTS

If accepting a loan of the time and psychic affirmation of others were contractually enforceable, I would stand in chains before a debtors' court magistrate.

First, I am grateful to Tor/Forge's publisher, Tom Doherty. From the very first day Tom approached me about publishing my novel *Dragon Fire,* I could sense the depth of his concern about the sustainability of life on our planet. In every discussion about possible themes, narratives, and story lines, Tom displayed a sincere and profound concern for man-made threats to the continuation of human and animal existence on Earth and urged me to ring alarm bells to arouse a citizenry that seems to have overdosed on lotus leaves.

Bob Gleason, Tor/Forge's editor extraordinaire, is a man on fire, obsessed with our lack of obsession about the existentially destructive nuclear weaponry that remains on hair-trigger alert in too many countries. Bob is an intellectually armed and dangerous man — a jazzologist and a Tarot-card mystic to boot — whose imagination knows no limits and whose editorial pen, no mercy. He has been uncommonly patient and forgiving of my travel excursions and diversions even as he gently reminded me that deadlines are not made to be broken.

I am unquantifiably grateful to my friend Tom Allen, an accomplished author of fiction and nonfiction works. I first met Tom in 1983 when he was asked to edit *The Double Man,* a novel that I had coauthored with Senator Gary Hart and that became a Featured Alternate Selection of the Book of the Month Club. Ten years later, Tom and I decided that we should collaborate to write a mystery novel called *Murder in the Senate,* a story that we fervently hoped would always remain in the realm of fiction. Since that time, I have turned to Tom on multiple occasions to make sure that my hand remained steady as I tried to weave imaginary tales that both inform and entertain.

A special word of thanks to copy editor Terry McGarry, who has the eye of a jeweler. Terry caught every mistake and miscue in the many manuscripts she scrutinized, and her mastery of the story line was remarkable.

At my writing desk (iMac) I have a model of Yoda of *Star Wars* fame, whose buttons, when pushed, offer wise and ethical counsel. Tom is my Yoda, and he remains for me a repository of information about life on Earth and in the galaxies of the mind.

Enormous thanks go to Army Colonel John Urias (Ret.), who first alerted me to a research report that he helped write for the Air Force in 1996: "Planetary Defense: Catastrophic Health Insurance for Planet Earth." The report is stunning and stark in the analysis of asteroid threats that most people have chosen to ignore.

I am indebted to one of America's best and brightest, NASA director Charles Bolden, a Marine Corps major general (Ret.) and former astronaut, who directed my script to Dr. Donald K. Yeomans, manager, Near-Earth Object Program, Jet Propulsion Laboratory, and to Dr. Bill Barry, NASA chief historian. Both Dr. Yeomans and Dr. Barry provided me with very precise and insightful comments that contributed to the accuracy of the calculations and suppositions contained in the story.

I am also grateful to many of the

extraordinarily talented colleagues with whom I am privileged to work, namely: Bob Tyrer, Jim Bodner, General Joseph Ralston (Ret.), Lieutenant General Harry Radugue (Ret.), General Paul Kern (Ret.), Admiral Jim Loy (Ret.), former ambassador Marc Grossman, and attorney Tommy Goodman, who offered so many constructive suggestions on both the substantive and legal issues involved in the story.

Finally, I must reserve the greatest share of my gratitude to my wife, Janet, an accomplished author and playwright. Patience is said to be a virtue, provided it is not eternal. Contrary to my every promise to seek moderation and balance in my life, there have been times when I simply disappeared for days into my man cave and lingered there with my Muse, a jealous and demanding mistress. To err is said to be human, but for Janet to forgive, well, that's divine.